"What's the name of the guy who told you to kill me?"

Kofi's eyes were fixed on the illuminated knife in my hand, and he sneered. "What? You gonna start cutting me open if I don't confess?" He ran his tongue around the inside of his mouth, spat out something, and muttered, "Shee-it. You damn near knocked my teeth out with that sucker punch."

"Tell me about the contact."

His face twisted in agony, and he shuddered. When he finally spoke, his voice was full of sad surprise. "Y'know? I hurt like hell inside."

"Where?"

"Left. Maybe broken ribs. You came down hard on me, but I traded you some. Should see your face!" He took a ragged breath, then flashed me a bloodstained grin.

"You're somethin' else, Hel. Know that? Dodged the sea-toad, got rescued off that damned comet, bisected ol' Bron Elgar like a bagel out there on Cravat . . . How the hell you get away from those damn fish down in the Glory Hole? Man, you got more lives than a New York alley cat."

"The name," I repeated. I brought the blade down in front of his eyes, keeping torchlight on his face . . .

By Julian May
Published by The Ballantine Publishing Group:

ORION ARM

The Rampart Worlds: Book 2

Julian May

A Del Rey® Book
THE BALLANTINE PUBLISHING GROUP
NEW YORK

A Del Rey® Book
Published by The Ballantine Publishing Group
Copyright © 1999 by Starykon Productions, Inc.

www.randomhouse.com/delrey/

Library of Congress Catalog Card Number: 99-91747

ISBN 0-345-39519-0

Manufactured in the United States of America

First American Edition: April 1999

10   9   8   7   6   5   4   3   2

Prologue

His Daimler-Tori hoppercraft hurtles down from the ionosphere on its programmed course. The time is 0247 hours and
the appointment with Alistair Drummond is at 0330. Below,
the land is hidden by a thick layer of clouds, but the ship's
ground display shows the enormous expanse of the capital
conurbation and its satellite residential communities, spread
along the entire northern shore of Lake Ontario.

The hopper joins a sparse swarm of other light aircraft
hovering within a holding pattern at nine thousand meters.
The ship's navigation unit says: *"Now arriving Toronto Conurb
ATZ. Please supply next routing."*

He has dozed fitfully most of the way from the Sky Ranch
in Arizona, exhausted by the stress of the general board meeting and fearful of the challenge that lies ahead. Rousing with
a muttered curse, he removes the templets of the dream machine and says: "Wait."

The navigator acknowledges.

He leaves the flight deck and enters the Daimler's tiny lava-
tory. After relieving himself, he fumbles at the convenience
console and calls up shave-gel, mouth rinse, an astringent
towel, and a mild stimulant. As he completes the grooming
ritual and the drug takes hold, his reflection in the mirror
changes. The features lose the blotched puffiness of fatigue,
becoming keen and judicial, and the sunken, haunted eyes
take on a counterfeit sparkle. He combs his hair low on his
forehead and to the side, concealing the prominent widow's
peak that characterizes so many members of his famous
family.

1

Returning to the flight deck, he opens a locker, removes a hooded featherweight soft-armor jacket with a one-way visor and puts it on over the tropical business suit he had worn to the board meeting. The personal weaponry can wait until he's on the ground.

He addresses the ship's navigator again. "Go to Blue Disenfranchised Persons Reserve. Prep for manual touchdown at junction of Mamertine and Borstal streets."

"Warning. This area is outside the jurisdiction of Toronto Conurb Public Safety—"

"Cancel advisory."

"Warning: Touchdown in a DPR is at your own risk. No aid units will respond to emergency summons—"

"Cancel."

"Warning. Touchdown in a DPR will render all vehicle insurance coverage null and void. The following precautions are—"

"Cancel all advisories and go."

"Air access to Blue DPR visitor landing sites requires barrier override code. Please enter code."

His fingers tremble only slightly as he plugs in the data-dime furnished by Galapharma's Arizona covert op. The navigator blinks in approval.

"Confirmed. En route."

The hoppercraft drops through the cloud deck to an altitude of less than five hundred meters. It comes in from the south, over the dead-black lake. Rain is falling heavily, blurring the pinpricks of colored light delineating the cityscape below. Only the Toronto core and its adjacent maze of islands to the east are clearly visible, shielded in the tenuous golden glitter of a Class One force-umbrella nearly forty kilometers in diameter. Protected from the weather, handsome government buildings and the proud bright crystalline towers of the Hundred Concerns defy the stormy summer night.

The panorama is gorgeous, but he is in no mood to appreciate it. He calls up a triple-shot espresso with a tot of cognac and sips it, speaking the magic words aloud:

"Calm. Competence. Courage."

He possesses all three qualities in abundance, and they will carry him through the upcoming ordeal. However, since he is the bearer of disappointing news, he rehearses the spin angle he has calculated will be most effective with Alistair Drummond. Galapharma's CEO will probably be furious at the setback, but Drummond is no fool, and he'll have to concede that the Rampart takeover can be leveraged only with inside assistance.

His assistance.

There is really nothing for him to be afraid of.

Coventry Blue is finally gone, along with the other wretched excesses that were tolerated by a compliant CHW government under the corrupt thumb of galactic Big Business. Nowadays, white-collar criminals — like him—get their comeuppance in a more humane, if less colorful, manner.

Too bad.

He deserved Coventry Blue if anyone did, the treacherous bastard. But I suppose I'm prejudiced . . .

Before the Haluk War, the penal institution that combined the worst aspects of an ancient Soviet gulag with anything-goes 2050-vintage Las Vegas was situated on the western outskirts of Toronto. It was the largest and most flagrantly mismanaged Disenfranchised Persons Reserve in the Commonwealth. Nobody seems to know how the dark carnival aspect first invaded this particular Coventry, but it undoubtedly persisted because the Hundred Concerns found it useful as a tangible deterrent to corporate disloyalty. Among other things.

The DPRs were originally designed as walled, self-contained penitentiary villages, providing their lifer inmates with an environment that was supposed to allow them a limited amount of independence and dignity. Self-government by the highly educated felons was one of the prime organizing principles, and in most of the Coventries the system worked well enough. Guards kept order, but under the original charter, they operated more like a small-town police force than like jailers. The convict population lived in apartments instead of cells. They didn't have to wear uniforms. There was no onerous regimentation. The prisoners had ample opportunity for gainful employment and recreation, and according to regulations, they were allowed visitors once a week. Life in a conventional Disenfranchised Persons Reserve wasn't all peaches and cream, but it wasn't a lunatic jamboree of Neronian depravity, either.

The same couldn't be said about Coventry Blue.

Most of the luckless felons sentenced to permanent residence there (some having been apprehended by me, when I was an enforcement agent for the Interstellar Commerce Secretariat) would have sold their souls to be elsewhere. At the same time, naughty-minded free citizens on the Outside were paying good money to get into the damned place!

Blue's transient clientele came from all over the home world and from adjacent planets of the Orion Arm. The goal: to party down and dirty. Libertine tourists romping along the notorious Blue Strip could count on rubbing elbows—if nothing else—with distinguished local citizens, many of them members of the capital's political and corporate uppercrust who might deplore the place's wickedness in the public forum but didn't hesitate to indulge illicit Blue itches when the need arose. To the more vicious variety of well-heeled thrillseeker, the sort who could afford the stiff bribe for the night entry code and the outrageous fees charged for the unique attractions, Coventry Blue was the carnal cruise destination of choice: zero-K cool, the ultimate hoot, where vile amusements weren't bloodless virtual reality, but shockingly, deliciously, perilously *actual*.

And legal, within the walls. After all, the inmate purveyors were Thrown Away, stripped of citizenship, nonpersons. In law, not even the probationary disenfranchised—such as I was, in those days—had any civil rights. Throwaways condemned to Coventry Blue were the lowest of the low, officers and middle management employees who had violated important statutes of their Interstellar Corporation or Amalgamated Concern, threatening the very economic foundation of the Commonwealth of Human Worlds.

A certain percentage of Blue inmate newcomers—especially naifs who had disbelieved the dire rumors they'd heard about the place—committed suicide when they realized that the prison was under the absolute control of exploitative convict gangs; but the majority just caved in to the inevitable and decided to go with the flow, accepting employment in the illegal enterprises operated by inmate kingpins. If life became too unbearable, oblivion was available in the form of cheap drugs, buzzheading, or old-fashioned alcohol that could be purchased with the monthly dole if one skimped on frivolities such as food and clothing.

Religious leaders, left-wing media pundits, Reversionists, and other powerless moral guardians of the time called Coventry Blue a pervert's playground, a stinking sore on the backside of the capital conurbation, the epitome of everything that was rotten in the Commonwealth of Human Worlds during those bad old days of yesteryear. Right-thinking citizens were gratified when Blue was finally shut down during the sweeping reforms that followed the war and the downfall of the Hundred Concerns.

Lots of wrong-thinkers were relieved, too. Including *him*.

But I still get a smidgen of wicked satisfaction imagining how it must have been on that night of January 18, 2233, when he visited the infamous den of iniquity—under strong protest, of course.

He prided himself in knowing almost nothing about Coventry Blue. Its sordid activities went unreported by the legitimate media, and he would never have dreamed of entering its restricted-access smutsite on the PlaNet. He wasn't interested in *that* sort of thing.

The quest for power was his besetting sin, and in pursuit of it he had conspired to betray his own family's Starcorp to a predatory business rival, allying himself with a megalomaniac who might or might not decide to feed him to the wolves when his usefulness was over.

Corruptor and corruptee had conferred face-to-face only once before, at the very beginning of Galapharma's bid to take over Rampart Starcorp. Since then the two men had communicated via intermediaries, covert ops belonging to the big Concern's security organization who would mysteriously appear to request progress reports or deliver instructions. He had no idea why Gala's capricious CEO had elected to set up this meeting in Coventry Blue instead of in a more seemly venue.

Unless he'd done it for educational purposes.

So here goes our corporate antihero, an upright, uptight respected executive of Rampart, on a quickie tour of hell. His perilous game is approaching its climax. If he wins, he'll get everything he's ever wanted. If he loses, he could come to Coventry Blue to stay . . . for the rest of his life.

The hoppercraft flies slowly at a low altitude, reined in by the computers of Traffic Control. Even in the wee hours the Shore Freeway and Queen Elizabeth Way are crowded with cars and transit vehicles flowing in orderly streams to and from the radiant central umbrella. Luminosity reflects from low-hanging clouds, revealing the residential districts and industrial parks of Mississauga and Etobicoke, their wet streets gleaming beneath neatly spaced streetlamps.

To the north is a less tidy enclave of about nine thousand acres. Its irregular perimeter is outlined by bright sapphire lights that surmount a ten-meter-high wall topped by razorwire and Kagi guns on pivoting stanchions. At the eastern side of the complex is a gatehouse and security checkpoint. A single garishly illuminated thoroughfare—Peel Road, a.k.a. the Blue Strip—leads from the gate into Coventry's interior.

The main drag of the prison village is solidly packed with upscale cars. The byways, almost deserted, have meager streetlighting or none at all. There are no trees or other ornamental vegetation anywhere. Except for the bizarre come-hither architecture of the clip joints, pusher palaces, and bordellos along the Strip, the structures of Coventry are built of drab plascrete—dismal apartment blocks and jerry-built flops for the more peaceable Throwaways, lockups and warehouse facilities for the wig-outs and immobile sickies, unsanctioned fortified town houses inhabited by the convict elite who exploit their lesser fellows, and a guard barracks near the prison entrance. Smaller boxy units accommodate inmate services, tacky small shops and take-out food joints, storefront churches and charitable institutions, and the innumerable enterprises of Blue's illegal economy. Windows of the off-Strip buildings are mostly dark, in obedience to the selectively enforced midnight curfew regulations. In a few, oleum-flame lanterns and even candles cast a wan yellowish glow. Burnt-out ruins and heaps of rubble occupy some of the weedy open areas. Others serve as parking accommodation for visiting hoppercraft or cars and have bonfires burning to signal available space.

His Daimler reaches its destination and hovers until he takes over the controls. Borstal Street runs parallel to the Blue Strip. Its intersection with Mamertine is at the western end of the penal complex, nearly five kilometers from the gate. He descends toward the parking lot designated by Alistair Drummond.

The Daimler's terrain-scan monitor shows a level area crowded with at least sixty expensive hoppers, incongruous amidst the squalid surroundings. Their security shields throb faintly crimson in the rain, warning that intruders will be shocked into insensibility. Only a handful of the private aircraft show visible registration alphanumerics on the roof. The rest have ID illegally obscured for the duration of their stay in Coventry.

For a brief moment he hesitates. (Calm! Competence! Courage!) Then he lands in a space as near to the lot's bonfire as possible. A parking attendant comes out of a shanty and slowly approaches over the muddy ground. The figure waits at a safe distance for him to emerge.

He buckles on twin holsters, checks the load in his Ivanov stun-gun and the charge indicator on the Kagi photon pistol. He programs the remote control gorget for the hopper and locks it around his neck, zips the armor jacket and pulls down the visor. He stuffs his wrist wallet with cash and a single blind draft credit card, then pulls on zapper gloves.

The Throwaway attendant stands motionless as he climbs

out and touches his gorget to lock the aircraft and engage the security system. He can hear the noise of the Strip a block away: high-db rock music with yelping electronic toms and seismic bass, obbligato horn honks from the traffic jam, a volley of mystifying animalian howls. Underlying it all is the roar of carousing humans.

"Morning, guv," says the attendant. "That'll be two hundred fifty."

He can't help being outraged. "So much!"

The convict shrugs. "Take it or leave it, citizen. That's the fee. You have a complaint, file it with King Kwadena Akosu. The lot belongs to him. You'll find him at Casino Royale."

"Hmph. I suppose you want a tip as well."

"Your gratuity would be deeply appreciated. And bless you, guv."

A barely legible name badge identifies the Throwaway as GAVIN D. He is gaunt, scraggily bearded, and his grin reveals two chipped front teeth. Between his glazed red-rimmed eyes is a metallic button identifying him as a buzzhead, addicted to electronic stimulation of the pleasure centers of the brain. His rainsuit is old and ill-fitting, patched with duct tape, smudged in soot, stained repugnantly about the crotch. Only his voice, hoarse but still retaining the inflection of an expensive education, reveals that Gavin D. was once more than human debris.

Who was he when he lived Outside? A too clever corporate lawyer? A financial officer caught with his hand in the till? A data thief? Another faithless executive who sold company secrets to the opposition?

Gavin D. waits patiently, holding out a filthy hand with broken black fingernails. "Cash or plastic. Your first visit to Coventry Blue?"

"Yes," he growls. Sort out the money, fork it over. A grudging twenty for the tip. The man's stink penetrates the closed visor. He backs away in distaste but Gavin D. follows, rummaging in the side pocket of his rainsuit.

Is he going for a weapon? Panic! Drag the Ivanov out of its holster. "Stand back, damn you!"

"Easy—easy does it, guv." A contemptuous snicker. "No

one here will hurt you." Wink. Grin. "Unless you pay them to." The convict pulls a cheap e-book from his pocket and proffers it. "Complimentary guide to the local scene. What sort of action are you looking for? Sex? Dope? Gladiators? Gaming?"

He waves away the book. "Which way to a place called the Silver Scybalum?" This is the rendezvous specified by Alistair Drummond.

Silenced in mid-spiel, the attendant's eyes show a spark of revulsion before reverting to practiced blankness. "So you're one of those . . . Well, different strokes for different folks. I hope you brought your niobium Visa card. You're looking at ultra-pricey show biz at the SS."

"Never mind. Just tell me how to find it. And what's a scybalum, anyhow?"

"Look in the display window when you get there." The Throwaway hesitates and then the grin returns, sly and vindictive. "I wouldn't want to spoil your fun, but you ought to know that the performers there are genengineered humans, not the real thing. Neither are the baby ho's in the shorteye joints. Genen adult inmates, every last one. No real kids in Coventry. The female cons—"

"Which *way*, goddammit?"

"Don't get your twat in a twist. Go down to the Strip, hang a left, go two blocks. You can't miss it." Gavin D. turns away and shuffles back to his hovel to await the next customer.

He sets off, moving cautiously on the broken pavement and repeating his soothing mantra over and over. Calm, competence, courage! This is a test. He'll ace it, and to hell with Drummond's mindfucking control games.

He passes a row of dark, ramshackle flophouses. The only illuminated place is a Catholic mission with a holosign that SAYS FREE MEALS 24 HRS. The projection depicts a smiling Jesus sketching a blessing with one hand and offering a steaming-hot burger plate with the other. A vagrant slouches in the mission doorway, chugalugging the last of a bottle of fortified plonk. Inside, a brother in a white karategi with a black belt waits to unlock and admit him, sans booze.

Farther along the street are shuttered storefronts: a day-labor exchange, a noodle shop, a minimart with an iron grille across the door and windows. Ragbaggy forms huddle in some of the doorways, wrapped in foil blankets against the pelting downpour.

One calls out to him as he hurries by, an elderly woman whose face is barely visible. "Spare some small change, citizen? Brings good luck to feed the animals at the Blue Zoo, you know."

He is superstitious enough to stop and toss her a small-denomination bill, which she deftly snatches out of midair. He asks, "Why in the world are you sleeping outside on a night like this?"

"Safer here than in the dormitory blocks," she tells him. "No lushrollers, no pussy bandits or bugnuts crawling in bed with you, no screaming meemies, no psychoid icemen looking to waste you for the fun of it—" He shuts his ears to the catalog of horrors and hurries away, finally reaching the blazing clamor of the Strip.

Here the sidewalks are thronged with roisterers wearing costly rain gear. Many of the pedestrians are anonymously hooded and visored, as he is, but fair numbers of the most youthful men and women go bareheaded in spite of the bad weather. Flashily dressed, shrieking with sycophantic laughter as they cling to the arms of their incognito escorts, these can only be professional whores imported from Outside. Coventry Blue's population of upper-echelon corporate felons probably has a perennial shortage of inmates who are young, attractive, and reasonably priced.

The funhouses stand cheek by jowl, tricked out with giant holograms, flashing strobes, laser pattern generators, neon constructs, even blinking incandescent-bulb marquees. He cannot help gaping at the outrageous displays and the signs that shriek and blare the Blue Strip's extravagances:

LIVE YOUR WILDEST WET DREAM GORGEOUS GALS FAB FAGS KLASSY KIDDIES LOVERLY LIVESTOCK PSYCHODELICADO BOU-

TIQUE LE POT DE CHAMBRE CORRECTIVE WHIPPERSNAPPERS
ORGY PORGY HELGA'S HOUSE OF PAIN ROCKET FUEL DEPOT
NARC NOOKY CESSPOOL FOLLIES PETER PUFFER'S POOFTAH
PALACE BLOOD GLADIATORS OF ANCIENT ROME CASINO
ROYALE—LOWEST ODDS ON EARTH BOOGIE BOMBITA BANDITA
RUSSIAN ROULETTE VAMPIRE PLANET ELECTRIC BREATHING
LESSONS SALADIN'S SNUFFBOX—100% REAL DEATH DRUGS
DRUGS DRUGS SEX SEX SEX XXX . . .

Grimly, he shoulders his way through the mob, fending off
the stoned and the importunate. Barkers and strong-arm touts
aggressively seek his custom, but a warning gesture with his
zapper glove sends them off with a cheery "Fuck you, guv!"
flung after him. The teaser spectacles in the show windows
startle him, nauseate him, even arouse him—to his shame
and consternation, for he is a cultural snob who had thought
himself to be above such vulgar titillation.

Calm. Competence. Courage.

And God damn Alistair Drummond.

At last he sees his goal, a surprising oasis of conservatism
amidst the crashing hullaballoo. The large building's facade
is slick black, with a bas-relief frieze that appears to wriggle
and contort, as though trapped living things are attempting to
escape a river of tar. A modest sign above the sheltering por-
tico says SILVER SCYBALUM. The entrance is flanked by two
gargantuan doormen in imitation spacesuits of glolamé with
reflective helmets. On either side of the doorway are large
windows. The one on the left is curtained with silvery drapes.
The other, artfully spotlighted, features a curious grotto of
pitted white rock thickly mottled and veined by black and red
minerals. Some of the cavities are lined with beautiful ruby-
colored crystals.

He approaches and joins a group of idlers who stare at the
xeno creature behind the glass. It has the general shape and
bulk of a sea lion. The body is roughly pear-shaped, clad in
a greenish pebbled hide, possessing only two front limbs
armed with oversized claws with which the thing has anchored itself to the irregular sidewall of the artificial cave.

The hideous wrinkled head is oversized, naked, leathery, with
tiny red eyes. Wormlike feelers surround its open beak and
apparently guide interior mouth parts that work like recipro-
cating drills, pecking industriously at the rock. A larger ap-
pendage, like a warty tongue, laps up mineral dust as fast as it
is produced. The hole the creature has gouged sparkles with
minute raw metal surfaces and freshly broken crystals that
look like scarlet flecks of pepper.

He reads the descriptive sign at the front of the exhibit.

The sapient denizens of Gwalior [Sector 8], requiring arsenic and sulfur in their unique metabolism, consume native rock containing the red mineral proustite (silver arsenic
sulfide) together with free silver. The latter is egested as a
waste product.

After a few minutes the Gwaliorite detaches itself from the
wall and flops down with comical abandon, inspiring considerable mirth among the observers. It slithers clumsily to a
pool of steaming liquid and drinks daintily. Then it rears back
and begins to shiver.

"Yes!" cries one of the crowd. "Do it, sweetheart!" Others
contribute encouraging shouts.

The trembling intensifies and the Gwaliorite utters a series
of prolonged screams, broadcast electronically to the world
at large. He recognizes the exotic ululation he had heard earlier, in the hopper park.

After a final tortured cry the alien wriggles backward to
a depressed area of the floor where there is an in-spiraling
gutter. At its center is a sensor knob that suddenly starts to
blink red. A roll of recorded drums rattles from a loudspeaker.
The Gwaliorite lifts its massive legless posterior slightly and
excretes four golfball-sized droppings of gleaming solid metal that roll down the gutter, strike the sensor, and trigger a triumphant display of multicolored strobe lights and a flatulent
tuba fanfare.

The crowd applauds raucously, the silver scybala disappear through a little trapdoor, and curtains sweep shut on the

window, hiding the now motionless creature. Simultaneously, the drapes of the second window open, revealing a smaller Gwaliorite already munching minerals.

He remembers the lot attendant's chilling remark about pseudo-alien performers. But surely . . .

He questions one of the spacesuited doormen. "They're animatronic, aren't they? Just robots?"

The giant deopaques his helmet and looks down on him with a patronizing smirk. "The exhibits are alive, Citizen Frost. Perfect genen transforms. The procedure is illegal on the Outside, but there are no such restrictions in Coventry Blue."

"But why would even a Throwaway—"

His queasy speculation is cut short by a sudden chilling insight: the doorman has recognized him, called him by name. His supposedly scannerproof visor has been penetrated by some high-tech gadgetry and his iris pattern analyzed and identified.

Alistair Drummond lied when he said that their meeting would be secret.

The doorman is saying, "We've been expecting you. Here, take this. Your entry fee is already paid." In the palm of the outstretched gloved hand is a shining sphere of xeno ordure. "The Silver Scybalum will be your passport to erotic delights beyond human comprehension. If you choose to accept them."

With a curse, he knocks the thing aside. The ball falls into a filthy puddle on the street, where shouting bystanders scrabble eagerly for it. Both doormen ignore the fracas, swing wide the double doors and gesture for him to enter. Having no choice, he does.

The establishment's lobby simulates a funky 1930s-style Buck Rogers starship, all brushed multicolored metal with gemlike rivets, obsidian panels, and round portholes framing astronomical scenes. Three heavily muscled ushers, dubiously female, insist upon divesting him of his outerwear and weaponry. They wear topless "space-girl" uniforms of bias-cut satin with cantilever support for their enormous bare breasts, elbow-length silver gloves, silver high-heeled boots, and open silver helmets topped with goofy little antennas. When they attempt to outfit him in an iridescent bodysuit with strategic cutouts he balks and threatens to leave.

"Be like that," one of the attendants sniffs. "You'll find it *very* inconvenient for the activities."

They open an inner portal that imitates an antique airlock with a handwheel. "Please follow the illuminated floor guides to Citizen Drummond's private box."

He squares his shoulders and moves forward slowly. It's dark in there. Music swells around him and the turgid air is redolent of musky perfume. Amplified moans and other wordless human cries mingle with insistent Stravinskyesque discords and thudding tympani. At his feet is a trail of tiny green lights shaped like arrows. They lead him down a short corridor that opens into a great murky bowl-shaped chamber, a theater-in-the-round with a central stage surrounded by tiers of spectator boxes that look like imaginary space vehicles conceived by a retro comic-book artist. Some of the boxes are open; others are enclosed for complete privacy, with mirrored one-way windows.

The ceiling is velvet-black, sparkling with colored stars and projections of interstellar gas clouds and galaxies. On the eerily lit stage, where hologrammatic plantlife impersonates an otherworldly jungle, four naked men struggle in the clutches of an enormous barrel-shaped alien resembling a feather-crowned purple sea anemone equipped with dozens of glistening opaline arms.

At first glance he thinks that the human performers are being devoured by the gorgeous monster. Their torn treksuits and broken weapons are scattered among the scenery. Then he realizes that the men are engaged in bizarre sexual congress with the extraterrestrial, convulsing and uttering delirious wails as the final movement of the *Rite of Spring* rises to an overorchestrated crescendo.

He tastes bile in his throat and turns away, fighting for self-control. When he is finally able to pull himself together, the music has reached a thunderous climax—and so, evidently, have the human participants in the spectacle. He dares to look again and sees the performers lying spent in the beautiful creature's grasp. There is a blinding flash. When his vision recovers, he discovers that the stage is empty except for a ring of blue footlights.

He pauses, irresolute. The lights fade, a new tritely erotic theme begins—de Falla's *El Amor Brujo*—and a column of whirling flames momentarily curtains the circular stage. The blazing barrier lowers to reveal a more ominous species of exotic seducer, insectile, skeletally thin, and studded with atrocious black thorns. It sways hypnotically and its amber eyes glow as a woman in ornate bondage harness slowly approaches it with outstretched arms.

The trail of green arrows still glows on the floor. He follows it down a long aisle of shallow steps to the lowest tier, which is entirely taken up by six exceptionally large enclosed spectator boxes. One of them is his destination. He raps firmly on the compartment's side door and it slides open, emitting a cloud of sweet narcotic fumes.

The Chairman and CEO of Galapharma Amalgamated Concern stands there, dimly backlit by interior wall sconces. His princely features have the perfection of genen rejuvenation, and every hair of his elaborately styled leonine coiffure is in place. Alistair Drummond is a tall man, and his shoulders are massive and his hands very large. He wears one of the obscene shiny bodysuits, mercifully covered with a belted scarlet brocade dressing gown. Poised artfully in his right hand is an antique jade cigarette holder with a smoldering giggle stick.

"Come in, lad! I'd nearly given up on you."

"Hello, Alistair." He is a good thirty minutes late but does not apologize.

Drummond motions his guest inside and shuts the door, diminishing the volume of the music. His voice is pitched low, peculiarly soft, with a slight Glaswegian accent. "I see that you didn't let the ushers dress you for the occasion. What a shame. I had some interesting entertainment planned for us before we got down to mundane matters."

"No, thank you," he says with polite regret. "Pseudoalien sex isn't really my style."

Alistair Drummond laughs. His ice-colored eyes show no sign of intoxication, and as always, they are completely unreadable. "The Silver Scybalum can furnish any sort of amusement you'd like. Anything the Blue Strip has to offer. Don't tell me that none of the attractions you saw on the way here appealed to you."

He mutters, "Not really."

"You're lying," Drummond says, without rancor. "It had better be your last lie. Do you understand me, lad?"

He swallows. "Yes."

"Excellent. Would you care for a drink?"

"Scotch and water would be fine."

The box seems much larger on the inside and apparently extends back beneath the steeply raked auditorium floor. The opulently cheesy interior continues the Art Deco starship theme. The place resembles the private retreat of Ming the Merciless or some other out-of-date science-fiction potentate. Its most conspicuous piece of furniture is a very wide couch covered with burgundy leather that takes up most of the compartment's far end. Three matching armchairs stand before a long one-way viewing window overlooking the stage. Underfoot lies black carpet as lush as mink fur. An onyx and silver food and beverage bar backed by softly illuminated erotic stained-glass murals occupies part of the rear wall, where there is a second door with a small electronic service panel mounted beside it.

For a brief, blood-quickening moment he wonders what might have come through that inner door if he had accepted the "entertainment" offered by his host. Then he feels a quaver of revulsion. Whatever it looked like, it would have been human once.

Drummond goes to the bar, stubs out the smoldering narcotic joint, and pours thirty-year-old Lagavulin single malt into two crystal tumblers, adding water to one. Before returning with the drinks, he touches a pad on the service unit and speaks.

"Will you join us now, Baldwin? There's been a slight change in plan."

Surprise, consternation. "Alistair, I thought we'd agreed that this meeting would be private!"

"Did we?" Drummond hands him the drink.

He struggles to keep his composure, sipping the marvelous smoky liquor. The inner door slides open upon a tunnel that leads into the bowels of the theater. He half expects a loathsome xeno facsimile to appear, but the smiling man who enters has a perfectly ordinary, even genial, appearance—except for the jarring steely intensity of his eyes. He appears to be in his mid-forties and has a narrow face that is slightly freckled. His curly auburn hair is cut very short. He is dressed in a neat business suit of oxblood worsted with a matching silk turtleneck. Grimacing at Drummond, he mops at one sleeve with a pocket square.

"Some kind of damned slime on the corridor wall got all over me. You wouldn't believe the geek collection hanging out back there in the green room! . . . Or perhaps you would."

Drummond chuckles, turns to his guest and says, "This is Ty Baldwin, head of Galapharma Security. He'll sit in on our conference."

"Glad to meet you, Citizen Frost." Baldwin heads directly to the bar. "Don't mind me. I'll set myself up. You two just go ahead with your business."

Indignation and suppressed fear. "We can't talk in front of him!"

"Certainly we can," Drummond says easily. "Come and sit down with me by the window. We can watch the show while you tell me about the Rampart board meeting." He turns up the music. On the stage outside, rings of dancing flame encircle the performers. The spiky entity has enfolded the woman in its multiple arms and penetrated her. She is bleeding from scores of small wounds.

He turns away in disgust, almost spilling his scotch as he sinks into one of the oversoft leather chairs. "I have some disappointing news. The Rampart Board of Directors turned down your acquisition tender again."

Alistair Drummond speaks so quietly that he can hardly be heard above the driving Spanish rhythms. "You stupid shit. You assured me that this time we'd win."

He forces himself to show no emotion. "The decision was extremely close. I was able to pass a resolution calling for a new vote at the end of six weeks. By then the ICS will have ruled on Rampart's application for Concern status. They're almost certain to turn us down. And then the board will have no alternative but to accept Galapharma's offer—even if it's *lower* than the present bid. In the long run this temporary setback will redound to your advantage."

Drummond grunts dubiously, failing to affirm the attempt at damage control. "Who was the holdout? Scranton and her mob of Small Stakeholders?"

"No, it was Katje Vanderpost. Her action was totally unexpected because Beth and I had worked very carefully to bring her around. I took a quiet poll yesterday before the meeting, when everyone but Katje had already arrived at the Sky Ranch. All the stakeholders except Simon Frost were in favor of the Gala merger this time—even Thora Scranton. I suspect that Simon found out that Katje had been pressured. The old devil went to work on her as soon as her hopper landed. She caved in at the last minute—saying she couldn't vote for the merger and betray her late brother's dream for the Starcorp."

"Sodding sentimentality! Trust a damned woman to ignore logic. Her quarterstake would eventually double in value."

"In retrospect, I wonder if Katje's poor health might have influenced her decision more than any twaddle about Dirk Vanderpost's noble aspirations for Rampart." He pauses, swallowing a fair amount of his drink. "She could be thinking ahead. Intimations of mortality. Afraid that her children might contest her will and cut off the major source of funding for her precious Reversionist Party if Rampart merges with Galapharma." He utters a dry little laugh. "As might very well be the case! Asa tried to get her to set up a trust benefiting her pet causes, but she vacillated—thank God. I'll keep hammering away at her. We'll get her vote on the next go-around."

Drummond is obviously uninterested in these tactical details. His gaze is riveted on the increasingly lurid theatrics outside, and from time to time he moistens his pale, finely chiseled lips. "Just make bloody certain that she favors the merger next time."

"You have nothing to worry about. When the board meets again in six weeks—"

"Six weeks!" Once more the gentle intonation of Drummond's voice belies the brutality of his words. "I've been waiting four fucking *years* for you to make good on your promises, lad. But your pissant little Starcorp still owns the Perseus Spur, and the Haluk trading embargo remains firmly in place. Inside of six weeks the Secretariat for Xenoaffairs could launch an official inquiry into Gala's role in the fiasco on the planet Cravat. And then *my* cock could be on the block."

"Put your mind at rest. There won't be any Cravat inquiry, and no action will be taken on the Tokyo University findings, either. My source inside SXA spoke to me on Thursday. There's insufficient evidence to justify involving the Special Counsel at this time. The genetically modified Haluk cadaver can't be linked to illegal human activity, and the secret xeno establishments on Cravat were completely demolished. That left only the verbal testimony, and it was finally disallowed."

"Did the evidentiary hearing reject Eve Frost's deposition, then?"

"It was never officially submitted to SXA, nor was the corroborating material provided by Matilde Gregoire, the new Rampart Security VP. Simon himself convinced them not to affirm the previously recorded testimony, for fear of prejudicing our status-upgrade petition and the pending civil action against Galapharma. You can understand how there might have been a jurisdictional dispute between Xenoaffairs and the Interstellar Commerce Secretariat if Rampart dragged in an allegation of a Haluk-Galapharma conspiracy."

"I can't believe Simon would simply sweep the Cravat affair under the rug."

"He intends for it to be a significant part of Rampart's civil

suit later on. But Simon doesn't give a damn that you and
some of the other Big Seven Concerns are violating trade in-
terdictions with an unsanctioned alien race. Nor is he particularly worried about Haluk skulduggery, so long as it doesn't
menace any other Rampart Worlds. All he cares about right
now is averting the clear and present danger—saving his
Starcorp from a Gala takeover."

Drummond considers the matter for a few moments before
saying, "And Eve Frost went along with Simon's decision not
to depose the Cravat incident to Xenoaffairs?"

"She gave in very reluctantly," he admits. "She's become
almost paranoid about the Haluk since her kidnapping. Eve is
convinced that the aliens have sinister designs on the Human
Commonwealth itself and intend to use their Spur colonies as
staging areas for expansion into the Orion Arm."

"That's completely absurd!"

"Asa may have influenced her thinking on that matter. Unfortunately, he saw the Servant of Servants' big new flagship
with his own eyes. And you may recall that he also has personal knowledge of the Haluk prototype speedsters. His
smuggler crony Bermudez blasted one to bits en route to
Cravat."

Alistair Drummond's glass is empty, and he hisses a pe-
remptory command to his unobtrusive security chief, who is
seated on the couch in a shadowy corner of the box. "Baldwin, get me another double."

The man silently complies. Drummond sips and scowls.
"What about Asahel Frost's evidence? And that of Bermudez?"

"They insisted on filing their depositions. Simon couldn't
stop them. But their material was thrown out on grounds of
testimonium non probum. My source inside the Secretariat
tells me that any SXA investigation of a Haluk-Galapharma
conspiracy should be considered quashed—at least for now."

"*Non probum,* eh?" A cold smile. "I like that. Untrust-
worthy witnesses!" Drummond's moment of good humor
fades. "But Eve and the Gregoire woman can resubmit their
testimony without prejudice at any time, can't they?"

"Once Galapharma has absorbed Rampart, they can only

file as private citizens, without the stature and legal resources of a Starcorp to bolster their case. We can handle that."

Drummond stares thoughtfully into his drink, finally asking, "What's Simon's strategy, as of now?"

"All efforts are to be concentrated on the last-ditch push for Concern status, since an upgrade would eliminate any possibility of a hostile takeover of Rampart once and for all. This will take priority over everything else—including the civil action against Galapharma. You know that our legal department has sent nothing to the ICS Prosecutor's office yet, even though we've given first notice of intent to file. Nazarian's people are still gathering data to verify Gala's felonious infiltration and its role in the sabotage incidents. Thus far, the corroborating evidence is none too conclusive— unless they find out where we've stashed Ollie Schneider. And there isn't a hope in hell of that."

"We've got nothing to worry about, then," Drummond decides. "It's no secret that Simon himself is the principal stumbling block to a status upgrade. The Commerce Secretariat will never make Rampart a Concern so long as that vacillating old fart stays at the helm."

"We had a frank discussion about that at the board meeting. Simon knows ICS has no confidence in his leadership, but he won't step down unless the board nominates a new CEO who meets his approval—one he's absolutely certain won't turn around and immediately sell out to Galapharma. The only candidate acceptable to the old man is his daughter Eve, the First Vice President and Chief of Transport and Distribution. Fortunately for us, she's chosen to make herself unavailable."

"That's news to me. How?"

"To be effective, the new CEO belongs in the Perseus Spur, at Rampart Central on Seriphos. *But Eve doesn't dare leave the Sky Ranch.* She can't let anyone see her in a demiclone state, except the members of the board and a few loyal ranch employees."

Drummond is incredulous. "Are you saying that Eve Frost

still hasn't submitted to restorative dystasis treatment? It's been six months since her rescue from Cravat!"

"She has high principles. She insists on preserving incontrovertible evidence of the Haluk demiclone scheme—even if her evidence is held in abeyance for the time being. It's imperative that she remain in seclusion. If the media found out about her condition, Xenoaffairs would be compelled to open an official inquiry into the Cravat can of worms."

"There's no chance that Simon will persuade her to change her mind and go into the tank?"

"Not even to save Rampart. Eve is willing to postpone a public revelation in order to give Simon his precious six weeks' leeway. But after the status decision comes down, she says she's going straight to SXA and instigate a probe of what she calls Haluk aggressive expansionism." He hastens to add, "That won't happen, of course. We'll find a way to force dystasis on her."

"You'd better," says Alistair Drummond, with ominous kindliness. "This is very bad news, lad. Very bad." He ponders the implications for some time. "Meanwhile, Simon will certainly have to choose another new CEO if there's to be any hope of upgrade. Either you, or—"

He cannot help the bitterness that colors his reply. "Yes. We two are the obvious candidates. But unlike the goddamned Golden Girl, both of *us* have problematical executive track records. The Commerce Secretariat might have been willing to grant Rampart immediate Concern status with Eve as CEO. She's proved her abilities. But with either of us in the top slot, ICS would probably postpone a decision."

Drummond bursts out laughing. "Then Simon's up shit creek without a paddle. He's got to appoint one of you. There are no other suitable candidates. And whomever he chooses, Galapharma wins."

"There's . . . something else you should know, Alistair." Calm! Competence! Courage! "Eve made an alternative proposal. It was her contention—preposterous on the face of it, but perhaps understandable in the light of the Cravat affair—

that her brother Asa has the potential to solve the problems facing Rampart."

Alistair Drummond frowns and turns to his security chief. "Baldwin, didn't you tell me that Asahel Frost had a blazing row with the old man and his sister last week and resigned his rump vice-presidency?"

"Yes, sir. Our agents report that he left Rampart Central on Seriphos and went back to that little freesoil planet, Kedge-Lockaby. He and Simon had been estranged for years. Asa joined Rampart only because he loves his older sister Eve and decided that he needed the Starcorp's resources to rescue her. Once she was safe, Asa's commitment to Rampart became less than solid. He was frustrated by his inability to locate the fugitive Rampart Security personnel who were in our employ, and apparently enraged by certain actions of Simon's. Asa finally quit in a huff. Our informant on K-L reports that he has publicly stated his indifference to the fate of Rampart."

"What was his quarrel with Simon about?" Drummond asks his guest.

"Asa took violent exception to what he called his father's cop-out strategy on Haluk involvement in the Cravat affair. He even castigated Eve for siding with Simon."

"By resigning from the Starcorp," Drummond points out, "Asahel Frost reverts to his former disenfranchised state and becomes a legal nonentity."

"Unfortunately," he explains, "Eve's alternative proposal took all that into account. She said she *would* accept the top slot—become CEO—provided that the board agreed she could make Asa Chief Operations Officer, effectively restoring his citizenship. He'd work directly under her and be accountable only to her. She'd remain in seclusion on Earth, overseeing corporate strategy through subspace com from the ranch, while Asa takes personal charge of the Spur operations."

Drummond seems stunned. His handsome, supercilious face changes into something momentarily more human and vulnerable. "Good God. How did the board react?"

"Oh, they were violently opposed," he says. "Of course, no

one dared to say a word against Eve personally. Her proposal was finally tabled on consideration of how the Commerce Secretariat might react to Asa's appointment. They'd never in a million years upgrade a Starcorp with a convicted felon in top management."

"A *framed* felon," Ty Baldwin interposes, smiling thinly.

"Oh, for Christ's sake! Asa's out of it! Thrown Away! Eve never consulted with him before nominating him as her right-hand man. If she had, he would have turned her down flat. It's not in his nature to be a corporate team player."

"You're probably right," Drummond says. He seems to have recovered his Olympian aplomb. "On the other hand, we can't afford to have this—this bloody *beach bum* interfere with our plans again. Our man on Kedge-Lockaby will have to take Asahel Frost out."

"It shouldn't be difficult to arrange," Baldwin says.

"Your late assassin, Quillan McGrath, underestimated Asa," the visitor says.

Drummond's tone is glacial. "He paid the ultimate price, and so did several hundred of our Haluk allies. The bastard is an ex-ICS agent and he's proved he can be mortally dangerous."

"Rely on me to see to the matter, sir." Baldwin pauses, then: "Perhaps we should also consider a permanent solution to the other grave threat hanging over Galapharma Concern and the Haluk. I refer to Eve Frost. In my opinion it would be a mistake to think she can be neutralized through forced dystasis."

The visitor says, "Well, your corporate hit men will never get to Eve so long as she stays at the Sky Ranch. The place is impregnable."

"Not to you," the security chief retorts.

"You don't give me orders, Baldwin! There's no way I could . . . deal with Eve without compromising myself."

Drummond hastens to soothe his guest. "And we wouldn't want that to happen, lad. By no means. Eve Frost can wait. And you are absolutely correct. Ty doesn't give you orders. I do."

The Galapharma CEO falls silent, apparently intent upon the culmination of the sadomasochistic drama out on the stage. When the final blackout comes, he rises from his chair and returns to the refreshment bar, where he begins scrutinizing flasks of exotic liqueurs. "You have six weeks, lad. At the end of that time I expect Rampart's petition for Concern status to be denied. I also expect you to turn Katje Vanderpost around. One way or another her vote must affirm the Galapharma merger. This is absolutely crucial."

"I understand."

"I hope you do. I needn't remind you that Katje lives in a Phoenix, Arizona, penthouse apartment, not at the Sky Ranch. If she rebuffs your persuasive wiles—if exceptional measures become necessary to ensure an appropriate outcome—*you* will be the one to remedy the situation."

He feels the blood rush to his face. Not trusting himself to speak, he stands rigid, fists clenched at his sides. The Galapharma security chief takes a step toward him. But almost at once the abrupt surge of rage and panic dissipates. "You'll have her vote."

Drummond nods. He lifts an oddly shaped bottle containing a milky mauve concoction, uncorks it and sniffs the contents. "Ever tried this stuff? Gemmulan absinthe. Females of the Y'tata race use it to enhance labial dexterity. It's supposed to do interesting things to the male human anatomy, too."

He manages to say, "Is there anything else we should discuss? If not, I should be going."

"You'll be contacted when it's time for us to meet again."

"Not here," he declares adamantly.

"Killjoy." Alistair Drummond laughs, turning his back dismissively upon his guest. "Baldwin, did you see any Y'tata analogues on deck when you were waiting in the green room?"

The guest doesn't wait to hear the security chief's reply. Slipping out of the box, he closes the door and almost races up the aisle to the exit.

The three lubricious usherettes sneer as they retrieve his

outerwear and weapons from the cloakroom, but he takes petty revenge by slapping down a measly fiver for a tip before lurching outside into the rowdy commotion of the Strip. The rain has stopped and dawn is breaking. The rose and gold radiance of the summer morning sky overwhelms the tawdry artificial lighting of the clip-joints. They seem dingy, shrunken, and unutterably sad.

But his ordeal is over.

Except for the matter of Katje.

Realizing what he might yet have to do, he staggers through the mob of diehard revelers and vomits into the gutter. No one notices. After a few minutes he recovers and heads back to his hopper, while the carnival music plays on and the human Gwaliorite screams in its silver-draped show window.

Chapter 1

I'd been home for three days, and it still didn't *feel* like home.

Trouble was, I was depressed. Not just about bailing out of the Rampart mess, but about the resolute way that Matilde Gregoire had spoken to me after I'd quit, saying we were through. There was no place in her life for a Throwaway charterboat skipper . . . and evidently no place in mine for a dedicated Starcorp loyalist.

Half dressed and barefoot, I stared into the open refrigerator, wondering what I was going to eat for breakfast. I'd had my heart set on a monster Tabasco scramble, but all the eggs were gone. There were no green peppers, either. I still hadn't done a real grocery buy since my return, and the garden had been destroyed in the sea toad attack.

Just as an interesting alternative popped into my mind, the phone buzzed. I went out of the kitchen onto the field-screened front porch of my beach shack, which serves as the office and scuba equipment sales area.

"Cap'n Helly's Dive Charters."

The caller was female and apologetic. "This is Jenny Chung, Captain. My husband and I were supposed to go out with you today, but I'm afraid we'll have to cancel. The weather is just awful here at the Big Beach. We checked the report for the Out Islands and—"

"The tropical depression isn't due to arrive in this area until late tonight," I said pleasantly. "We're expecting a sunny, calm day in the place I'd picked for our dive."

"We really don't want to risk it. And we're returning home

to Plusia-Prime tonight, so we won't be able to reschedule the trip. I'm very sorry. Of course, you may keep our deposit—"

"No," I said, with polite fatalism (and a craven desire to keep on the good side of the irascible booking agent at the Manukura Nikko Luxor). "The concierge at your hotel will credit you with a refund. Maybe we can go out together the next time you visit Kedge-Lockaby. Have a nice day, Citizen Chung." I poked the disconnect pad and said, "Rats."

The Chung couple would have been my first clients since my return from the planet Seriphos, and I'd been looking forward to the trip as an affirmation of my reacquired independence: I was free of Rampart responsibilities, free of my father's convoluted intrigues, free—alas!—of my emotional relationship with a lovely woman who disapproved of my undisciplined and feckless ways.

Well, the choices had been my own.

I picked up a mesh catch bag and went down the porch steps onto the beach in search of marine edibles. The morning sun was still behind the island so the sand was cool, shaded by the grove of mint palms that crowd close to my house on three sides. Eyebrow Cay's lagoon was mirror-smooth, reflecting a blue sky adorned with a few puffy cumulus clouds and countless silvery paintbrush strokes of the comets that infest Kedge-Lockaby's solar system. Glasha Romanov's classic fishing smack trolled the calm waters out near the reef. A nifty motor-sailer based at Manukura came slowly around Cheddar Head, outward bound with a party of tourists after spending the night moored at Gumercindo Hucklebury's marina. (I know: impossible name. But almost everybody on Eyebrow uses an alias. Mine is Helmut Icicle.) The big sailboat would probably ride out the upcoming storm in the shelter of Alibi Island, our larger neighbor to the west, after sending its clients back to the Big Beach on the hopshuttle.

Eyebrow Cay is a crescent, as its name indicates, about twenty-five kilometers from end to end. The jagged reef, with only two safe passages, extends from each tip of the island, completing a lopsided circle and enclosing our lagoon. Almost all of Eyebrow's population, under fifty souls, live on the inner shore where there are attractive sand beaches. The island's largest natural harbor holds the marina and Sal Faustino's boatyard, a few guest houses, a kite shop, and our little general store.

Many of the folks on Eyebrow Cay are Throwaways, and quite a few others have personal histories that don't bear close scrutiny. I definitely fit into the latter category; and if Rampart's personnel office was on the ball in upgrading their database, I would already have rejoined the former group after a brief sojourn among the franchised citizenry of the Commonwealth.

Two friends share the cove where I live. To the south, half visible through the palm grove, is the deceptively modest bungalow of Mimo Bermudez, who may be the wealthiest man on Kedge-Lockaby. He is certainly one of the most enigmatic. My neighbor on the other side is Kofi Rutherford, another dive charter skipper, whose tumbledown dump lies out of sight behind a small rocky rise.

Both men had come to the rescue when my previous home had been gobbled by a giant sea toad, six months earlier. Mimo had shot the monster dead and Kofi helped search its stinking guts for salvageable household items . . . among other things. Not much of my stuff had escaped the brute's invincible digestive juices. But with help from Mimo and Kofi and other good buddies on Eyebrow, I'd ended up with a new little house even better than the old one. It still wasn't quite finished.

There are about four hundred Out Islands strung in a loose archipelago a couple of thousand kilometers west of the Big Beach, Kedge-Lockaby's single continent. Manukura, our planetary capital, boasts a tiny starport, the best hotels, a clutch of boutiques and craftshops, the independent casino that supports K-L's schools, and the rest of what passes for Kedgeree civilization. Most permanent residents live on the BB, and most Perseus Spur tourists go no farther abroad in search of recreation. The islands are much more primitive, more gorgeous, and utterly lawless. This has advantages and disadvantages, as I had already discovered and was shortly to reaffirm.

But first, breakfast!

I rolled up my jeans and splashed around the shallows, grabbed a dozen yolkworms before they could burrow out of reach, and stuffed them in my bag. They're repulsive-looking greenish squirmers about twenty centimeters long with a fringe of tiny paddles along each body segment. The edible part is a yellow sperm sac the size of a small plum, which cooks up better than the yolk of a fresh-laid chicken egg.

I cleaned the catch and tossed the leftovers to an eager flock of elvis-birds that glided down out of the mint palms, humming melodiously. Slogging back to the kitchen, I thought about how to spend the rest of the day before the storm hit.

I could paint window frames. (Yuck.) I could design a spiffier brochure to entice more sport divers from Big Beach hotels. (Double yuck.) I could start another vegetable garden, since the last one had been totaled by corrosive slobber from the shack-eating toad. (Exponential yuck, and besides, the impending storm would mess up the new plantings.) There were other chores, too, but the prospect had absolutely no appeal.

Ah, to hell with doing anything useful. I'd spent the last three days unpacking the stuff I'd brought back from Seriphos, evicting the vermin who'd snuck into the house during my long absence, and testing some new diving gear. Why shouldn't I goof off now and visit the Glory Hole? It's my second favorite place in all the galaxy, *numero uno* being the Sky Ranch in Arizona, where I was born.

(But I hadn't been there for thirteen years. Not since I had announced, fresh out of law school, that I was joining the Corporate Fraud Department of the Interstellar Commerce Secretariat rather than coming into Rampart Starcorp, as my father had expected . . .)

I whipped up the scramble and served it on soda biscuits, garnished with locally smoked faux lox. Then I called Kofi Rutherford to ask if he'd be my dive buddy. He wasn't answering his phone, but I figured maybe I could catch him over at the marina. I began to pack a lunch for two, and while I was building sandwiches the phone in my pocket buzzed again.

"Helly, it's Mimo," said a suave, familiar voice. "You have a subspace call. From Earth. Your sister, Eve."

"I'm on my way," I said, hitting the End pad and loping out the kitchen door. My phone was a cheap model without video, much less a patch option, so there was no way I could have the call transferred.

The only private SS com on our little freesoil planet was just where you'd expect it to be—in the home of Guillermo Javier Bermudez Obregon, semiretired Smuggler King of the Perseus Spur and my closest friend on K-L. He's beyond middle-aged, extravagantly generous, and inclined to keep mum about his past and present affairs. For reasons that are not quite clear to me, I have told him far too much about my own sorry history.

I trotted along the path through the palms in my bare feet, dodging scissor-shells, sandtacks, and the sharp-pointed fallen fronds of the exotic trees, certain that Eve was about to deliver the melancholy news that Rampart's Board of Directors had approved the shotgun marriage of my family's Starcorp and Galapharma AC.

I'd figured it would happen. The expectation had been one of my main reasons for opting out.

Mimo was waiting for me behind his screen door, a tall and skinny figure dressed in a fawn pashmina dressing gown, beat-up huarache sandals, and nothing much else. His habitually uncombed gray hair was even more frowsy than usual, and his lean, deeply furrowed face wore a look of grave concern.

He said only, "This way," and led me down a hallway decorated with primitive *santo* paintings, Maria Martinez pottery, and illuminated wallboxes holding ancient Aztec figurines.

The room that served as his study and command center was finished in cream-colored adobe and had a beamed ceiling. The floor was patterned red Mexican tile, softened with striped throw rugs. A fireplace, ready for the impending rainy season, held split fingertree logs resting on heavy andirons. Cushioned wicker chairs and a sofa stood before it. Above the plank mantelpiece with its twin wrought-iron candlesticks hung the portrait of a dark-haired woman dressed in the fashion of thirty years ago—my friend's late wife. A huge Mexican desk of elaborately carved oak stood before a window that overlooked the sea. Along the left-hand wall were two antique *bibliotecas* crammed with data-dime files, reader-slates, e-books, and conventional volumes. Between them, gleaming in modern ceramalloy incongruity, hulked a tall gun cabinet that I knew held an awesome collection of photon beamers and other portable arms. The communications equipment occupied an alcove of its own, framed by exotic plants growing in black Oaxaca *ollas*.

The old smuggler gestured for me to sit down at the transceiver console. "When you're finished, I'll give you coffee." He left the room.

I touched the Open pad, then went through the rigamarole of iris-ID verification and establishment of a Phase XII encrypt filter. When that was complete, my big sister's awful face appeared on the monitor screen and she spoke to me across the fourteen thousand light-years separating the Perseus Spur from Earth.

"Asa, the Galapharma merger bid was turned down again by the Rampart board. Thanks to Mom."

"Katje voted with Simon?" I was thunderstruck. "But I thought she'd switched over to the other side!"

"So did all the rest of us, going into the meeting. But somehow, Pop talked her out of it. Cousin Zed, Leo Dunne, and Gianni Rivello were livid. Even Dan and Beth were shocked to the socks." Eve was smiling, and it broke my heart to see her semimorphed features, partially human and part Haluk as a result of the interrupted demiclone genetic engineering procedure instigated by her kidnappers.

"The bad news is," she continued, "there'll be another vote taken in six weeks, immediately after ICS rules on Rampart's status upgrade. If we don't make the jump and gain Concern immunity, I'm afraid we're wiped."

"So Simon refused to retire?"

"On the contrary. He agreed to step down if the board elected what he called a suitable successor—one whom the ICS would have confidence in. The consensus was that neither Zed nor Dan really fit the bill. The only viable candidate left was *moi*."

"Yes!" I enthused. "I knew it! Congratulations, Evie—"

"Not so fast, little brother. I turned Simon down. Conditionally."

"What the hell does that mean?"

"I don't dare travel to Rampart Central on Seriphos, where an effective CEO rightfully belongs. I'd be a sitting duck for the media or even Galapharma hired guns. But I can't run the Starcorp from Earth, either, hiding out at the Sky Ranch. It would be an administrative nightmare, given the horrendous problems we're facing. I told the board that I would accept the CEO job under one condition: that they elect *you* Chief Operations Officer, immediately under me."

"What!"

"Zed could retain the presidency—nominally—but he'd no longer be in a position to give orders and screw things up. On purpose or otherwise. I'd remain on Earth and call the shots very broadly. You'd be on Seriphos or wherever else you were needed, doing what had to be done any way you saw fit. Between the two of us, we can pull the show back on the road and impress the pants off ICS. What do you say, kid?"

I couldn't say anything. I only sat there, open-mouthed, in a state of total disbelief.

Four days ago at Rampart Central on the planet Seriphos, when I still held the ad hoc title of Vice President for Special Projects foisted on me by my father, I'd taken part in a three-way conference call with Simon and Eve, who were back on Earth. We wrangled about what I perceived as the Haluk threat.

I had just learned that my Cravat deposition to SXA had been shitcanned. Mimo's statement and that of our young associate, Ivor Jenkins, had also been disallowed on the same legal technicality. I demanded that Eve show her Halukoid self immediately to Assembly Delegate Efrem Sontag, an old university friend of mine who was now Chairman of the Xeno-affairs Oversight Committee. Eve's mutation, together with a formal complaint that the Haluk had been stealing the genen viral vector PD32:C2 from Rampart and conducting a secret demiclone project on Cravat, would provide valid grounds for suspicion that the aliens were up to dirty work, possibly aided and abetted by Galapharma. My pal Sontag could be counted on to light a fire under the feet of the secretariat, forcing it to launch a full-scale investigation into dubious Haluk activities in the Perseus Spur.

But Simon had his own reasons for refusing to file a complaint about the vector theft and the Cravat shenanigans immediately, and for pressuring Eve to remain in hiding until after the status upgrade decision. He explained everything to me in words of one syllable, and also stoutly maintained that he could stave off the Gala acquisition bid at the upcoming general board meeting.

I told my father that his reasoning sucked. And if the takeover did go through, Galapharma would be in a position to conceal the vector theft evidence and fatally weaken Eve's deposition against the Haluk.

Our conference deteriorated into a shouting match. I berated Simon for putting the welfare of the family Starcorp ahead of a possible alien threat to the human hegemony in the Spur worlds—and maybe in the Orion Arm itself.

Simon told me I didn't understand the Big Picture.

I told him what he could do with said picture.

Eve tried to soothe the pair of us.

I lashed out at her for compromising her principles.

Finally, I tendered my resignation as VP Special Projects, announced that my tiny department was herewith dissolved, and wished my father, my sister, and Rampart Starcorp the best of left-handed luck.

Simon called me a traitor to the family honor, a sorry-ass bent cop, a born loser, and a cowardly coyote. Then he cut out of the conference. Eve remained calm and said she'd call later to let me know how the board meeting went.

After announcing my bail-out to Matt and to Karl Nazarian, my associate and nominated successor in Special Projects, I left Seriphos with my tail between my legs. Home again on my little tropical island, I tried to expunge from my mind the improbable events of the past six months that had torn me out of my beachcomber's paradise and plopped me back into the turbulent mainstream of the Commonwealth of Human Worlds.

The mental delete job hadn't been going too well.

And now my sister had come up with *this* . . .

"Evie, you're stark staring loco. I can't run Rampart."

"Of course you can, with competent support. Once upon a time, you were an excellent bureaucrat, Divisional Chief Inspector Asahel Frost."

"Oh, sure. And how would the ICS Upgrade Committee react to my appointment?"

She laughed. "The Board of Directors asked me the same question. Dan and Cousin Zed figured ICS would go seriously apeshit, and so my proposal was tabled. But not formally rejected! I didn't force a vote because I wanted to ask you whether you'd accept. In my opinion, ICS will react to your COO appointment in the same way that they did when Simon made you VP Special Projects: they'll judge your performance by *results* and not quibble about your shady reputation. You did a hell of a job on Cravat, Asa. And there are still people at Commerce who don't believe you were guilty of malfeasance and all the rest of it. You aren't without friends in high places."

"Horse apples."

The half-alien face was almost impossible to read. She spoke very softly. "You don't have to give me a decision immediately. Think about what I've said. The moment that Rampart makes Concern, I'll institute a civil action against Galapharma. Jump on 'em with rowel-spur boots. Throw the Cravat affair in their teeth. Expose that damned Gala hit man, Elgar/McGrath. Implicate him in my kidnapping and demicloning and the attempts to murder you. Let the media know how Gala has tried to undermine and devalue Rampart to force the merger. And their secret dealings with the Haluk aren't merely violations of interstellar commerce. They're *treason*, Asa! We'll crush those bastards. You and I!"

"Evie . . . we don't have enough evidence for any sort of case against Galapharma. Not without Ollie Schneider as a star material witness."

"Then find him, goddammit!"

"I've tried," I said wretchedly. "Karl and Matt and I combed the Spur from one end to the other, using all of Rampart's security resources and whatever help we could pry out of Zone Patrol. Schneider and his passel of Gala infiltrators have vanished without a trace. They must have escaped to the Orion Arm. And we haven't a prayer of tracking them there, among so many human worlds."

"Find other evidence, then. Play the Qastt angle. Put the screws on those Squeak pirates we've still got locked up on Nogawa-Krupp. They were dealing directly with the Haluk. Maybe some of them had contact with Bronson Elgar or other Galapharma covert agents."

"I never thought of that. It's a long shot, but I can put Karl Nazarian on it—"

"I want *you* on it!" Oh, God. Tears were running down her blue alien cheeks.

"But Evie—"

"Please work with me, Asa. Simon can call an extraordinary session of the board and ram both our appointments through. All the directors will remain on Earth for another week."

"I don't see how—"

"Will you at least think about what I've said? Give me your decision tomorrow. Whatever it is, I'll accept it."

I hesitated, then said, "All right, Evie. Tomorrow."

"Love you, Asa. Goodbye." My older sister's mutated face winked out and I shut down the subspace communicator.

Why the hell didn't I have the guts to say no to her, once and for all?

Because I'm a cowardly coyote, that's why.

I left the study and went to find Mimo. He was sitting at his dining room table, a polished wooden slab supported on wrought-iron legs, reading the morning news on a jumbo magslate. He had put his clothes on and now wore pressed slacks and a madras plaid sport shirt. His hair was still fly-away frizz.

"Sit down, Helly. Let me pour you some coffee. It's real Colombian Nariño. One of my colleagues just brought in a new shipment."

I accepted a big stoneware cupful and drank the embargoed elixir in silence for several minutes. Mimo read his slate without further comment.

Finally, I said, "Rampart's still alive. A six-week reprieve, courtesy of my mother."

"Good. I hope she's well."

I didn't respond to that. As of four days ago, Katje was very far from being well. Simon had slipped in that sad piece of intelligence during our acrimonious confab. My parents had been divorced for twenty-three years, but they were still coolly friendly. Katje had always voted her corporate quarterstake as Simon advised her to, until Eve's kidnapping and the threats against my life and those of my older brother Dan and younger sister Bethany had terrified her and nearly convinced her to capitulate to the Galapharma takeover bid.

I said, "Eve was offered the Rampart Chief Executive post. She said she'd accept only if I became her ops officer."

"*Caracoles!* And what did you say?"

"That I'd let her know tomorrow. But I'll have to turn her down. The situation is hopeless. She seems to think that Rampart still has a shot at making Concern status. I don't. There's no way she and I could ever turn the Starcorp around inside of six weeks, corral a heap of fresh venture credit for expansion, and prove that Galapharma had used criminal pressure tactics in the takeover bid. Rampart's a goner. If only we'd tracked down that fucking turncoat Ollie Schneider . . ."

"Ah." Mimo looked thoughtful, even sly. Perhaps I should have suspected something, but I was immersed in my own frustration—to say nothing of my guilt.

"I've had a bellyful of Rampart, Meem. What I really have

to do is figure out a way to force the Commonwealth to take the Haluk threat seriously. At the moment, I haven't a clue. So I'm going scuba diving, and fuck the fate of the galaxy."

My friend nodded tolerantly. "Can I prevail upon you to bring back some nice fish for dinner? Perhaps a few flapjaw demons. I'll grill them and make my special sweet pepper salsa if you'd care to join me."

"Happy to. We can watch the storm roll in."

"The colleague who smuggled the coffee also provided me with a case of 'twenty-nine Woodward Canyon Reserve Chardonnay from Washington State that I'd like your opinion of. It received the highest rating in *The Wine Advocate*."

"Sounds excellent."

As I was leaving, Mimo said, "Oh—one last thing. There's a remote chance that another guest might join us for dinner."

Something in his tone made me leery. "This person wouldn't be female, by any chance?" I wouldn't put it past the romantic old fart to try to fix me up with a new sweetie—or even lure Matt Gregoire to K-L in hopes of reconciling us.

"He's a business acquaintance of mine who is flying in from Callipygia. Masculine . . . most of the time." He shrugged.

"*No problema* then. Catch you later."

I went back to my place, put on my OK Corral sweatshirt and a pair of Teva sandals, and grabbed the sack of sandwiches. Then I got my personal dive gear off the porch, loaded it on my new antigrav tote, and headed down our island's single marl road to the marina. On the way I stopped in at Billy Mulholland's Mercantile and augmented the sack of lunch with two liters of rozkoz-gold milk, a six-pack of Pepsi-Cola chillinders, and a couple of bananas. Then I gave him a grocery list I'd prepared, and said I'd pick up the food around sundown.

"Taking *Pernio* out today, Helly?" Mulholland asked me.

"Yep. My charter fell through, so I'm just gonna knock around. You see Kofi anywhere?"

"He was in earlier for a cappuccino, fresh off the dawn hop-shuttle from the Big Beach. Try his boat."

Billy Mulholland was a poker player nearly as artful as my

old man, and the only other Eyebrow denizen besides myself
and Mimo who was born on Earth. He was a handsome devil
who got busted and Thrown Away for operating a Ponzi in-
vestment scam that plundered the stock portfolios of a few
hundred credulous old ladies in Sydney, Australia. After serving a five-year term in a DPR in Goondiwindi, he dug up the
small stash he had managed to hide from the law and bought a
ticket to the Perseus Spur.

He finished adding up my bill on an old-fashioned calcu-
lator. "Should I put this lot on your tab, mate?"

"Nah, I'm flush again." I proffered an EFT card primed
with the obscene amount of severance pay I had received
from Rampart. If I was discreet, the sum would take care of
my modest domestic needs for the next ten years or there-
abouts.

Leaving the store, I passed Jinj & Peachy's Bed & Breakfast.
The gals were sweeping their veranda and watering hanging
baskets of flowers. The Tallhorse sisters were a sweet-natured
pair, parolled and Tossed after serving time for armed rob-
bery on Fanning-Alpha. I gave them a wave and a grin, then
moved on downhill to Gumercindo Hucklebury's marina.
Goom himself, a rumored wife-murderer from Tikchik, was
engaged in a furious argument with Seedy McGready over
the old fisherman's penchant for dumping piscoid guts off the
dock after cleaning his catch.

I said, "Hi, guys." They halted their squabble long enough
to bid me a friendly good morning, then went at it again,
hammer and tongs.

Kofi Rutherford's rattletrap sport submersible, *Black Coffee,* was in its slip, and he lay on his stomach on the aft flat, in-
stalling a new surefoot covering. His rinky-dink boat was
down for repairs more often than not, so he frequently served
as first mate on mine.

"Yo, my man," he called as I hove into view with the tote
wafting after me. "Come aboard. Time I took a break anyhow.
This job is a megabummer."

He climbed to his feet and stretched, working the cramps

out of his splendid mahogany body. Kofi is a couple of centimeters taller than I am but less heavily muscled, a top-notch diver who knows more about the Kedgeree underwater realm than anyone else in the islands. He was wearing chartreuse shorts patterned with pink flamingos, and a duckbill gimme cap bearing the Macrodur AC logo.

Next to Mimo Bermudez, Kofi was my closest pal on K-L. He was an embezzling accountant from Cush in the Orion Arm, on the run from the enforcers of Omnivore, the Big Seven food and beverage Concern. He managed to escape his planet with a briefcase stuffed full of high-end negotiables but lost the loot when Qastt bandits boarded his starliner in the no-man's-land around the Fungo Bat Nebula. His temperament tended toward the morose, perhaps because of the fiscal disaster, but he was dependable and hardworking and knew how to keep clients happy.

I had let him use *Pernio* during my late stint with Rampart, and I swear there were tears in his eyes when I told him I'd come back to the islands to stay. Could be that the poor guy's emotions were somewhat mixed.

"How's about coming out diving with me?" I offered. "My sports cancelled and it's a perfect day for a dip. Won't be too many more like this before the rainy season sets in for good."

He sighed. "You're tempting me somethin' fierce, man. But I gotta get this flat patched, then go fix the roof on my shack . . . Where you figure on heading?"

"Glory Hole. Maybe see a giant cometworm. They come into the shelves before bad weather. Aw, c'mon, Kof. You know I don't like to dive alone."

"Maybe you can find someone else to buddy up with." He thought about it, frowning. "Damn. Might be tough to do today. Oren's at the Beach, picking up a new load of fritzware from his Dumpster-divers, Glasha went fishing, and Tewfik told me he was gonna hop over to Alibi to see his girlfriend."

"Never mind. I'll do a solo. What're rules for if you can't break 'em once in a while?"

"Tell you what, Helly. If there's anything left of the day when I finish, I'll come on out and join you. If I don't make it, stop by my place on your way home and we can pop some hops."

"You got a deal. Be seeing you."

Pernio was tied up temporarily at Sal Faustino's boatyard across the tiny harbor from the marina. My sub is a forty-year-old Mawson with a lot of good years left. A portion of my corporate gratuity had financed a complete overhaul of the sturdy old bucket's engines and systems, plus a fresh coat of buttercup-yellow paint. Her name is the medical term for frostbite. Sneaky little play on words there, a veiled reference to the exalted family moniker. She's equipped with a retractable flybridge for surface running, a stereo system featuring recordings of golden oldies by the Beatles and Jimmy Buffet, a big underwater viewport, and a framed copy of my personal motto: SPORT DIVERS ARE ALWAYS IN OVER THEIR HEADS.

I went aboard with my gear and spent a half hour checking the sub out. She looked great and the engines purred like the big fat Persian cat that guarded the door at Jinj & Peachy's guest house. I left *Pernio* idling at the slip and went to pay the bill.

In response to my hail, Sal Faustino emerged from the machine shop and gave me a cool greeting. She's the best marine engineer in the Out Islands, a square plascrete block of a woman whose flaming temper conceals a heart as soft as a creamed ham pie. Sal used to love me like a foster son until she found out that my real name wasn't Helmut Icicle.

"I'm taking *Pernio* out today, Sal. She looks great."

"Thanks." She didn't offer her hand, maybe because it was covered with grease. And maybe not.

"I'd like to settle up with you."

She hmphed. "Rampart plastic, I suppose."

"That's right," I said mildly.

"Yeah. Well, c'mon into the office."

A few folks on Eyebrow Cay really got their knickers in a knot when they discovered I was the son of Rampart's *queso grande*. The piss-off quotient maximized when I actually signed on with the Starcorp in order to expedite the search for

Eve and her kidnappers. Even though K-L was a freesoil world, Rampart still exerted a chilling influence over the little planet's economy—most especially its Orion Arm imports, which largely made the trip on Rampart transport and had moderately appalling price markups as a result. The situation was only partially alleviated by the Spur's thriving smuggler community.

Sal was one of those who disapproved of my family connections on general principles. Now that I'd quit Rampart and reverted again to Throwaway, she was still grumpy, but inclined to let me worm my way slowly back into her good graces.

"Keep an eye on the starb'd propulsion unit," she muttered, handing back the EFT card. "Had to use a rebuilt injector when those snots at BB Nautical wouldn't let me have a new one. 'Reserved for regular customers,' they said! I suppose I should've mentioned the Holy Name of Frost—"

"I'm sure a rebuilt will be fine."

"You know about the storm coming, right? Where you heading?"

"Place I know near Teakettle. I plan to be back long before the weather turns. So long, Sal. Thanks for rushing the refit."

Ten minutes later my yellow submarine and I chugged through the reef passage into the calm blue alien ocean.

Any real sailor will tell you that a glory hole is a place on shipboard to store odds and ends. Mine, however, is a genuine hole in the bottom of the sea, as celebrated in the old barroom ballad.

In my alter ego of Cap'n Helmut Icicle, I never took sport-diving clients to my secret spot. Mimo, Kofi Rutherford, and a handful of other close friends on Eyebrow Cay have shared the Glory Hole's heart-stopping beauty with me, but for the most part I've kept it for myself as a sort of private sanctuary—maybe the closest thing to a sacred place that my battered psyche will acknowledge.

To get there you have to go nearly two hundred kilometers southeast of Eyebrow to the treacherous, uncharted shoals south of Devil's Teakettle Island. Then, if you're driving a sub, you crank up the flybridge and navigate on the surface, eyeballing your way through a skimpy serpentine channel full of razor-sharp lava rock and half-submerged coralline heads, trying not to tear the bottom out of your vessel. Eventually you come to a dead end in the midst of a featureless shallow flat some seven kilometers offshore.

Now it's time to anchor the boat and start walking or swimming, depending on the tide. It was on the ebb this morning but still at armpit depth, so I was able to swim to the hole.

I dressed out in the brand-new gear I'd splurged on before I'd left Seriphos: a Phoque skinsuit and BC, an ultralightweight NeLox rebreather helmet with a depth spectrum compensator lens, and a Rolex dive computer with sonicom, magfield navigation, and lots more bells and whistles. Sitting on the forward flat of the sub, I donned another new toy: Corby jetfins, a lazy man's way to move around underwater that I'd long lusted after but hadn't been able to afford prior to my Rampart gig. They were controlled by means of a single shell-glove worn on the left hand.

I butt-scooted onto the starboard descender, tapped its control pad, and let the mechanism lower me into the water. Easing myself prone, I did a small buoyancy tweak, then clamped the fingers of my gloved hand together mittenwise and flexed them slightly to activate the fin waterjets.

Hot damn! I was off and steamin', gliding effortlessly just beneath the surface at a minimum rate of knots with nary a splash, one with the fishies.

The preset navigation display on my faceplate showed me the way to go. There was almost no current on this side of the volcanic island and the waters were transparent as air, with visibility almost unlimited—not that there was much to see as yet. The bottom was mostly featureless grayish sand, pocked here and there with odd small craters. Most of them were no more than twenty or thirty centimeters wide, dark blue at the center, densely edged with lacy pink, lavender, and lime-green sessile animals. The only free-swimming piscoids on the flat that day were tiny golden creatures no larger than terrestrial guppies. They fled ahead of me in panicky schools before spiraling en masse into a handy bolthole, as though they were glittering confetti being sucked down a drain.

The moored yellow submarine was nearly invisible against the background of wooded Teakettle Island when I finally reached my destination, over two kilometers away. From the surface the Glory Hole appears as a perfectly round azure aperture about two meters in diameter, sited mysteriously in the midst of pale shallows punctured by countless smaller openings.

I turned off my jets by splaying my fingers and flippered along with the most exquisite caution, for the hole's timid denizens are easily spooked. Drifting to the rim, I planted a locator-float with a dive flag. Then I adjusted my buoyancy compensator to permit the slowest possible descent, feet first, body motionless. The NeLox rebreather gives off no noisy bubbles and its little tanks can sustain an adult human for nearly half a day at moderate depths. The water, uncomfortably warm on the flat above, cooled as I sank through a short shaft of white rock alive with colorful sea-daisies, waving banners of blue-green seaweed analogues, and colonies of miniature firecracker spongids that "exploded" scarlet defensive nematocysts as I passed by. Unlike the deadly weaponry of their larger cousins, these tiny poison darts bounced harmlessly off my skinsuit.

I emerged from the tube into a kind of underwater arcade, a unique realm that lies beneath the enormous shelf reef that partially encircles Teakettle. The coral ceiling was perforated by hundreds of small openings that admitted narrow bright beams of angled sunlight like theatrical spots, illuminating the gorgeous creatures that inhabit the Glory Hole as though they were precious specimens on display in a museum. Every nuance of color that would ordinarily be lost at depth was restored to vivid perfection by the compensating mechanism of my faceplate lens.

Huge amber filigree sea fans, peony-worms with cerise gills, and iridescent violet plum-tunicates grew on the rocky piers supporting the shelf. Hanging beneath some sections were dense thickets of dainty shrub-corals and bryozoans. Their fragile branches glimmered like faceted jet or pink mother-of-pearl and harbored slowly creeping emerald and cobalt molluscoids.

The floor of the Glory Hole was pure white sand separating a series of fantastic gardens browsed by slow-moving schools of autumn-leaf fish, calico cheepers, and fearless hula-hoop microsharks. Blue and silver toadstool algids grew amidst cannonball crinoids streaked with neon red. Flowering vine gorgonians festooned gigantic translucent barnacles. From sheltered crevices among the encrusted rocks, alien crustaceoids in shiny armor watched me with calm, fiery eyes.

There were plenty of sleepy-looking flapjaw demons hanging about, ugly but delicious fish analogues about half as long as my forearm with sharp little triangular teeth, strabismic eyes, and leathery muddy-red skin. Normally, demons are sluggish and inoffensive; but they go into a feeding frenzy when there's blood in the water, so I didn't want to bother them until it was time to leave. Then I'd capture the designated dinner subjects with my hands, pop them into my catch bag, and dispatch them when I got back to the sub.

Twenty meters or so from the entrance to the hole was a flat rocky area the size of a billiard table that hosted very few bottom-dwelling organisms. In its center floated a cheap plastic lawn chair, tethered to a rocky knob with two short lengths of cord. This was my nautical throne, in which I was accustomed to rock in the cradle of the deep.

I brushed a few clinging marine animals from the seat and settled down gratefully. The chair touched bottom, then tilted gently to and fro. Doing my best to empty my mind and surrender to the Glory Hole's soothing enchantment, I breathed slowly and steadily, attempting to achieve an altered state of consciousness that would wipe away my malaise and persistent sense of guilt. Now and then curious scavenger fishes or creeping arthropodal life-forms would investigate my swaying body. When they found that I was inedible, they went away. My eyes began to close . . .

What was that?

I snapped out of my reverie, aware of a sudden anomalous movement among the indigo shadows on the landward side of the arcade. The sea floor rose in there, coral pillars thickened into virtual corridors, and the illuminating holes in the ceiling were few and far between. Something was fitfully thrashing around in the twilit caverns, and it was very large.

A rush of adrenaline banished my mystical mood in a nanosecond. I gripped the arms of the plastic chair and asked the dive computer to do a targeting scan. My faceplate darkened slightly. The fairy-tale scene lost most of its color and seemed to flatten into two dimensions. A huge shape seemed to be tied in a knot behind one of the thicker columns. The targeter gave its range as 33.2 meters.

"Identify," I whispered. The display confirmed what I already suspected: PROBABILITY 86%: GIANT COMETWORM— THALASSOKOMETIS MAGNIFICA.

Most members of the Kedgeree diving community rated the creature as the most beautiful marine species on the planet. It was also one of the rarest.

I switched the faceplate back to normal mode and finned toward the fabulous beast. Within a few moments it was clearly visible to my enhanced eyes. The rounded head was about the size of a big beachball, blue and gently fluorescent, with enormous white-glowing eyes and a luminous golden mane of hairy filaments. Its mouth gaped, revealing multiple rows of sharp glassy fangs. The body was thick as a man's thigh, matte-black, adorned with horizontal lines of glowing crimson, amber, and white sparks that were brightest and most numerous near the head and faded to invisibility at the tail. Swimming freely, the creature would have been at least six meters long.

But this specimen was unable to swim. It was entangled in the tenacious meshes of a crude drift-net.

"Aw, shit," I whispered.

As I hovered at a safe distance, the cometworm ceased its impotent struggling. The head turned and looked straight at me, then tilted slightly to one side. Slowly, the formidable jaws closed. The headlight eyes blinked. I remembered that these animals were reputed to be very intelligent. Was there a hope that this one might let me cut it free?

I drew my knife from its leg-scabbard and held it in my extended right hand. The worm tilted its head to the other side, as if in puzzlement. Holding my left arm tightly against my side, I performed a brief mime show, pretending that the limb was stuck. Then, beginning at the wrist, I simulated short chops with the blade that gradually "cut" the arm free of its invisible bonds.

"I can do this for you," I said quietly. "How about it?"

The worm blinked again.

I shifted the knife to my other hand and repeated the demonstration. The cometworm stared. I swam toward it with infinite caution, keeping the knife extended in my right hand. If it lunged at me, I was prepared to activate the jetfins and haul ass. But it remained motionless, waiting.

"Okay, big guy. Here's how it works."

I grasped a trailing end of the net and sliced off a hunk, letting the mesh float free. The worm didn't move. I ventured closer, took hold of a section that enveloped the creature's midsection, and began to cut in earnest. Its skin was like black velvet studded with tiny gems. It trembled slightly when I inadvertently touched it, but otherwise remained still, suspended a meter or two above the sandy sea floor. I worked carefully, slicing apart the tangles, while the eerie eyes watched me and seemed to approve.

Finally, the job was done. I wadded up the net shreds and tucked them into my catch bag, finned backward, and put the knife away. "That's all, fella. You're free."

The great serpentine bulk undulated gracefully and the creature opened its mouth wide. Then it gave a final blink and eeled off into the darkness.

A voice in my helmet earphone said, "Nice going."

I spun around in delighted surprise and saw a familiar skinsuited figure equipped with scuba gear. He was back in the well-lit section of the Glory Hole, coming toward me, and he carried a gas-powered speargun under his arm.

"Kofi! Hey, man, you made it after all!"

"That's right. The thought of you out here all alone in a place almost nobody knows about . . . I just had to come."

I swam to meet him, chuckling. "Well, you won't need the gun. The cometworm was tamer than a pussycat. It seemed to know I was there to help."

"Yeah. I saw. Damnedest thing. I've heard those worms are smart. Must have been a fluke, the critter getting caught in a net. Some of those back-to-nature clowns over on Sindbad Cay go in for primitive fishery techniques."

"Well, all's well that ends well."

"Too bad it doesn't," my friend said.

He was less than four meters away when he lifted the speargun, aimed it squarely at me, and pulled the trigger.

Chapter 2

I clenched my left hand and the jets blasted me upward at an oblique angle. The spear missed, but I smashed headfirst into the coral ceiling and nulled out amidst a cascade of exploding colored stars and shellshocked marine life.

When I came to my senses, skull throbbing, Kofi was almost done with the job of lashing me securely to my plastic throne with duct tape.

"What the hell?" I moaned.

"Getting you ready for the deep six, old buddy. Sorry about this. Nothing personal, you understand. The word came down while I was back in Manukura. Seems that some very important people are torqued 'cause you still exist. Thought they'd forgotten all about you, but I guess they were just hangin' back till some shady stuff clarified. Anyhow, I've been designated to finish some previously bungled business."

"Kofi," I said. "Kofi . . . for God's sake!"

"I really hate this," he told me, with what seemed like genuine remorse. "But you gotta understand, Helly, it's my ass or yours."

He finished fastening my flippered legs, slicing off the end of the tape neatly with his dive knife. "See, yesterday this seriously dire dude sidles up to me in the Raiatea Bar on the BB. He tells me that I either polish you off in a tidy and workmanlike fashion *tout de suite*, or somebody'll notify Omnivore's gorillas that I'm hiding on K-L. That happens, the Foodies give me a five-minute trial, call me guilty of grand larceny and embezzlement in the first degree, then haul my handsome black butt back to Earth and lock me up in Coventry Blue till hell chills out."

I shook my head in disbelief. My pal Kofi. We'd worked together, got drunk together, saved each other's lives once or twice on hairy dives. He'd even helped build my new shack after the sea toad ate the original when I should have been inside but wasn't.

"Were you in on the toadster caper, too?" I asked sadly.

"Only in an advisory capacity. Bron Elgar screwed that job up all by himself. Never did like that sadistic motherfucker. Slow on the payoff, too." He tucked the roll of tape into a waist pouch and honed the blade's razor edge gently against one of his BC straps to get the sticky stuff off. He didn't put the knife away.

"So you're just gonna leave me here to die? Jesus, Kofi! There's nine more hours of NeLox in my tanks. Can't you rip off my helmet and at least make it quick?"

He shook his head. "Wish I could, but I've got my orders: no bod for autopsy, but enough residual DNA in the bones and scraps to confirm your ID. You had a tragic accident, see. Except, your mother will get the real message and quit trying to stave off the inevitable—"

"My *mother*!" I surged violently against the duct tape. It got me nowhere.

"Hold still now," Kofi admonished, "and this'll hurt less."

He started to work on me with the dive knife. Beginning with my upper arms and proceeding down the areas of my trunk unencumbered with equipment and onto my thighs, he sliced through my skinsuit and into the flesh beneath. I screamed and cursed, writhing helplessly and blinded by tears of pain.

"Almost done!" he soothed me. "One more time. There we go."

I howled into my helmet as saline water flooded into the shallow wounds, intensifying the pain. Kofi released his hold, and the tethered chair with me taped to it jolted and lurched like an amusement park ride until I finally stopped struggling and subsided, spent and motionless. Dark little strings of blood oozed slowly from at least a dozen small cuts.

I muttered, "Shit. The suit was brand-new. A genuine Phoque from France. Paid full duty, too."

Kofi chuckled and slipped his knife back into its scabbard. "Yeah. Really sharp-looking outfit. Oops! Didn't mean to commit a pun."

"Fuck you, funny man."

"Hey, no hard feelings. I liked you, Helly, even if you were an ex-cop. We had us some good times." He glanced at the dive computer on his wrist. "Well, I guess it's time for me to go. I'll rig *Pernio* to ride out the storm, then come back to-morrow to search for my poor lost bud—collect your remains and whatever scuba gear the flapjaws don't scarf down. I hope those Corby jetfins survive. Always wanted a pair of those."

"You lousy shithead," I said bitterly. "You could have told me about Gala's blackmail threat. I'd have talked to Matt Gregoire, had Rampart Internal Security take you to another planet and give you a new identity—"

"I thought about that. Really! I mean, it was okay to earn a little spare change just lettin' Elgar know what you were up to during the past couple years, but I had to do some heavy thinking when this other dude ordered me to blow you away. Weigh the alternatives. If I'd come clean to you, I'd have had to leave K-L. And the place grows on you, y'know? With you deceased, I figure I'll take over *Pernio* and all your neat stuff. Our pals on Eyebrow'll appreciate that you would have wanted it that way."

Out of the corner of my eye I saw sinister dull red shapes moving through the water. The vanguard of the flapjaw demons was zeroing in, drawn by the scent of my corpuscles. "Just don't toss my Jimmy Buffet dimes," I croaked. "They're worth a bundle."

"I'll play one of his songs at your funeral," Kofi promised. "How about 'Fins to the Right, Fins to the Left'?"

Laughing merrily, he picked up his discarded speargun,

gave me a farewell finger waggle, and swam away into the Glory Hole's access shaft.

Several dozen of the carnivorous piscoids had assembled now and were milling around tentatively, crossed eyeballs pooched out in excitement and toothy mouths oafishly agape. They were a wee bit suspicious of the alien hemoglobin, but they'd get over their inhibitions quickly enough. There were damn good reasons why smart divers wore full skinsuits in waters frequented by this species. Flapjaws weren't all that large, but they were strong and voracious. One coral scratch on your bare skin and you were fish chow.

The pain of the superficial wounds was rapidly diminishing. Kofi had only cut deep enough to draw blood. I strained against my bonds but the tape didn't give a millimeter. Good old duct tape . . . For two hundred years the stuff has been the best friend of plumbers, electricians, mechanics, engineers, sailors, astronauts, householders, and billions of other folks desperate for a quick fix. It's very tough—almost impossible for human musclepower to burst. You have to tear it, beginning at one edge, or poke a starting hole in it with something sharp. But there was nothing near my plastic throne but sand and well-worn rock.

And about thirty flapjaw piscoids with teeth like piranhas, getting ready to sample some exotic fast food.

In time the frigging fish themselves would tear me loose. But by then I'd be a goner. Kofi, with careful forethought, had refrained from slicing me anywhere near the wrists or the ankles. The demons were going to start feeding on my leaky parts—upper arms and thigh muscles, and the soft flesh of my abdomen. Eventually the crazed brutes would consume the rest of me, together with my tattered suit and the tape and every other part of my rig soft enough for their teeth to handle.

A single intrepid flapjaw, larger than the others, darted in as fast as lightning and took a chomp out of my right shoulder. I balled my fists and screamed, *"God!"*

Damned if he didn't answer . . . sort of.

My jetfins swooshed as I inadvertently activated the control glove. I flipped over violently backward until the chair reached the limit of its twin anchor cords and I was almost flat on my back. When I unclenched my left hand the jets cut off and I floated back to an upright position.

The enterprising demon had fled. Its comrades gathered in a nervous huddle at a safe distance.

Well, well.

I punched the jets again and again, setting myself gyrating crazily, hoping the movement would scare the predators away permanently. But after a few minutes they seemed to decide there was nothing to worry about and began to close in. I shouted obscenities into my helmet, goosed the fins until I bobbed like a toy balloon in a gale, but the fish kept coming.

I savored the irony of it: that which I had planned to have for dinner was shortly to dine upon me.

The attack came abruptly, but this time I had no sense of being bitten. I felt blow after stunning blow, as though I were being struck by catapulted rocks. At each impact, the demons tore away a bit of my suit. Some of them also took small hunks of meat. I bounced and roared as the vicious creatures swirled around me. My blood began to cloud the water. I shut my eyes to the horror and howled in brokenhearted desperation.

And missed seeing my savior arrive.

But I felt it, a great glancing thump against my left knee that set me twirling. My eyes flew open and I saw a sinuous black body squirm about me like a gargantuan serpent. Its eyes were shining white and it had a luminous blue head and a streaming golden mane, and it was snapping up flapjaw demons like a bull terrier catching butterflies.

The cometworm had come to my rescue—perhaps out of gratitude, like the lion in the fable who saved the life of that Roman slave, what's-his-face, after the guy pulled a thorn from the big cat's paw. Or more likely, the worm just had a really serious attack of the munchies.

I began to whoop with hysterical laughter.

The water around me turned a sickly greenish-brown hue,

the color of demonic vital fluids mixed with those of humankind. The frenzied cometworm crashed into me again and I felt myself drifting laterally, out of the melee. My rescuer had somehow snapped the cords holding down the chair.

I curled the fingers of my left hand. Accelerating, I moved through the murk toward one of the larger coral pillars that supported the shelf-reef. Tiny creatures fled at my approach, swimming off or withdrawing into crevices in the rock. I let the propulsion wedge me firmly into a niche, then wriggled about until my right wrist was in contact with a rough coralline peg. I rasped away, enfeebled by shock, and after an interminable interval the duct tape confining that arm shredded and came apart. By the time I had freed myself completely from the chair, only a few morsels of demon flesh were left bobbing about the sandy sea floor, pursued by interested crustaceoids. The cometworm was gone.

A sweet, deceptive sense of relief flooded through my brain. My willpower had been sapped by terror, pain, exsanguination, and the effort to escape my bonds. I floated aimlessly about the Glory Hole, slipping in and out of rational consciousness. A remote part of my mind realized that if the upcoming storm caught me under the shelf-reef, the surging currents would almost certainly sweep me into some submarine cul-de-sac where I'd be trapped and perish.

I decided that I didn't care.

Indeterminate time passed. The beauties of the hole surrounded me, and my miseries had mercifully faded away. Kofi's treachery was forgotten, as was Eve's desperate plea for help, my fear that the Haluk were planning an attack on humanity, and even the fact that I might be bleeding to death. In a state of neutral buoyancy, wafting along faceup with my arms and legs flaccid, I drifted immediately beneath the hole's main access shaft . . . where the water was breathing!

A faint curiosity roused me from my torpor. The tendrils and other trailing appendages of the marine life encrusting the vertical tunnel were alternately sucked upward, then downward by increasing wave motion at the surface of the sea. I watched the undulant phenomenon in uncomprehending fascination. The bright colors of the creatures had faded in spite of my spectrum compensator lens. This vaguely puzzled me, but I was too far gone to realize that the sunlight was dimming. I experienced a muddleheaded urge to check out the "breathing" more closely and once again activated my jetfins. The abrupt thrust propelled me toward the lower rim of the shaft, directly into a colony of miniature firecracker spongids.

Their stinging nematocysts fired and my torn suit was hopelessly inadequate to protect me. I felt as though I had been struck by a hundred flaming needles. The sudden agony banished my fatal languor and turned me into a convulsing madman, shrieking and caroming off the sides of the passageway as my spastic left hand involuntarily turned the jetfins on and off.

Something or other, maybe Providence, finally prompted me to punch the buoyancy compensator's emergency ascent pad. Still flailing and shouting, I shot up the shaft to the surface, which was less than seven meters above.

I broached and thrashed about in delirium. Some small functioning part of my mind took command, and little by little I forced my body to relax and ride the waves. The pain from the spongid venom was excruciating, giving a sensation of being roasted alive. But the exploding stingers of the miniature species didn't kill; they only caused slow paralysis of the voluntary muscles.

I had about five minutes to reach *Pernio* and administer the antidote. After that I'd be helpless human flotsam.

Unexpectedly, as my burning body began to go off-line my woozy brain switched back on, with every sense seemingly tuned to preternatural sharpness by sheer agony. The wrist computer's chronograph told me it was late afternoon, which surprised the hell out of me. I managed to look around. The sea had turned from limpid turquoise to muddy olive, the wind had picked up considerably, and clouds were thickening toward the south. The storm might be coming in faster than anticipated. A lenticular cloud that resembled a flying saucer was perched over the summit of the Devil's Teakettle volcano, another indication that the weather was changing for the worse.

There was no sign of *Black Coffee*, but *Pernio* was a reassuring golden speck in the distance. If only the water had been deeper, I could have used my dive computer to turn on the sub's autopilot and summon it. But that was no option. Even with the tide now at its height, the sea around me was still less than four meters deep.

The reconnaissance had taken only a few moments. In my extremities, the ghastly burning sensation was gradually giving way to a more bearable tingling. I clamped my arms to my sides and made a tight fist with my left hand. The jets kicked in at max and I surged off, head partly out of the water like a charging grampus, crashing through the stiff chop. It would have been more efficient to move underwater, but I had a desperate urge to keep my yellow submarine in sight.

Prickly numbness invaded my toes, my fingers, my nose, and my lips. I began to consider what I would do after I reached the sub and administered the antivenin to myself. Kofi's sub was slower than mine, but he would almost certainly reach Eyebrow Cay ahead of me. That was all to the good. He'd phone his Galapharma controller in Manukura with news of my putative demise, but I doubted that he'd leave the island. He had to be in place to go hunting for my bones tomorrow. I could return home under cover of darkness, nab him, do a little rough and ready interrogation, and—

I was slowing down, with half a kilometer still to go.

Cursing, I realized that my entire left arm had lost sensation. The damned nematocysts had mostly struck that side of my upper body, and the hand wearing the fin control glove was almost completely paralyzed. With my right hand I squeezed the useless left fingers into a ball. Immediately, my speedy forward progress resumed. But weakness was creeping down the good arm as well, and a few moments later I felt its grip also failing.

Shit. I was losing momentum again, and *Pernio* was still at least two hundred meters off. I moved at a snail's pace through the waves, which now bore small foamy crests. My right arm functioned, but its fingers were nearly impotent. My feet were full of pins-and-needles now in what I feared was the prelude to paralysis, while my legs still felt relatively normal.

I was dead in the water again before it occurred to me to thrust my hands into my crotch with my last remaining bit of arm strength and press my thighs together.

The jets reactivated momentarily, then cut out again. Somehow, the inner-finger contacts on the glove weren't closing properly. I wriggled my legs, trying to work the pinioned hands into an effective position. Both of them fell free, as useless as lumps of lead.

Well, there was always low-tech methodology . . . until my legs gave out.

Taking a deep breath of the canned neon-oxygen mix, I lowered my head into the water to decrease resistance, turned on the Rolex's navigator, and began scissoring with the stiff, heavy fins. In my weakening state it was desperately hard work. The Corbys weren't meant for serious muscle-powered swimming and they seemed to weigh ten kilos apiece. By now my feet were switched off and I could barely bend my knees, so the entire burden of propulsion fell on my thigh muscles. After a few minutes they were screaming. I ignored the new onslaught of pain and forged on.

I made slow progress while the muscle ache steadily worsened, spreading into my groin. Even my balls hurt. Was I still bleeding? Kofi certainly hadn't opened an artery, and I didn't think the fish had, either. They'd torn my suit to ribbons but I was pretty sure that the bites themselves were mostly small. K-L's seawater is mildly astringent, and minor wounds will often close spontaneously on an immersed body. I was overdue for some good luck and hoped for the best.

I kept kicking woodenly. With my head underwater, the encouraging view of *Pernio* was lost and I concentrated on the faceplate navigation display. Its tiny sub icon was green, the color of safety, while my body was represented by a white blip creeping crazily along like a drunken slug.

Whenever I veered off course, the navigator squeaked at

me to signal a correction: *beebeep* for bear right, *boop* for bear left. At first the incessant *boop-beebeep-boop* drove me nuts; ordinarily, I never used this guidance feature, but I didn't trust myself to swim a straight line under the circumstances. After a time the squeaks became mere background noise, a dreary counterpoint to my misery that I obeyed automatically.

The swim was taking forever. The gap between my icon and the sub's seemed to have stopped closing. Was I making any headway at all?

What if the dive computer wasn't working properly? How many times had my right wrist smashed into coral rock during my struggles down in the Glory Hole, jolting the thing's delicate innards? Surely it wouldn't hurt to break stroke and take a peek above water, just to make sure I was traveling in the right direction . . .

I didn't dare give in to the temptation. If I knew the real distance I still had to cover, rather than the virtual, I might give up in despair.

Maybe I'd do that anyway! What the hell. I was tired enough to die.

But I kept on feebly kicking.

My eyes rebelled against the strain of focusing on the lens display, went bleary, and finally drifted shut. I was on total cruise control now. *Boop-beebeep*. My heart and lungs labored in anguished overdrive. The water of Kedge-Lockaby's ocean is warm, but a cold feeling was creeping up my thighs now, tagging after the deadly pins-and-needles. My face had gone numb. Below my knees there was nothing. Below my shoulders there was nothing. I moved slower and slower.

I wasn't going to make it.

Never mind, Helly. Remember why you came to K-L in the first place, after they threw you out of the ICS. How many times did you aim a "borrowed" sailboard out to sea when you were a drunken derelict living on the Big Beach, intending to make an end of it? Half a dozen times, at least! But you always lost your nerve. Tough to deliberately decide to die when you're a burnt-out case. But no decisions are necessary now. All you have to do is let go . . .

You fucking loser.

That's what my father had called me: a loser. He believed that I'd lost my nerve.

Was it true? Had I turned my back on Rampart Starcorp because Simon was an idiot and I'd done my damnedest before reaching a hopeless dead end . . . or was I just ducking the challenge, as the old man had said?

God damn him, expecting me to come to his rescue! Did he stand by me when I was up against it during my trial for malfeasance? Fuck if he did. He still believed I was guilty of the trumped-up charges. But he'd *use* me any whichaway if it meant—

Bonk.

Oh, Jesus.

I opened my eyes and saw a freshly painted yellow flexihull. I'd kept on kicking throughout my incoherent bitch session and I swam right into *Pernio*'s flank.

Now what? Look, Ma! No hands . . .

But the descender platform was still down, a mechanism designed to spare effete sport-diving clientele from having to leap ignominiously off the sub into the sea or strain tired muscles climbing back out. I hoicked my fanny onto it, tapped the control pad with my faceplate frame, and upsy daisy! I was flopping on the aft flat like a gaffed halibut. Even though the anchored vessel wallowed in the choppy waves, the stanchions and their narrow railing were still deployed so I managed not to fall overboard.

Kofi had retracted the flybridge, battening down for the storm, but it was easy enough to tell the computer to open the main hatch, which was nearly flush with the dorsal surface. All I had to do then was maneuver myself over the coaming and descend the ladder to the command deck without fracturing some vital part of my anatomy.

Easily said. I wore large, awkward jetfins, smallish tanks, and a helmet that had seemed featherlight when I donned it this morning but now threatened to snap my neck with its oppressive weight. There was no helping it: the gear had to come off.

Getting rid of the fins was easy. I slithered into position on the heaving flat and used the leverage of a stanchion to pry the Corbys off, cringing as the expensive things fell into the water and sank out of sight. The helmet, attached to the gas tanks and rebreather unit by its feed lines, had to come off next. Then I could hit the quick-release buckle on the main harness and dump the rest of the equipment that was strapped to my body.

I squirmed and I tumbled. But no matter how I tried, I was unable to remove the headpiece. It was secured by a tenacious neck-hugging skirt of flexible plastic, impossible to budge without the use of my paralyzed hands. I briefly considered and rejected the notion of discarding the harness and letting the deadweight of the attached diving gear pull off the helmet. But the sub was bouncing too violently. I might be dragged back into the sea along with the equipment.

I decided that I had no time left to waste. Rolling to the open hatch, I pulled myself into a sitting position and allowed my nearly deadened legs to drop into the opening. The ladder was angled slightly. I intended to descend it with my back to the rungs, as though it were a flight of steep stairs, performing a sort of jolting slide and praying that the tank module didn't get snagged.

The helmet made it hard to see my insensate feet. When I decided they were resting securely on one of the ladder rungs, I started to wriggle downward, arms dangling limply. My dying thigh muscles quivered like jelly with the effort of lifting my inert legs, and I whacked my backside atrociously at every bump of the descent.

When I was halfway down, a big wave broke over *Pernio* and the sudden flood of water nearly knocked me off the ladder. Fighting not to panic, I told the computer to close the hatch. I reached the bottom miraculously standing on my dead feet, but almost immediately the sub rolled. I lost my balance on the wet sole, went sprawling, and banged my head so hard on the flybridge enclosure that I knocked myself silly.

The mishap was a fortuitous one. When I recovered my wits, lying on my stomach, I discovered that my chin had somehow popped through the helmet's snug-fitting neck seal. With a little more head-bashing and prying against the support of the command seat, I was finally able to pull the damned bucket off my head. The tanks and BC fell free when I hit the buckle-release against the seat's footrest.

Centimeter by centimeter I wormed my way to the first-aid locker beneath the navigation console, struggled up onto my benumbed knees, and poked the code numbers into the simple safety lock with my unfeeling nose. My teeth served to pull out the tray of biotoxin antidote self-dosers. I dumped them onto the wet sole, oblivious of sterility considerations, collapsed, and rooted around in the heap like a dying pig until I found the correct doser. Never mind taking it out of its transparent plastic envelope. I flipped the med with my nose so that its explosive injector sleeve faced up, then fell on my face, shooting the antivenin into my numb cheek.

Yes!

A surge of idiot exultation blazed through me. I was slashed, bashed, semiparalyzed, half conscious and running on the fumes. But I was going to recover and make it back to Eyebrow Cay. And when I got there, my old friend Kofi Rutherford had better look sharp, because his ass was grass and I was the Grim Reaper.

I waited for the lifesaving drug to kick in, reviewing the situation, considering my new options, wondering where I'd stowed my own roll of duct tape.

Chapter 3

Fifty-six years ago, in 2176, Galapharma Amalgamated Concern decided that its remote Perseus Spur colonies were no longer economical and retreated to the Orion Arm of the Milky Way. Seven years later a spunky shoestring outfit called Rampart Interstellar Corporation, founded by my uncle Ethan, my father, and their friend Dirk Vanderpost—my mother's brother—came along and proved that the Concern had made a big fat mistake.

It had been Gala's policy to treat preindustrial alien natives as virtual slave labor. Ethan Frost decreed that Rampart would pay the Insaps fairly. In return the Zmundigaim folks of Seriphos gave their new human employers a little present that they had kept secret from the Gala exploiters: a basket containing a candylike treat they called rozkoz, said to "gladden both the mouth and the mind."

Ethan realized immediately that the confection, more delicious than chocolate, was a potential goldmine. It founded the fortunes of Rampart and brought modest affluence to the Zmundigaim who chose to work for the Starcorp.

By 2232, Rampart had claimed and exploited sixty-four of the most resource-rich Spur worlds. Its ICS mandate also gave it conditional title to nearly three thousand other terrestrial-class planets in the Spur, excepting the handful inhabited by the stargoing Qastt and Haluk races, which were off-limits under Statute 44 of the CHW Code.

Insaps lacking interstellar technology had little to say about human exploitation of their territory, whether in the Perseus Spur or in other parts of the Commonwealth. If the

Earthlings who invaded them were reasonably enlightened—
as Rampart was—primitive Indigenous Sapients often pros-
pered. But if the encroaching Concern or Starcorp treated
alien peoples unjustly, they had very little recourse in CHW
law. Certain humans, including myself, thought this was deplorable; but we were a powerless minority during the heyday
of the Hundred Concerns.

The Qastt and the Haluk were not consulted when CHW
awarded the vacated Perseus Spur Mandate to Rampart. Why
should they have been? During the Galapharma occupation,
the two races refused to trade or even conduct polite di-
plomatic relations with big bad scary humanity. Since the
weaponry and ultraluminal transport technology of the aliens
were inferior to Gala's, the Concern just kissed 'em off.

The trouble was, they didn't stay kissed for long. Instead
they turned pirate, attacking vulnerable human starships and
raiding the weaker Spur colonies. An armistice, brutally
forced upon the Qastt and Haluk during the Galapharma
years, was still nominally in place. In spite of it, depreda-
tions by both alien races, officially attributed to "uncon-
trollable lawless elements," had continued virtually unabated
throughout Rampart's tenancy.

The diminutive, falsetto-voiced Qastt, who occupied thirty
two Perseus worlds and were the most persistent bandits, represented a relatively minor nuisance.

The allomorphic Haluk were something else altogether, as
I'd discovered through personal experience. No one trivial-
ized *them* with droll nicknames. Their hijackings and planet
raids were always well-planned, ruthless in execution, and
targeted toward specific high-tech commodities. Currently,
they had only eleven outpost colonies in the Spur, but they inhabited tens of thousands of other overcrowded planets in a
satellite star cluster off the Spur's tip. Haluk emigration to the
Milky Way Galaxy had been very slow because of their
primitive interstellar transport system, as well as certain limiting peculiarities of the racial physiology.

Both those problems were in the process of being solved,

thanks to egregious meddling by Galapharma and certain of its Big Seven allies.

Of the as yet unclaimed Rampart mandated worlds, 206—including Kedge-Lockaby—were freesoil human colonies, former wards of Galapharma presently governed by the Commonwealth until Rampart chose to move in and assume responsibility for the infrastructure of civilization as we know it. The other planets of the mandate had no permanent human settlements and were informally classified as "wildcat," theoretically wide-open to squatting or plundering, but in actuality too inhospitable or economically challenged to attract small-time opportunists.

CHW Zone Patrol, overworked and underfunded, kept an eye on the freesoil and wildcat worlds and tried to prevent any significant incursions by human or alien predators. Rampart ExSec was responsible for maintaining law and order on most of the Starcorp-settled planets, although a few of the more remote worlds were policed by Rampart Fleet Security.

Under the leadership of the late Ethan Frost, Rampart had flourished and grown apace. In fact, it was on the verge of making the quantum leap from Interstellar Corporation to Amalgamated Concern, whereupon its growth would have become explosive, fueled by venture credit infusions available only to members of the Big Boys Club. However, when Uncle Ethan died in 2227 and my father took over the CEO slot, the company lost its momentum. Simon had never possessed his older brother's entrepreneurial zeal. He lacked the imagination and energy necessary to advance the corporate fortunes and he made a number of very bad strategic decisions.

Among other things, he halted the acquisition of new freesoil planets, cut back on new product research and development, was stingy with employee and Small Stakeholder benefits, and spent too much on ill-considered marketing schemes designed to give Rampart an impressive image that he hoped would dazzle the politicians in Toronto and speed the upgrading of Rampart to Concern status.

Among the worst of Simon's mistakes, to my mind, was his

choice of Ethan's son Zared to be Rampart's President and Chief Operating Officer. Zed Frost was a very smart and charismatic frontman who talked a good game; but when it came down to nitty-gritty operating decisions, he was overly conservative, even more cautious than Simon or my older brother Dan, Rampart's top legal eagle. Zed's handpicked top management men—Leonidas Dunne, Chief Technical Officer, and Gianliborio Rivello, Chief Marketing Officer—were cut from the same bolt of stodgy cloth. The pair served on the Board of Directors and invariably voted along with Cousin Zed.

A sudden string of costly setbacks and several blatant instances of sabotage turned Rampart's stagnation into a genuine downhill slide. It was ripe for a takeover when Galapharma made its first tender offer in 2228. Zed, Leo, and Gianni declared themselves in favor of the merger. So did Emma Bradbury, Ethan's widow, who controlled 12.5 percent of the corporate shares, voting them as instructed by her son, Zed.

The attempt by the colossus to gobble Rampart made Simon's blood boil. He rallied opposition among the stakeholders and Gala's initial bid was voted down.

As time passed and disasters multiplied inside the Starcorp, Simon's principal boardroom allies—my brother Dan, Thora Scranton, who was the Small Stakeholder mouthpiece, Gunter Eckert, the financial chief, and even my mother, Katje Vanderpost—began to have second thoughts about the wisdom of linking up with the big Concern. Alistair Drummond submitted new offers, sweetening the pot each time and applying more and more pressure.

By the time I came onto the scene in 2232, after Eve's kidnapping, Simon was fighting a rearguard action with the Rampart board. He suspected that one or more of them might have made an under-the-table deal with the enemy.

Corroborating that belief was an enigmatic remark that had been made by Gala's late assassin, Bronson Elgar, implying that a member of the Frost family—presumably a secret Galapharma partisan—was responsible for the diabolical suggestion that Eve be demicloned. This pointed strongly to Cousin Zed as the viper in the corporate bosom. He certainly had a bitter resentment of my older sister. They were open rivals for the top executive position, and Simon had been very nearly ready to promote Eve and repudiate Zed at the time of her abduction.

I had found no firm evidence of treachery by Zared Frost during my own investigations, undertaken during the six months following the rescue of Eve from her kidnappers. My associate Karl Nazarian, who had been Simon's original head of corporate security and knew more about cyberespionage than anyone else in the Perseus Spur, had analyzed Zed's spoor within Rampart CorpNet over the previous several years and come up with *nada*. Not even my cousin's open endorsement of the Gala takeover proved he was a traitor. He might just as well have been motivated by expediency and honest greed as by perfidy.

The only other thing even remotely suggestive of incrimination was Zed's close relationship with the turncoat security Vice President, Oliver Schneider. He'd nominated Schneider as Nazarian's successor when the old man decided to retire, and he'd strongly supported Schneider when the latter made certain controversial—even disastrous—security decisions. But Zed seemed to have done so without any devious motives.

Karl Nazarian had proved Schneider's guilty association with Galapharma by following his secret data-trails; but none of those trails had led to the office of Rampart's incompetent President and Chief Operating Officer, Zared Frost.

If only it had been possible to interrogate Zed and Ollie with psychoprobe machines! But my cousin's high corporate position made such a fishing expedition inconceivable, while Schneider and his four asshole buddies, who'd engineered the campaign of subversion and sabotage, were gone with the wind.

Matilde Gregoire, the former Fleet Security Chief who had taken over Schneider's position as VP Confidential Services, had ferreted out a number of other low-echelon saboteurs and dirty-tricksters emplaced in various departments of Rampart; but these perps knew nothing at all about any upper-level treachery. Machine probing affirmed that they were all in the game for the money alone. They had taken their orders directly from Schneider's minions and knew nothing about any Gala connection.

Our attempts to find other material witnesses implicating Galapharma in a conspiracy to devalue Rampart had failed. Without them the investigation had reached a dead end.

Or had it?

There were still the captive Qastt pirates Eve had mentioned . . . and Kofi Rutherford.

As I lay helpless on my submarine in a pool of blood and seawater, waiting for my poisoned nervous system to recover, I did some serious thinking about the new suspects.

The Squeak buccaneers had an unusual history. Several weeks before Eve's kidnapping, they'd got into a firefight with a heavily armed Rampart freighter and were forced to surrender. When a human prize crew boarded the Qastt vessel, they discovered a Haluk passenger who had just committed suicide. The Squeakers were narrowly prevented from destroying the body.

Now, it was totally unprecedented for Haluk to travel on Qastt starships. The two races had almost nothing in common except their hatred of humanity. When the Qastt crew were interrogated by Rampart security agents on Nogawa-Krupp, they admitted that the Haluk had been on board to broker an instant deal for the Rampart freighter's cargo, should the bandits succeed in grabbing it. Subsequently, I discovered which portion of that cargo was particularly coveted by the Haluk. It was the obscure genen vector PD32:C2, produced only on the Rampart planet Cravat.

At the time, neither Eve nor the authorities on N-K suspected that the Haluk corpse on the pirate ship had any sinister significance. Because this particular alien race was still little known to human science, the body was sent to Tokyo University for study. The Japanese researchers' findings had been astonishing, providing the first clue to the nature of the

Haluk's mysterious genetic engineering project. But in no way did the Tokyo data implicate Galapharma. The scientists very properly decided to keep their discovery secret until the study was completed.

They'd tried to keep it a secret from Simon, too, but he pried it out with a combination of threats and bribery.

Eve's suggestion to me that the Qastt prisoners might provide a clue linking Gala to the Haluk seemed highly unlikely. It was more logical that the Haluk would have told the Squeakerinos as little as possible about their reasons for wanting PD32:C2, to keep the price down. I'd have to ask Karl Nazarian to reinterrogate the Qastt pirates just in case they knew something, but the odds were that they'd be just another dead end.

Kofi might not be, if he could lead me to the Galapharma agent who'd ordered my death.

It took over an hour for the spongid venom antidote to take effect completely. I was up and about even before the paralysis had completely faded, shucking the remnants of my skinsuit, standing in a shower screaming my head off as cold and then hot water laved my wounds, shooting up with antibiotics and painkiller. My cuts, bites, and bruises were numerous and picturesque, but not as serious as I had feared. I found everything I needed to treat them in *Pernio*'s well-stocked meds locker.

When the doctoring was done, I dressed in a set of sweats and rain gear, cranked up the flybridge, and started the sub's engines. I'd have to take her out of the dangerous shallows running on the surface—and do a damn quick job of it. The first rain squall of the approaching tropical depression now lashed the waves with gale-force winds, and the old boat wallowed like a drunken sow, as she always did riding topside in rough seas.

Finally we reached a safe depth. I went below again and submerged, and the chaos of the storm vanished miraculously. *Pernio* picked up twenty knots of headway. I fed the course into the MFGS, engaged the autopilot, and went to my bunk.

I'd intended to sleep during the three hours it would take to get home, but my damned imagination wouldn't let me. I brooded about what I was going to have to do to Kofi. Then I thought with growing dismay about Eve's overly optimistic notion that she and I could save the Starcorp by dint of fancy footwork that would impress the ICS Status Review Board.

It wouldn't happen. Not unless we could nail Galapharma to the wall before the crucial six weeks were over—that is, come up with evidence that would justify immediate and massive legal action against it.

Alistair Drummond wouldn't sit quietly by, watching Rampart straighten up and fly right under a new regime. If Eve and I openly took command and somehow made Rampart look good to the ICS, Drummond would have no choice but to accelerate his assault to a red-line pitch. He'd destroy Rampart rather than let it slip out of his grasp, because the takeover was no longer a mere matter of profiteering.

Galapharma's own survival, and that of its Big Seven allies, was at stake.

The more I thought about this angle, the more certain I became. Sending Kofi to kill me had been a bizarre step smacking of panicky improvisation. I'd been working on Seriphos for months, vulnerable to professional hit men, and yet Gala had done nothing. That Alistair Drummond was actually worried about the prospect of my rejoining Rampart as Chief Operations Officer seemed ridiculous on the face of it; but try as I might, I couldn't figure any other motive for a sudden attack by an amateur killer. It only made sense if Drummond felt he was engaged in a desperate holding action that he could not afford to lose.

In her eagerness to have me consent to her plan to save the family farm, Eve had discounted what we'd learned in the caverns of Cravat from a pathetic woman named Emily Blake Konigsberg, the former lover of Alistair Drummond. Emily's story had been almost beyond belief, but Matt Gregoire and I had both seen the proof of it with our own eyes.

And Eve herself was *living* proof.

This is what Konigsberg had told us:

When the Galapharma CEO cast avaricious eyes on the Perseus Spur, he had a greater goal in mind beyond simply getting back the valuable properties that his predecessors had foolishly let slip away. Drummond envisioned a vast new market among the teeming Haluk, whose star-cluster boasted an abundance of valuable ultraheavy elements—a market not only for the drugs and biologicals of Galapharma, but also for the products of Bodascon, Sheltok, Homerun, and Carnelian Concerns. Which Galapharma would broker, for a stiff percentage of the take.

Emily started it all.

Until she convinced him otherwise, Alistair believed, like everyone else, that the Haluk were a hopelessly treacherous and xenophobic lot who nursed an implacable hatred of more scientifically advanced humankind. Emily Konigsberg, who was an academic of distinguished reputation and naive idealism, had made a special study of the Insaps of the Perseus Spur. She persuaded her lover that the antagonism between humanity and the Haluk was rooted in misunderstanding, together with a tragic envy by the aliens of our more efficient racial biology.

Together, Emily and Alistair conceived a daring strategy that they were certain would win the Haluk over . . . and generate colossal profits for Galapharma and its allies as a felicitous side effect. Never mind that it was highly illegal for a nongovernmental organization—even one of the mighty Big Seven Concerns—to negotiate a secret pact with an alien race, bypassing the Commonwealth Assembly. The two conspirators believed that if CHW was faced with a successful fait accompli, it would be forced to grant retroactive approval to a project so objectively worthy.

And so advantageous to Big Business.

Armed with conditional offers of support from four other members of the Big Seven—Omnivore, the food and beverage colossus, was not invited to join the cabal because the aliens didn't favor human comestibles, while the Chairman of Macrodur was a notorious straight arrow who couldn't be trusted to place his bottom line above his moral principles— Drummond's agents presented the proposal to the Haluk leadership. In exchange for enormous quantities of unhexocton, unhexseptine, and other transactinide treasure, Galapharma pledged to set aside no less than fifteen hundred terrestrial-class Perseus Spur planets for Haluk colonization, said worlds to be delivered when the expected Gala takeover of Rampart was accomplished. In advance of that, as a supreme gesture of good faith, Emily and a team of other Galapharma scientists would assist the Haluk with a certain complex genetic engineering project that the aliens deemed crucial to their racial destiny. The human assistance came at a high price, which went without saying, but the Haluk eagerly accepted.

The genen aspect of the scheme had gone into operation about four years ago. Participation by the four other big Concerns followed later, as Drummond demonstrated the enormous profit potential of Haluk trade. Bodascon supplied top-of-the-line starships that were needed by the Haluk to step up emigration from their home star-cluster. Sheltok provided advanced fuel additives needed to propel the vessels, as well as energy generators and force-field projectors. Homerun sold heavy equipment and machinery that the aliens required to upgrade their industrial base. Carnelian supplied a wide variety of robotics, sophisticated communications equipment, and electronic controls.

The grand conspiracy had worked beautifully . . . until I came along with my unlikely crew of spoilers and threw a monkey wrench into the works on the planet Cravat. Emily Konigsberg had died there, trying to escape an underground holocaust. The Haluk genetic engineering project she had supervised, a crucial component of the secret trade deal, went up in smoke along with her.

Drummond and his cabal were undoubtedly hard at work attempting to repair the damage. But it seemed certain that none of those corporate hotshots had the least notion that the xenophobic, needy Haluk might have other goals in mind besides upgrading their inconvenient physiology, finding a little *Lebensraum*, and taking care of business.

I now had a pretty good inkling of the awful truth. But since no one in authority would listen to me, I was merely a Throwaway version of Chicken Little, yammering that the sky was about to fall.

In my present depressed and frustrated mood, I was damn near ready to let it.

Only maybe not quite yet.

When *Pernio* made a cautious passage through the surf-pounded reef of Eyebrow Cay, the lights on shore were barely visible in the torrential downpour. I didn't want to tie up at the marina, in case Kofi was still on his boat. There was also a chance that he'd be spending the stormy evening hoisting a few with the gang in the back of the general store, where Billy Mulholland operated a shebeen that purveyed alcoholic cheer as well as espresso drinks and simple pub food.

I moored my sub in the lagoon just outside the cove where I lived and went jouncing ashore in the inflatable. I was wearing a rainsuit with a fanny pack full of necessary stuff buckled over it. My dive knife in its scabbard was hidden beneath the jacket. Wind roared through the trees like a stampede of Brahma steers, and the surging sea nearly reached the steps of my house; but the shack was on high pilings, like most of the other island dwellings, and safe enough from most of the local weather. As I reached the top of the rocky rise that separated Kofi's place from mine I saw a glimmer of light among the thrashing palms and fingerwoods and gave a satisfied grunt. He was probably home.

There was no need for a cautious approach with the storm making such a racket so I just stole up his front steps. They sagged alarmingly. Like the rest of the tumbledown old building, they were rapidly biodegrading. Kofi had the shutters lowered on the windows facing the raging sea. I went around the open deck to the side of the house and peeked in. There was my treacherous bud, taking his ease in a ratty old recliner before the television. A nice fire was burning in his glass-door Franklin stove. He hadn't gotten around to fixing the leaky roof, having killed the day (so to speak) with me, and a bucket was set out to catch drips. He had a brew in one hand and the remote in the other. The screen on the wall was showing previews from the Purple Pipeline featuring frisky ladies doing unlikely things to one another.

I crept back to the front of the place and began to pound on the door and shout in a strangled, high-pitched voice. "Kofi! Open up, it's Mimo! Help me, for God's sake!"

The door suddenly flew open. I stood out of arm's reach. The rainjacket's hood hid my face. I teetered from side to side like a sick old man.

Kofi said, "What the fuck?"

I whimpered, *"Ayudame, amigo!"* and took a faltering step backward.

As he came out the door, I straightened and brought up my right fist in a short, wrecking-ball uppercut that took him square on the chin. Any ordinary guy would have gone down like a sack of sand. (Any ordinary embezzling accountant would have gone lullaby for a week!) But Kofi Rutherford just rocked on his pins, gave a bellow of rage, and tried to envelop me in a rib-crushing bear hug. I thumb-fisted him in the balls. He leapt back screeching and landed a solid blow to my left eye.

We danced around and I charged him with a body block. The two of us crashed to the rough boards of the deck and rolled about, grappling and howling, neither one daring to release his grip on the other. He got hold of my ears and pounded my head into the floor. I broke his pinky finger. Roaring with pain, he nevertheless trapped me in a headlock. I turned my face into the crook of his elbow to stave off strangulation, raked his flesh with my nails through the thin fabric of his T-shirt, caught him with my legs in a scissor lock, and rolled. We cannoned against the deck railing, and the half-rotten supports snapped like matchsticks. Still clamped together, we went over the edge and fell more than two meters. The rain-hardened sand was like plascrete.

I landed on top, but even so, the impact stunned me. Kofi

woofed and was still. I lay there for a minute or two, then felt him stir beneath me. He began to mumble, "Ah shit ah shit ah shit." It was black as midnight under an iron skillet and pouring fit to drown a frog.

I found Kofi's north end from the noise he was making, fitted my hands around his throat, and was pressing my thumbs into his jugular when he gurgled, "Quits! Quits! Fuckin' leg's broke. Something wrong with my arm, too."

I eased on the strangling a mite. "If you're lying—"

"Get off me and see for yourself. I ain't going nowhere."

"Don't move!" Still sprawled on top of him, I groped for the small flashlight I carried in my fanny pack and turned it on. A portion of the smashed railing lay beneath us, partially driven into the sand. He moaned as I slithered off his body. I drew my knife from its sheath, let him see it in the beam of the flashlight and said, "I'm gonna get up."

"Yeah, yeah." His left leg was bent at the knee in an unnatural way, either broken at the joint or badly dislocated. His left forearm, flung wide, was lacerated and bleeding, pierced by a splinter the size of a bayonet. He reached across his chest with the other hand, the one with the broken finger, touched the wood shakily, and cursed.

Struggling to my knees, I took stock of myself. One of my eyes was swelling shut. There was a throbbing knot at the back of my skull. I tasted salty blood from a split lip and my ears were on fire. My jacket had come unsnapped and blood was smeared all over the front of me, probably from old shoulder wounds that had torn open. My bones seemed to be intact.

I said, "What's the name of the guy who told you to kill me?"

His eyes were fixed on the illuminated knife in my hand and he sneered. "What? You gonna start cutting me open if I don't confess?"

"I need a description and his phone code at the Big Beach."

Kofi ran his tongue around the inside of his mouth, spat out something, and muttered, "Shee-it. You damn near knocked my teeth out with that sucker punch."

"Tell me about the contact."

His face twisted in agony and he shuddered. When he finally spoke, his voice was full of sad surprise. "Y'know? I think I'm really fucked, man. Hurt like hell inside."

"Where?"

"Left. Maybe broken ribs. You came down hard on me, but I traded you some. Should see your face!" A soft giggle. He squeezed his eyes shut as another spasm of pain washed over him. To my surprise, he asked, "How you doing?"

"Okay. You broke my fall."

"That, too?" He took a ragged breath, then flashed me a bloodstained grin. "You're somethin' else, Hel. Know that? Dodged the sea toad, got rescued off that damned comet, bisected ol' Bron Elgar like a bagel out there on Cravat . . . How the hell you get away from those damn fish down in the Glory Hole? Man, you got more lives than a New York alleycat."

"The name," I repeated. I brought the blade down in front of his eyes, keeping the flashlight on his face. Falling drops bounced and beaded on the bright metal. His dark cheeks were streaming. There were tears mixed with the rainwater. I said, "Please, Kofi."

"Hey, now!" He gave a crazy kind of laugh and winced at the effort. "Interrogating the suspect *po*-litely! You crazy? Go ahead—start slashing! Carve me like a pork roast. I deserve it, right?"

"All I want is the information."

"Don't wanna do the torture thing? Not even a teensy bit of revenge? Get some satisfaction for the way I sold you out, poked holes in you, wouldn't even let you die easy down in the hole? Come on, make me talk. See if you can!"

I held the knifepoint a few millimeters above his right eyeball. "Tell me, Kofi."

"You gonna do it," he whispered, "do it!"

For a long time I didn't move. Then I withdrew the blade, replaced it in its sheath, sat back on my heels and stared at him. The rain cascaded down on us. Waves were thundering on the rocks below Kofi's house, and the leaves of the alien trees clattered in the fury of the gale. I was soaked to the skin in spite of my rainsuit. I'd lost one sea boot. My wound collection ached like blue blazes and I had dribbled blood all over the broken man lying on the sand.

"Do it!" Kofi screamed.

"Shut up."

I unclipped my fanny pack, rummaged, found the phone and tried it. The case was cracked. The thing was dead as a chunk of corned beef. "Is your phone up in your house?"

The sound he made was half a sob. He writhed, trying to pull his arm off the impaling splinter. "Left it . . . on the boat to charge. House charger unit fritzed out. I was gonna ask Oren to fix it."

"Terrific. Lie still."

I'd have to go back to my place to get help. The nearest Medic Unit was on Gingerbread Island, over three hundred kilometers away. I thought it might be better to fly Kofi over in Mimo's speedy Garrison hopper rather than wait for an evacuation, but he'd have to be stabilized first.

I used the flashlight to find my missing footgear and gather loose deck palings that would serve for splints. The arm would be a tricky job for somebody whose first-aid skills were as rusty as mine. That dagger of wood couldn't be left in place, but he'd probably bleed like a son of a bitch when I removed it. I dragged as much of the shattered railing out from under Kofi as I could and then shed my rainjacket. The knife served to slice off one of the long sleeves of my sweatshirt. I chopped the thick cloth into pieces.

"Can you hold the flashlight?" I asked him.

He took it. "About that button man on the Big Beach—"

"To hell with him." I took the roll of duct tape out of my pack.

"What you gonna do with that?"

"Boy Scout stuff."

A despairing chuckle. "Why bother? You think I'm dog shit."

"Wrong. I think you're guppy shit."

"Hah! I know why you can't torture me, muthahfuckah.

Because it'd *lower* you to my scumbag level. You're a Boy Scout for real! Can't stand soilin' your lofty moral principles—"

"I've got to lift this arm off the wooden spike poked through it. It'll hurt. I'll try to be quick."

As I did the job, he yelled, "Shiiiit!" and dropped the flashlight.

I caught it and held it in my mouth. Blood was pouring from both ends of the puncture but I didn't see any strong arterial spurting. I held the pressure point in the bend of his elbow until the flow eased, simultaneously clamping wads of cloth over the holes. I really needed another hand. I could feel at least one broken bone moving inside the lower arm. Blood continued to ooze slowly as I wrapped it firmly with the wide tape and applied a splint.

"Now I'm going to cut your shirt and check your side."

Kofi spoke in a faint, strained voice. "Can't you do this . . . repair work someplace dry? Feel like I'm freezin'."

"Soon."

He cried out weakly as I felt along his side. There was no external wound and it was impossible for me to see any bruising on the dark wet skin. "You feel ribs grating in there? Take a breath."

"Yeah . . . Jesus, it's bad, Helly."

"Right. I'm too wrecked myself to carry you into the house, but in a minute I'll be able to drag you underneath it, out of the weather. First I have to do a quickie splint on the leg. Here, cover up with my jacket. Keep the rain off you at least."

"Too . . . damn nice."

His voice was barely audible now and his eyes had glazed. He was probably going into shock. God knew what was busted inside him besides the ribs. Maybe his spleen or his liver. Could be internal bleeding.

Working as quickly as I could, I immobilized his leg between two slats and wrapped the result with duct tape. More of the sticky silver stuff secured his wounded arm to his chest, slingwise. I ignored the broken pinky finger. That was the least of his problems.

After hauling him to the driest spot beneath his shack, I limped up the stairs and collected bedding, a plastic tarp, and a big lantern. When I returned with the stuff, his skin had turned the color of clay. I cut off his wet clothing as best I could and swathed him with the blankets. His eyes opened.

"Helly."

"Don't talk. I'm going to my place and—"

"The guy . . . name he used was Lee. Garth Wing Lee. Oriental, one-seventy-five centimeters, stringy build, maybe martial artist, long black hair in a tail, ultra clearcut threads. Staying . . . Alhambra Lagoon, Bungalow 40. But he was leaving K-L. Maybe already . . . gone."

After pulling the blankets closer around his head, I arranged the tarp in a kind of tent, tucked under him, to keep wind-blown rain and spindrift at bay. "Thanks, pal. I'll check it out."

"Gone," he repeated. Then he was still.

It didn't register. But of course I was in pretty shitty shape myself by then. I finished fumbling with the tarp and said, "Hang in there. Be right back."

His mouth hung slack. The eyes in the gray face were wide open, their pupils dilated to onyx circles. I felt for a pulse in his neck but found nothing.

Should I have tried CPR? No use, given the circumstances. And besides, I wasn't *that* much of a Boy Scout.

Chapter 4

Back at my place, I called the Alhambra Lagoon Hotel on the Big Beach. Citizen Garth Wing Lee had indeed checked out, not quite an hour earlier. By now he was either at the starport or hightailing it into the void. It was futile for me to think of going after him, given my state of physical decrepitude. Only one person could help me now.

Jake Silver is the Superintendent of Kedge-Lockaby's small Public Safety Force. Prior to my temporary rehabilitation, he was the only one on K-L who knew the true identity of the hapless beach bum called Helmut Icicle. On several occasions he prevailed upon me to share my special expertise in corporate-style criminality. We had become warily chummy. Cranky, ponderous, and on the wrong side of fifty, he is much too tough and intelligent to be running a twenty-officer dog and pony show on an insignificant planet in the back of beyond. I figured that somewhere, sometime, he had made some important enemies.

Just like me.

"It's Helly Frost over on Eyebrow Cay," I said, as he picked up my call. The poor guy is on duty ten hours a day. "Do me a swift and enormous favor. This is no joke! See if one Garth Wing Lee has departed Manukura Starport, and if so, via what." I rapped out the physical description. "If the guy is still landside, have your special weapons team take him down with a stun. He's extremely dangerous and he might try to self-destruct."

"Mother-o'-pearl!" Jake drawled. "You're not home a week yet, and already you're throwing your weight around.

79

May I remind you that you're Thrown Away and no longer a facecard Rampart exec to whom I must bow and tug my graying forelock?"

"Jake, there's no time for bullshit. Lee could be another Bronson Elgar. One of my friends is dead because of him and I had the crap beat out of me. You gotta pull this fucker in."

" 'Gotta' is not a word I want to hear from you, Hell-Butt."

The Throwaway population of the Out Islands lives and dies beyond the jurisdiction of Commonwealth Public Safety authorities. Undertaking a hazardous collar on behalf of Rampart Starcorp is not a top priority of the freesoil constabulary, either.

"Do it, Jake, for chrissake!"

After a long pause he said, "I'll get back to you," and cut off.

I carried the phone into the bathroom so I could take another hot shower, pop more painkiller, and treat the latest damage to my long-suffering carcass. The right eye was reddish black and almost swollen shut. I pricked the contused flesh with bruise-diffuse and tied coldpacks over the shiner and the lump on my occiput by knotting a blue bandanna around my head, making me look like a cartoon Captain Kidd. The split lip needed AB and a strip of Novepiderm. So did the reopened wounds and my lacerated knuckles. My scarlet ears benefited from anti-inflammatory salve.

While I struggled into a fresh set of loose-fitting sweats, I debated whether to collapse on the bed and pass out immediately or get a glass of milk and some snickerdoodle cookies first to raise my cellar-dwelling blood sugar and calm my queasy stomach. I hadn't eaten since breakfast but I had no appetite. Being on the receiving end of mayhem'll do that to you.

The phone buzzed before I sorted out a decision.

"Jake?" I inquired.

But it was Mimo Bermudez. His dinner invitation had slipped my mind completely. I apologized. "It turned out to be a dismal day on the water, *hombre*. Sorry, but I wasn't able to bring back any flapjaws for you to cook."

"There's plenty of other food I can prepare for us. You must come over, Helly. The business associate I told you about this morning is here and very anxious to meet you."

"I'm really whacked and not very hungry. Much as I'd like to chat with your colleague—"

"He has vital information for you. If you're too tired to eat, then so be it. But you must hear what this man has to say. We'll come to your house."

"No!" I interposed hastily. "Give me a few minutes and I'll be right over." I severed the connection, moaning. I felt like I had one foot in the grave and another on a banana peel. There were gory clothes all over the place and the floor was bloody, too. No way was I going to explain to Mimo what had happened to Kofi and me. Not in front of some stranger.

Plodding back into the bathroom, I treated myself to a stimulant. I still felt terminal. The rainsuit was a mess so I put on an old yellow slicker and sneakers without laces and shambled out into the storm. When I knocked on Mimo's door, he opened immediately.

"Come in! Let me take your coat and get you a drink—" He surveyed my visible dings. "*Madre de dios,* what have you done to yourself?"

"It's a long story and I'd really rather not go into it just now. A neat shot of Jack would be great."

I followed him into his study. Blazing logs crackling in the hearth were the only source of light. Sprawled on the sofa in front of the fire was the guest, an enormously fat man with dead white skin. Either he was unaware that gross obesity can be treated by metabolic tweaking, or else he was one of those weirdos who take perverse satisfaction in cultivating corpulence.

Given the rest of his appearance, it had to be Option B.

His hair, which was teased into an intricate beehive, his eyebrows, and his bushy beard were an improbable buttercup color. He wore a tentlike garment that resembled a crazy quilt stitched together from countless scraps of expensive fabric: velvets, satins, brocades, glacé leathers, even bits of tapestry, trapunto work, and see-through tulle embroidered in gold and silver. Black leather cuffs bulging with little closed cases were clasped about his pudgy wrists. The nails of his oddly slender fingers were filed to sharp points and painted black, and he wore a multitude of jeweled rings. The feet of the grotesque apparition, absurdly small and dainty, were shod in Aladdin boots with turned-up tips. An ornate chain around his neck bore a tiny gold-plated Davis DM-22 derringer pistol as a pendant.

Mimo said, "Helly, may I present my former business associate, Captain Zygmunt Cybulka. Ziggy, this is Asahel Frost."

The seated personage made no attempt to shake hands. He smirked at me, showing discolored pointy fangs, and raised one of my friend's crystal tumblers, half full of amber liquid, in a mocking salutation.

"I'm glad you could join us after all. I did come to see you at considerable inconvenience." He chuckled throatily, a sound like pebbles pouring onto a bass drum. "But Mimo assures me that I will be generously reimbursed."

What the hell?

Mimo held up a bottle of bourbon. "I'm afraid I have no Jack Daniel's. Ziggy was kind enough to bring me a gift of Maker's Mark Limited Edition from his latest import shipment."

"I'll manage to gag it down," I said. It was probably the best American whiskey in the known universe.

He poured me a snort of the magnificent booze and I lowered myself into one of the cushioned wicker chairs and sipped. It warmed my gullet all the way down, pooled igneously in my empty stomach and seeped into my veins, bringing blessed ease. Rain pelted the snuggery's windows and the surf sounded like rhythmic cannon fire.

"You look somewhat the worse for wear, Citizen Frost," remarked Captain Zygmunt Cybulka.

"I'm just fine. Small accident on my boat. You may as well call me Helly. I'm not a citizen any longer."

Cybulka expelled another rattling laugh. "A temporary setback, I'm sure, my dear Helly. I can't believe that your illustrious family would allow you to remain disenfranchised for long."

I was not in the mood to trade small talk with creepy low-lives. My pal Mimo was an honorable sort of outlaw, but cop's instinct told me that this "associate" of his was crooked enough to have to screw on his socks. "Do you have something to tell me, Captain Cybulka? I'm tired and I want to go to bed."

"Call me Ziggy. I have interesting information for you, but I do not intend to vouchsafe it gratis."

Mimo said to him quietly, "The two million is yours if the tip pans out. You know I'm good for it."

What?

The eyes under their shaggy yellow brows were small and reptilian. They darted back and forth between me and Mimo. Then Cybulka seemed to come to a decision and nodded. "In the course of my business travels throughout the Spur, I happened to see a parked starship designated RES-1349—"

"The ExSec cutter Schneider stole!" I croaked. "Where?"

The fat man went on as though I hadn't interrupted. "An acquaintance of mine said that the vessel had been there for a long time. Its dockage fees were paid up to date, however. I was told that five individuals had been escorted from the ship and off the port premises by a highly placed local official. My confidant had no way of knowing what became of the cutter crew after that. They may still be on the planet or they may not be. I departed at once and headed here at top speed, notifying Mimo of my intent to claim his reward."

I jumped to my feet, pain and fatigue forgotten. "My God—it must be Schneider! But how could our sweep have missed a ship parked in plain sight?"

Zygmunt Cybulka's face bore a self-satisfied simper. "Easily. You looked in all the right places, ignoring the wrong ones."

I stared at Mimo, who shrugged and said, "While Rampart and Zone Patrol mounted their search, I spread the word amongst . . . *los bajos fondos de la sociedad,* requesting that they keep their eyes open. I took the liberty of offering a generous gratuity."

"So where is the cutter?" I plopped down again.

"On a Qastt planet!" Cybulka quivered in seismic glee.

"Surely you jest." This was crazy. The fugitives might conceivably have gone to a *Haluk* world with the connivance of Galapharma, but hardly one belonging to the Lilliputian brigands.

"I saw the vessel with my own eyes." The fat man's voice was suddenly level and as cold as ice.

According to the terms of CHW Statute 44, human starships were forbidden to approach even the outermost perimeters of Qastt or Haluk solar systems without permission from the aliens. Which was never granted—except to shady operators such as the plethoric captain.

"From time to time I undertake commercial transactions with the Squeakers," he continued. "Dreadfully devious and high-strung little sods, but they do have an insatiable appetite for certain recreational narcotics. I condescend to supply their needs when it suits my schedule. Imagine my surprise when I visited—hem!—a world of theirs and saw the missing Rampart External Security ship."

"Which Qastt world?" I asked.

An intriguing idea lurked coyly at the threshold of my mind. There were numbers of Qastt planets in the vicinity of Cravat, source of the coveted genen vector PD32:C2, but the nearest Haluk colony was nearly seven hundred light-years distant. What if the Haluk had set up a genetic engineering facility on a Qastt world for the sake of convenience? We already knew that they had other operations besides the very specialized one on Cravat. Knowing what I did about their grand demorphing scheme, I figured there might be excellent political reasons for them to site the facilities outside their own colonies.

And Ollie Schneider and his lads might be usefully employed there, until the heat was off.

"Which Qastt world?" I repeated.

"Two million," the drug-runner crooned, "was the posted reward."

"Rampart Starcorp will give you half the amount immediately," I said, gritting my teeth. "You'll get the balance when we confirm the presence of the stolen cutter on the Squeak planet. I'll call Rampart Central on Mimo's SS com right now and arrange for the transfer of funds. Just give me your account code."

"Make it a blind draft," Ziggy said crisply. He opened one of the small compartments on his left cuff and handed me an EFT card. "And I want all of it now."

Mimo broke in. "Helly, I was the one who offered the reward—"

I rounded on him. "Rampart will pay. If this overfed scagpeddler really has the goods."

Cybulka chortled. "Oh, I do. Two million immediately, or I take my business elsewhere. I'm sure there will be other interested bidders."

I surged to my feet and grabbed a fistful of patchwork caftan. "Don't you play games with—"

He tapped one of my arms casually with his right leather cuff. A few thousand volts sparked from a concealed taser electrode into my frayed nervous system. I flew backward and crashed to the floor on my hypersensitive contused ass.

"*Three* million," said Ziggy, tossing off the contents of the crystal tumbler.

I disparaged his sexuality and that of his mother in hackneyed terms.

He cocked his head roguishly. "Do I hear four?"

Mimo helped me into a chair and murmured, "Let me take care of this. He means what he says."

I hissed, "Dammit, Meem, why the hell didn't you tell me what you were doing?"

"The odds were very long and I couldn't risk Matt Gregoire or Karl Nazarian interfering." He eyed Cybulka. "Or putting pressure on my more skittish underworld contacts."

"Fuckin' A," averred the fat man. He poured more whiskey from the bottle that sat on the low table before the fire and smiled at me benignly. "I forgive your impulsive behavior, Helly. It's plain that you've had a bad day. The information is yours for three million: two as a down payment, and the balance upon verification."

I asked Mimo, "How can we be sure this joker isn't just shining us on? And that he won't pull a double cross?"

"Ziggy would not dream of lying to *me*." Mimo Bermudez regarded his former colleague as though he were something he had just scraped from his sandal. "Nor would he entertain any thought of warning the Qastt of our interest, or speak of this delicate affair to anyone else."

"No, indeed." Cybulka's voice had lost its archness. "I'm too fond of living."

There was a silence. Not for the first time, I wondered about my courtly friend, Guillermo Javier Bermudez Obregon, semiretired Smuggler King of the Perseus Spur.

I said, "Okay, Ziggy. I apologize sincerely for doubting you and for the roughhouse. You get *all* the money up front tonight. Now which Qastt planet did you see the Rampart ship on?"

"Dagasatt, about one hundred ninety lights from Nogawa-Krupp."

Yes—and only thirty or so from Cravat!

Cybulka went on. "The cutter is docked at an auxiliary starport near a city called Taqtaq, on the edge of a conspicuous landform called the Great Bitumen Desert. But don't ask me to take you there! That's not part of our bargain. As I said, my boy, I'm fond of living."

"What kind of world is Dagasatt?" I asked.

"Ugly, but clean. No inoculations required. Imagine a desert, scads of sand, but with plenty of water available beneath the surface. No resources *we* could possibly be interested in. It's a very old Qastt colony, but a planet that only xenos could love."

He burbled on about the uncongeniality of the wee aliens, but I wasn't listening. An idea had burst into my mind like a supernova. Maybe it was impossible for Rampart Security or

Zone Patrol ships to land on a Qastt planet, but I had a notion how the trick might be managed.

"Mimo, can I use your SS to call Eve right now? She can authorize Cybulka's payment draft by spinning some yarn to Simon. It may take a few hours—"

"Let me suggest a simpler solution. I'll advance the amount to Ziggy now, and you can have Rampart reimburse me at your convenience."

"A splendid idea, Mimo!" The fat man levitated out of his chair as though he were inflated with helium or wore an anti-grav jockstrap. He presented the EFT card to my friend with a flourish. "I intend no offense, but the inclement weather of Kedge-Lockaby is really not to my taste, and I have urgent business back on dear old Callipygia. So if you don't mind—"

The phone in my pocket buzzed and I started like a goosed moose. "Excuse me. I was expecting an important call."

I lumbered out of the room, tapped the Open pad, and whispered, "Yes."

"Your chum Garth Wing Lee had a very impressive private cruiser waiting at the starport," Jake Silver said. "A Bodascon Y700 prototype. Groundcrew never saw one like it before. It must be even faster than the souped-up crate your Mexican bootlegger pal flies."

"Shit. Well, thanks anyway for—"

"The cruiser was still at the fueling bay when my team arrived. They found Citizen Lee in the general astrogation office, calling the cashier impolite names because her card reader was malfunctioning and she was having difficulty completing a manual transaction of the fuel sale."

"You had her stall!" I yipped joyously. "Did your team nab Lee?"

"The subject is resting in the port authority lockup, out colder than a frozen wonton. You owe me a big one."

"Superintendent, start making out your Christmas list."

"Hanukkah list," he corrected.

"Whatever. Listen—"

"No, you listen up, Hell-Butt! I want this schmuck and his

ship off my world ASAP. As far as CHW is concerned, Lee was never here. We both know he's Concern-connected, and I don't need any fallout from high places. Get on Mimo's SS and tell Rampart Security to collect Lee without any fuss."

"Meet you at the port lockup in about ninety minutes. I'll take care of everything personally when I get there."

"I was afraid you'd say that." He punched out.

Leaning against the wall, I let loose with a jubilant "*Yee-haw!*"

Mimo popped out of the study, aghast. I lowered my voice. "More good news! I'll fill you in later. Can I prevail on you to give me a ride to the Big Beach?"

"Certainly. I was returning Ziggy to his ship there anyway."

The drug dealer, wreathed in smiles, was donning a rain poncho the size of a bedspread. I presumed he'd been paid off. "So very kind! Much as I would love to avail myself of your island hospitality, I have special needs that can best be served aboard my own vessel."

"I'll just bet," I said.

I had suddenly become ravenous, so Mimo nuked some tacos to take along, spreading them with the sweet pepper salsa he'd prepared for the postponed flapjaw feast. To wash them down, he brought up a pony keg of Yucateca Leon Negra from his cellar coldroom. Then all three of us piled into my friend's Range Rover and bumped and splashed along the half-flooded marl track to the primitive hopper pad a kilometer away. Mimo was the only island resident prosperous enough to own a private aircraft. The other two parked at the muddy field were beaters belonging to our local taxi outfit.

We whisked upstairs to the peaceful ionosphere, high above the raging storm, where a voluptuous Moon of Manukura was shining amidst a rabble of multihued comets. Cybulka, overflowing the four-seat passenger compartment, polished off the lion's share of the food and beer and then promptly went to sleep, snoring like a phlegmy oboe.

To ensure our privacy I asked Mimo to close the flight-deck door. Then I told him everything, beginning with Eve's call and ending with Jake Silver's timely pinch. The beer loosened my tongue and comforted my hurts. I also found it was cathartic as all git-out to recount the events of my devastating day to a sympathetic friend who would never in a million years consider judging or second-guessing me.

Mimo listened in silence, smoking one of his expensive contraband Cuban cigars and staring out the windshield of the aircraft. When I finally finished, he asked, "What do you intend to do now?"

"Take Jake's prisoner to Rampart Central on Seriphos. They've got psychoprobe machines there that'll make him sing like a Mormon choir. Even if this Lee is only a third-string operative, he's bound to be a direct link to Gala. Whether his evidence alone will be sufficient to prove Rampart's case against the Concern is a tougher call. Probably not. I was trained as a lawyer myself, you know, and it usually takes a truly humongous pile of shit to bury an elephant. Especially when it's fighting for its life to crawl out from under."

"But if you had Oliver Schneider as well . . . ?"

"Bingo," I affirmed succinctly "We prove the whole megillah, civil and criminal cases. The very fact of the conspiracy to devalue Rampart, and the tort—the civil wrong committed by Gala against the Starcorp, entitling Rampart to killer damages that would effectively dismember Galapharma AC. Aside from that little matter, Ollie had to be involved in the murder of Yaoshuang Qiu, Rampart's former Chief Tech Officer. He could connect Gala to that. Ollie and his apparatchiks might even provide a direct link to Elgar/McGrath, who supervised Gala's entire covert operation in the Spur, including the Haluk lab on Cravat."

"Schneider and his men may all be dead. Silenced."

"That would have been the safest course for Gala. But Matt knew Ollie well, and she told me that he was slick as snot on a doorknob. I can't believe a man like that wouldn't write himself an insurance policy when he agreed to be Alistair Drummond's main mole."

"Schneider might certainly still be useful to Galapharma,"

Mimo conceded. "His intimate knowledge of Rampart security measures would be invaluable—up to a certain critical point in time."

I smiled wolfishly. "*Exactamente.* And it would be the job of whoever nabbed him to explain that the critical point was rapidly approaching. And turn him! Even using the machines, you get superior poop from a cooperating witness."

"That 'someone' capturing Schneider . . . will it be you?"

"I'll have to disappear," I said, not acknowledging the question, to which I did not have an answer. "Maintain the fiction of my death. Leave K-L and do a damned good job of covering my tracks, or Gala will just send a better class of assassin."

"There is that." He blew a smoke ring.

I reclined the copilot seat, leaned back and closed my good eye to match the puffed-up one hiding under the coldpack and bandanna. Hurting, used up, and bummed out didn't begin to describe the shape I was in. Down in Arizona, folks would describe me as feeling lower than a roadkill horntoad.

"Christ, Mimo, I thought I was back on K-L to stay. I was out of Rampart! Resigned to letting it be gobbled by the monster. Now I'm right back in the middle of the corporate shitstorm. It's Eve's fault that Gala came after me again. It's *your* fault that I'll probably have to scope out Dagasatt."

Mimo said nothing. He would never call me a cowardly coyote, God bless him. On the other hand . . .

"You knew I'd kissed off Rampart," I grumbled, "but you still had to dangle that damned Ziggy in front of my nose rather than telling Matt or Karl Nazarian about him. A meanspirited Anglo might suspect you of deliberately trying to reinvolve me in the Starcorp. You Mexicans have convoluted notions of family obligation and honor."

"We do," he agreed. "Of friendship also."

"Hah! Saving me from myself—is that it?"

"Who could do a Dagasatt penetration better than you?" he asked gently, returning to dangerous ground.

For a few minutes I sulked behind my shut eyelids. Then: "Nobody, probably. Certainly not a Rampart Security force."

"Would you care to explain?"

"An operation like that is against Commonwealth law, unless Rampart's Legal Department can furnish solid proof—not hokum and hearsay from a crook like Ziggy—that the aliens are harboring a corporate criminal fugitive and refuse to surrender him. Of course, if such proof did exist, and if Rampart were simpleminded enough to make an official request through CHW channels to mount a Dagasatt search, Ollie'd be out of there faster than chain lightning with a link snapped. A deniable penetration is the only option. Bounty hunter stuff."

"This would be legal?"

"The statutes are vague enough to make such an operation feasible. If a Throwaway like me dragged Ollie in and sold his ass to Rampart, there'd be no danger at all of his deposition being thrown out on grounds of illegal apprehension."

Mimo said, "So you *do* intend to lead a raid."

"Everything depends on what we wring out of Citizen Lee. Maybe his evidence will be so sensational that we won't even need Schneider."

"Then you'd be off the hook." Mimo's voice held the faintest tinge of reproach.

"Except for having to go underground to prevent another attempt on my fast-withering life."

"Concerning that, there are matters that will have to be taken care of. The disposal of Kofi's body, and so on. How shall I proceed?"

"Let me think." I hauled myself back upright and ruminated for a while. "You're going to need help. I think we can trust Sal Faustino, don't you? If any Gala covert op came sniffing around later and tried to put the squeeze on her, she'd turn him into sushi."

"I agree that Sal is the perfect choice for an accomplice. And Oren Vinyard, if another person is needed."

"How about this, then. You guys put the body into *Black Coffee* tonight. Sal uses her tugboat to tow Kofi's sub to the Blue Gut and scuttles it deep. Then she tows *Pernio* out and does the same thing. I hate like hell to lose the boat, but it's full of blood and other suspicious shit. You'll have to clean up inside my house and take care of the mess at Kofi's place."

"The rain will help with that," he said.

"Right. Tomorrow, when Kofi and I turn up missing, you inform the Eyebrow gang that Kofi told you he was going out in the storm last night to look for me. You argued with him but he insisted. Now we're both presumed lost. The grief-stricken gang has a nice wake for the pair of us. Jake Silver reports the double tragedy to the local media because I'm a VIP, albeit a tarnished one. A Manukura webstringer snatches up the story and passes it along to the cosmos at large. That'll cool Gala's jets and give me room to maneuver—whatever I decide to do."

"Mmm. It could work." More smoke rings, concentric this time.

I tipped a nod toward the closed passenger compartment door. "We'll have to make sure that Captain Cybulka doesn't blow my cover. Are you absolutely certain he'll keep his trap shut?"

Mimo looked hurt.

"Lo siento, don Guillermo," I apologized, "but if he blabs, I'm gutted."

"He won't."

My friend finished his cigar. I had a large cup of coffee to counteract the beer, visited the ship's bathroom, and considered the matter of Lee's interrogation on Seriphos. I'd have to supervise that myself, preferably with Karl Nazarian's assistance. If Lee's evidence proved to be as crucial as I hoped, we'd have to ship him off to Toronto by the speediest and most secure means possible.

We were almost to the starport when Mimo broke into my thoughts. "Perhaps it's not my business to ask, Helly, and if I'm out of line I want you to tell me so. But if you did decide to penetrate Dagasatt, how might you go about it?"

I told him and he burst out laughing. "I was about to suggest that very thing."

"Wiseass beaner."

"Have you had field experience in high-tech Insap penetrations?"

"I led a few," I said cautiously.

But that was a long time ago, and in the Orion Arm of the galaxy, far away. With my expensive legal education—and my goddamn famous name—I'd been a natural for ICS's career fast track. I made Divisional Chief Inspector by the time I turned twenty-eight, and had more important things to do besides chasing Y'tata gunrunners or busting cyberflea-markets on Kallenyi worlds. There were even those in the Commerce Secretariat who had called me brilliant.

They'd changed their tune fast enough when I was framed for malfeasance . . .

"Who would accompany you to Dagasatt—assuming you went?"

"Well, I really don't know jackshit about the Qastt," I admitted. "But Matt will probably be able to put me in touch with some experienced people who might like to earn a few mil pulling hazardous private duty."

Mimo's dark eyes were glittering. I'd seen that glitter before. "Why don't you take a human contraband trader along with you—one who knows the Qastt customs and can provide a useful cover story for the operation? No, not Ziggy! I know another crook who has been to Dagasatt more than once, even though it was many years ago. One who is eminently trustworthy."

I glared at the old man in horror. "No! Abso-fucking-lutely *not!*"

"Nonsense," laughed the semiretired Smuggler King of the Perseus Spur. "I'd enjoy it. Things have been very dull since Cravat. Sal and Oren can take care of Kofi's body and all the rest of it. We can call them right now, on a contingency basis. Your options will remain open."

"Got an answer for everything, haven't you, *compadre*?"

"Not always. But often enough." He lit another cigar.

We reached Manukura Starport a little after 0100 hours, and Mimo guided the hopper down through the heavy tropical rain. Our console ground display showed only a small number of starships docked at the tiny port. Most of them were cargo vessels. A single commercial carrier was parked at the passenger terminal, together with three private cruisers. One was Mimo's pride and joy, *El Plomazo*—"the bullet"—a nifty Y660 cutter. The second was an aging Iridion-16 that I presumed belonged to Ziggy. The radical conformation of the third was evident even on the small screen. Its transponder ID was BXX-0021, an experimental Bodascon designation.

"Cielos!" murmured my friend. His eyes were sparkling again. "What a lovely ride our villain came in on! How I'd like to check her out."

"Well, you could. That's a Y700 prototype. I promised Jake I'd get Lee's ship off K-L, so how about swiping her for me? You shouldn't have any problem figuring out her goodies. Fly her to Seriphos and put down in the restricted area of Rampart Starbase."

"I may not want to give her up!"

"Actually, you may not have to . . . if you're serious about wanting to go along on the Dagasatt raid."

He hoisted one shaggy gray eyebrow. "You know I am."

"Fly the Y700 to Seriphos by yourself while I schlep Lee there in your *Plomazo*. Assuming that I do decide to lead Operation Q, we'll use the Gala ship and you can pilot her. We'll need a blitz buggy in a job like that, especially for the getaway."

If we got away.

Mimo said, *"Plomazo* might also come in handy for your operation."

"If you don't mind, I'd rather use her to carry Garth Wing Lee off to Toronto as fast as possible after we finish tossing his brain. Rampart hasn't got anything in the barn to touch *Plomazo*. She can get to Earth in ten days, and she's also more heavily armed than any of ExSec's cutters."

He nodded. "I'm agreeable. You know, Helly, it would be a good idea to examine the contents of the Y700's computer before putting her in harm's way. It might hold interesting data about Lee's work in the Spur."

"Good thinking. Contact Karl Nazarian when you arrive on Seriphos. He'll get someone to do a data dump and get started on the analysis. I'll tell him that you're coming."

"Perhaps I should also have the prototype's identification modified. Just in case."

"Yeah. Right." Why did I have the feeling that I stood on the rim of a slippery slope and any second I'd go over— taking my friend with me? "Assuming we do go to Dagasatt, and assuming we survive, the Y700 will be yours to keep—to make up for my losing *Chispa* at Helly's Comet. I'll fiddle the registration transfer somehow through Rampart, and Gala won't be in any position to squawk. Maybe you can call the new starship *Chispa Dos*."

"Helly, Helly. I think you've lived with Throwaways and rascals too long."

I laughed. "Found my natural moral milieu, that's all. We'll talk about this later, on Seriphos."

The hopper touched down and I went into the passenger compartment to wake the Sleeping Beauty.

"Rise and shine, Zig. We've arrived."

"I had the most amazing dream," the fat man burbled as he pulled himself together. A robolimo was waiting to take us to the terminal. "I dreamt that Rampart Starcorp hired me as a marketing consultant to the Qastt. I went before their Great Congress and gave a magnificent presentation, with the result that a *stupendous* new era of trade opened between humanity and the nasty little Squeakers!" He simpered. "My stipend from Rampart was princely."

"Dream on, sweet prince," I growled. We exited the starship and crossed the rain-lashed apron, after which Ziggy departed rather sniffily to his own vessel and Mimo and I went into the terminal.

A smartly uniformed young Public Safety officer approached and inquired, "Is one of you Chief Inspector Helmut Icicle, Rampart ExSec?"

Mimo smothered what might have been a cough. Damn Jake and his sense of humor.

"That's me." The hood of my old yellow slicker was up to obfuscate my identity and hide the wraparound bandanna. I was still wearing the sweatsuit and the sneakers without laces.

The cop gave me a dubious look. If he was expecting credentials and a snappy salute, he was doomed to disappointment. After a beat he said, "Superintendent Silver is waiting. Follow me." He spun on the heel of his boot and marched off with us trailing behind.

At this hour, the terminal was tenanted only by service personnel and sparse numbers of travelers. We took an elevator into the bowels of the building and eventually arrived at the security offices. Jake, dressed in rumpled civvies, was asleep in a chair in the anteroom. He awoke the instant we walked in.

"It's about time you got here," he snarled. Climbing to his feet, he yawned prodigiously and rubbed goop from his pouchy eyes. "What happened to you, Helly? You look like a fugitive from a back-alley production of *Pirates of Penzance*."

I pushed back my slicker's hood and removed the kerchief and the coldpacks. The eye was feeling much better. I could even see out of it again, a little. The back of my head still hurt. "Might have known you'd make fun of a man's disabilities. Actually, I ran into several doors."

Jake gave a disbelieving grunt and turned to Mimo. "And how are you, Captain Bermudez? Giving the Chief Inspector a little assistance tonight?"

"I'm always willing to help a friend, Superintendent."

"And you've got some beauts. Is that freakazoid pusher pal of yours out of here?"

Mimo nodded. "Ziggy indicated that he would be leaving immediately."

"He better be. Even on a world like K-L we have minimal standards."

Jake reminds me of an English mastiff, a breed favored by my former wife, Joanna. Not in appearance, because mastiffs are trim-looking dogs and Jake is slightly potbellied and sartorially challenged, but in his watchful, melancholy air of having seen it all—and God help you if you try to perpetrate any of it again in his territory.

I told him, "Thanks for the bust. I'll take the subject in charge and Mimo will remove his vessel."

Silver said to the waiting officer, "Nikitenko, please escort Captain Bermudez, here, to starship BXX-0021 at the general astro gate. Expedite his departure."

"Sir, under the circumstances, that will require authorization—"

"Get it," Jake said. He turned to me. "This way."

We tramped hither and yon through deserted corridors until we came to a door with a simple sign: DETENTION. Outside of it was a rider-type antigrav baggage transport holding a coffin-sized container.

"What's this?" I asked.

"A coffin, dummy. Did you think you were going to push a shackled, unconscious Galapharma spook through the terminal in an invalid chair? I told you we were going to draw a veil over this arrest. The officers involved think Lee is a well connected Rampart exec wanted for nameless database perversions. We Kedgeree Kops are discreetly giving him the boot back into Starcorp jurisdiction."

He swiped a card through the detention room lock slot and the door opened. We went inside, where there were two small cells fronted by force-fields. Chained hand and foot to a bunk in one of them was a handsome Oriental male wearing a designer business suit and impressive jewelery. He was out cold. I stood staring at him for a few moments. It was still hard to believe he'd been netted so easily.

"Lee might be a real prize, Jake. If his probe comes up aces at Rampart Central, it could help save the Starcorp's bacon."

"I thought you didn't care."

I sighed. "Sometimes I do, sometimes I don't. It's a puzzlement."

"It's your damn daddy's fault," snorted Jake Silver, "and I really hate Freudian shit like that."

"You're nuts, Super."

"And you're a poor putz in search of a father figure. Thank God you latched onto Bermudez instead of me. Come on, help me carry the prisoner." He shut off the confining field and we went into the cell. Jake readjusted the restraints.

"Did you sweep Lee for suicide devices?" I asked. I wasn't about to touch the psychoanalytical wisecrack.

"Don't be silly. You can do a full body scan in your corporate torture chamber on Seriphos. The magnum stun-dart he took during the scuffle is good for about three more hours. All the same, I'd keep his cuffs on."

We lugged the body out into the corridor and boxed it. Jake had thoughtfully bored holes in the plastic casket's sides. When the lid was closed and fastened, he climbed into the antigrav cart's driver seat. It was only large enough for one.

My face fell. "You mean I have to walk? I'm not a well man."

"So ride on the coffin, cowboy."

I mounted with creaky caution, feeling like the actor Slim Pickens in the last scene of the classic film, *Dr. Strangelove*. In due time we reached *Plomazo*'s berth and stowed the cargo. The Y700 had already taken off and it would certainly reach Vetivarum Conurbation on Seriphos long ahead of me. Mimo's personal starship cruised at a zippy enough sixty ross, which would get me and my prisoner there in about two and a half hours.

At the last, I explained to Jake how I'd be playing dead, and what his role in the upcoming media farce was to be. He began bitching before I'd even finished.

"You get somebody else to play straight man in your scam! I have no intention—"

"It's a small thing, Jake. You won't be compromised in any way by issuing a simple announcement of my apparent death, and Kofi's. You can qualify the news release any way you like to cover your ass. You 'received a report.' It's hearsay."

"Well . . ."

We were standing on the open tarmac, getting wet. I switched to wheedle mode. "Earlier, we spoke of Christmas—I mean, Hanukkah! Would you consider leaving K-L and taking a highly remunerative executive security position in the corporate sector? Provided that the sector doesn't go belly-up, that is."

His lip curled in a wry smile. "If we're talking pie in the sky, I'd rather rejoin CCID back in Toronto. My wife misses the grandchildren and I wouldn't mind seeing snow again before I die."

"Ah."

"But you don't have that kind of clout, Hell-Butt."

"I'll give it my very best shot, Jake."

He made a raspberryish sound that mingled cynical disbelief and tired resignation. "Just get out of Dodge and make damn sure none of your Rampart *tsuris* comes down on me or my little planet."

Superintendent Jacob Silver turned and squelched off into the rain. I climbed into *Plomazo* and called the tower for a tow to the launch pad.

Chapter 5

Light snow was sifting down when I landed at Rampart Starbase on Seriphos. During the few days I'd been gone, winter had arrived on the planet. The huge port facility had most of its docking accommodations tucked away underground, but I made special arrangements so my prisoner and I could bypass the terminal.

A gobot truck towed the starship into one of the elevator sheds, out of the weather. Instead of programming a descent to the service area, I waited. After a few minutes a hoppercraft bearing the Rampart crenellated-wall logo came gliding across the field, meter-high. It wafted into the shed along with a swirling cloud of snowflakes and settled. A stocky figure dressed in winter gear climbed out and waved. Karl Nazarian had come to meet me as I had requested.

Karl was one of the charter Rampart Small Stakeholders, a contemporary of Simon, Ethan, and Dirk Vanderpost. Sometime during his long life he'd had a course of rejuvenation, but his face still looked like a topo map of the Caucasian mountains divided by an aggressive buzzard-beak nose. He had founded the Starcorp's security force and headed it for over thirty years, prior to the regime of Oliver Schneider. Until he joined my infamous Department of Stupid Projects, Karl had pottered his twilight days away working on Rampart's archives. When I told him I was quitting, he had threatened to go back to Earth and retire to a lakeside cottage in Armenia. I wondered if Simon had persuaded him to change his mind.

I gathered my stuff, such as it was, donned a nifty Burberry jacket of Mimo's with a scannerproof visor hood that I found in the flight-deck locker, and came down the cargo ramp with my boxed and still-snoozing prisoner trundling behind on a tote.

En route from K-L, I'd warned Karl via SS com that Mimo was coming in with a stolen starship that would require immediate cosmetic detailing and a counterfeit registration. I also told him that I was supposed to be dead, had a Galapharma covert operative in custody, and urgently needed help in a top-secret psychoprobe gig. My former colleague had reacted to this news with his usual equanimity, reining in his curiosity until he could question me in person.

Karl shook my hand after I buttoned up *Plomazo* and sent her downstairs to a berth. "Welcome back, Helly! I rather thought we hadn't seen the last of you."

"I'm not rethinking my resignation, if that's what you mean. And I was a little surprised to find you still holding down the fort at Special Projects when I called. I thought you were going to disband the outfit for me."

"The letter of intent is in my computer, but "

"Send it. Dated three days ago. I mean it. I have a job for you and a few other adventurous SP souls that'll require your instant severance. You'll be going to Earth, driving the speedboat I just rode in on. Pardon the cliché, but Rampart's life could depend on it."

"What about *your* life?"

"Karl, I told you I'm a dead man. For the time being, anyhow."

"Is your resurrection contingent on what we can squeeze out of the person inside that box?"

"Maybe. It might depend even more on you and your crew hauling the person safely to Toronto when we finish pumping him. Did Mimo come in okay?"

"Over half an hour ago. The new ship is docked in the restricted area, under guard, being refueled and modified according to his instructions. Lotte Dietrich is helping with the computer data-dump. How about if I take her along to analyze it en route to Earth?"

"Good idea." She was Special Projects' best encrypt breaker, one of the faithful little band that I'd left in the lurch when I skipped out. "Let's take our friend here to the Library and get started on the quiz session."

When Simon had dragooned me into being VP Special Projects, in essence forming an independent internal investigation force that reported only to him, I'd set up a secret command center in the subbasement of the Vetivarum Public Database. Presided over by Karl, our tiny gang of counterespionage agents and cybermavens had been completely divorced from Rampart Central and what was then the undesirable scrutiny of Vice President Schneider and his suspect Department of Confidential Services—which included both the External and Internal Security divisions. We called our lair the Library. For reasons of my own, I wanted to question Lee there, rather than at the now sanitized InSec facility inside Central.

But Karl's black eyes did a shifty little dance and he raised one shoulder in apology. "Um. There's been a slight change of plan. It just wasn't practical to move the heavy-duty psychoprobe equipment across town from InSec on such short notice. And you know the Library isn't really set up to handle high-risk prisoners, either. We'll do the work at Central."

"But I told you—"

"Don't worry. Matt Gregoire will stay out of the way to spare your wounded male ego."

"That's not it at all," I mumbled.

"The hell it isn't."

"Dammit, Karl! I'm not trying to avoid Matt. There's still a remote chance that Rampart Central might harbor a Galapharma spy. It's vital that news of this prisoner's capture and interrogation doesn't leak out. And the same goes for my still being alive."

"Don't worry. I've got everything arranged." My hood was still pushed back, and he seemed to become aware of my battered face for the first time. "You know, you really look terrible."

"Damn right I do, and I'm sick of hearing about it. Among

other things, I'm cruising on two hours' sleep, and I can't hit the sack until you and I finish grilling this Galapharma turkey."

"Do you want to tell me what's been going down?"

"I'll fill you in during the flight into town. Help me load the prisoner and let's get going."

The city of Vetivarum, home to almost all of the half-million human inhabitants of Seriphos, is sited on a picturesque bay at the edge of the planet's rugged north polar continent. In summer, the climate is pleasantly temperate and the days are long and sunny. In winter, storms sweep down from the interior icefields and produce weather conditions similar to those of terrestrial Greenland. As the days shorten and become frigid, the Zmundigaim Insaps of Seriphos, whose culture is somewhere in transition between paleolithic and technogalactic, abandon their primitive camps in the geothermal mountain valleys where they earn a living gathering rozkoz spores and migrate to coastal villages. There, in huts loaded to the rafters with modern Earthling comforts, they basically party all winter long.

Human Rampart employees and the service personnel who cater to them, trapped in the work ethic, just hunker down and endure until spring. My former colleagues had told me that most folks didn't mind the dark Seraphian winter. Those who did took their holiday breaks then, fleeing to planets with milder climes. Such as Kedge-Lockaby.

Flying above the sprawling conurbation, where dusk was already coming on at 1500 hours and powerful streetlamps shone fuzzily in the snowfall, I silently wished I were back on good old K-L myself. Or just about anywhere else except the headquarters of my family's endangered Starcorp.

The ziggurat bulk of Rampart Central, three hundred stories high, glowed against the darkening sky like some monstrous wedding cake spotlit beneath a scintillating canopy of sparks. It was the only structure in Vetivarum with a protective force-field umbrella, a white truncated pyramid ornamented with blue and gold, which proclaimed its domination of the planet and every person living on it.

We touched down on the landing pad atop the building and were met by Matt Gregoire and three armed paramedics. She didn't say anything to me, but of course I was incognito by then, behind my mirrored face-shield. Garth Wing Lee was immediately transported to the interrogation chamber of the Internal Security Division, where a doctor waited to revive him and prep him for the procedure. Matt took Karl and me to a small observation booth above the chamber.

I doffed my disguise. "Thanks for helping us, Matt."

"I haven't yet assigned anyone to record your prisoner's deposition," she said briskly. There was no smile, not even a greeting for me. "Will Karl be handling that?"

"I need his assistance with the questioning. If you would, I'd like to ask you to supervise the recording and witness it officially. It's best if as few persons as possible are involved at this point."

"Very well. I presume that you do know how to operate the psychoprobe equipment."

Interrogation wasn't my specialty when I was with ICS, but I'd learned the basics, just like all the other agents. I kept my expression neutral when I replied. "I can handle it. You may recall that I also had personal experience being hooked up to the machines on Cravat."

"Yes." She looked away.

And when I regained consciousness in an underground cell, pain-racked and weeping from shame, my head was lying in Matt's lap . . .

Karl asked me, "Didn't they ream you when you were accused back on Earth?"

"As a noncorporate defendant I had the option of not submitting. So I didn't. Psychoprobing can sometimes do permanent brain damage, and my lawyers didn't want me to risk it. They thought they could prove my innocence by conventional means, since the trumped-up evidence against me was so circumstantial. They were wrong."

A voice came through the annunciator. "The prisoner is ready, Vice President Gregoire." The physician and her aides looked up at us.

"Thank you, Dr. Krasny," Matt said. "He'll require intensive resuscitation later, since he's being transported offworld. We'll call you when we need you."

The medics filed out.

Matt turned to Karl and me. "Do what you have to do."

One of the first things Lee confessed was that he had been fitted with two ingenious microminiature destructive devices, in addition to a conventional suicide implant. Matt, Karl, and I hastily took cover while the unflappable Dr. Krasny returned, wearing bomb-disposal gear, and removed the lethal trinkets from Lee's body cavities through neat keyhole incisions under local anaesthetic.

When the prisoner was no longer in a position to kill us or himself, Karl and I questioned him for nearly five hours. Rampart's legal justification under CHW law for taking a *depositio sub duritia* was thin but valid: that Lee had conspired to murder a high Rampart official—to wit, me—since my resignation had not yet been completely processed and finalized at the time of Kofi's attack.

Theoretically, the high-intensity psychoprobe procedure is capable of emptying the entire memory bank of a subject; practically, results are limited not only by time considerations but also by the amount of neuron destruction the inquisitors are prepared to inflict upon the inquisitee as they obtain the deposition under duress.

Lee was by no means scrubbed clean, wrung out, and hung up to dry at the end of the session, since I wanted to keep him in reasonably good shape for further questioning on Earth; but we had gleaned a fair amount of raw data from him.

Garth Wing Lee—his real name, to our surprise—was a high-ranking agent of Galapharma AC, having the innocuous title Deputy Chief of Client Services. His immediate superior was Tyler Baldwin, Gala's top spook. He was originally based at Concern headquarters in Glasgow but had been working in the Perseus Spur for two years. Regrettably, he had not been a close associate of the late Elgar/McGrath.

Lee did not know the precise whereabouts of Oliver

Schneider, who was apparently the responsibility of an another Gala operative named Erik Skogstad; but he did confirm that Schneider and his men were alive and working for
Galapharma somewhere in the Perseus Spur.

The most important information that we obtained from
the prisoner involved his formal assignment—to spy on the
Haluk while overtly expediting the aliens' illegal purchases
from Galapharma, Bodascon, Sheltok, Homerun, and Carnelian Concerns. Lee thus was a material witness to, and a
participant in, a grand conspiracy by the five Concerns to vio-
late CHW Statute 50, which prohibited trade of certain high-
technology equipment and disclosure of certain scientific
procedures to nontreaty alien races. Going by the letter of the
law, it was treason.

This chunk of evidence comprised what is known in the intelligence trade as platinum poop, or a Gotcha. Small wonder
our prisoner had been a veritable walking booby trap.

An emergency order from Baldwin had sent Lee hightailing it from the Haluk planet Artiuk, the aliens' principal
Spur colony and a center of Galapharma huggermuggery, to
procure my homicide on K-L. Lee was not privy to the motivation behind the order. I asked him why in God's name
Baldwin had sent a hypersensitive operative such as himself
to waste Little Old Me—and why he hadn't chosen to stick
around long enough to ensure that the job was done properly.

Lee had been told by his superior that my immediate death
was deemed "crucial." No other explanation was given. Erik
Skogstad, an experienced assassin who might more logically
have been sent on the assignment, had been unavailable, so
Lee was pushed into the breach. He had delegated the job to
Kofi because he himself was "a specialist in xenorelations,
not wet affairs." His overhasty departure from K-L was occa-
sioned by a nasty flap back on Artiuk involving some drunken
Carnelian robotics engineers, a much-prized xeno domestic
animal, and an enraged Haluk bureaucrat. Soothing the latter
was judged to require Lee's personal intervention.

Interesting as it was, this portion of the confession was
worth diddly squat relative to Rampart's case against Gala-

pharma. Since I was now well and truly disenfranchised, neither Gala nor its agents could be convicted of instigating my botched murder. Under Commonwealth law, Throwaways might be slaughtered with impunity—although the deed was mercifully rare in civilized venues—provided that their deaths did not inflict a "consequential" civil wrong upon any citizen or corporate entity, or result in a public nuisance.

When the questioning was finally over, I had come to an unhappy conclusion. Garth Wing Lee was a vitally important material witness for the Commonwealth. All by himself, he would provide sufficient evidence to bring in an indictment against five Concerns for illegal alien trading and possibly for treason. Unfortunately, he wasn't worth chickenshit in Rampart's life-or-death battle against the Galapharma takeover.

To win that one, we still needed Oliver Schneider.

Dr. Krasny and her paramedics returned to take Lee to a secure recovery facility, while Karl went off to supervise the disbanding of Special Projects as an arm of Rampart Starcorp in the Perseus Spur. Most of our hastily recruited SP agents would be returning to private life, but Karl had invited three peculiarly talented individuals to accompany him to Toronto on *Plomazo*, the computer analyst Lotte Dietrich, a cunning old InSec operative named Cassius Potter, and Hector Motlaletsie, a retired Fleet Security spook. Some stealthy business needed doing back on Earth, and Karl and his associates were the only ones I could trust to handle it.

When I rejoined Matt Gregoire in the observation booth, she gave me a plastic case.

"Here are two data-dime copies of Lee's deposition, witnessed by me and encrypted to Phase XII as you requested. The computer is swept clean. Is there anything else you need from us?"

I did my best to match her detached professional demeanor—a tough job when you're suffering from terminal fatigue, semistarvation, and a lively collection of physical miseries and emotional collywobbles. "Keep one of these dimes in a safe place. Give it to Eve or Simon if you get word that the bad guys have stopped my clock. Karl will take the other copy to Earth."

She seemed unperturbed at the renewed prospect of my demise. "Is that all?"

"I'd like the use of a private-channel subspace com. I'll have to tell my sister Eve about the results of this interrogation. After that, I need to eat and sleep. I could use your help recruiting seven or eight volunteers for a highly unorthodox and very dangerous operation of mine. My old Special Projects gang didn't have quite the right people."

She frowned. "What kind of operation?"

I put my finger to my lips. "Can't tell you."

"How long will the operation last?"

"Maybe a week, if all goes well. If it doesn't—" I shrugged. "The mission will be Rampart-deniable. The participants will earn four million each, with double indemnity in case of death."

"Good grief! Who's paying for this?"

"Simon. He doesn't know it yet, but he will after I've talked to Eve."

"I see," she said doubtfully. "What type of personnel do you require?"

"I need one pilot with combat experience and seven others with special weapons and assault training. Familiarity with the Qastt race would be a plus. The people can't have any connection to Rampart. Former Zone Patrol agents would be ideal."

"I might be able to round up a short list of possibles. When would this operation begin?"

"As soon as I can get my broken ass in gear. No later than noon tomorrow."

"Then you aren't going back to Earth with Karl and the prisoner?"

"No. I'm needed elsewhere."

She finally smiled. "Poor Helly. And you thought you were home free when you resigned from Rampart! Are you sure you can't tell me what this is all about?"

"I'm a free agent embarking on an unsanctioned and very

illegal mission with a handful of low-life henchpersons. First I'm going to Nogawa-Krupp. You'll be asked shortly to authorize the release of certain notorious prisoners being held there. A mysterious benefactor is about to bail them out of the hoosegow."

She stared at me, mystified. A wild surmise began to dawn. "Those Qastt pirates? Don't tell me that—"

"Stop right there! Don't even think it."

She gave an exasperated sigh. "Oh, Helly."

"Oh, Matt," I replied sadly.

She is my age, thirty-six, although she looks ten years younger. Her hair and eyes are very dark and her skin is the color of cinnamon. She had been Chief of Fleet Security at the time of Eve's disappearance and had directed the early, fruitless search for my sister. An impulse that was at least partially hormonal had inspired me to ask Matt to join the team of Baker Street Irregulars that had engineered Eve's rescue. Post-Cravat, while I concentrated mostly on the Ollie hunt, Matt took over Schneider's job and cleaned out the moles and incompetents in Rampart Security like an avenging angel.

Matt Gregoire had been my professional colleague, my companion in peril, and my lover. The day I quit, I asked her to come away with me and share my carefree life in the islands. She had turned me down without an explanation.

"I have a secure SS unit in my inner office," she said, "in a cabinet on the right-hand wall. I'll tell my secretary to expect you."

I nodded meekly. "Since I'm officially dead, I'll have to hide behind a scannerproof visor. Will this badge Karl gave me serve as a laissez-passer for a masked weirdo?"

"No one on this floor will stop you. There's a sofa bed and facilities in my office's little back room if you'd like to stay there. It's totally secure. You can order whatever kind of food you like through the servitron and then get some rest. If you like, I'll come and wake you at"—she consulted her wrist unit—"say, oh-six-hundred hours. I'll bring you the list of eligible candidates for your team of commandos."

"Pick eight of the best. I trust your judgment. Send them to

Mimo for kitting out and briefing. He's aboard the stolen Bodascon Y700 prototype that snuck into Starbase for a clandestine refit."

"So Mimo's going on this mysterious mission with you."

"He invited himself. You know how he is."

"Yes. And I know how you are, too."

As she turned to leave the observation booth, I said, "One
last thing, Matt."

"What is it?"

"I don't want to find your name on the volunteer list. This
isn't the kind of mission a Rampart executive can participate
in. And I won't have you quitting your new position to
qualify."

She smiled, once again distancing herself from me behind
a facade of remote professionalism. "No danger of that happening, Helly. The circumstances are entirely different now,
aren't they?"

Before I could reply, she was out the door and gone.

I skulked down the corridors of the 220th floor of Rampart
Central, ignored by uniformed InSec agents and civilian personnel alike, and finally came to an impressive executive
suite with a silver plaque that said, MATILDE GREGOIRE—VICE
PRESIDENT FOR CONFIDENTIAL SERVICES.

The flunkies in the outer office didn't even look up from
their computers as I slipped in. Matt's secretary, Boris Brago-
nier, glanced at me incuriously and silently pointed to a
familiar door, which stood ajar. I went inside, engaged the
manual lock, and stripped off the overly warm hooded jacket.

The room was large, with a window overlooking a panorama of snow-dimmed city lights. Matt's crowded desk held
an antique green-shaded reading lamp, a brass cup full of
computer stylomikes, pens and Hi-Liters, a data-reader, three
e-notebooks, an overflowing tray of papers, a magslate entitled DEPARTMENTAL BUDGET—THIRD QUARTER, and a slender
ceramic vase with a small spray of brown-and-gold hothouse
orchids. The framed holo of Matt and me standing arm in arm
on the aft flat of my submarine was gone.

I got something to eat on a tray, then pulled the private sub-space communication unit down into position and flopped into a swivel chair in front of the screen. During the twenty-five minutes it took to establish the encrypted subspace link to Earth without benefit of corporate priority, I gobbled a rare sirloin steak, six baby red potatoes, and a side of steamed broccoli in Dijon mustard sauce. I washed the food down with a tall glass of Rainier ale and then began to nod off. The sight of Eve's face abruptly appearing on the com monitor shocked me back to alertness.

"Good God, Asa," my older sister said peevishly. Didn't you check the Zebra Clock? It's the middle of the night in Arizona."

"It's evening here at Rampart Central. Wintertime, too."

She did a double take. "What are you doing on Seriphos?"

"Poking into Rampart business again. Can't you tell by looking at me?"

Her eyes widened in dismay. Their irises were still human—green with amber rings around the pupil, like my own. Un-like mine, her "whites" were a vivid, alien azure as a result of the partial genen procedure she had undergone. "What happened?"

"I'm stabbed, fish-bit, punched to a pulp, and mad as a peeled rattlesnake. But I've got good news all the same. We caught us a Galapharma agent, Evie."

All sisterly concern vanished and she snapped, "Tell me!"

Once again I recapitulated the events of the long day, adding the results of Garth Wing Lee's interrogation. From time to time Eve broke in with questions to clarify my slightly muddled narrative.

When I ran out of steam, she said, "This is fantastic! But . . . you do realize that we'll have to keep this man on ice, rather than turn him over to CCID immediately when he ar-rives on Earth."

"I've thought about that—"

She swept on urgently, telling me what I already knew. "Lee is a stellar witness for Xenoaffairs, implicating the five

Concerns in crimes against the Commonwealth. But his evidence doesn't bolster Rampart's case against Galapharma the way Oliver Schneider's would. From what you've told me, it seems plain that Lee operated in an entirely different province."

"Evie, we can't just sit on this deposition. It's too important. Rampart might even lay itself open to an obstruction of justice charge—"

"And what do you think will happen when Alistair Drummond discovers that Galapharma is about to be indicted for a Statute 50 violation, based on evidence that *Rampart* submitted? He will find out, you know."

I just shook my head.

Eve's voice fell to a harsh whisper. "Asa, he might try to have Pop killed, or Mom. Thinking either death could force an immediate merger. Pop has willed his majority stake in the Starcorp to Dan, Beth, and me in equal portions. I'm certain Dan and Beth would cave in if Pop was gone. Mom's entire stake will be inherited by her Reversionist Party charities. They'd approve the merger because of the financial incentive. Once Rampart is swallowed by Gala, Drummond will find a way to suppress or impeach Lee's deposition. He'll certainly destroy the other evidence we have."

"I don't see how he'd be able to quash this confession," I said stubbornly. "Not with Matt's certification and Karl as interrogator of record."

"Drummond might *think* he could. The man's not sane, Asa."

Neither was he a certifiable nutcase. Megalomaniacs like Alistair Drummond have become emperors and führers, served by underlings who never questioned their most irrational orders. Eve was probably right about the potential dangers, but I felt we had to accept the risk.

"I'm not going to stand by and let another cover-up happen, Eve! You can't hide this evidence the way you've hidden your demiclone condition. We have an obligation to humanity—"

She pressed ahead with relentless logic. "Suppose that we blow the whistle. Drummond commands his minions to do their worst. One or more members of the Frost family die. Rampart is absorbed by Galapharma. All of the other circumstantial evidence we have pointing to a Haluk threat is suppressed, but Gala and its cohorts *are* indicted for illegal trading as a result of Lee's deposition. I don't think a treason charge would stick. What happens next? Your average Commonwealth bureaucrat sitting on the judicial panel might look at the Haluk trade conspiracy and see only an insignificant technical violation of Statute 50. A Mickey Mouse rap! Galapharma and the other four Concerns might very well be able to beat it or escape with a wrist-slap by using that legal principle Carnelian cited when it conspired to peddle robotics to the Joru twenty years ago."

I groaned. "*Non detrimentum*—no harm done. It could happen."

"Of course it could. Because thus far, trading human high technology to the Haluk hasn't hurt anyone. Garth Wing Lee can't help us prove that the aliens have a secret agenda hostile to humanity. Not even my mutation proves that conclusively. Our other evidence is even less persuasive. Secondhand statements by Emily Konigsberg—a dead woman! Our personal observations of a suspicious Haluk genen facility, now inconveniently demolished. A Haluk body that's been genetically engineered with human DNA. What do they really prove? Nothing! I say that we should keep Lee under wraps at least until—until you go to—" She fell silent.

"Until I go to Dagasatt," I finished. "And find Ollie. And save Rampart from Galapharma. That's a lot of eggs you're putting in one ratty old basket, sis."

"*Are* you going to the Qastt planet, Asa?"

"Yes."

"Then you know I'm right! So we hold back Lee's deposition."

"Evie, the mission to Dagasatt could fail. It's possible we'll never get any solid proof of malicious intent by the Haluk. Not until the xenos decide to put their secret game plan into operation. Then Drummond and his shortsighted greedy buddies will be shocked by the wicked underhandedness of their clients. And the Commonwealth could find itself fighting a war."

"Asa—"

"You and I have to make certain that what we believe to be true about a possible Haluk threat becomes known to the Commonwealth. Even if Rampart goes down the drain. Even if Alistair Drummond destroys our whole family. We've got to tell someone in the government about this right now. No more goddamn waffling and agonizing and—"

The anxiety drained out of her face and relief bloomed as suddenly as springtime flowers in rainwatered desert. "Sontag!" she said.

"What?" My head seemed stuffed with cotton wool. I had no idea what she meant.

"We'll tell your friend, Efrem Sontag. The man you wanted me to show myself to . . . earlier."

Yes. Before Simon had convinced her to remain in seclusion. Before I'd abandoned Rampart in disgust.

Efrem Sontag, Commonwealth Assembly Delegate, Chairman of the Xenoaffairs Oversight Committee, was more than an old friend from my law school days. He was also a powerful legislator and one of the few people who hadn't believed in my frame-up. He'd keep the Lee evidence confidential for a few weeks while I tried to nail Schneider, but he'd have no compunction about blowing the lid off if worst came to worst.

"It'll work," I told Eve.

She was radiant now, full of renewed confidence. "Tell me what I should do."

"I'm sending Karl Nazarian to Earth with Lee in custody. He and his people should get to Toronto in about ten days, flying Mimo Bermudez's Y660 smuggler's pride. Ask Sontag to meet them in Rampart Tower, under conditions of strictest secrecy. Karl will have a data-dime with the original deposition we took on Seriphos. I'd prefer that we didn't show that one to Ef because I'm one of the interrogators. A Throwaway could taint the evidence—and besides, I need to stay dead, even to Ef. So we'll have Karl repeat the most critical phases of Lee's psychoprobe interrogation. Ef can witness it personally. Karl will make three certified holovid copies—one for Ef, one for Rampart, and one other that's to be kept sealed unless some 'accident' befalls Sontag himself."

"Who gets the third copy?"

"A former colleague of mine, Chief Inspector Beatrice Mangan of the ICS Forensic Division."

"The one who helped you finger Bronson Elgar as a Gala mole?"

"Right. Now listen! The news of my alleged accidental death on Kedge-Lockaby will be webcast within a few hours. Use that as an excuse to call Sontag in Toronto—on a phone without video, of course. Tell him Galapharma ordered my death as part of the overall Haluk conspiracy. It's the truth, and Karl will see that Lee's new deposition corroborates it. I want you to also tell Ef why Gala feels it has to grab Rampart, no matter what: in order to hand over those fifteen hundred Spur planets that Drummond promised to the Haluk. Strictly speaking, that's not illegal. But it's imprudent as all hell and tends to bolster our contention that xeno hordes covet T-class worlds in the Milky Way."

"Can we be sure Sontag won't feel obligated to go public with this information at once?"

"I'm certain he'll be willing to wait, if there's a chance we can come up with additional substantiating evidence within a reasonable period of time. Convince him! Tell him a team of freelance agents has gone to a certain Spur planet to try to get the vital skinny. Just don't say that one of the agents is me. Rampart *must* officially deny invading Dagasatt."

"Asa . . ." Eve paused. Her petite alien form on the communicator screen, incongruously garbed in a thin nightgown and negligee suited to the high desert summer night, leaned closer. She was smiling, and for an eerie moment I seemed to see her as she had been before the mutation. "In view of all this, I'm going to ask Simon to call an extraordinary meeting of the Rampart board immediately. I'll have him renominate me to the CEO position. I'm going to accept this time, without condition, and the board is going to vote me in. By acclamation."

"Christ! Do you think you can you pull it off?"

"I don't see why not. The Gang of Three and Aunt Emma will see it as a last futile gesture of defiance before the inevitable." She gave an ironic chuckle. "Besides—what can I possibly accomplish in six weeks, hiding out at the Sky Ranch?"

"You tell me."

"Well, for starters, I'll ask Gunter Eckert and Dan to come to Arizona and help me work out details of my new financing strategy."

"You've got a strategy *already*? Fast work, Madame CEO."

"I haven't just been brooding among the cacti for the last half year, you know," she remarked tartly. "I've considered a number of sneaky ways to get hold of the venture credit Rampart will need for major expansion."

"Does a rank outsider get to hear how you intend to pull off the miracle?"

"Not until I've firmed my ideas with Gunter."

He was Rampart's Chief Financial Officer and another charter stakeholder, a board member whose progressive ideas had too often run afoul of Simon's conservatism, Zed's lack of vision, and my older brother Dan's penchant for micromanagement. Dan, Chief Legal Officer of the Starcorp, would have to approve any plan of Eve's before Gunter attempted to implement it; but I had confidence in my sister's ability to twist his arm. She'd been doing it since we were kids.

"By the time I get the financial business squared away," she went on, "Karl should be in Toronto with Garth Wing Lee. And do you know what, Asa? I intend to be there for the meeting with Assembly Delegate Efrem Sontag. In person."

I gaped at her like a dumb damn flapjaw demon. "My God."

"Why not? As long as we're sharing secrets, I'd like to let Sontag see for himself what the Haluk did to me on Cravat. Karl Nazarian can hook me to the psychoprobe machines to prove the truth of what I say about my condition. Hey! Don't you think it would be a hell of an attention-getter if I gave my deposition first? The reinterrogation of Lee can be Act Two . . . and a bit of an anticlimax, if I do say so myself."

"You know, Evie, that's rather brilliant."

Her expression was almost smug. "Of course it is. And as the newly elected Rampart CEO, I'll have additional credibility."

"Just be careful what questions you let Karl ask you during probing. Remember that I'm dead. To Ef Sontag and to everyone else except you and Karl."

"Surely we'll have to tell Mom and Pop—"

"Fuck Simon! Don't you dare tell him *anything* about me or Lee's deposition or Dagasatt! That goes for every other member of the Rampart Board of Directors as well. For their own safety, if for no other reason."

"Asa, Mom has got to know. She's slipping away and she refuses to let the doctors do anything. If she believed you'd been murdered, it would finish her."

"All right. Tell Katje right now. But for God's sake impress on her how vital it is to keep the information secret. Remember that someone in the family is hand in glove with Alistair Drummond and Galapharma."

"We don't really know that for certain."

"Do you want to chance it?"

She let her intent gaze fall. "No. It fits too well. All right. I promise to beware of the unknown ratfink in the Frost bosom."

"I'm serious about the safety considerations, too. I think you should make a firm recommendation that the entire Board of Directors remain on Earth under heavy security. Until I nail Schneider or . . . we all fall down in six weeks' time. Get the family members to stay at the ranch if you can. And when I say family, I *don't* include Cousin Zed. He'll explode into solar orbit when you tell Simon that you want the CEO job. Even if Zed isn't the Gala mole, he might try to dry-gulch you out of sheer pique."

"I'll deal with Zed. Coping with Pop might be more of a problem. He'll demand to know why I've changed my mind and want to lead Rampart now that you're dead and things look blacker than they ever have."

"You can tell Simon this much in strict confidence: say

that Matt Gregoire has a new and important lead on Ollie Schneider and his fugitive associates. Following through will require the expenditure of thirty million dollars—"

"Yikes!"

"—deliverable to Matt Gregoire immediately. The money has to come from Simon's private accounts, not from Rampart."

"Pop will try to pump Matt, you know."

"Good luck to him. Just tell him to send a blind EFT draft to her home in Vetivarum within six hours. I can't carry out the Dagasatt mission without the *cojonudo dinero*."

"You'll get it. Do you need anything else?"

"Two matters have to be taken care of. Neither will help Rampart, but they may be useful additions to the circumstantial evidence proving a Haluk threat."

"Just tell me."

"First, the matter of the Haluk cadaver with the human DNA that went to Tokyo for study. Get it away from the university researchers and hide it. Xenoaffairs received a transcript of the analytical data from Professor Shibuya, but it's been classified Cosmic Secret, and SXA might deny its existence. Get another copy from Shibuya and tell her to watch her back. You'd better pray that Drummond's spooks haven't gotten to Japan first."

"Oh, my . . . Yes, all right. What's the second thing?"

"More body-snatching. You'll have to find someone dependable to dig up Fake Emily and secure the remains. And this time let us pray that her loving brother didn't have her cremated before interment in the family plot in Swaledale, North Yorkshire."

Eve was frowning. "You mean—"

"Emily Blake Konigsberg's doppelgänger, the Haluk demi-clone duplicate of her that was accidentally killed in a starship accident before it could wreak unspecified mischief. No one knew the corpse wasn't human when it was released to her brother."

"Yes, I recall you telling me about that. I'd completely forgotten . . . or perhaps I put it out of my mind because of the appalling implications. But we never knew for certain where the Haluk clone was heading, or what it intended to do."

"Fake Emily and its mission aren't what really concerns me, Evie. I'm worried that there might be other Haluk disguised as humans—and I'd like Ef Sontag to worry about them, too. That bastard Elgar planned to duplicate you and me as part of the plot to take over Rampart. But if we can believe what Real Emily told us, none of the Galapharma agents knew that the Haluk were *already* copying humans as part of some secret scheme of their own."

"Sontag will have to be told about that even if we don't find the demicloned body. I'll see to it. Do you have the brother's name?"

"Hubert Blake Konigsberg. He's a chemistry prof at some university in Leeds. Emily studied there before going out to Stanford in California and becoming a big wheel in xenobiology."

"I'll do a data scan on her burial myself. If the body exists, perhaps your forensic friend Beatrice Mangan can advise us on how to have the DNA analyzed."

"Excellent idea. Those findings should also go to Sontag." I tried to think if I'd forgotten anything. If I had, I was past remembering now. "I guess that's about all, sis."

She grimaced at me in a comical fashion, pushing her human hair away from her face with a grotesque alien hand. "All? Oh, Asa!"

"Hey." I managed to smile back at her. "Up, up, and away, kiddo. Blue Supergal and cashiered Supercop, fighting to save the day."

"There's that," she said in a low voice, the humor suddenly faded away. "But there's Rampart, too. For me, at any rate. I know you don't really care about the Starcorp. But the thought of losing it to a madman like Alistair Drummond—"

"Evie," I broke in gently. "Leave Drummond to me."

She seemed to freeze. Then she whispered, "Can I really do that, Asa? When you finish on Dagasatt—"

"If the mission succeeds, you won't have to worry about me tossing Ollie Schneider onto your doorstep while I go back to my old beach-bum lifestyle. I've had enough of Drummond's games. He needs burying. Like a rabid skunk. I'm ready to take on the job."

"Thank you," she said quietly. "Please be careful."

"Can't do that. But maybe I'll finally get lucky." I touched her image on the screen. "Gotta sleep now. Goodbye, sis."

She nodded and the com unit went to standby.

I slumped inertly in the office chair, staring at the remains of my supper, wincing in embarrassment as my fatigue-drugged brain replayed the John Wayne stand-up-sheriff speech I'd just delivered. Had I really said that?

Yep, I had.

A wonder Eve hadn't laughed in my face.

I'd worry about it tomorrow. Like one of the living dead, I shuffled into the back room of Matt's office, stepped out of the floppy sneakers and dropped onto the sofa bed, not even bothering to open it.

A rabid skunk . . . a steak bone . . . dredged up from child-hood memories of vacations at the Sky Ranch . . .

It's a late spring evening in the high desert country of the Sierra Ancha. Getting kinda chilly. Stars galore, the faint noise of a creek in the canyon below, faraway howl of a coyote. There's Simon, tall as a ponderosa pine in his jeans and pearl-snap shirt and shearling jacket and old Tony Lama boots and curly-brim Stetson. There's me, no more than seven years old but dressed about the same, helping Pop clean up the supper dishes before we bed down for the night.

He'll sleep on the ground beside the dying campfire, long gun at his side, like a real cowboy. I'm stuck with a tiny screened pup tent and strict orders from my Mom: "Never mind if your father wants to risk a blacktail rattler snuggling inside his bedroll! You sleep in that tent, Asa. Do you hear me? And be sure to keep the screen zipped."

I toss our steak bones and leftover beans and apple cores into the ashes at the edge of the fire, zap the last plate clean in the laser stove, and pack the cook kit away. After a while Pop and I go off together with a lantern to check on his black stallion, Bandido, and my paint pony, Charlie, picketed a couple dozen meters away among some paloverdes smothered with blossoms.

The mounts are fine. Simon and I stand side by side, peeing against the broken trunk of a huge dead saguaro cactus looming skeletal in the starlight. Then we go back to the campfire. Flickering orange flames illuminate my little tent, which stands on the opposite side of the fire with its mesh curtains neatly tied open.

"Pop! Look!" I freeze in horror.

Something's inside the tent, sitting on my sleeping bag and gnawing one of the bones I'd failed to dispose of properly: an animal smaller than a house cat, dark fur strongly blotched and marbled with white. It sees the encroaching humans and does something so bizarre as to be nearly unbelievable.

Leaps into a perfect handstand, body in the air, jittering and bouncing and waving its plumy tail.

"Little spotted skunk," Simon murmurs.

I'd seen them road-squished, but never alive. The critter is in a frenzy, dropping onto all fours for a moment and then standing up on its hands again. It repeats the goofy maneuver over and over as I watch, thunderstruck. Then it hisses, picks up the bone and resumes chewing.

"Damn fool kid," says Simon. "Told you to burn up the leftovers."

"How can we chase it out of there?" I whisper in dismay. "It'll spray stink on my sleeping bag—maybe on the saddles and all the rest of our stuff!"

"Don't move, boy. Stay right where you are. I'll be right back."

He retreats, taking the lantern, and returns a minute later with one of the dry saguaro ribs, over a meter long. Cautiously, he pushes one end of the cactus stick into the fire. He grabs his rifle. When the stick blazes up, he takes it in his other hand and moves slowly toward the tent with the burning brand held ahead of him.

The flames come nearer and nearer to the little skunk. It

sits petrified for a moment, just inside the tent door, then drops the bone and skitters away into the dark desert night.

"Oh, wow!" I groan. "That was close."

"Most animals are afraid of fire." Simon makes certain that the skunk is gone. "It was acting a mite peculiar. Had me worried."

"The handstands?"

"Nope. That's the usual way they warn you off. The nervous twitching and the way it hissed is what bothered me. Sometimes a skunk will have rabies. They catch it when they're bit by an infected bat. These little spotted guys are normally bold as brass, kinda cute, but a rabid one will come runnin' right at you. Crazy fearless, scared of nothing. You better be ready to shoot if that happens, and never mind about gettin' stink on you. That's the least of your worries! You got to shoot a rabid skunk dead and bury it without touching it. Got that, boy?"

I say, "Yes, Pop."

"Okay. Go to sleep now." He unstraps his bedroll.

I kick the stupid steak bone out of my violated shelter and into the center of the campfire. Then I zip the mesh curtains shut and lie on my sleeping bag fully clothed, my hunting knife clenched in my fist, listening fearfully for the scratching of tiny sharp claws against the outer fabric.

Eventually, my eyes close.

"Helly?" Rapping, rapping. "Helly?"

No sooner had I managed to fall asleep than a horrible noise woke me up. I cursed and rolled off the sofa and crashed onto the carpeted floor. Ooh, that hurt. More rapping. I struggled to my feet and remembered where I was. Limping to the door, I opened it. Matt stood there holding a large stack of packages. The big office window behind her still showed the luminous dark gray of snowfall in the nightbound city.

"It's oh-six-hundred," she said. "Here are some fresh clothes. If you'd like to pull yourself together, I'll order breakfast for us out here and give you a status report on Operation Q."

"Thanks. Be with you in a sec."

I retired to the impressive executive john, showered, and got rid of my beard. The wounds were much improved, and most of the bruises had responded to treatment and were fading to a sickly greenish-purple hue. I ate a few analgesic tablets, combed my hair with a towel, and put on the black mock turtleneck, lightweight khaki pants, matching short jacket, and the sturdy desert boots Matt had provided. The outfit would serve very well for the hot, arid climate of Dagasatt.

. . . But how had she known?

I slouched into her office, scowling. "I suppose Mimo spilled the beans about the mission destination."

"No. It was Eve. When she sent me the funding for your expedition, she told me everything but the planet's name, which was easy enough to deduce."

Someone had rolled in a small table, complete with white linen, elegant place settings of silver flatware, and china with the Rampart Starcorp logo. Nothing but the best for top management. Matt sat there eating a chilled orange-grapefruit cup. I plopped into a waiting chair and poured myself some coffee.

"Dammit, I wanted this mission totally deniable."

"Did you seriously think I'd be able to organize the logistics and personnel while you kept me completely in the dark?"

"I was going to take care of things myself. When my brain was back up to speed." I broke open an oat-walnut muffin and slathered it with rozkoz confiture. "Didn't you order any eggs? Sausage? Ham?"

"Eat your fruit. It's good for you."

She had always tried to reform my breakfast menu, which tended toward chuckwagon cholesterol. And now that small bit of domesticity was over, too. I felt a sudden awful pang of loss and regret.

"I really missed you back on K-L, Matt."

Her smile was ambiguous. "Separated five whole days. Or is it six?"

"That's not the point."

"The point, Helly, is that it was great fun—but just one of those things. You were a marvelous complication in my life. Really marvelous. But a complication all the same. Your quitting Rampart was just a—a final denouement to a decision I'd already made months earlier."

"To leave me." The muffin tasted like sawdust and the mellow sweetness of the rozkoz had turned cloying. "But we were good together, Matt. Those three weeks we had on the island, recuperating from Cravat. You told me then that you loved the place."

"Eyebrow Cay was wonderful. But not forever. I know what I want to do with my life. You still haven't figured that out."

"I'm back with Rampart, if that's what you mean." I tried to keep my tone free of sarcasm.

"Not permanently."

"For as long as it takes. And I intend to give it my best shot."

"And then you'll go back to the islands again and vegetate."

"I didn't sign on to the Starcorp for life, the way you Small Stakeholders do. What will you do if Galapharma wins? Stay on in your great new Vice President job under Alistair Drummond's regime?"

She flushed at the unfair jab but refused to lose her temper. "Galapharma is not going to win."

"Why don't you come right out and say it, Matt? Even if you do abandon the sinking ship, you still wouldn't want to live with me."

"That kind of a decision would require love on both our parts. And what we had together wasn't love at all. We both knew it, Helly. It was plain from the beginning. You always held back, never made me feel that you really wanted to know me. Or let me know *you*. Eve says—" She broke off, biting her lip.

"Go ahead. Tell me what my busybody sister says about my sex life!"

"This is all beside the point. Let's forget it." She activated a slate and handed it to me. "Here's the roster of volunteers. I was only able to recruit three people who fit your requirements. All of them are highly qualified."

Only three? . . . But I didn't want to think about that. "Tell me what Eve said about me!"

Matt ignored the question again. "Two of the recruits, Ildiko Szabo and Zorik O'Toole, took early retirement from Zone Patrol SWAT units. They're in their middle forties. Joe Betancourt is thirty-two, a former ExSec cruiser pilot with extensive combat experience. He left Rampart because of a personal conflict with a coworker, but that shouldn't affect his ability to work with you. He's been working as a shuttle pilot. None of these three have dependents, and they understand the risks involved. All of them have had experience with the Qastt. Mimo felt you needed at least one additional person, so he drafted Ivor Jenkins, who was very eager to work with you again. God only knows why."

"Matt! Tell me what my sister said."

She wouldn't meet my eyes. "Eve is my closest friend, Helly. We worked together for nearly ten years on Tyrins. I love her. And she loves you so very much. She and I had every right to—"

"To talk about *us*?"

"Why not?" she exclaimed hotly. "You've never been exactly forthcoming about your past, have you?"

"I thought you'd researched all my felonious little secrets pretty thoroughly."

She shook her head. "That's not the part of your life we spoke about."

"Then what, for chrissake?"

"Eve believes you're still in love with your former wife, Joanna."

"Jesus!"

Matt plowed ahead. "She said that you were the one who insisted on a divorce after your conviction and disenfranchisement, while Joanna had tried unsuccessfully to change your mind, and even wanted to accompany you on your self-imposed exile."

"Eve had no right—"

"She also said that you used to wear two wedding rings on a platinum neck chain."

The furious words died in my throat. Kofi Rutherford had rescued the rings from the marauding sea toad's guts. I'd left them in Mimo's safe on Eyebrow Cay when I came back to work at Rampart Central, when it seemed that Matt and I . . .

I stared at the table. "I'm not in love with Joanna. And she certainly doesn't love me."

"Whatever you say." Matt's dark eyes were blazing with some emotion I couldn't fathom. She rose to her feet abruptly, rattling the coffee cups.

"Career histories and psychoprofiles of Szabo, O'Toole, and Betancourt are in the slate. I've also primed it with all the data we have on the planet Dagasatt—which isn't much. Mimo has the money your father forwarded. You'll need a local contact to arrange details of the Qastt release at the Justice Center on Nogawa-Krupp, but Mimo says he knows somebody. I'll call the operations manager at the Nogawan starport myself and have the impounded pirate ship cleaned up and fueled."

"Matt, can't we—"

She was standing beside me. "Your crew is waiting for you at Starbase. Good luck, Helly. And goodbye." She bent down, took my head in both hands, tilted it up and kissed me long and hard. "Now get out of my office. The day's just beginning and I've got work to do."

Chapter 6

The bad ship *Chispa Dos*, sporting a new name and newly registered to a citizen with known connections to the underworld, made the long journey to the Rampart world of Nogawa-Krupp in a phenomenal twenty-two hours, barely enough time for me to work out a revised plan of attack, based upon my pared-down personnel roster, and brief the team.

Because they'd been with me on Cravat, Mimo and Ivor Jenkins already knew the complex details of Operation Q's background. Prudence dictated that I keep Szabo, O'Toole, and Betancourt in the dark about the more sinister aspects of the Haluk involvement in the Galapharma plot against Rampart, at least until I knew them better. The trio had been aware from the beginning that our mission was both clandestine and illegal—which didn't bother them—but they were amateur mercenaries, not pros, and I didn't want to confuse them with galactopolitical considerations. The corporate politics of the affair were murky enough.

During our briefings, I informed everybody that we could certainly expect lethal opposition from Gala agents and possibly from the Haluk as well. I declined to explain why Schneider and the other fugitives were hiding in a Haluk installation on a Qastt world. The three newcomers professed not to give a damn.

Actually, the team orientation sessions went very well except for one notable fly in the ointment. Zorik O'Toole took me aside after our first meeting and sternly asked me if I was "that" Asahel Frost. I admitted I was, and wanted to know if it was a problem for him. He said probably not. I said that if

he'd prefer to withdraw, I could always arrange his passage
home from N-K. He pointed out that he needed money and I
needed him, so he'd stick with the team, subject to reviewing
the situation if unspecified "difficulties" arose.

We left it at that. But I wondered—with good reason, as it
turned out—whether keeping him on was a serious mistake.

Optimist that I was, I had hoped we could touch down
briefly on N-K, grab the Squeak pirates and their ship, and
zoom off to invade Dagasatt. To expedite matters, Mimo had
contacted a Nogawan shyster of his acquaintance before we
left Seriphos and hired him to process the legal paperwork
connected with the prisoner release. The lawyer had promised to have the Qastt pirates ready to hand over when we
landed.

Eleven hours had gone by since then, proving the ancient
rule of "hurry up and wait." *Chispa Dos* still sat in the transient spacecraft holding area of the N-K spaceport, the pirates were still in jail, and the wheels of the overloaded
Nogawan justice system were grinding with glacial slowness.

Joe Betancourt, the former Rampart ExSec fighter pilot, was
aboard the impounded Qastt starship, waiting for the takeoff
order. He was a quiet moody little guy with an air of invincible
confidence, who knew all about weird xeno crates. He'd even
served on a prize crew that had brought a Squeak bandit in. Joe
had told me that his ambition was to operate a sky-shuttle service on a pretty freesoil world called Chaguaramas, back in the
Orion Arm. His fee for the mission would put a down payment
on his dream.

Mimo, Ivor, Zorik O'Toole, and Ildiko Szabo were playing
poker in the forward salon, unwinding from a series of tedi-
ous documentary holovids on Qastt culture. I was in *Chispa*'s
wardroom, sitting at a table studying the systems schematics
of a medium-sized Qastt aircraft called a tuqo, commonly
used as a Squeak emergency vehicle. My revised plan called
for us to steal and use one on Dagasatt, and although Mimo
had assured me he would be able to fly it with ease, I wanted
to check the thing out myself.

Outside *Chispa*'s large view window, a mist-laden drizzle hid most of Nogawa-Krupp Starport. It was early evening. I'd visited the planet only once before, during the earlier fruitless search for Schneider, and at the time I couldn't get away fast enough. An unattractive, foggy-bottom sort of place out near the tip of the Perseus Spur, N-K had cloudy skies that never stopped weeping and soupy air with too much carbon dioxide for human comfort. The most prominent feature of the local biota was a species of tree that had foliage like purple noodles. I also recalled that leeches with teeth were apt to pop out of puddles and nibble your boots as you walked about the bustling capital city.

One single natural resource made this dreary planet supremely desirable to Rampart Interstellar Corporation: the richest platinum-group ore body in Zone 23.

A brisk knock sounded on the wardroom door. Mimo stuck his head in. "The lawyer's here. To explain the delay. We've got trouble."

"Never would have guessed it." Sighing, I put away the schematic printouts. "Send him in."

A florid-faced chap of mature years, wearing a handsome Barbour rainjacket over custom-made business attire, bounded in and pumped my hand with enthusiasm. "Delighted to meet you, Captain Icicle! Cadwallader Cassini, Esquire, at your service. Always happy to do business with a friend of Guillermo Bermudez. What a fantastic ship! I don't believe I've ever seen such a luxurious interior. How many ross can you squeeze out of her?"

"Over sixty." Actually, the hyperspace cruise capability of the prototype was closer to seventy-two light-years per hour, but I didn't want to advertise it. "Please take a seat, counselor. Why don't you tell me what seems to be the difficulty with the Qastt prisoners."

His cheery demeanor cooled a couple of degrees. "Well, to put it in a nutshell, they don't want to be released into your custody."

"What the hell?" Of all the potential screw-ups, I'd never anticipated one like this. "Do you mean they have a choice?"

"Apparently there's an obscure stargoing-Insap rights clause under Statute 44 that applies even to convicted felons."

"Well, what's the beef?"

"I'm afraid I still don't understand their objections fully. The Qastt language—all those squeals and whistles and peeps—isn't processed very well by the mechanical translator, you know. Yesterday, after Captain Bermudez sent your authorization, I took care of the transfer of the twelve million dollar draft to cover the fine, forfeiture, and incarceration expenses, vessel impoundment fee, board and lodging, service charges, and Zone tax. Then I visited the prisoners in the PJC—the Planetary Justice Center—to tell them the good news about their impending freedom. Naturally, I thought they'd be delighted. Instead, they seemed terrified at the prospect of going away with you."

"You told them that we were unofficial agents of the Qastt Great Congress?"

"As I was instructed. The leader—his name is Ba-Karkar—declared that the Congress would *never* authorize humans to pay their ransom. He seemed to believe . . ." Cassini hesitated. "He seemed to believe that he and his people would be in mortal jeopardy if they were remanded into your custody."

"Shit," I said. The damned Squeakers probably thought we were Galapharma goons in cahoots with the Haluk. These pirates had let themselves be captured with an incriminating Haluk passenger aboard their ship. Maybe the penalty for that was death.

Cadwallader Cassini remained blandly silent. The disastrous cover story was my mistake, but a prudent solicitor doesn't rub the client's nose in it.

"There's only one way to resolve this matter," I told him. "I'll have to talk to the Qastt myself."

"I'm sorry, Captain Icicle. Only legal advocates or Rampart Security personnel are allowed to interview alien detainees in the PJC."

I smiled and rose from the table, signaling to Cadwallader Cassini that the conference was over. "Trust me, counselor.

That won't be a problem. You just carry on with what you were doing."

"Actually, all of the legal work is complete except for activating the voucher of remand."

"I'll want to do that personally. Do you have the document with you?"

He handed over a data-dime in its little envelope. "Right here. It's irregular, but I suppose—"

"Excellent!" I picked up the intercom unit. "Mimo, will you come to the wardroom, please? Counselor Cassini is ready to receive his fee. And please tell Ivor, Zorik, and Ildiko to stand by for a foray into town. We'll need some ground transport."

The lawyer said, "If you intend to go to the PJC immediately, I should warn you that it's Saturday night on Nogawa-Krupp. The place is apt to be rather busy. All those fun-loving miners, you know."

"Thanks for warning me. It's been a pleasure, counselor."

I passed him on to Mimo. The other three members of my merry band were waiting in a jellybean van on the wet tarmac by the time I'd collected my coat and hat and a few other necessary things.

Ildiko Szabo was driving. I took the seat beside her. "Where to, Helly?" she inquired.

"To the local slammer. They call it the PJC."

She told the van our destination and we roared off into the night.

Half an hour later four arrogant offworlders came swaggering into the crowded Nogawa-Krupp Planetary Justice Center. They shoved their way through a mob of soggy Rampart ExSec officers, suspects both cowed and belligerent, shysters in fancy stormwear trying to calm agitated clients, and depressed-looking relatives and friends of the recently apprehended. Indignant shouts broke out from those who were shouldered aside, but the pushy quartet moved forward as relentlessly as a human landslide. Its apparent leader was a tall rogue who wore a floor-length oilskin drover's coat over a tan ranchman's outfit, a dripping Stetson with a snakeskin band, scanner-defying mirrored glasses, and peace-bonded sidearms.

As he neared the armored dispatch and reception booth, the gunslinger bellowed, "Stand aside! I got me a court order here. Gonna spring my poor li'l *amigos* outta this jerkwater joint right now!"

The crowd muttered ominously. One furious lawyer, who'd had his Chasseur-booted foot stomped on, exclaimed, "Who the bloody hell do you think you are, elbowing into the line like this?"

"I think I'm ahead of *you*," chuckled the cowboy, with studied insolence.

Angry growls from the throng. A learned obscenity from the lawyer. Snickers from the cowboy's oddly assorted companions. One was a woman. Two were men.

Inside the booth, the InSec dispatch sergeant slowly looked up from her computer. She was a strawberry-blonde about forty years old and her eyes were hard and knowledgeable. The name tag on her left breast said KENNELLY, J. Shielded from the importunate crush by everything-proof windows, she spoke through an annunciator in a bored voice. "Take a number, citizen. Wait your turn."

"Number? I don't need no stinkin' number!" The tall cowboy whipped a Rampart Red Card from his breast pocket and pressed it against the glass. "I got this."

The affronted lawyer with the mashed foot turned away without another word. Bitter babbling arose from the disappointed crowd. "Hot shit honcho . . . big noise from Central . . . korpo kuhnockers throwing their fuckin' weight around."

The dispatch sergeant rolled her eyes. VIPs were always a pain in the ass. This one and his associates looked to be even more anally agonizing than most. The Red Card checked out. It was issued to one Helmut Icicle and enjoined every person employed by Rampart Starcorp to cooperate fully with the bearer under pain of instant dismissal and disenfranchisement.

"What is your business with us tonight, Counselor Icicle?"

The long drink of water with the obnoxious grin didn't bother to correct her misperception of his professional status. "Me and my posse are here to bail out some detainees."

"Do you have a remand microdisk with the names and case numbers of your clients?"

An envelope was flourished. "There you go, Sergeant Kennelly. What's the J stand for?"

She ignored the question. "Please insert the dime into the data input receiver below. And would you please take off your eyeglasses for iris ID verification?"

"Nope. Don't need to, with a Red Card. You forget that, Sergeant Kennelly, J?"

"Thank you," she said obscurely.

The cowpoke's companions also wore scannerproof glasses. One of the men was of very modest physical stature and stood stiffly erect, feet apart and hands clasped behind his back in a military "at ease" posture. He had an almost lipless mouth and a gray military moustache. His expression was fiercely intent. The spacer's coverall and billed cap that he wore had no insignia, but they were almost identical in their cut and dark blue color to those worn by CHW Zone Patrol. He carried a black leather case.

The woman beside him was the only other armed member of the quartet, equipped not only with bonded sidearms, but also with an Allenby SM-440 magnum-fléchette stun carbine in a dorsal scabbard. The vaguely Oriental cast of her broad face was contradicted by tightly cropped straw-colored hair, dotted with raindrops. She was of medium height and wore a baggy ensemble of desert-camo Repeltex. One metal toecap of her ballistic-cloth boots still had a forlorn leech clinging to it.

The fourth intruder, a titanic young man in his early twenties whose demeanor was sweetly shy, stood two hundred centimeters tall and might have weighed in at 160 kilos. None of his awesome mass was fat. Overdeveloped pectorals and deltoids threatened to burst the seams of his wet workout jersey, which bore the logo PROPERTY OF IVOR'S ATHLETIC

CLUB—VETIVARUM—XXXXL. He wore a Sony EMS-3 myo-
stimulator collar capable of augmenting his muscle power by
a factor of three.

"Remand data transfer from Magistrate's Court is complete," the sergeant said, studying her computer display. "But
I note that the Qastt prisoners have declined to place themselves in your custody."

"Why don't I just have a word with my little buddies and
clear up the misunderstanding," the cowboy suggested with a
grin. "You want to roust 'em into an interview room for me,
Sergeant Kennelly, J, ma'am?"

She addressed her computer mike. Following a brief
pause, a map projection appeared on the armored window.
"Very well, counselor. Your associates will have to wait here,
but you may proceed to Visitation 3, the room indicated in
blue on the directory. Your clients will be waiting."

The magical Red Card appeared again. The cowboy was no
longer smiling. "My associates will not wait here. They'll go
with me."

"As you wish. Have a nice day, counselor . . . or whoever
the hell you are. *Next!*"

We moved through corridors swarming with uniformed
Rampart Security personnel, civilians, even detainees in
acid-green jumpsuits who wandered blithely at large with
electronic monitors clamped about their upper arms.

"Wasn't that performance of yours a bit over the top,
Chief?" Zorik O'Toole remarked to me.

"Just thought I'd have a little fun. Won't hurt if the local
yokels think we're a gang of Rampart Central clowns."

"Hmmm." The face of my new colleague was eloquent
with disapproval. "I still think we might have been less obtru-
sive. But it's your call."

I thought: Damn right it is, and don't you forget it.

O'Toole's dossier had checked out five-star. A sawed-off
Napoleon type, he was a former SWAT unit commander in
Zone Patrol, retired two years ago with a list of valor com-
mendations as long as my arm. He'd willingly put aside

writing his memoirs and joined up. His early retirement pension wasn't adequate to sustain his preferred lifestyle; and besides, no Earthside publisher seemed to be interested in a book about law enforcement among the boondock Perseus planets.

Our other patrol recruit, Ildiko Szabo, had made lieutenant before she left the service. Her retirement occupation was listed as Floriculturist, Wholesale. She'd had considerable experience dealing with Qastt captives face-to-face, and her stories about irascible Squeaker pirates she had known were both amusing and discouraging. Ildiko opined that Operation Q might be in for a tough time of it on Dagasatt.

Ivor Jenkins had shared the Cravat mission with Matt, Mimo, and me while AWOL from his low-paying job as a junior bodybuilder. Rampart rewarded him so generously after Eve's rescue that he was able to open his own gym. But being a businessman was harder work than the young man had anticipated, and he said he was overjoyed when Mimo invited him on another adventure. I had reservations about Ivor's participation that I kept to myself. He was only twenty-three, and he'd barely escaped with his life from the caves of Cravat. It didn't seem fair to put a nonprofessional like him in jeopardy again. If there had been anyone else available for our team, I would have insisted that Ivor Jenkins stay home on Seriphos with his barbells and Nautili. On the other hand, he was not only strong, but seriously smart. He knew how to cook, too, and had already put his talents to work for us in *Chispa*'s magnificent galley.

We found Visitation 3 on the floor below, just outside the main cellblock, and filed inside. The Qastt hadn't arrived yet.

The room was about four meters square. Its walls and ceiling were finished in glossy beige enamel like the inside of a refrigerator, and the beige tile floor had a central drain. Hard plastic chairs and a long conference table were solidly bolted down. Maybe the place was hosed down and disinfected after each visit, like public toilet cubicles.

"Sweep it," I told O'Toole.

He took an electronic bug-detector from his black case and prowled around, brandishing the device and scowling. "Clean," he said at last.

We arranged ourselves in chairs on one side of the table and waited. After a few minutes an inner door slid open. A guard ushered four entities inside, consulted a magslate, and whispered:

"Prisoners Ba-Karkar, Ogu, Tisqatt, and Tu-Prak are authorized to confer with Counselor Helmut Icicle and party of three."

"That's us," I declared, flashing a hearty smile. The Qastt, who were wearing translator pendants, huddled together and glared.

The guard studied his slate. He seemed to be suffering from laryngitis. "Um . . . says here the Qastt have been processed for release pending final activation of a voucher of remand, which they've refused to eyeball." He shook his head. "That's one for the books."

"Let me talk to them," I said. "It's only a misunderstanding. I'll clear it up in a jiffy."

"You'd better," the guard murmured on his way out. "Or these inmates go right back to their cells. Press the call-pad when you get things sorted out." He closed the door.

I had never met any Qastt before. They were only about a hundred and twenty centimeters tall, almost humanoid, dressed in garish chartreuse jailhouse jumpsuits that hung loosely on their twiggy frames. Their pink-skinned faces had sharp little noses and close-set golden eyes with peculiar cross-shaped pupils. Bloated cheeks gave them an uncanny resemblance to gophers with their mouths stuffed full of food. They had no external ears, but twin organs like bottlebrushes that served as auditory sensors sprouted from the top of their hairless heads. The antennae differed in shape and color on each individual.

I pasted a big shit-eating grin on my face and said, "Hello there! Which one of you is Ba-Karkar?"

The Qastt remained frozen. Finally the one with the lumpiest cheeks and large black skull-brushes uttered a prolonged, grating shriek. His mechanical translator decoded its approximate meaning:

"Castrate you, boomer! May you putrefy!"

Talk about a failure of communication.

"Helly, let me try. I've had experience with them." Ildiko Szabo rose from her seat and approached the diminutive aliens very slowly. She placed both hands over her mouth, then removed them and whispered, "Holy silence be to you all."

"To you also," squeaked the Qastt who stood closest to the lumpy-cheeked nutcracker. The brushes on this one's head were frilly and coral-red, and its eyes were slightly larger than those of the others.

Ildiko sank down onto her haunches so that she and the entity were eye-to-eye. "My leader apologizes for loudspeaking," she breathed. "He did not understand that it is hurtful. Please let him talk to you. He is not an enemy. He wants to help you. He wants to set you free."

Coral Brushes gave a kind of hiccup. "Untranslatable expression of fearful skepticism."

I stood up and repeated the mouth-covering gesture, then whispered, "Let's begin again." I beckoned to Ivor and Zorik O'Toole. They followed my lead as I tiptoed away from the intimidating table and too-tall chairs and sat on the floor with my back to one of the walls.

Ildiko joined us. "Speak slowly and simply," she told me. "Avoid figures of speech and idioms."

I pointed to Lumpy Cheeks and said softly, "Are you the one called Ba-Karkar?"

He glowered wordlessly and finally said, "Yes. I Ba-Karkar, corsair captain."

"Please come closer. All of you. Let us speak."

Reluctantly, the Qastt complied. They stood in a ragged line, with Ba-Karkar and Coral Brushes to the fore.

I whispered, "Thank you. Now please tell me: Why do you refuse to be set free?"

"You not agents of Qastt Great Congress," the irritable

little pirate captain said. "Guard lie when he say human Congress agents pay ransom, come take us home. Humans never do this! Who you? What you really want?"

"Call me Asahel. You are correct. I am not an agent of the Great Congress. This was a misunderstanding. But I will pay your ransom and set you free. If you agree to help me."

"Help putrid boomer humans? No! Never!"

Coral Brushes kicked him in the shin and addressed me in a voice like an eager, cheeping bird. "Really free? No more putrid human odor in horrid damp air? No more garbage food? No more boomer guards bully us? Really really free?"

"Yes," I said. "If you help us, I'll take you home."

"No!" Ba-Karkar screeched. His antennae were vibrating in fury. "You lie, boomer Asahel!"

"Rest in holy silence," Coral Brushes told him waspishly. Then to me: "What kind help you want?"

Ildiko Szabo said, "Please. Who are you?"

"I Ogu, wife and partner to Corsair Captain Ba-Karkar."

Uh-oh. A crack in the dike!

"This putrid abomination," he blatted cantankerously. "This undermines my authority. This significantly diminishes my pride."

"Untranslatable!" his wife shrilled. "Eight human equivalent months we stay putrid prison. No ransom comes. You say it comes soon. It not come. You want die here? Not me! Not Tisqatt or Tu-Prak, either. Ask them!"

The other two Qastt hiccuped diffidently. One had molting buff-colored brushes, and the other's vibrissae were slate-blue. They showed no inclination to join in the marital spat.

I said, "I will tell you why your ransom didn't come: because you carried a Haluk on your ship. This made my people very angry. The ransom was refused."

"Eeeeee," sighed the Qastt.

"But Haluk say pay me double for quick transfer of untranslatable human cargo," Ba-Karkar crabbed. "This why ride."

Ogu made a sound like a throttled sparrow. "So now we stay prison for ever? Greedy untranslatable epithet you!"

"It doesn't have to be that way," I pointed out. "I'm a very powerful and important human. I'll pay the ransom and get you out of here. But you must promise to help me."

"Tisqatt?" Ildiko Szabo whispered. "Tu-Prak? What do you say about this?"

"They say nothing!" the little captain raged. "They only putrid gunner, ship engineer. I, Ba-Karkar, must speak for all!"

Ogu kicked him again. "Then ask what kind help Asahel wants, untranslatable epithet male. Or no more untranslatable for you! Never again in putrid boomer prison."

Her husband gave a choked gasp. "Cruel female!"

"No more sex, either," she added.

The pirate leader's golden eyes squeezed shut. His defiant black bristles collapsed into flaccid snarls on his bald pate. He chirred almost inaudibly, and the translator decoded: "Misery. This what happens when poor hardworking corsair listens to putrid rich Haluk."

"Yes," I agreed. "Haluk bring misfortune to Qastt and humans alike."

His eyes popped open. "Asahel, what?"

"I hate the Haluk," I murmured. "Let me tell you why. They give shelter to my enemies. My human enemies. I want to punish my enemies, but they're hiding with the Haluk. This is why I want your help. My enemies are hiding with the Haluk on the Qastt planet Dagasatt, near a place called Taqtaq."

"Impossible," scoffed Ba-Karkar.

Scraggly Buff Brushes contradicted his boss softly. "Not."

Ba-Karkar whirled around to confront the crewman. "Tisqatt, you know what this human speaks about?"

"I once live Akakoqoq, city at edge Great Bitumen Desert same like Taqtaq. Everyone know Haluk build untranslatable facility in desert. Dangerous weapons guard facility. No ordinary Qastt person can go near. Haluk kill bonehunters, others who try. Some say that castrating Haluk pay Qastt Great Congress significant money to allow facility on Dagasatt that too dangerous to build on Haluk world. Putrid scandal, but you know politicians."

I knew. Everywhere in the galaxy, on human and nonhuman worlds alike, there were always slimy boodlers ready to deal.

"What kind of a facility?" I asked.

"Untranslatable. It significantly large."

"Is this Haluk facility near Taqtaq Starport?"

"Not very near," Tisqatt said. "Human distance equivalent from Taqtaq 922.2 kilometers. Much farther from Akakoqoq."

I said, "I want to go to Dagasatt and look for my enemies. I want you to help me get to Taqtaq."

"Impossible!" The Qastt captain semaphored his vibrissae violently.

Ogu silenced him with a vicious chirp. "Explain precisely what kind help you want, Asahel."

I did. The whole bunch broke out in horrified squealing. Ba-Karkar banged his little fists against his chest and shrilled, "No! No! No! Castrate you and your companions also! That plan of action unacceptable. It seditious. It putrid. It get us into significant trouble."

Shrugging, I said, "You can go back to jail if you prefer. No more sex and no more untranslatable."

Holy silence fell. I let him stew for a minute.

"Ba-Karkar," I whispered at last. "I swear we won't deliberately harm you or any innocent Qastt on Dagasatt. There will be some danger. We can't avoid that. But I will do my best to keep you and your people safe. The only ones who will surely suffer from this operation are the conniving politicians, the Haluk, and our human enemies."

"Putrid castrators!" he snarled.

I wasn't sure if he was referring to the Qastt pols, the Haluk, Ollie and the wiseguys, or us. Probably all four.

Smelling victory, I played my trump card. "Help us and I'll let you have your starship back after the raid."

"Starship!" He was aghast. "You say humans not demolish my beautiful ship while we in putrid prison?"

Rampart routinely chopped up captured xeno privateers

for scrap before releasing the ransomed crews. During the early stages of our hunt for Eve, I'd told Matt to hang on to this particular pirate craft and its people, thinking they might hold some clue to my sister's disappearance. Then I'd completely forgotten the poor jailed Squeakers—until Eve herself had recalled them to mind.

"Except for the guns, your ship is pretty much intact," I told Ba-Karkar. "It's fueled and ready to fly. What do you say?"

The pirate captain's small head tilted to one side. His bulging cheeks rippled, as though he were munching nuts. God only knows what the mannerism signified. Finally he spoke with sly insinuation. "You pay us significant money also?"

"Don't push your putrid luck, pecwee!" I hissed. "No more pussyfooting around. Are you in or fuckin' out?"

Ba-Karkar blinked. "Your boomer comments not translatable. But I comprehend nevertheless. I think we cooperate."

I gave a profound exhalation of relief. "Right. Just let me call the guard and arrange for finalizing your release. Then we'll go to the starport." I pointed to Zorik O'Toole. "This man and I are going to ride with you and Tisqatt in your ship. Another human will also go with us and pilot your ship to Dagasatt. Our own armed vessel will follow closely. Ogu and Tu-Prak will ride in our ship."

"Not separate me and husband!" Ogu pleaded.

"I'm sorry, Ogu. I wish we could trust you. But Qastt people and humans have been antagonists for too long. You and Tu-Prak will be hostages for the good behavior of Ba-Karkar and Tisqatt."

"I think this human can ride Qastt ship." Ba-Karkar indicated Zorik. "But not you."

"I'm going." I smacked my sidearms, having had a bellyful of Squeak intransigence. "No more arguments, dammit!"

"He not argue," Ogu cheeped. "Translation bad. He means if you ride, you sorry."

And I was, too.

Have you ever visited a kindergarten class where all the

furniture and even the rest room fixtures are miniaturized for the tiny children, and you feel like Gulliver trapped in a doll-house? Well, the Squeaker pirate ship was sort of like that to a man of my bulk and altitude. Low overheads, narrow little corridors, a cramped flight bridge with toy instrument consoles and command seats so dinky I couldn't cram my butt into one to save my life. God knows how Rampart ExSec ever brings in captured Qastt ships.

Maybe the members of the prize crews are all runts like Betancourt and O'Toole. They coped beautifully. Joe piloted the alien starship and Zorik kept an eye on our two alien passengers. Meanwhile, I crouched in the deactivated weapon-system cubicle just behind the flight deck during the five interminable hours it took the privateer to reach Dagasatt, poking along at its maximum pseudovelocity of forty-one ross. *Chispa Dos* tagged behind, throttled back, while Mimo kept the tractor-beam generator and photon cannons at the ready in case Ba-Karkar and Tisqatt tried anything cute aboard the bandit.

They didn't—unless you count ripping off the hated human-style jail uniforms and stuffing them into the matter converter to the tune of malevolent chirps. Then they dressed themselves in voluminous white garments that resembled Bedouin robes augmented with floaty gauze scarves. I already knew about these typical robes from the Qastt cultural orientation holovids, and since they had an excellent potential for disguise and weighed almost nothing, I had Mimo duplicate a set for each of us, using *Chispa*'s malle-armoire unit.

In addition to changing their costume, the two mini-buccaneers also drenched themselves with xeno perfume to counteract our disgusting human stench. After they finished their toilette, the pirate tub smelled like a cross between a crude-oil cracking plant and a Tijuana cathouse. Zorik O'Toole and I nearly coughed our brains out until Joe flushed the environmental system with a blast of pure oxygen. I confiscated the perfume flasks for the rest of the trip.

After Ba-Karkar programmed his ship's navigator with the entry codes for the Dagasatt solar system, there was very little more he could, or would, do to help us, so we let him go off and sulk in his teeny-weeny captain's cabin for the rest of the flight. Meanwhile Zorik and I pumped Tisqatt, the gunner, for useful information about the planet of his birth.

Much older than his cross-grained skipper, Tisqatt was a milder and more obliging soul. He told us what he knew about the Great Bitumen Desert, then willingly called up a detailed chart projection of the region from the pirate ship's database, which was in such an appalling state of confusion that Joe had given up on it early in the game.

The mysterious Haluk facility wasn't shown on the map printout—no surprise—but Tisqatt indicated its approximate position in the far northeastern corner of the strange landform. The desert was sprinkled with cautionary notices warning of unstable and hazardous surface conditions.

Zorik and I conferred and debated the various options for carrying out Mission Q without getting caught, consulting frequently with our tiny pal, who gave useful input on the groundside emergency procedures we intended to subvert during the penetration. Finally, after a lot of second-guessing of my tactics on Zorik's part, we firmed things up—including the best spot for the crash.

"But I think Corsair Captain not like," Tisqatt warned timidly.

I grinned at him. "We not give damn."

Zorik fetched Ba-Karkar. I showed him the printout of the Great Bitumen Desert and told him what his role was going to be in the upcoming charade. It was more complex—and more hazardous—than the earlier scenario I had spun for him back in Visitation 3 on Nogawa-Krupp.

As predicted, he raged, cursed untranslatably, smote his little chest, and told me that the plan was significantly idiotic. When he subsided, we all rested in holy silence for a long time.

Then I spoke, reminding him of the freedom now nearly within his grasp. I allowed as how we could probably carry out our plan without his active cooperation, but the operation would then be even more dangerous. And more likely to leave poor Ogu a widow, since Ba-Karkar would have to accompany us anyhow . . . with a gun pointed at his head.

The gopher cheeks were munching tentatively again. "Asahel, you say only I must go with you to Dagasatt surface. Ogu and other Qastt crew can stay safe in orbit on human ship."

"That's right. Ivor and Ildiko and Mimo will join you and me and Zorik in this vessel. Joe and Tisqatt will transfer to the human ship where Ogu and Tu-Prak are. The human ship has a dissimulator mechanism—a way to hide its shape. It will wait in a distant orbit. No one on Dagasatt will see it. If we are killed on the planet, then Joe will fly your three people home. If we succeed, you will have not only your freedom but also your ship to keep."

The Qastt captain turned away from me and gazed somberly at the bridge's main viewer. We were rushing through the sparsely strewn stars of the Spur's tip, the uttermost part of the Milky Way Galaxy. The indeciperable ideographs of the alien instrumentation were transposed into human parameters by a portable navigator unit Joe had spliced into the console. We were presently three light-years from Dagasatt, ETA four and a half minutes.

In the viewscreen's upper right corner was a faint ball of fuzzy diamond dust, the satellite star-cluster over seventeen thousand light-years distant that was the original home of the Haluk race. Ba-Karkar pointed to it.

"Only twenty human equivalent years before humans come," he said, "Qasst own Perseus Spur. No other star-traveling people here. We move from planet to planet, colonize slowly. Then Haluk come from out there, invade our stars, take one two three four planets, very quiet. We not know. Soon Haluk become bold, not so quiet anymore. They take eleven planets, tell us we can colonize no more. They despise us. They rich, we poor. They never share. When they trade, they cheat us. Haluk stop taking more planets only when humans come. Humans tell Haluk and Qastt: Now all useful planets where you not already live belong to humans! If you try take, we kill you. You believe this good and correct, Asahel?"

I said, "No. I believe it's neither good nor correct. But the human government doesn't care what I think. I am only one man."

"Zorik. You believe this good and correct?"

"Yes," said O'Toole matter-of-factly.

Ba-Karkar asked Joe Betancourt the same question. The pilot said, "I don't know whether it's good and correct or not. I do know that human science is stronger than Qastt or Haluk science, and strong people often take what they want."

"Significant," said Ba-Karkar. "This why strong people feared by people not so strong."

"Some humans," I said carefully, "want to help people who are not so strong. Share science. Undertake honest trade."

The pirate hiccuped. The machine said, "Untranslatable expression of fearful skepticism."

Zorik O'Toole shot me a look and chuckled. "You want to go down that road, Chief, you're gonna need a lot better map than the one you got."

"This not translatable," Ba-Karkar said.

"You don't know the half, little buddy," I told him.

The Qastt navigation unit gave a gentle triple *ping*. The main viewer went white as the ship dropped out of ultraluminal drive and exited hyperspace. An instant later the viewscreen showed a yellowish sun and the apparently motionless red-blue-and-white crescent of a sizable T-2 planet blotched with clouds.

"Dagasatt," said Joe Betancourt laconically. "Gee-synch orbit five hundred kay kilometers, beyond casual landside detection range of known Q equipment. No artificial sats in evidence. *Chispa* matching our intrinsic vee and closing in for docking and transfer."

"Will you help us?" I asked the little pirate.

He said, "You show me again printout of Great Bitumen Desert. Then I decide if your untranslatable plan can work."

Chapter 7

Our landing party crammed itself into the tiny privateer, and at one point I jokingly suggested that we might have to strap Ivor to the outside, like an elk carcass lashed to a pickup truck. The young giant took the joshing in good humor and finally found a place in the cargo bay among the pods of weaponry, assault gear, and supplies. Ildiko and Zorik huddled in the Qastt messroom while Mimo stayed on the flight deck and I took my previous position among the dead weaponry controls.

Ba-Karkar was in the command seat. He had said he would cooperate, under strong protest, with the condition that we allow him to select the precise landing site within a more broadly drawn target area.

Joe Betancourt wished us good luck as he withdrew *Chispa*'s docking tunnel. The Y700 drifted away into space, her external ID and transponder code illegally blanked out so she couldn't be identified. With the dissimulator on, the starship was virtually invisible so long as she stayed in orbit or traveled at minimum sublight velocity. I knew for a fact that the more advanced Haluk/Bodascon starship hybrids had dissim-detect capability; but the Haluk themselves were still unskilled in the equipment's use—they had failed to spot Mimo in *Plomazo* on a couple of occasions—and I was confident that Joe would be able to hide *Chispa* successfully while we carried out the first phase of Operation Q.

Later on, if Galapharma hotshots got wind of our invasion and came sniffing around, all bets might be off.

We were taking two portable CL-4 lasercoms with us, as

146

well as a number of personal LC units. Using orbiting *Chispa* as a satellite relay, the communications system was undetectable by all but the most advanced type of sensors—at least during the daytime. We'd use it at night only in case of a major emergency event such as a call for an evacuation via *Chispa*'s gig.

The privateer began its descent to Dagasatt. I was still not sure that we could trust Ba-Karkar completely, so I kept the holster of my Ivanov stun-pistol unfastened while I crouched behind him. He followed orders well enough, breaking orbit and guiding his ship manually through the outer atmosphere, but his responses to my attempts at friendly chitchat were grudging and curt. The Qastt's bottlebrush antennae had gone droopy again, which I took as an indication of deep anxiety.

Hey, in his position I'd have been depressed, too.

When Mimo saw that I was getting nowhere in my attempts to calm the alien, he gave me an almost imperceptible signal and took over the small talk himself. He told Ba-Karkar about his own background as a smuggler and scofflaw, which instantly made him *muy simpatico* in the skipper's eyes, and spoke of his experiences trading contraband on various Qastt worlds. He apologized for my brusque manner even more elaborately than Ildiko had done, trying to excuse me by painting a highly exaggerated picture of my importance in Rampart Starcorp. This emboldened the pirate to once again bring up his hope of a bonus payment.

"You and Asahel give me money in addition to starship," he said to Mimo, doing the cheek-munch grimace again, "I not only cooperate, I cooperate *significantly*."

I nodded my agreement above Ba-Karkar's head. After all, my father was the one who'd pay, not me. Mimo went into a long rigamarole of bargaining and a sum was finally agreed upon. The flight-deck ambience perked up noticeably after that, along with the little Qastt bandit's auditory antennae.

Money: maybe not a universal solvent of life's intestinal blockages, but it does make the shitclogs more bearable.

Because of technical limitations in our translator equipment, Mimo and I were able to understand only Ba-Karkar's side of the routine space-to-ground transmissions during reentry; but he appeared to be proceeding in a straightforward manner. He requested permission to land at Taqtaq Auxiliary Starport and it was granted. As part of our plan, he also notified Ground Control that his ship's subluminal powerplant was behaving somewhat erratically, although he was not yet prepared to declare an emergency. The controller told him he could descend to thirteen thousand meters, a lower altitude than normal for starship approach. His vector would be monitored closely by Taqtaq Control when he was within its range.

"What kind of a place is Taqtaq?" I asked Ba-Karkar.

"Not know. Never go there. Everyone say putrid."

"It's a petroleum refinery town," Mimo said. "One of several at the edge of the Great Bitumen Desert. These people still make wide use of fossil hydrocarbons in their fuel and plastics industries. I peddled some contraband chemical equipment at Taqtaq over twenty years ago. The smog was cosmic-class and the auxiliary starport was very small and poorly equipped."

"We'd better scope it out as we pass over," I said. "Twenty years is a long time."

We were traversing a largely flat, arid continent with a broad underwater shelf, situated in a pale blue ocean ominously named the Empty Sea. It wrapped around most of the planet's north subtropical zone and had a decidedly odd appearance. The rocks and soil were ochre or vivid red, sprinkled with thousands of rounded lakes having borders of blue-green vegetation. Denser rings of plantlife encircled the cities, which were sited on larger lakes and connected to one another by networks of ruler-straight high roads and forested parkways. Overall, the Dagasatt landscape looked like an intricate connect-the-dots puzzle drawn upon a long, blotchy apple peeling.

I knew from the orientation holovids that much of the planet's rainfall sank immediately through the sandy soil into shallow aquifers, from which it was easily pumped to the surface and utilized for irrigation. Eroded mountain ranges rose along the northern coast of the continent, some of them snow-capped. Streams flowing from their forested inland slopes fed ribbons of cropfields before disappearing underground.

We flew eastward, toward the night, at moderate velocity. From time to time Ground Control made contact to make sure we were still airborne. The unintelligible squeaks of the controller didn't sound particularly worried. Our own aerial tracking display showed only small numbers of conventional aircraft sharing the stratosphere with us. On Dagasatt it appeared that people and commodities flew mostly at low altitudes or traveled on the ground.

The main forward viewer finally showed the eastern edge of the continent in the purpling distance. Along the coast lay what seemed to be a mosaic of hundreds of adjacent lakes or lagoons covering a hazy oval basin of enormous proportions. The dry land within the basin was very dark in color.

"Great Bitumen Desert," Ba-Karkar informed us.

It was vast, nearly three thousand kilometers from north to south and a thousand kilometers wide, surrounded on three sides by a waste of barren red sand traversed by highways that had oases strung along them like beads. Our ship was approaching the basin's western boundary, where there were six widely separated refinery cities. Smoky pollution trails streamed out from them, carried on the prevailing west wind. The opposite side of the Great Bitumen Desert was narrowly separated from the sea by a long arc of cloud-girt volcanic peaks called the Barrier Range. Short rivers flowed from the highlands into the desert basin, creating the myriad shallow bodies of water covering much of the natural hydrocarbon deposits. The area of bitumen was a "desert" only in the sense of being an uninhabitable wasteland. It wasn't arid at all.

"Taqtaq northernmost city," Ba-Karkar said. "We decelerate now, turn over desert for approach."

"Give me a closer look at the surface," I requested.

He activated the privateer's terrain scanner and showed me how to use it. Some of the dry land between the iridescent, oil-slicked ponds was rough, slate-gray or pinkish in color. Other areas were much smoother, almost jet-black, and marked with peculiar concentric ringed features like huge whirl-pools. Due east of Taqtaq, the desert had a slightly higher elevation and less water coverage. Parts of it looked almost like solidified lava. In the far northeastern quadrant of the basin, adjacent to the Barrier Range separating it from the Empty Sea, was an area where fantastically eroded red sandstone buttes thrust up out of a plain of pitch. Scattered plumes of smoke rose from the surface.

The Haluk facility was supposed to be located somewhere in there. I ordered Ba-Karkar to do a multiphase scan of the region, but none of the primitive sensors of the privateer found any trace of a structure or any other anomaly, and it wasn't feasible to use our more sensitive portable equipment inside the Qastt starship.

"It could be shielded from overhead detection by human technology," Mimo suggested. "A GBD horizontal projection unit would do it. With luck, they won't have bothered with perpendicular dissimulation fields—only a roof to foil scans from space by Rampart or Zone Patrol. You'll probably be able to find the place easily enough once we're on the ground."

I asked Ba-Karkar, "Is there any way to take an aerial photograph of this region—or do a topographic scan in hologram and make a printout?"

Both were feasible. He showed me how to do it, and I clicked off shots of the entire northeastern portion of the desert, plus the adjacent mountains and seashore. The printouts had Qastt alphanumerics, of course, but they were a hell of a lot better than the chart we'd retrieved from the ship's databank.

Then I adjusted the scanner to survey Taqtaq itself and the adjacent starport. It was larger than I had expected. At least sixteen spacers of various sizes sat on the ground, as well as numbers of conventional aircraft. I spotted something else that made me frown, but at that moment Ba-Karkar spoke up.

"Asahel, now time we begin final approach and then undertake your untranslatable subterfuge. You understand: disaster impact simulation might become genuine disaster under unforeseen circumstances. Warn your people take precautions."

There really wasn't much we could do, since the Qastt crash harnesses would only accommodate human nine-year-olds. But I sent Mimo aft to alert the others.

The pirate spoke briefly to Taqtaq Starport, notifying the controller that we were on final approach. I was expecting a relatively sedate human-style descent pattern, but instead Ba-Karkar threw the privateer into a precipitous auger spin that didn't flare out until we were less than three hundred meters above the ground. We were inertialess, of course, but I still clung white-knuckled to the back of the command seat as the various flight-deck displays reflected the giddy maneuver.

"Holy shit! Did you have to drop out of the sky like a god-damn rock?"

"I great corsair captain," Ba-Karkar growled. "I drive starships when you mere embryo sleeping in untranslatable of your putrid mother. Now be silent, Asahel! I must drive with significant cleverness."

He punched some controls and the engine power faltered. The ship did a wild dance before abruptly losing more altitude. It leveled out again at a hair-raising 125 meters above the asphalt, moving very slowly on a 280-degree course toward Taqtaq. I hoped we hadn't fallen off the starport's tracking equipment. We needed to have them find us.

Ba-Karkar touched the com pad and said calmly, "Attention, Taqtaq Ground Control, this incoming starship untranslatable."

The controller answered.

"I now have significant emergency. Untranslatable maneuvering apparatus malfunction. Altitude human equivalent 124.6 meters. Engine power very erratic."

Ground Control responded with what sounded like a query.

"No, Taqtaq. Impossible. Power failing."

We maintained our westerly course. The desert surface was much more rugged than it had appeared from upstairs. Heaped broken blocks the size of houses that looked like an aggregate of asphalt and red gravel formed what might have been pressure ridges. Among them were gleaming black mirrors, pools of some liquid that I didn't think was water. By now the sun was almost on the horizon, shining straight at us, and every irregularity on the dark ground threw a long, confusing shadow.

More interrogatory squeaks came from Ground Control.

"No no! I must attempt desert landing. You track my vessel? Yes?"

A more urgent hum, chirp, chitter.

"Descending, Taqtaq. I now proceed with emergency landing. I activate locator beacon and await rescue craft." The little pirate captain cut off the com.

"Do they still have a lock on us?" I asked him. "Dammit, you weren't suppose to let them lose us."

"Silence, untranslatable fool, or we all maybe die!"

I shut my mouth and crouched on the deck, watching the navigation display. Our position was about six hundred kilometers east of Taqtaq, on a beeline between the city and the presumed location of the Haluk facility. We were almost exactly where I had ordered Ba-Karkar to put down—far enough from the starport so the Qastt would be obliged to do an aerial search-and-rescue operation at an inconvenient distance from base, far enough away from the Haluk facility so its guardians wouldn't be suspicious.

The main viewer showed the ship almost skimming the dark ridge tops. We flew slower and slower. Ba-Karkar turned skillfully to avoid a collection of bristling scarlet crags and we passed out of the chaotic jumbled area into a level region cracked like a dried playa. A host of blobby black pinnacles had broken through the surface here and there like columnar mushrooms. The tallest rose at least fifteen meters high and measured about four meters in diameter.

"This looks like a good landing place," I said. "We can conceal the ship among the outcroppings."

"If we land here," Ba-Karkar said, "ship sink within human equivalent fourteen minutes. All soft bitumen under cracked surface." He pointed to a small console display. "Also, air have excessive noxious components from gas seepage out of cracks."

"Oh."

We continued to waft along at what would have been treetop level had there been any trees. The sun had set and daylight began to wane. The pinnacled poison plain gave way to a wide lake blotched with oil slicks, and on its opposite shore were more of the jagged black pressure ridges. Some of their fissures vented thin ribbons of vapor and were rimmed with a dirty yellowish crust that I suspected might be elemental sulfur.

Then Ba-Karkar uttered a squeak of triumph. "You look!"

Beyond the ridges lay what seemed almost like tarmac—a nearly round expanse of unblemished gray pavement over four kilometers wide. In the middle of it hulked a black excrescence that looked almost exactly like a gigantic tree stump. It had spreading buttress "roots" and a snaggly top. The entire formation was perhaps sixty meters high. The upper portions steamed gently, giving it the aspect of a charred victim of a recently extinguished forest fire.

"What the hell is it?" I asked, forgetting to whisper.

"Untranslatable. Chart say many other untranslatables like it exist this area. We land beside this one. Little water there but not much. Surface here very tough rind covering sizable reservoir of viscous pitch. Firm enough to support starship." And then he made my stomach lurch by adding, "I think."

"You're not positive?"

"Who positive?" he demanded rhetorically. "Great Bitumen Desert significant enigma with imperfect data. I study data, I decide where we land. We go down now . . . Untranslatable!"

The last defiant squeal almost sounded like a battle cry, a Qastt *banzai*. He had deployed his crash harness.

I shouted for the others to brace themselves as we headed straight for the peculiar black formation, came to hover in midair, and then descended as lightly as a feather into a steep narrow V between a pair of buttresses. It would have been a flawless touch, except that the skipper had miseyeballed the deeply shadowed inner angle of the notch by a scant half meter. Two of the six legs of the splayed landing gear scraped the walls on the way down. I heard a couple of loud reports and a grinding scrunch. The privateer lurched and shuddered.

Ba-Karkar slapped the power kill-pad and 1.1 gravity took hold of us. We hit the pavement with a sublethal impact and I was flung to the deck.

"We arrive," said the pirate captain. He retracted his crash harness and peered down at me. "Emergency beacon on. You want me contact Taqtaq on voice communicator?"

"Is the ship badly damaged?" I checked my own chassis. It was operational and I climbed to my feet.

"We take off easily. Land again maybe very dangerous. Starship tip over and break. But I think two support-legs not difficult to repair. I look and see. We now very well concealed from casual aerial observation, just as you command."

"Well done!" I shook hands with myself, which is the Qastt way of indicating enthusiasm and a generalized slap on the back. "Do not communicate with Taqtaq Ground Control. Will our ship's scanner be able to detect the rescue aircraft approaching?"

"When aircraft attain sufficient proximity."

"Okay. Do you have any idea of the rescue craft's top airspeed?"

"Maybe human equivalent three hundred kilometers per hour."

That gave us over an hour and forty minutes, even if they scrambled instantly, which wasn't likely. I asked him for an atmosphere analysis and wasn't too surprised when he told me that the air was filthy with volatile hydrocarbons, sulfur compounds, and smog particulates. But it was breathable by humans—at least for a few days—and if we hadn't accomplished our mission by then, it wouldn't matter.

Mimo, Zorik, and Ildiko pushed forward cautiously on the canted deck.

"Only light damage," I reassured them. "The caper's still on track. How you guys doing?"

Ildiko was super, Zorik was excellent, and Mimo told me that Ivor had survived the minor crash in good spirits but was very anxious to be released from the cargo bay because it had no latrine facilities.

"Open both hatches," I told the Qastt skipper. "We'll all go outside for a little while. Ba-Karkar, while I talk to my people, you can inspect the broken landing gear. Do not reenter the ship without my permission."

"I understand," he said. "You fear I commit some bad act alone in ship. No fear. I cooperate *significantly*."

That was nice to know. But I still wasn't about to trust him.

We trooped down the forward ramp into evening on Dagasatt. The air was very warm, about thirty degrees. Its petroleum stench was occasionally alleviated by cooler gusts of untainted north wind that blew straight into the shadowed cut between the tall black buttresses. The starship rested in a pool of water no more than a couple of centimeters deep, which was obviously a condensate of the vapor that wreathed the upper part of the stump. Bits of material scraped from the root walls by the ship's glancing collision lay about the two broken legs of the landing gear.

Ildiko bent down and fished a black chunk of debris out of the puddle. "Look at this. It's chock-full of tiny bubbles, almost like Zanderian pumice stone or even burnt toast. Weighs hardly anything. Do you suppose Stump Mountain is some kind of a volcano?"

Mimo asked her for the specimen, sniffed it, and studied it briefly. "Not exactly, although volcanic heat probably accounts for its birth. I think this formation must be a carbonized mass of fossil organic material—not petroleum, but perhaps more like coal. The bubbles in it were probably produced by a subterranean cooking process that yielded carbon dioxide and steam. Since the spongy mass was much less dense than the rock strata and molten bitumen surrounding it, it rose slowly to the surface and cracked the hard crust in a starlike pattern. Then it squirted through the crevices like a thick paste and gradually assumed the stump shape as it cooled and hardened."

Ildiko regarded my friend with admiration. "Are you a planetologist, Captain Bermudez?"

Mimo shook his head, smiling as he extracted a cigar from a gold case. "No, *querida,* but I have visited many strange places in the galaxy during the course of my checkered career, and it pleases me to study their natural history. There are often evolutionary parallels on the different worlds because creation tends to be economical."

Ivor came splashing over to us and the task force was complete. I told Ba-Karkar to carry on with his damage inspection. The rest of us moved a few dozen meters down the wedged-shaped black canyon onto the dry natural pavement, as firm and perfect as a newly laid asphalt parking lot. The rescue aircraft would find us without any trouble, and our ship was ideally sited for an ambush.

The little pirate captain had certainly earned his bonus. Even the broken landing gear was fortuitous, adding plausibility to the crash scene.

I began the briefing without any preamble.

"I've been reconsidering having Ivor remain here alone guarding the Qastt prisoners while the rest of us hit the Haluk installation. My objections are based on a worst-case scenario, and I'd like your input."

Everyone looked at me with professional blankness except poor Ivor, who probably thought I was about to impugn his abilities.

"Initially, based upon information that I got from Mimo, Ba-Karkar, and the pirate gunner Tisqatt, I thought that Taqtaq city was a dinky little place, and we could count on only a single overworked search-and-rescue team to hunt for us. But during our overflight I took a close look at the starport. It was larger and more modern than I'd expected, and there were *three* search-type aircraft parked there. The Qastt call the ships tuqo. They were unmistakable, colored blaze-orange and with wide ski-type landing gear suitable for soft sand or gooey bitumen."

"Mierditas," Mimo swore. He lit his cigar with a wooden match.

I said, "My sentiments exactly. There's no real problem if the Qastt send more than one aircraft on the first reconnaissance, following our beacon. We can deal with two as though they were one."

"But not three," Zorik O'Toole said.

"No," I agreed evenly. "If three tuqo come, we're out of here and the mission is an abort. But I think the odds of that happening are small. Okay, back to my worst case: What worries me is the prospect of a second or even a third search team coming out *later* if it seems that the first one pranged in and disappeared. We'll try to set up the destruction legend with the help of one of the prisoners, of course. And we'll camouflage the privateer with filotarps and turn off the emergency beacon. But there's always a chance that the first team will have reported our exact position to base before landing. We'll try to question our prisoners about this, but we may not get any good answers." I turned to O'Toole. "Zorik, take a translator pendant along when you hit the aircraft. If it's possible to question any Qastt aboard about a position report, do it."

"Understood," he said.

"We'll do the same with the prisoners that we take inside the privateer. But if another search team comes out and zeroes in, we'll know for sure that this site is fucked. The second team will have to be taken prisoner and the second tuqo demolished in a plausible fashion. After that, the privateer will have to be moved stealthily to another hiding place by our little buccaneer bud, to preclude a *third* team coming out after the second—along with God knows what kind of a generalized flap."

O'Toole said, "We could neutralize that problem by moving the privateer to a new position immediately after securing the first tuqo and its team."

I said, "Ba-Karkar told me that his ship can take off easily enough with broken gear, but landing again could be dangerous. I don't want to risk it unless it's absolutely necessary. Unless this site is compromised." I smiled at Ivor Jenkins. "Now, Ivor is a good man and I have every confidence in him. But he doesn't have the experience to contend with the worst-case scenario I've just described. No one, working alone, could cope."

"I agree, Helly," the bodybuilder said humbly.

Zorik and Ildiko remained impassive. They knew I wasn't about to ask that either of them, combat-trained veterans, remain behind.

Mimo said, "You want me to stay with Ivor."

"Yes. Together, you could handle just about anything."

"Are you certain of that?" O'Toole murmured.

I said, "Ask Mimo."

My friend calmly puffed smoke as he stared up at the bizarre Stump Mountain. "You need have no doubt that Ivor and I would deal effectively with this hypothetical situation, Commander O'Toole."

"There *is* another option," Zorik said to me. "Under these new circumstances, it's one that might be superior to your original plan if you've got the—if you're willing to consider it."

Great. He didn't quite say that there was another option if I had the balls to make use of it.

I just smiled and said, "What?"

"Once you have a single tuqo in hand, force one of the Squeakers to call the other two units for backup. When they land, grab one additional ship and destroy the third. Forget about taking Qastt prisoners. Use 'em to propagate the destruction legend to Taqtaq Control, then waste 'em. Blow up the privateer. We don't need it for evac—we can call down *Chispa*'s gig. This way, we have two aircraft for our raid instead of only one and a SWAT team of four, as originally planned. Ivor can guard the pirate and the aircraft while the rest of us make the ground assault."

I said, "You know that I promised Ba-Karkar we wouldn't harm innocent Qastt. They don't come any more innocent than search-and-rescue personnel. I also promised him he'd get his ship back after the operation."

Zorik O'Toole shrugged. "That was then, this is now. You can't see eliminating the Qastt, just leave 'em on the blacktop."

Six hundred kilometers from nowhere. "Thanks for the suggestion, Zorik, but it's a no-go."

"Suit yourself."

Mimo said to me, "There is another matter to consider. If I remain here, who will fly the Qastt aircraft?"

"I studied the schematics," I said. "The tuqo utilizes a primitive antigrav generator for lift, and a bank of small pivoting thrusters for propulsion. It's all manual, seat-of-the-pants flying. No computers, no really vital instrumentation except the fuel gauges and inertial compass. I can translate them."

Mimo grinned around his cigar. "You may actually be better off unencumbered with a feeble old *pedorrero* like me on this raid of yours. Unless, of course, you get yourselves into a really hairy firefight."

The veteran smuggler's prowess with weaponry, both portable and shipborne, verged on the phenomenal—which is why I'd had no serious qualms about including him on the team in spite of his age.

I said, "I think I assessed the situation correctly when I assumed that this facility wouldn't be defended any more elaborately than the one on Cravat. It's logical that the Haluk and their Galapharma protectors will rely more on sophisticated intruder-detection equipment than defensive firepower. The worst they can expect here are Qastt snoopers, and from what Tisqatt said, the locals are scared stiff of the place. I'm betting that the facility will have a medium-splendacious perimeter alarm system with robosteered Kagi blasters or the equivalent, a few Mickey Mouse antiaircraft guns, and a security force that spends most of its time playing gin rummy."

"You may very well be right," said Zorik O'Toole. He did a brief take. "And if it works out differently, why, we'll just have to improvise."

Uneasy looks from Ildiko and Ivor. A flat stare from Mimo, who recognized the whiff of insubordination for what it was. From me: "If I get whacked, improvise all you like. Until then, I expect you to follow orders."

"Goes without saying," said O'Toole, meeting my gaze without flinching. "You're the chief and we're the grunts."

I'd been away from Zorik's type too long—not that we'd had that many hardasses like him in the ICS Enforcement

Division, an outfit known for a certain lack of military formality. He was a man with no sense of humor, no inclination to accommodate human frailty, and no respect for a leader who failed to measure up to his draconian ideal of competence. I had no doubt that Zorik O'Toole would be a stone whiz in a combat situation. It was just too damned bad that he knew about my past history . . .

"Okay." I flashed the inimitable Frost grin at one and all. "Does anyone want to comment on the plan revision? No? Right, let's move on to a quick review of the upcoming action and then get back to the ship and suit up. I'd like each of you to go over your part in the ambush of the Qastt rescue personnel. Be as detailed as possible. Zorik, why don't you start?"

Dagasatt night.

The temperature has dropped over twenty degrees. The sky overhead is surprisingly clear in spite of a foul ground haze, decorated with broken patches of Milky Way, meager stars, and the Haluk Cluster, which looks like a small luminescent fingerprint on black velvet. There are no animal or insect sounds; only a faint hissing and an occasional fairy tinkle from high on Stump Mountain as it steams, cools, and endures an occasional minuscule landslide.

Out of the west a bright light approaches, first silhouetting the pressure ridges, then blazing clearly in the sky. A sound of primitive reaction thrusters. The engine noise changes pitch momentarily as the aircraft descends to a lower altitude, skimming the tarmac, vectoring in on the presumed site of the crash. A laser spot lances out toward Stump Mountain, discovers the slightly tilted starship nestled among the roots. An ominous plume of smoke rises from the wreck. Its cargo-bay hatch gapes wide open. There are no signs of life.

The Qastt rescue craft lands a cautious kilometer away. It has a no-nonsense shape, like a squared-off loaf of human bread, and measures about ten meters in length. The landing gear consists of two broad skis. Projecting from the roof is a short pylon bearing a brilliant site-illumination lamp. The laser spot shines from a housing below the cockpit, which has a broad windshield through which several figures are visible. They remain in place as the engines throttle back to idle. A side hatch opens and a robot probe trundles down the ramp and speeds toward the derelict starship.

The robot is small, equipped with a multitude of sensors. It reassures the crew of the rescue craft that the starship's potentially hazardous subluminal engine is turned off. Aside from the smoke, which is of unknown origin and may not even emanate from the wreckage, there are no fumes and no poisonous or flammable vapors in evidence. No obvious onboard conflagration registers on the infrared sensors. The robot glides through the shallow pool of water and ascends the derelict's ramp. It enters the cargo bay and begins casting about for indications of survivors.

A figure shrouded in white robes lies beneath a tumble of blue, yellow, and red cargo pods. They are human-style containers, and the rescue crew judges that the crashed starship is one of the valiant band of Qastt corsairs that plies the void, preying upon the hated race of putrid boomers.

As the robot eye zeroes in on the pathetic body trapped beneath its heap of booty, there is a slight movement. No clear view is possible, but the sensors confirm that the person is alive.

The robot spins about, scanning for other survivors. It finds another robed shape lying just inside the small interior hatch that connects the cargo bay with the forward accommodations and the flight deck. This person lifts his head and speaks directly to the robot in a wavering squeal.

"Help us."

The voice of the rescue-team leader responds. "Help has arrived. How many people aboard?"

"Six," says the crash victim. Then he falls motionless.

A large pod blocks the robot's way and it can go no farther forward. It turns about and completes its scan of the cargo bay. Finding no other survivors, it exits the privateer and waits, oblivious to the shallow water.

The rescue aircraft has closed its hatch. The antigrav unit

lifts it a dozen centimeters above the smooth asphalt and the thrusters scream thinly. It glides to the mouth of the small black canyon, only a stone's throw from the wreck, and once again descends, landing at the puddle's edge. This time the engines wind down to a full stop and there is a moment of silence. The laser spot has been turned off but the xenon site-illumination lamp mounted above the aircraft casts a clear white light on the scene.

Then the hatch reopens and four members of the rescue crew emerge, dressed in orange coveralls with a single ideograph written across the back, weighted down with gear. A single Qastt remains behind in the cockpit, bent over the flight console.

The small rescuers enter the privateer to begin their mission of mercy, speaking softly among themselves. They do not notice another figure that emerges from beneath a camouflaging filotarp among the dark chunks of detritus and flits over to the aircraft.

The figure is dressed in voluminous white Qastt garments. A tallish individual, it assumes a hesitant, slouching gait as it enters the rescue craft and moves forward. The pilot hears a noise, leaps up in surprise, recognizes that the newcomer is a member of the hated boomer race, and reaches for a weapon. She falls senseless as a dart from a stun-gun strikes her in the chest.

Back inside the cargo bay of the privateer, three of the rescue team are working to shift the containers from the half-buried victim. The plastic pods are surprisingly light. In fact, they appear to be empty. Meanwhile the fourth rescuer, who is a medic, squats to assess the injuries of the Qastt victim lying near the interior hatch.

The unconscious man rolls over, pulls a species of exotic pistol from beneath his robes and rams its muzzle into the neck of the flabbergasted medic.

"Silence! No movement or I shoot!"

The other three members of the team pause in their efforts, paralyzed by shock. Before they can react, a hideous xenoid rises from among the pods, shedding the robe that had concealed his monstrous size. He also holds a weapon, which he fires with lightning speed—*zzzt! zzzt! zzzt!* The rescuers crumple helplessly to the deck.

"Why?" cries the Qastt with the gun in his throat. "Why?"

I slipped the Ivanov back into its holster and pushed out of the tumbled pile of empty pods. Mimo and Ildiko shoved aside the container that had blocked the inner hatch and came out of the forward compartment into the cargo bay.

"Nice job, Ba-Karkar," I said.

Ildiko seized the arms of the medic while Mimo relieved our Qastt accomplice of his uncharged Kagi pistol. Deftly, the former Zone Patrol officer manacled her captive's wrists, then clipped a translator pendant to his blaze-orange coverall His angry chitters were decoded into a string of "untranslatables."

"Tell him the situation, Ba-Karkar," Ildiko commanded.

The pirate captain addressed his indignant compatriot. "You human prisoner. I human prisoner also, compelled to cooperate. Rest in holy silence. They not harm me. They not harm you either if you obey orders. You not obey, they shoot you like others."

"You kill agents of mercy!" the prisoner shrilled in my direction. "Untranslatable epithet boomer you!"

"They aren't dead," I said. "Only sleeping for a while."

I told Ildiko to take him outside. Ba-Karkar and I followed on her heels. Mimo was already snapping restraints on the wrists and ankles of the three unconscious Qastt. Hurrying down the ramp, we met Ivor, who had been concealed under a filotarp deeper inside the canyon.

"Shall I begin the unloading, Helly?" he asked.

I nodded. "Bring everything to the Qastt aircraft as fast as you can."

He opened the forward hatch and began hauling out the weapons and equipment we had previously unpacked from the pods.

Ildiko frog-marched the little medic to the tuqo while I followed with Ba-Karkar. The dazzling site lamp had been turned off and Zorik was coming down the ramp of the rescue craft with a Qastt body flung over his shoulder. He was no longer wearing his robe disguise.

"Had to take it down when it reached for a weapon," he remarked. "It didn't seem to be using the com. Probably waiting for a situation report from the others before calling into base."

"We'll check it out," I said. "Dump the snoozer with Mimo and then give Ivor a hand transferring gear. And kill that locator beacon inside the starship."

"Affirmatory," said Zorik O'Toole.

Ildiko and I let Ba-Karkar precede us into the cockpit of the rescue aircraft. He fumbled about the console for a few moments. "Asahel, their communicator not in operation."

"Turn it on and see if anyone at Taqtaq is trying to talk to these people." I said to the captive: "Listen to me. The lives of your comrades depend on what you do within the next few minutes. If you obey me, none of you will be harmed. We will keep you prisoner for a short time and then let you go. Ba-Karkar, confirm this."

"He mean what he say. He putrid boomer but he not lie. What honorable name you have?"

"Gogatar," muttered the medic. "I qualified healer."

"Okay, Gogatar," I said. "This is what I want you to say to Taqtaq Ground Control."

I told him, and he performed the expected song and dance of defiance, whereupon Ba-Karkar, Ildiko, and I worked on him with both threats and reassurances. He capitulated in a shorter time than I would have expected. We sat him on the pilot's bench, still shackled.

"I'll control the transmitter," I said. "Speak the first phrase over and over. You won't know when the words are being broadcast, so it won't do you any good to attempt to speak a warning. Ready?"

Gogatar hung his small head. His emerald antenna-brushes had wilted into doleful dishmops. In a monotonous chirr he intoned: "Taqtaq Control, you hear me? Taqtaq Control, you hear me?"

I keyed him in, then listened for a response. It came immediately, and Ba-Karkar translated it: "We hear. Speak."

I forced the medic to say in halting phrases that his colleagues were dead and he was the only survivor. The searchers had found the crashed starship on a strange, cracked bitumen formation. They landed, and four of them reconnoitered and entered the starship in the usual manner. No sooner had they gone inside than the asphalt crust around the vessel began to heave and fracture. A cataclysmic eruption of tar surged up. The slab holding the starship tilted and the ship was engulfed.

A cacophony of horrified squeaking from base greeted this ghastly tale, but I didn't bother to have Ba-Karkar translate. Following my lead, Gogatar told the controller that the slab on which his own aircraft rested was also sinking slowly into the bitumen morass. There was no possibility of escape.

"Now tell them goodbye," I commanded.

He started up from his seat. "Nooooo!"

I cut him off in mid-scream. "That was very good. Even the last bit. Do him, Ildy."

The small dart took him between the shoulders and she caught him as he fell.

"Not necessary!" Ba-Karkar protested.

"Expedient," I said. "All the prisoners will awake at about the same time tomorrow morning."

Ildiko hoisted the medic with ease and took him away in a fireman's carry.

The pirate shot me a glance of bitter resentment. "You plan render me unconscious, too, for sake of putrid expediency?" He was probably having second thoughts about cooperation after seeing his compatriots mowed down.

I asked him, "How long will it take you to repair the landing gear on your starship?"

He seemed caught by surprise. "Two human equivalent days. Maybe significantly less time if boomer-mountain help me. I have all parts."

"Do the job and don't make trouble. Then you won't be rendered unconscious or put into shackles. I'm going to take this aircraft and go fetch my enemies who are hiding with

the Haluk. Two of my people will go with me, and two—
including the boomer-mountain—will stay to guard you and
the other Qastt."

"*Eeeeee.* What if you die far away, Asahel? What happen to
us then?"

"Then you and the others will be in a shitload of trouble, so
you better pray to your Qastt gods that I have nothing but
good luck. Does that translate?"

"Significantly," said Ba-Karkar.

I slipped into the bench seat before the alien control console. There was more room for my boomer physique than
there had been in the privateer's flight deck. I wouldn't have
to fly the tuqo with my knees tucked under my chin, provided
that I sat just a wee bit sideways.

Ba-Karkar watched me uneasily as I pulled an e-book out
of my pocket and began to compare the aircraft instrumentation with diagrams flashed consecutively on the book's small
monitor.

"You fly Qastt tuqo before—yes, Asahel?"

"No. But I'm a fast learner."

"*Eeeee!* Crazy boomer you!"

"Probably," I agreed, sighing. "You feel like giving me
some flight instruction?"

"I think it better I go back to my starship and pray."

Chapter 8

His gods must have been listening.

After performing a complete external and internal inspection of the tuqo, I did a thirty-minute checkout flight at minimum altitude, skipping over the tarmac like a stone and dodging among the pressure ridges, getting the feel of the craft's controls and fuselage clearance. The bus wasn't hard to fly once my mind sorted out the fact that antigrav and propulsion weren't linked, the way they were in a human-designed hoppercraft. It was moderately tricky keeping a suitably delicate grip on the child-sized double joysticks and avoiding a ham-fisted boomer tendency to overcontrol.

When I was satisfied, I returned to the crash site and told Zorik to jury-rig the external units of our specialized scanning and stealth devices on the outside of the tuqo. Back on Seriphos, when the Rampart ExSec Equipment Manager had asked what we wanted to take along, I'd described Dagasatt's terrain without identifying the planet and told him to give us whatever he thought might be useful for a small-force assault. He'd assembled half a ton of costly gear, which we'd picked over and marveled at while *Chispa* was en route. Some of the stuff we had was so cutting-edge that we never could figure out what it was for. If Operation Q tanked, it wouldn't be for lack of top-line equipment.

Inside the privateer, I found the cargo bay had been converted into a makeshift brig by Ildiko and Mimo. Clamshell pods lined with bubblewrap padding had been made into beds for the unconscious agents of mercy, who were already tidily sacked out. Other empty containers of varying sizes made an improvised table, seats, and even a toilet cubicle for their use.

Ildiko and Ba-Karkar had been stowing away packets of Qastt food, containers of water, and other spartan necessities for the prisoners. The two of them finished as I made my inspection, and Ildiko sent the exhausted, grumbling little pirate to his cabin to take a breather.

"What next?" she asked me.

"Why don't you give Zorik and Ivor a hand. And see if you can find a way to mount guns on the outside of the tuqo."

"I have my doubts," she said, "but I'll do my best."

Mimo was stacking unneeded and empty pods outside the starship to give the five Qastt captives as much room as possible. "I don't anticipate any difficulty with them," he remarked. "After all, they're rescue technicians, not soldiers. If everything goes well, we can allow them outside for exercise. They might even help Ba-Karkar with the repairs. Just the sight of Ivor will probably frighten any notion of misbehavior out of their heads."

"Wait till daylight before contacting Joe with the lasercom," I said. "The smog will thicken as the night goes on, and the laser's UV will make the particulates fluoresce. The beam could be visible to passing aircraft if somebody's looking sharp. I'll get our team's relay set up as soon as I can tomorrow."

"How long do you plan to be gone?" Mimo asked.

"Give us three days. Seventy-two hours. We'll try to keep in contact via LC relay, but there may be blackouts, depending on the terrain. If we don't get back to you at the end of the three days, you can assume we've bought it. Hit the trail as fast as you can."

"Helly, don't be so pessimistic. I agree that the privateer should leave the system if you're delayed, but there's no reason why *Chispa* shouldn't stay. She'll be in no real danger unless the opposition calls in heavy reinforcements. Even then . . ." He smiled craftily, knowing full well that the Y700 could fly rings around any starship in the cosmos.

I flipped a hand, conceding the point. "All right. You and

Joe lurk out there in your overgunned blitzboat until hell freezes over if you feel like it. But remember that Ba-Karkar's unauthorized departure is certain to alert Dagasatt Ground Control, and they might pass the news along to the bad guys. We don't know what kind of liaison the Haluk facility has with the locals. Or with Galapharma."

"We'll cope. Don't worry."

"Got to. It's my job." I tapped my friend on the shoulder. "Well, I'm out of here. I'll send Ivor back when he's finished with the loading. You two can deploy the camouflage filotarps and then kick back with a bunch of beers. Be sure to give old Ba-Karkar a major snort of exotic booze, too. He's okay. Take care of yourself, Meem."

"*Vaya con dios,* Helly."

I left him standing on the ramp, thoughtfully chewing on an unlit Montecristo No. 2.

The distance between our crash site and the presumed position of the Haluk facility among the high redstone buttes was roughly 380 kilometers. I hoped we could get within striking range and find a good hiding place before dawn, thirteen hours away, since our wave-bender would not be able to conceal us from observers using powered optics. A more efficient vehicular stealth system required more power than the tuqo could supply; and even our small bender, being a species of force-field, sucked juice like a black hole. I was gambling that the Haluk installation wouldn't have very-long-range perimeter sensor arrays, and that their optical lookouts would only be stationed near the building compound itself, or possibly atop the adjacent buttes.

Our tuqo was equipped with a simple radar navigation system that would have pinpointed us to the foe like a bug on a bedsheet: useless. So I was obliged to utilize my own skull-mounted wetware, augmented by a rather decent photon-amplifying system in the bus's windshield that I'd been happy to discover during my study of the specs. Without it, a night approach by starlight would have required me to wear power optics all the way, leaving me with poached eyeballs.

The aerial photos and the holographic terrain maps made during our overflight in the privateer were invaluable guides. Even so, we had some narrow escapes early on when I misjudged our airspeed and had close encounters with deceptive bits of the local geography. As the night progressed, my tuqo piloting improved. Zorik and Ildiko had sense enough not to backseat-drive, but I could tell that the ex-commander was sorely tempted.

Our carry-on detection equipment included a powerful wide-angle light amplifier scope, as well as a scanning system that would warn us of the more conventional types of intruder alerts such as PHBA. Luckily for us, the really high-tech sensing defenses had blatant signatures that would have been easily spotted from space, so they weren't an option for a clandestine installation such as this one. I figured that the worst thing we might encounter was a platterstack EUV-laser micropulse array; but if I flew no higher than ten or twelve meters, even that would never tag us.

Zorik and Ildiko took turns operating our detection gizmos and sleeping, while I drove on and on and on, listening to old-time country music on a portable stereo—Willie and Waylon and Kenny and Garth, Reba and Patsy and Barbara and the Austin Lounge Lizards, singing about a simpler world long ago, where the heartaches and the frustrations and the laughs bore a curious correspondence to those of the twenty-third century.

The nightscope didn't reveal a single living thing abroad on the bitumen, nor were aircraft of any sort flying overhead—which was to be expected since the only other Qastt settlements in this remote region of the continent were situated far to the north. Eastward, in our direction of travel, lay only a wilderness of petroleum deposits, the narrow Barrier Range of volcanoes, the eponymous Empty Sea, and a hidden Haluk facility that might or might not harbor Oliver Schneider.

I tried not to think about the very real possibility that Operation Q was only a dangerous wild goose chase. Or that the facility would be so secure that our small force wouldn't have a prayer of penetrating.

The smog finally blew away, improving visibility. We zoomed along like a hovercraft, close to the surface of the ground—making good time over the lakes and flats, wafting more cautiously among the pinnacles, ridges, untranslatable stump mountains, and rugged areas. Our average speed was only 45 kph, about as fast as a four-wheeler moving on a rocky dirt track in the Arizona backcountry, but we were keeping well within our designated time frame.

We ran into the first array of ground-based automated PHBA motion sensors when we were 120.3 kilometers from our hypothetical destination. Ildiko shut off the scan alarm and I brought the tuqo to a jolting midair halt, then retreated until we were out of range.

"It's okay," she said. "We barely touched the signal underbelly before backpedaling below its horizon."

I mentally gave thanks that I had been forced to slow down to a relative crawl by a thicket of the black mushroomlike outcroppings. A few minutes earlier we'd been bombing along over a lake at 200 kph.

Zorik had been awakened by the scan alarm and came forward. "Think they made us, Chief?"

I'd told him to call me Helly at least half a dozen times. He still hadn't loosened up enough to do it.

I said, "No. We were still in the ground clutter zone."

"Here's a fascinating thing," Ildiko pointed to the monitor, which was in replay mode. "The six units of the phased array within range are precisely three klicks apart. And they seem to form a perfect arc of a circle."

I blinked. For an installation that was supposed to be hidden, the implication was ridiculous. "A *circle*? Galapharma engineers must have supervised the sensor setup. They wouldn't be that stupid."

Ildiko had a marvelous silvery laugh. "Why not? The ground-based dissimulator hides the facility from space observers. Landside, all they have to worry about are naive little Squeak snoopers and the odd human smuggler flitting around.

The horizon break fits the numbers pretty well, given the rough terrain. I'll bet you a tenner cash money that this array encircles the target precisely one hundred klicks out!"

"Compute it," I said.

A few minutes later she marked the holo printout of the area with a stylus and drew a bull's-eye around it. "Your Haluk facility has got to be right there. Small fuzzed-out open area surrounded by high rock formations that poke through the dissim umbrella."

"The dumb galoots!" I chortled. "They might as well have hung out a Kick Me sign."

Zorik smiled minimally. "Methodical to a fault."

Now we wouldn't have to waste valuable time just searching for the target inside the area shielded by the GBD. I was happy as a burro eating prickly pears.

"Okay, Ildiko. You get your winnings when we're back aboard *Chispa*. Now analyze that coverage and figure what we need to ooze through it."

She had the answer within a few minutes. Zorik fed the data into our wave-bender generator, which he had mounted on the aircraft's site-lamp pylon, and the tuqo continued stealthily on, now invisible to automated high-band sentinels. We passed within spitting distance of one of them, and I had Zorik shoot a holo of it amidst the xeno landscape. The unit was camouflaged from overhead observation by a wave-permeable fake-rock umbrella, while the sides of the hide were wide open. We could even see the Sheltok AC logo on the antenna housing.

We found identical perimeter-defense rings at twenty-kilometer intervals the rest of the way in. Their coverage overlapped and a bat couldn't have overflown the area without being detected. There were no EUV-laser platterstacks or other gonzo sensor systems. The two innermost phased array installations had automated Kagi guns as well as motion sensors.

We crept past the blaster emplacements while holding our collective breath, but the bender did its job flawlessly and the tuqo got through scot-free. However, I was afraid that our good luck wouldn't last much longer. Sooner or later we were bound to run into sensors that the bender couldn't foil. Or guards with eyes. I was gambling that it wouldn't happen before we were within striking distance of our target. Ground-assault striking distance, that is. It had proved impossible to mount weapons on the outside of the tuqo, and the only option left to us was penetration on foot.

The aircraft now moved among huge sandstone buttes, some of them over a thousand meters high and eroded into spectacular turreted or perforated shapes, like the formations of Monument Valley in the ancient Navajo lands of the American Southwest. They thrust up from a dead-level, faintly wrinkled black surface that looked suspiciously like an immense pool of molten tar capped by a thin dry skin. Here and there were smaller versions of the smooth concentric formations we'd seen from the approaching privateer. We speculated that these might be fresh upwellings or even the remains of "popped" bubbles of petroleum distillates. Stranger yet were the huge bones that protruded from some of the ebony flats, remains of monsters engulfed ages ago and now upthrust again by the churning bitumen. In a few places the bones were so abundant that they looked like some alien Elephants' Graveyard.

The air had become calm with the approach of dawn. Rags of mist hung motionless among the formations like tired phantoms. The eastern sky was turning gray, and landscape features had become clearly visible through the aircraft's unamplified side windows.

Zorik was doing a final sweep of the rock tops with the big nightscope, which would shortly become useless as natural illumination intensified, searching for observation posts or spy-beam antenna towers. Ildiko continued to study her scanner intently, giving regular verbal reports as I had requested.

"Clear at nineteen klicks. No change in the phased-array freq. No laser beacons or gravitation scans."

We were very near and we needed solid ground now, a place to conceal the tuqo while we did our final reconnaissance afoot. I wanted to get as close to the target as possible, so I threaded a slow course among the buttes, doing my best to keep solid rock between us and the facility. We were now well within line-of-sight range from the top of formations that surrounded the place. If a photon or graviton beam swept us, we were dead meat.

But there were no beams, and Zorik found no rocktop structures.

"Clear at seventeen klicks," Ildiko said.

She had her own copy of the topo plot. Once, when I began to skirt a small butte clockwise, she said, "Go right, Helly. Better cover." She was correct and I was wrong, and I cursed silently and had to concede that after a stressful all-night drive, my judgment was slipping. Tension and fatigue made me ache all over, and my eyes were strained from the constant focus-shift back and forth between the windshield and the printout I was using as a map.

I called out, "Zorik, secure the nightscope and break out the powered day-glasses. Then come forward and help me navigate. I'm whipped."

"Right." He sounded almost pleased.

I didn't care.

Ildiko said, "Clear at fifteen klicks." And then, "Clear at fourteen. Approaching margin of dissimulator field. It's not a very strong one: a permeable smudger, maybe a GBD-2H, only about forty meters high."

More and more rock formations thrust up from the bitumen. As we moved beneath the dissimulator field, the higher portions of the outcroppings and crags assumed a faintly distorted aspect, but there was none of the "sparkle" effect typical of stronger force-fields.

"Clear at twelve klicks," Ildiko said.

"Zorik, call out the nature of the surface as it changes. I've gotta concentrate on dodging these damned rocks."

"Affirm. Surface is mixed petroleum and gravel."

The eastern sky had pinkened. Qastt have more sensitive vision than humans, and when external visibility reached a "bright dusk" level, I knew that the windshield light-amplifier system would automatically shut down. Then my tired eyes would be on their own.

Zorik said, "Rock needle dead ahead."

"Got it." I steered around the deceptive formation with a meter to spare.

Ildiko said, "Clear at ten klicks. Passing between Kagi-armed antenna units identical to those at the Twenty Perimeter. But now they're only half a klick apart."

"Surface is sand, gravel, and tar," Zorik said. "Is it wise to go much closer?"

"Just keep on trucking," I said through my teeth.

"Clear at nine klicks," said Ildiko.

"Surface is broken petroleum aggregate. Through-route to the left ahead."

"Got it." The windshield light-amp shut off just as I flew through a confusing cluster of red-rock towers, cursing under my breath.

We knew that the target was on a level plain hemmed about with high rock formations. However, the GBD projector that roofed the place had subtly distorted the near-surface features on our map, especially those within a four kilometer radius of ground zero, leaving us ignorant of the immediate target surroundings. It was possible that Galapharma and the Haluk had built their mystery facility on pontoons floating in the bitumen; but I fervently hoped that they'd chosen the easier option of solid ground. We had no easy way of traveling on foot over a treacherous morass of tar.

Ildiko said, "Still clear at eight klicks."

"Level surface is stiff petroleum," said Zorik. "Better slow it way down. Shitty terrain ahead."

"Right."

The contour-flying tuqo now resembled a small boat creeping through increasingly narrow straits that separated lofty barren islands. In some areas the closely crowded rocks made it impossible to skim the bitumen and I had no choice but to hopscotch to altitudes of fifteen meters or more. Our blaze-orange aircraft might have been invisible to sensor waves, but an intelligent observer could have spotted it with ease.

"Clear at seven klicks."

"Level surface is gravel, some shallow water over petroleum."

Then I saw what I had been hoping to find. And brought the tuqo to an abrupt hover-stop just above the tarry shore of a small lake.

"Yes!" I hissed in satisfaction. "Look—that squatty conical butte dead ahead of us across the water? It's an ancient volcano with a talus-slope collar. We've got a jillion of 'em in Arizona. First one I've seen here. I betcha there's good firm rocky stuff all around it. Check it out with the day-glasses, Zorik."

The dark-colored eminence was about three kilometers in diameter and half as high, mostly a heap of shattered basalt. Only a stub of solid rock poked out the top, the remnant of a vent plug. To the north were two lesser sister formations of igneous rock. According to the map, they seemed to be separated from Conical Butte by a precipitate narrow canyon. A stream running through it probably supplied the lake we were hovering beside. To the south loomed a colossal red sandstone outcropping. The corridor between Big Red and Conical Butte was wider than the northern canyon through the Sisters. The map showed a dense cluster of tall crags at South Corridor's far end . . .

Beyond which lay the flat with the secret Haluk installation.

"This is it, troops . . . Ildy, scan the tops of all these buttes with the whole spectrum. Zorik, scope 'em out as well as you can with the glasses. If this outfit is really security conscious, they'll have spy-beams up there. The GBD field isn't strong enough to seriously inhibit coverage."

But there was nothing.

I flew across the lake and zipped around the foot of Conical Butte counterclockwise, keeping the bulk of the degraded volcano between us and the facility. Viscous bitumen beneath the water gave way to asphalt aggregate and then to a rough stony surface with only a few traces of petroleum. At Kilometer 4.2 we reached the crags, which seemed to be a fragmented lava dike extending out from the tumbled talus slope of Conical Butte. Three spindly columns of black smoke arose from the crags' far side.

It was nearly full daylight.

I eased the tuqo into a deep niche with a rocky floor, touched down, and killed the engine. All three of us scrambled out and covered the aircraft with filotarps, which instantly assumed the colors of the surrounding shadowed rock. Northwest of us Conical Butte was rosy gray in the light of the rising sun. Above our heads to the south, the sunlit crown of the monster sandstone formation I'd dubbed Big Red appeared to be painted in fresh blood. An even bigger red-rock mountain to the east, which would later be named Jukebox Butte by Zorik O'Toole, glowed fiery around the edges. The cool air was foul, not only with the usual hydrocarbon odor but also with the acrid smell of oily smoke.

"Surely the Haluk wouldn't use these bitumen deposits for fuel as the Qastt do," Ildiko said. "They have efficient small fusion generators and matter converters."

"Maybe our friends across the way accidentally ignited a seep of crude oil or some volatile stuff," I said. "Or there might be a live volcanic vent that did the same thing. If petroleum products are smoldering underground in the rock fissures, they might be impossible to extinguish."

Ildiko made a face. "Let's get back inside the ship where we can breathe clean air."

We retreated and I put her back to work on the scanner. "All-band surveillance for at least another hour, with special emphasis on the com frequencies. We want to be sure no bad guys come cantering through the crags with guns blazing."

"One of us should do a fast long-range ground recon as well," Zorik stated. "I volunteer. I'll do an optical peek around those pointy-top rocks just north of here. Move less than a klick away from the ship. Scope out the Three Smokes and make sure there's no unusual volcanic activity. Might even be able to view the target if the terrain's favorable. What say?"

Oh, you spring-butt bastard. Just can't wait to get into action . . .

"Good thinking, Zorik. Gear up. I'll do the comlink right

away so you can keep in touch with us here through your helmet LC."

He went aft to prepare his equipment. Ildiko resumed her station at the scanner and I fiddled and diddled with the CL-4 until its thread-thin modulated laser beam found *Chispa Dos* in her geosynchronous orbit half a million kilometers above the Great Bitumen Desert.

Joe Betancourt reported that Ogu, Tisqatt, and Tu-Prak were very subdued and compliant. Three Qastt vessels had lifted off from the planet's central starport yesterday afternoon and left the solar system. The only human starships on the move were obvious Rampart vessels coming and going from Cravat, thirty-three light-years away. There was no trace of Haluk starship activity within a sixty-light-year radius of the Dagasatt solar system. Mimo and Ivor had just reported a quiet night aboard the privateer with no sign of additional search-and-rescue aircraft from Taqtaq.

I thanked Joe, gave a brief report of my own, then had him activate the relay system that turned *Chispa* into a very expensive private communications satellite. As I signed off I heard the back hatch of the tuqo close softly, but I thought nothing of it.

My mind was already on breakfast and I dug out the pod containing our selection of ready-to-eat meals. "Carnivore or veggie?" I asked Ildiko. "Coffee, tea, or juice?"

"Veggie, please. English Breakfast tea with two honeys, apple juice if you have it."

"Yo, Zorik!" I called. "You want to feed?"

No answer. I figured he'd gone outside for a dump. It was impossible for a human to sit down inside the incommodious Qastt amenity at the rear of the tuqo.

I started pinching hot and cold bags, loading food onto little degradable dish-trays. One order of walnut oatmeal, grilled soy bacon, hot apple-raisin compote, and beverages; one order of ham-mushroom omelette, mini-bagels and cream cheese, cherry-pineapple-blueberry yogurt, and black coffee. There was no activity on the scanner except signals from commercial and government stations in the refinery towns, scratchy solar wind, the enormously long waves of distant lightning, and a fluctuating IR emanation from the burning site beyond the crags.

"You're from Earth, aren't you, Ildy," I remarked after stuffing my face.

"Yes. How can you tell?"

"Elementary, my dear Szabo! I used to be a cop. Actually, it's the slight accent you give to your Standard English that betrays you. Colonials homogenize their speech within a generation and talk media-vanilla. Only people born on the Old World retain regional accents. I can't place yours."

"It's Hungarian. My mother and father have a hydroponics farm in a small town north of Budapest. They grow roses and freesia for the floral trade. I helped them from the time I was small." Her face took on a rather wistful expression. "They were marvelous parents, but I thought they were very bourgeois and boring. I couldn't wait to join Zone Patrol and take a posting as far away from Earth as possible. I wanted adventure and excitement among the stars."

"Did you find it?"

"Oh, yes. It was a good twenty-five years."

"But you opted for early retirement. Why?"

A mischievous flicker in her eyes. "Not for the reason O'Toole did! My girlfriend Cosa was invalided out. Bilateral arm replacement. I decided to go, too. Stand by her during rehab. She and I retired to Seriphos. We thought it would be amusing to grow flowers as my parents did, and it was great fun . . . until Cosa met someone else. Poof!" She shrugged.

"And why did Zorik leave the patrol?"

"Perhaps I shouldn't have mentioned it. He hung it up a year before I did. There's nothing on his record but gold stars, not the least hint of slime. But some of the ZP insiders said that Commander Iron Nuts was given a clear choice by the brass: retire or get flushed. It was never clear exactly what happened. There were rumors of some gross piece of insubordination. O'Toole never was one to suffer fools gladly—even if they outranked him."

Ildiko fell silent, studying the monitor of her instrument

with particular intensity. Eventually she shook her head. "Nothing transmitting out there. Just the usual, and the Three Smokes glowing beyond the pointed crags."

We ate without speaking for a time. Zorik still hadn't joined us. I began to describe my former life as a happy beach bum and charterboat skipper and told a few yarns that made her laugh. Then I got down to what was public knowledge concerning my devastated career in the ICS Enforcement Division, figuring she had as much right to know as O'Toole did.

She listened with sympathy. When I finished, she asked, "Do you think you were framed by some criminal type with a grudge?"

"No. Almost certainly by Galapharma AC. As a deliberate opening move in its corporate chess game with Rampart. It was a nifty piece of irony. I'd joined the Interstellar Commerce Secretariat in the first place to defy my father and thumb my nose at the family Starcorp. I was a flaming idealist when I was young. Ready to expose the heart of darkness in the Hundred Concerns and all the other corporate predators who think they own the galaxy. Pretty sappy, huh?"

"No," she contradicted me softly. "They think they're above the law, that the Commonwealth Assembly is a collection of puppets and they pull the strings. The big Concerns have even corrupted the patrol—some wings of it, at any rate."

"How do you know?" I'd heard the same rumors, of course. Not only about the patrol, but about the ICS as well.

"That was the reason I requested a transfer out of Zone 16. You must know about the dirty business involving Carnelian AC and the Joru years ago. Well, it never really stopped— just became more discreet. Among other things, the Carnies have been literally getting away with murder, liquidating uncooperative xeno gashrunners with the collusion of a patrol death squad. The involved officers have never been charged, but the rest of us all knew what was going on."

"Have you ever heard talk of ZP corruption out here in the Spur?"

"There were hints of payoffs by Galapharma. For unauthorized variations in patrol patterns, mostly. The grapevine had it that Gala was spying on Rampart as part of its acquisition strategy and didn't want its speedboats logged in certain areas."

"Near which worlds?"

"Mostly around Seriphos, Plusia-Prime, and Tyrins. The high-traffic Rampart planets. But also way out near the Tip where there arc hardly any human colonies at all. That was hard to figure." Her blue eyes suddenly widened. "Would it have had something to do with the *Haluk*?"

I stared at her for a moment without speaking. The rear hatch of the tuqo slammed.

Hurriedly, I said, "Ildy, what do you intend to do when this mission is over?"

She seemed flustered. "Well . . . if you're satisfied with my work, I hoped you might keep me on. Let me do prisoner-escort duty. Help take the perps back to Earth. I'd like to see my folks. Check out the family greenhouse." Her mouth twisted wryly. "Who knows what I might do if the right position comes along?"

"You're hired," I whispered. "But it'll be our secret, for now."

"Is that coffee I smell?" O'Toole sang out.

"You want some?"

"Damn right! Make it big, make it black, make it extra hot, and make it snappy." He barked out a laugh to let me know he was only perpetrating a little comradely whimsy, then called, "Anything on the scan, Lieutenant?"

"Nothing at all, Zorik." Ildiko winked at me. She wasn't falling for his rank-pulling bullshit. "It doesn't look as though the opposition expected anyone to get through the perimeter defenses."

"One jumbo java, coming up," I said.

When I took it back to him a few minutes later, he was already dressed in full battle gear, except for the helmet. He poured the coffee into an insulated flexcanteen and said, "I've decided on a tentative reconnaissance route. Want to see?"

I refrained from giving the question the response it deserved. "Sure."

He laid out a completely new topographic plot.

It had to have been made within the last few minutes, using our own portable photon-differential terrain mapper.

He caught my look of shocked surprise and incipient anger and smirked. "Not to worry, Chief. I drew it with a single pulse at the very instant the sun peeked over the mountains. Even if the hostiles noticed, they'd think the burst was a solar flare phenom. Just part of the dawn chorus. I used the same trick during a successful clandestine action on Bandusia."

"Zorik—"

"Check it out!" He was very proud of himself. He'd displayed creative initiative while I'd been playing short-order cook. "This copy's for you. I have another one in my pack. With the photons bouncing off this collection of buttes, I was lucky enough to get some really useful detail."

The single-shot holographic "shoot-around-corners" computer-enhanced image was necessarily imperfect, with no fine resolution of the topo features or true differentiation between tar and hardpan on the ground surfaces; but it was a hell of a lot better map than the one we'd made with the Qastt equipment. It clearly showed rocks as small as watermelons. It penetrated all but the final kilometer or so of the circular GBD field. There was even a fuzzy ghost image of the shielded Haluk facility itself, a central module with three equidistant projecting wings like stubby propellor blades. East of the structure was a very shallow expanse of water, and beyond that rose another monstrous sandstone formation with steep sides that he'd christened Jukebox Butte.

I said, "I wish you'd consulted with me before making this map."

"You'd have agreed, right?"

"Probably, but—"

"I remembered the solar-flash stunt in the last minutes before the sun popped up. There was no time for discussion." He continued, as though that were the end of it—and I suppose it was, "Now then, since we have this new map, there doesn't seem to be any really compelling reason why I shouldn't do a full target recon right away. I'm feeling great.

Got plenty of z's riding in. I estimate the round-trip would take five or six hours, max. Continuous feedback to base, of course. With the recce done, I'll still have plenty of time to rest up for our strike after nightfall. What say?"

"Explain in detail what you're proposing."

"First, I considered and rejected the idea of climbing Conical Butte and doing the recce from up there. Even though there's plenty of cover, I believe that the target's GBD umbrella would interfere with high-angle powered optical observations. We've no choice but to check out this target at ground level." He gave me a severe look. "After evaluating the adjacent terrain on the new map—a goddamn hedge of high rock surrounds the place—I'm provisionally accepting your assumption that there'll be no perpendicular dissimulator field hindering our direct observation of the building itself. Under the circumstances, the defenders wouldn't be concerned about low-angle spying from a distance."

"Go on."

"I'll make an approach this way, always keeping solid rock between me and the target, until I reach this point."

His finger traced a tortuous eastward-trending path among the volcanic crags and redstone outcroppings, well to the south of the area from which the Three Smokes emanated, until he turned north across a nearly level region and came to a narrow sandstone pinnacle over 140 meters tall. The facility lay only about fifteen hundred meters beyond it.

The pinnacle had a lot of broken rock at its base and was oddly twisted in its upper reaches, bearing a passing resemblance to a huge corkscrew. Relative to the target, it was the closest bit of useful cover to be had, and looked like the best place to launch a penetration.

O'Toole certainly thought so. "This is the most appropriate assault route. The new map indicates that the area between Corkscrew Pinnacle and the target structure is dry ground."

"*Seems* to indicate," I corrected him.

He waved that aside. "I'll confirm it optically, of course. No other potential line of attack looks nearly as promising.

East of the target is water: an impossible approach. The open area due west of the target, between it and the rough talus at the base of Conical Butte, is nearly three thousand meters across and has almost no cover, only a few widely scattered boulders that are less than man-sized. The region southwest of the target, in the direction of the crags where we're hiding now, probably has burning oil pools—my deduction from those three smoke plumes."

"The smokes concern me," I said. "The recon path you've chosen precludes any exploration of their source."

"Irrelevant, unless the primary assault route choice proves impracticable—in which case, we'll have to consider an approach from the north or the southwest. Time enough to check out the smokes then, if necessary."

"With all its twists and turns," I said, "this route of yours covers at least five kilometers one way. That's a considerable distance for a lone scout in a potentially hazardous alien environment."

"I don't see any real problems for an experienced man utilizing camo gear. Do you?"

"Not according to this map."

"Then do I have your permission to proceed?"

He was gung-ho and ready to ramble, and I couldn't think of any good reasons to hold him back—except the possibility of unexpected terrain hazards, and my resentment at the way he'd challenged my authority. To be fair, I tried putting myself in O'Toole's place. He wanted the mission to succeed so he could retire in style, but he was saddled with a leader who was a disgraced cop turned cowboy adventurer, clearly lacking in recent combat experience. He knew exactly what he was doing and suspected that I didn't.

Maybe Iron Nuts was entitled to a little attitude.

"Okay," I said. "Permission granted. You'll make a continuous holovid record of the recon, of course, blink-transmitting the compressed data back to us via the lasercom relay. I also want a verbal report from you every fifteen minutes. Sooner if you make an important find."

"Affirmatory. If there's a way to penetrate that target, I'll find it. Guaranteed."

He gave me a hard smile before clapping on his helmet. It enclosed his entire head and featured a multifunction power-optic visor, holovid camera with continuous map-revise data stream, laser communication capability, and an omnifilter respirator. Like his soft-armored combat jumpsuit, it had an environmental system to keep him comfy. His belt held a Kagi sidearm, a monster commando knife in place of the usual Ivanov stunner, small flexcanteens of water, coffee, and nutrigoo, and a bulb of trailblazer spray. He strapped on an open-frame instant-access backpack loaded with fifteen kilos of fighting equipment and survival gear. Its scabbard mounts held a Talavera-Gerardi 333 actinic blaster with auto targeting, and a compact LGF-18 30-mm grenade launcher that carried standard and magnum HE, flare, and the newly developed AG97 sleepy-gas rounds.

Armed to the teeth, tough as the calluses on a barfly's elbow, ready for anything, Commander Zorik O'Toole, CHW Zone Patrol SWAT (Ret.), opened the rear hatch of the tuqo and marched out into the Dagasatt morning without a wave or a backward glance.

I stared after him in wordless bemusement, knowing he'd make good on his "guarantee" if any man could. Also knowing there was no way I'd ever want him guarding my back.

Never rely on a man who won't call you by your name.

Ildiko and I agreed on three-hour watches. I crashed first, laying out a pad and sleeping bag in the aisle of the tuqo, the only place on the cramped aircraft where I could stretch out full-length. My sleep was dreamless and so profound that when the pillow buzzer woke me I found I'd hardly shifted position.

I went forward. Ildiko showed me the plot of O'Toole's progress on the computer's greatly revised map, which continuously incorporated topographic data sent in by his camera. The monitor showed him approaching the tall sandstone formation called Corkscrew Pinnacle. Gaps between the incremental dots representing his quarter-hour call-ins were getting closer and closer together.

"He's moving more slowly than I would have expected," I remarked.

"The surface has gone tricky." She passed me the e-book with details of his verbal reports.

I skimmed it. During the first couple of hours, he'd moved at a brisk pace among the crags on a winding easterly path, traversing firm ground that was mostly broken volcanic rock or level red sand and gravel. But as his route curved northward toward the Corkscrew, he encountered a floorlike expanse of deeply fissured igneous rock that he speculated might represent an old lava flow. Some of the crevices showed glints of oily liquid in their depths.

Zorik's last message had reported that areas of the fractured surface now had a cindery crust, as though the oozing petrochemical material had burned at some time in the past.

He noted that tiny wisps of vapor were rising from some patches of cinders.

I cursed. "He's over two and a half kilometers east of the Three Smokes. But it's beginning to look as though a similar region exists around the pinnacle approach. We could be facing serious shit if it's extensive."

"His next report is due in four minutes."

I did a quick check of her scanner log. The Haluk facility seemed to be under a total electromagnetic blackout.

Again I found myself speculating whether Schneider was still there, exiled to this godforsaken place until Galapharma's takeover of Rampart made it safe for him and his co-conspirators to resurface in the Perseus Spur and assume remunerative employment under the new regime. The notion of a life-preserving "insurance policy" was logical. But why hadn't Alistair Drummond simply commanded his minions to hook Schneider up to the psychoprobe machines until he disgorged any incriminating data?

Maybe they had. And maybe the reaming attempt had backfired. Knowing where the hot poop was buried and being in a position to dig it up and neutralize it didn't necessarily equate. Cunning old Ollie could have come out of the interrogation with his policy and his skin intact.

And very, very pissed off . . .

"O'Toole to base," said the lasercom.

"Copy," Ildiko replied. "Go ahead, Zorik."

"Position approx one-forty-five meters due south of Corkscrew Pinnacle eastern extremity. Attempting approach to vantage point, but I'm hampered by increasing areas of highly unusual terrain. Old volcanic crust has disappeared now and surface is mostly sand and red gravel with patches of black cinders. Some of the cinders are smoking. We have no gas vents, craters, or large plumes—just a kind of diffused fuming in the hot spots, like from a raked-over campfire. Incidental comment: these cinders don't resemble the substance comprising Stump Mountain. And the gassy emanations seem to be real smoke, not steam like the Stump gave off."

Ildiko said, "Copy that. Have you taken surface temperature readings?"

"Affirm. Every dozen or so meters since last report. Variable temps up to a max of 62.8 degrees on current leg of the trail. We definitely have increasing thermal activity in the region. We need that new portable subterrain scanner to figure what's under the ground here."

But he'd left it behind in the tuqo. The device weighed nearly eight kilos, and Zorik had probably figured he wouldn't need it since he didn't plan to explore near the Three Smokes.

I leaned toward the mike. "Helly here. Does the zone of smoking cinders extend all the way up to the base of Corkscrew?"

"Conditional negatory. It seems intermittent. Sometimes windblown sand makes it tough to spot the borders of the high-temp material. Not all of the really hot stuff smokes, either. Proceeding with care and marking the trail with frequent spritzes of Lublaze."

"I'm concerned about this situation," I said to him. "If

patches of subterrain combustion extend north of Corkscrew—between the pinnacle and the Haluk facility—we'll have to ditch the approach."

"I don't think the hostiles would build their installation on a firepit," Zorik remarked sarcastically.

"No," I said. "But they sure might have used them as natural perimeter defenses."

That shut him up.

Ildiko said, "Zorik, do you have ETA for vantage point at base of pinnacle?"

He gave the estimate in Zebra Time—ten minutes from now. "But I'll want to do a preliminary survey before reporting. I'll get back to you on the regular sked, Lieutenant Szabo. O'Toole out."

"Base out," said Ildiko. She looked at me over her shoulder. "What do you think?"

I shook my head. "He picked the south approach because it's the best available, and he really wants to make it work. But there's an old country song about playing poker that we sing where I come from. The refrain goes: 'You gotta know when to hold 'em, know when to fold 'em.' "

She nodded and sang softly. " 'Know when to walk away and know when to run.' We sang it in Hungary, too."

I gave her upper arm a gentle punch. "My turn at the monitor. Time for you to sack out. Three hours of sleep. By the time you wake up, old Iron Nuts will be on his way back."

But he wasn't.

Zorik's camera stopped relaying terrain data eleven minutes later. He didn't respond to my call and missed the next fifteen-minute sked as well. I checked the relay equipment, even queried Joe Betancourt directly. He confirmed what I already knew: the carrier beam from Zorik was out.

"You want me to try finding him with enhanced optical, Helly? We're at extreme range, but—"

"No. He's too far under the GBD umbrella by now. We'll have to risk a dissim-penetration scan from *Chispa*, extrapolating from his last known position. Use a minimum diameter punch-through."

"Copy. Stand by."

Minutes passed. Then Joe came back. "Negative for a human body at the LKP. But there is something. Here comes the image."

The holovid map on my monitor acquired new detail in the immediate vicinity of Corkscrew Pinnacle. I pulled in an extreme close-up and studied it, feeling my spine go icy.

It was a new column of smoke.

"Thanks, Joe. I'll take it from here. Out."

Had Zorik met with an accident—or did his abrupt disappearance signify something else altogether?

Unlike Ivor Jenkins, whose father was an old chum of Mimo's, and the Library irregulars, who had been recruited by Karl from his circle of over-the-hill ex-security personnel, the three newest members of my team were virtually unknown factors. Matt Gregoire's computer had vouched for their professional skills but very little else.

Of the three, O'Toole had always been the most problematical. I'd felt an instant empathy for quiet Joe Betancourt and competent, amiable Ildiko Szabo. With Zorik, it was just the opposite. And he'd been forced into retirement for some unspecified transgression.

Ildy had spoken of corruption in the Perseus Spur arm of the patrol. Belatedly, I wondered if Zorik O'Toole had been part of it, paid off by Galapharma to look the other way while Concern starships secretly prowled Rampart space, sabotaging Starcorp operations and doing God knew what else.

I'd offered Zorik a whopping fee for his services.

What if Gala had topped it?

I woke Ildiko and we both began to suit up in full combat gear.

Chapter 9

We were about 250 meters south of Corkscrew Pinnacle, emerging from a dense group of volcanic crags, when we caught our first clear glimpse of the new smoke plume rising straight up into the dead calm morning air. Its source was very close to the base of the twisted sandstone formation, concealed among large broken rocks at the far right-hand side.

Our excursion had so far been rapid and uneventful. I hadn't shared my fear that we might no longer be safe in the tuqo, nor my doubts about the loyalty of Zorik O'Toole. If Commander Iron Nuts had sold us out, Ildiko didn't need to know about it yet.

"That's the new smoke Joe spotted from orbit," I said. "Right about at Zorik's last known position."

"A lot smaller than the three plumes farther west," she murmured into her helmet mike. "Almost like a burning pile of rubbish or something."

I said, "Yeah."

Or something.

We hunkered down together behind a desk-sized fragment of black basalt. Our filo ponchos turned us into part of the scenery. The entire base of Corkscrew was hidden from our view, nor could we see anything beyond it because of other intervening formations.

Earlier, I had spoken about the very real possibility that O'Toole might have accidentally broken through the cinder crust and plunged into a fiery crevasse. Now Ildiko proposed a more hopeful scenario.

"Maybe he came under attack. I know you said Joe

couldn't find any live-body signatures, but how about this: a Haluk sniper hits O'Toole's packframe or one of his weapons with a glancing beam. The EM pulse fries his com equipment instantly. Maybe wounds him pretty bad. He takes cover, launches an HE grenade. Whammo! Exit the hostile sniper down a furnace hole that opens up. O'Toole dives deep into the rockpile out of sensor range and starts regrouping."

"Mmm." I was noncommittal, but it was a possibility.

Over two hours had passed since Zorik's scheduled transmission. We'd raced out from the tuqo as fast as we could, following coded polarized trailblazes that were only visible through our powered visors. I half expected Haluk fliers or Galapharma hoppercraft to appear overhead at any moment, but the sky remained empty.

So had the sublight communications spectrum on the portable scanner Ildiko carried.

An enemy force alerted and on the hunt would not be able to use a stealthy laser relay system to keep in contact, as we did. Hoppers or goons on the ground would probably communicate via ordinary radio because the Qastt planet had no com satellites. I doubted that they'd bother keeping radio silence during a search-and-destroy mission—ergo, nobody was out looking for us yet. And it seemed fairly certain to me that no ambush had taken down Zorik, either, or the sniper would have reported the incident to base.

Gently, I pointed the latter out to Ildiko. "Besides that, if O'Toole had been struck by a hostile shot, we'd have picked up a last squawk as his LC unit went out. There was nothing. But if he dropped through the cinder crust, the relay beam would have clipped off silently. Just as though he'd moved into a dead zone, out of sight-line of *Chispa*."

"But isn't there a chance he might have survived if he did go down? I mean . . . maybe it wasn't burning all that much where he fell in."

"Anything's possible. We're sure going to check out the smoke site and finish the reconnaissance."

And decide whether or not two people had a ghost of a chance of breaking into the Haluk facility.

Know when to hold 'em, know when to fold 'em.

I said, "We'll have to move along now. Sooner or later somebody in the installation will send a hopper to check out the new smoke."

Ildiko nodded silently. Her grotesquely helmeted head flashed in and out of view as the filo units in the poncho hood did their best to render her invisible.

"I'll take the point," I said. "I'm going to hoover along with the new subterrain scanner from here on in—make sure we don't end up in Crispy Critterville ourselves. I have to learn how to use this thing, so I'll go pretty slow to start with. You hang back about ten meters and watch for moving targets. Sweep the northern heights and the sky behind the pinnacle with your Tala-G scope. If you spot anything, give a shout. We both freeze under our ponchos. The hostiles won't find us unless they land smack-dab on our heads."

"Check."

Unshipping the STS wand and holding it just above the ground, I called up its device display on the left side of my visor and cut a test slice. The image revealed an underground cross section only two meters wide but fifty meters deep and about half that in length. The rock strata were neatly labeled in terminology that might have been crystal-clear to a geologist but was a trifle abstruse to the likes of me. I was able to rotate the slice freely with verbal commands and even magnify portions for close inspection. When you moved the wand from side to side, a lingering afterimage gave a wider section. Pretty neat.

"How's it look?" Ildiko asked.

"We got a layer cake. The frosting is a very thin skin of old lava, cracked all to hell and covered with sand in some places. Below that are broken-up sandstone strata shot through with intrusions of different kinds of igneous stuff, mostly basalt and andesite. The sandstone has little pockets of what the scanner calls 'complex liquid and volatile hydrocarbon compounds.'"

"Crude oil."

"Yep. What I was afraid of, Ildy. Let's go."

We set off in a northeasterly direction toward Corkscrew, crossing an open area nearly free of protruding red formations. The surface was largely fissured dark rock with scattered drifts of scarlet sand and gravel. In some places the oil seeps were clearly visible, soaking the sand or down inside the cracks. The petroleum reservoirs in the subterranean layers got larger as we approached the pinnacle, and scorched areas appeared on the surface where oil had burned once upon a time.

We came upon the first patches of cinders. The scanner called them "petroleum combustion residue and fused mafic mineral granules." They were associated with underground pockets of identical cold, slaglike stuff, each linked to the surface by a kind of clogged vent or natural chimney. As we moved north my visor display showed cinders mingled crazily with broken red rock beneath the volcanic crust in a manner entirely mystifying to my layman's eye.

Then my scanner indicated that we'd reached the first of the hot spots. I stopped suddenly in the middle of the flatland, forgetting how vulnerable Ildy and I were to enemy observation. A light wind had begun to blow, flapping our ponchos and compromising invisibility. Corkscrew towered ahead, 144 meters of eroded red and ochre sandstone, partially veiled by torn black smoke.

I told my helmet computer to expand the subterrain display over my entire visor, providing a stereoscopic vision of what lay beneath my feet. With the scanning wand in my extended right hand, I rotated slowly where I stood.

The Dagasatt of air and sunlight disappeared and I saw its amazing underworld in three dimensions. It almost seemed as though I were back in the caverns of Cravat, turning as I surveyed stygian galleries, corridors, and grottos. There were miniature natural catacombs beneath the surface of this part of Dagasatt, too—not carved by groundwater but born of some bizarre combustion activity. The rock underfoot was honeycombed with holes. Most of them were very small, but

others were as large as rooms, fantastic in shape, intercon-
nected with their neighbors by an intricate web of narrow
channels and an occasional chimney leading to the surface.

Almost all of the chambers were partially full of granular
cinders. In some the filling was dead black and cold. Others
had hearts that glowed a fitful deep carmine, like banked
furnaces. A very few, lying directly ahead of me and linked
together with vermilion veins, were pockets or seams of red-
hot living coals, burning oil-soaked mineral matter sand-
wiched between layers of rock. Cracks supplied the fires with
oxygen from the upper world and also let the smoke escape.

Ildiko's shout echoed in my helmet. "Aircraft! Aircraft!"

I dived flat, pulling my limbs beneath the camouflaging
poncho, shutting down the scanner, collapsing its sensitive
wand. The surreal technovision of hell vanished. Welcome to
a new and different kind!

"How many?" I asked. "Can you identify type?"

"One hopper, sixty meters above the deck. Popped out
from behind the pinnacle. It sure as hell looked human.
Maybe a Vorlon ESC-10."

"That'd fit if Galapharma agents are supervising and
guarding the Haluk facility, the way they did on Cravat."

We lay motionless. The humming sound of the engine
changed pitch but got only slightly louder, as though the aircraft was slowly circling the area near the pinnacle. Finally it
landed and we dared to peek out from under our concealing
ponchos.

The hopper was about seven hundred meters northeast of
our position, partially concealed by the heaps of fallen rock
that lay around Corkscrew. It was human-made, almost certainly a Vorlon, painted black, with no alphanumerics or other
identifying marks. At full magnification my visor showed at
least four moving figures but no decent detail.

"Ildy, can you bring your Tala-G scope to bear on them?"

"Doing it. Wait one . . . Oh, my. We got four homo saps in
simple Class One envirogear, sidearms only. One guy with
some sort of scientific apparatus that might be a portable ST
scanner, another with unknown gadget, two kibitzers. My

gunscope calls the aircraft ESC-10XA. It's the armored model, carries one Harvey HA-5 cannon, two Kagi BRB-200 blasters."

"Anything on the EM scan?"

"Wait . . . Affirm on that. Tuning. Dammit, the transmissions are encrypted and our descrambler can't hack it. Most likely they're just reporting the touch to base. Gone quiet now."

"It's okay. Keep watching. They look excited?"

"Not a bit. The scientific pair are passing out of sight among the rocks. Others hanging back, don't seem eager to get close to the smoke until the area is guaranteed safe. Apparently no attempt being made to search the area systematically. Now all subjects ex-visible."

About twenty minutes passed before the masked and hooded human figures reappeared, emerging from among the rocks in single file. They stood by the aircraft for a short time, conferring. Then everybody piled inside and the Vorlon flew away.

"You're certain there were only four of them walking around?" I asked.

"Positive. You were thinking they might have found O'Toole's body? It sure didn't look like they were carrying anything except small equipment."

"Never mind. Let's get on with it."

We climbed to our feet. I couldn't see her face, of course, but she seemed to be studying me. "Not a body . . . You were afraid O'Toole was alive and called the hostiles to pick him up. You thought he'd finked on us somehow."

I didn't reply.

"Doesn't compute, Helly. Why would he have waited this long to make a move?"

"So the Galapharma goon squad could grease us and the people in the privateer without endangering *him*. But it looks like I misjudged poor old Zorik after all. He was an asshole, but not a double-crossing asshole." I shifted into a more comfortable position and pulled out my coffee canteen. "Let's wait here five more minutes to be sure the hopper doesn't circle back, then get on with the recon."

We covered the final distance quickly. Zorik's trailblazes followed a circuitous path, avoiding the hot cinder patches. In a couple of spots my subterrain scan showed dangerously fragile crust above the smoldering firepits.

The red boulders heaped around the pinnacle were chunks of sandstone that had weathered off the larger formation and crashed to the ground. We clambered up on them as Zorik must have done and made our way east, toward the source of the smoke. I had to put away the scanner temporarily, needing both hands to climb.

The area immediately around the columnar base of Corkscrew opened, forming a flat-surfaced corridor strewn with drifted sand and small stones. I was tempted to jump down and travel where the footing was easier, but there were no boot prints in the sand, indicating that Zorik had kept to the partial cover of the rocks. So we did, too.

Damned good thing.

We found the smoke just short of the vantage point—the place where it was possible to see beyond the pinnacle into the region where the Haluk facility lay. Just below our position on the boulders was a broad expanse of windblown sand. A jagged hole about two meters wide, stained with a great splash of soot around the edges, had been punched into the surface right next to the rocks. Roiling black smoke rose from the opening and a red-orange glow pulsed obscurely in its depths.

There were no footprints near the hole. Zorik had obviously hopped down off a boulder onto what had looked to him like firm sandy ground.

And plummeted into fire.

"Aw, shit," Ildy whispered. "I wasn't any big fan of O'Toole's. But to go like that . . ."

I pulled out my STS unit and swept the area, describing what I saw on my display to Ildy. An infernal chasm underlay almost the entire flat tract of sand, which concealed a

volcanic-rock crust that was less than four centimeters thick
in some places. The underground chamber was as long as two
soccer fields and equally deep, containing a mixture of incan-
descent petroleum and mineral matter. It extended from our
rock pile to the great sandstone block that formed the under-
pinning of Corkscrew, and wrapped around the formation's
far side.

"Let me take your Tala-G while you set up the thermal
body-scanner right here," I said to Ildiko. "This little nook
in the boulders gives pretty good cover for a survey of the
facility."

Too bad Zorik had decided to get closer.

Creeping into the natural redoubt, I propped up the heavy
blaster and brought the scoop-shaped eyepiece to my visor.
There it was at last, a building standing on a small open plain
surrounded on all sides by soaring rock formations. The
shallow lake on the right side of it had begun to gleam as the
sun rose above the bulk of Jukebox Butte.

The place had only a single story but was fairly large. A
domed roof over the central module held a tall tower supporting the GRD projector and a collection of com antennas.
Only two of the three radial wings of the structure were
clearly visible to us. Their roofs were flat, and at the outer
edge of each was an efficient-looking blaster turret. The windows in the facility were small and there weren't very many
of them. The only door I could see was situated in the angle
between the wings.

The facility's hopper pad was a simple slab just west of the
building. As I watched, a ring of caution lights surrounding it
flashed and the aircraft parked upon it sank down on an elevator platform and disappeared. A sliding lid sealed the
opening in the ground. There were no fences or external
guard installations, but a ring of small sensor housings armed
with antipersonnel Kagis encircled the place about a hundred
meters out, just beyond the hopper pad.

A distinctly tough nut for two people to crack.

Sprouting at the back of my mind was the seed of an idea.

If it worked, then Zorik O'Toole's awful death might not have been useless after all.

"The sniffer indicates lots of warm bods inside there," Ildiko remarked. She had the hypersensitive thermal scanner set up in a little collapsible tylar tent that would shield it from the firepit's radiation. I came over to have a look at the monitor. She said, "We have excellent cross-sectional views of the east and west wings, but I'm afraid I have no idea how to interpret the data. Those regularly spaced indistinct blips are certainly ranks of individuals. Hundreds of them! But they're not moving, and I can't believe they'd be asleep in an upright position. And see—other people are walking among the lines of stationary ones. Most of the mobiles appear to be Haluk, but there are a few humans there as well. More humans and Haluk are moving about in the central part of the building. Total enemy complement—wow!—four hundred and seventy. What the *hell* are they all doing here?"

"I think I know what this facility is," I said. "It fits a theory I had about this place." I sat down on the rock beside her. "Keep an eye out for any indication that the hopper's coming up again. We'll hang out here for a little bit while I brief you on what Galapharma and the Haluk were doing on the planet Cravat. Then you and me are gonna start some serious trouble."

I figured they'd land the hopper fairly close to the place it had set down earlier, so we threw together a little stone fort in a convenient rock pile near there and crawled inside. Both of us carried LGF-18s. Since I was the leader, I had dibs on shooting off the fireworks.

After I programmed their timers, I launched three magnum HE grenades, one after the other. They plopped onto the sand that roofed the combustion chamber and exploded simultaneously in a multilobed fireball. The concussion stunned us for a moment. A cloud of sand containing bits of rock blasted over our tiny shelter.

When the dust cleared, we saw flames leaping half as high as Corkscrew Pinnacle out of three new holes. The fire subsided after a few minutes and columns of smoke much larger than the one marking Zorik's pyre billowed into the air, all but curtaining the twisted red-rock formation.

We waited, knowing that observation instruments inside the facility would be trained on the novelty. But would the hopper return?

"I don't think they're going to fall for it," Ildy said after twenty minutes had gone by with no sign of an enemy excursion.

"Give 'em time. They have to do a little arguing. The scientists have had their innings. Maybe this time a load of tourists will come. It's got to be stone boring duty, guarding four hundred dystasis tanks full of Haluk genetic engineering subjects."

"I don't understand why Galapharma built the facility here instead of on a Haluk planet," she said. "Even if Dagasatt was more convenient to the source of the genen vector they were stealing from Cravat, there's the huge expense and inconvenience of this remote site, and the need to maintain security against the Qastt."

"My guess is that the decision was political. The Haluk leadership might have wanted to keep the project secret from their general population—at least for the time being, when so few of their people are able to undergo the new treatment. Otherwise, there might be some serious unrest on the part of the have-nots."

"You think that only the Haluk elite are being freed from the allomorphic cycle?"

"It's likely, since their supply of PD32:C2 is still very limited. As I understand it, no other genetic engineering vector will work, and the stuff's not easily synthesized. The only reliable vector source the Haluk have at the present time is Galapharma. Except for the rip-off operation on Cravat, Gala agents have have been obliged to buy PD32:C2 from Rampart on the open market, then resell it at an exorbitant markup to the Haluk. Gala was also responsible for setting up the dystasis facilities and training Haluk personnel in the techniques developed by Dr. Emily Konigsberg. Emily's dead now. She used to be the lover of Alistair Drummond, the Galapharma CEO. The Haluk genen scheme was her idea. Ultimately, it spawned the whole illegal trade conspiracy."

"It's hard to understand why you think the genen project is so wrong," Ildiko said. "I mean, it's reprehensible of Galapharma to try to destroy Rampart in order to control the vector supply, and to engage in profiteering at the xenos' expense. But why shouldn't Rampart *itself* help the Haluk escape from this ghastly allomorphic thing? It could sell the genen vector to them at a reasonable price—"

"Ildy, there's more at stake here than correcting a highly inefficient alien physiology."

I hadn't told her about the demiclone threat. The advent of nonallomorphic Haluk was bad enough. In their gracile phase, Haluk are highly intelligent, perhaps even smarter than humans. They spend about one-third of their day sleeping and are active the rest of the time, just as we are. But they also exist for nearly half of every four-hundred-day year in a state of tightly cocooned suspended animation, and endure an intermediate lepidodermoid phase that turns them into lumbering feebs for another couple of months before they enter their shells.

I reminded Ildy about that. "Haluk allomorphism is the reason why their civilization has been so slow to progress, even though their race is much older than humanity and far more numerous."

"You're afraid that if Haluk acquire a human-type life cycle, they'll compete with us?"

"I think they'll wage war on us, babe. Their planets are vastly overcrowded, even with half the population zonked out at any given time. Think what'll happen when the Big Sleep is eradicated. Part of their devil's deal with Galapharma is an agreement that will turn over more than a thousand Rampart-mandate T-1 and T-2 worlds to the aliens for colonization once Gala owns the Perseus Spur. But the Haluk won't stop at that."

"How can you be so negative about them?" she demanded. "Heaven knows they're a contentious lot, and they seem to hate and fear humanity. But if Galapharma can work out a trade agreement with the Haluk, then why can't—"

"There's more. Besides the genen equipment, Gala is also selling them other high technology stuff. Brokering starships, computers, energy generators, all kinds of advanced hardware produced by colluding Big Seven Concerns. The short-sighted idiots think they're only helping the Haluk improve their quality of life. So far, the Concerns haven't traded weaponry or large quantities of important matériel—just enough to keep the alien payoff flowing. Do you know that the Haluk star-cluster is exceptionally rich in rare transactinide elements? That's all Alistair Drummond and his greedy cronies care about."

"So you're afraid that the reengineered Haluk will some-day be able to build advanced starships and weapons of their own, and the balance of political power in the Milky Way will be upset."

I gave a little mirthless croak of laughter. "Ildy, even the al-lomorphic Haluk are smart enough to copy our starship and energy technology right now! I've got personal evidence that they've already done it on a small scale. But there's worse dirty work afoot. The PD32:C2 process can do more than eliminate the allomorphic cycle in a Haluk. It can change a Haluk into a human . . . and vice versa. The process is called demicloning."

She uttered an astonished phrase in another language I pre-sumed was Hungarian. "But how is that possible?"

"Emily Konigsberg used human DNA to eradicate the al-lomorphic trait. That gives an altered Haluk entrée into our racial genome and makes demicloning feasible. The process itself is complex. I certainly don't understand it, except to know that it works."

"But why in God's name did the woman do such a thing?"

"She explained it to me once, not long before she died. An idealistic dream about improving human-Haluk relations through a temporary exchange of physiology. What it came down to was that Emily was a naive simp and the Haluk pulled the wool over her eyes. By the time she began to suspect that her xeno buddies weren't as committed to interspecies brotherhood as they claimed to be, it was too late. The Haluk had made the demicloning thing an immutable part of their deal with Galapharma."

"I can't believe that Gala didn't understand the potential danger!"

"They thought they had a handle on it. Konigsberg inserted a redundant DNA sequence—a kind of marker—into all of her Haluk-human transforms. Other than that, it's virtually impossible to tell a demiclone from a genuine human except by its actions. We presume Gala knows how to identify the ringers. We don't. Not yet, anyhow. We *will* know as soon as we compare a known demiclone's genome with that of a genuine human."

"These demiclones would make perfect spies—"

"Or thieves, once they sopped up enough of our culture to pass muster. We know of at least one perfect Haluk-human. It was a duplicate of Dr. Emily herself, and it might have been on its way to Earth when it was accidentally killed. I can't believe that Galapharma's agents knew that Fake Emily existed. The Haluk are playing a secret game of their own with at least some of the demiclones, and the Commonwealth of Human Worlds is the unsuspecting opposition."

"Have you alerted CHW to—oh, Christ! Look! A hopper's coming up on the facility's pad lift."

"Right. Get ready. Keep monitoring the com bands."

I scuttled out of the rocky redoubt and took up a position among some boulders a dozen meters farther north. If the hopper touched down in the same place as before, we'd have it flanked.

In a few minutes the black aircraft was hanging over our heads, doing a look-see for the sightseers aboard.

Come down! I begged them telepathically. You can't savor the real experience unless you smell the oily smoke through your inefficient respirators, and feel the heat, and imagine what it would be like to plunge feet first into flaming death . . .

Finally it landed, farther east than I would have liked but almost out of sight of the facility. Good enough.

When its hatch opened, five humans emerged, clad in the simplest class of envirogear. Two of them wore Kagi pistols. Their leader carried a subterrain scanner and the others crowded around to study the monitor's depiction of the fire down below. When that thrill palled the crew began tramping through the boulder field to obtain a closer view of the smoke holes.

"Any com traffic?" I asked Ildiko.

"Negative."

"Wait for my shout."

I made certain that nobody remained behind in the aircraft. When the tourists had Corkscrew's solid rock between them and the Haluk facility, I said, "Hit 'em, Ildy."

Each of us launched a sleepy-gas grenade. They soared in a very low trajectory and exploded, *phut phut*. The targets were wearing Class One breathers fit only for filtering smoke, dust, and microbes. The AG97 went right through them. The hopper crew staggered, turned around and made a desperate attempt to retreat. One of the armed men nearly managed to make it back to the aircraft, collapsing as he attempted to pull a communication unit from his belt.

Ildiko and I were up and running as the last one went down, sheathing our launchers, drawing our Ivanov sidearms in case of opposition. But all of the enemy were snoozing.

"Let's haul 'em aboard," I said.

We dragged the nearest body into the aircraft. It was damned heavy. The Vorlon was without passenger seats, the roomy compartment behind its cockpit open to accommodate freight or the bulky gear of combat personnel. I spotted an antigrav tote clamped to a side bulkhead and let out a yip of appreciation.

"Now we're in business! I'll use this cart to gather up the rest of the baggage, and you climb into the pilot seat and make sure the base isn't trying to raise us on the com. If they do, simulate a gronk-out."

"Affirm."

I retrieved the other four hostiles, slammed the hatch, stripped off their masks, and set off a gas-neutralizer cartridge. All of the captives were human males. While I disarmed and restrained them, Ildiko lit the hopper's engine and turned on the environmental system. A few minutes later we were able to pull off our helmets and lose our heavy packs and other combat gear. We lounged side by side in reversed command seats, slurping hot coffee and nutrigoo from our canteens and surveying our inert quarry laid neatly side by side on the deck. Given the neutralizer, they'd wake up within ten minutes or so. Without it, they'd be gorked for half a day or more.

"Nice going, Lieutenant, ma'am," I said.

"My pleasure, Chief Superintendent, sir. I suppose it's too much to hope that one of these birds might be the coveted Ollie."

"Sorry. We're not that lucky. Could be we nabbed some of the small-fry fugitives, though. I'll check 'em out in a few minutes. I really need this caffeine."

She got up with a smile. "Well, what I need is to visit a decent-sized ladies' room." She went aft.

I glanced idly about the interior of the Vorlon. God, it was great to be in a ship designed for humans again! This one was a beaut, armed and armored and equipped with an oversized powerplant. I wondered how many more 10XAs were stashed in the facility's underground hangar. Outside, the sun shone brightly on the bloodred wall of Corkscrew. The smoke was diminishing.

A muffled groan came from one of the figures lying on the deck. I rose and went over to them, pulling the little e-book from my jumpsuit pocket. It contained mug shots and dossiers of Oliver Schneider and the four ExSec officers who had fled with him from Seriphos. Except for Ollie himself, I didn't know any of them by sight.

I began comparing faces. Nobody matched.

"Rats," I muttered.

Ildiko reappeared. "No joy?"

"Not in this bunch. It looks like we'll have to break into the facility after all. There must be a tunnel connecting it to the underground hangar."

One of the men opened his eyes and mumbled something incomprehensible. He lay on his side, hands fastened behind his back, a massive young tough with dark brows, a potato nose, and a prim rosebud mouth that he'd tried to hide beneath a soup-strainer moustache. He eyed me woozily and whispered, "Wha'?"

"Gag the others," I told Ildiko. "This beauty will do for interrogation."

I went to my pack's med kit and got a couple of penvcrol dosers, not nearly as effective as psychotronic machines but much more portable. Turning his head, I pulled open the captive's collar, laid the tiny purple pillows on either side of his larynx, X side down, and pressed them firmly with my thumb and index finger. Microexplosions injected the drug into his carotid arteries. His eyes rolled and the preposterously dainty mouth sagged open.

"What's your name?" I asked after a few minutes had passed.

He stared at me in pained puzzlement. "Mmm . . . mmm."

"Name," I repeated.

He spoke in a slow, affectless voice. "Mmm. Darrel . . . Ridenour."

"Are you employed by Galapharma AC, Darrel?"

"Ye-es."

"What is your position?"

"Ex-external s-security agent . . . fourth grade."

"What is the nature of the facility where you're stationed?"

"It's . . . a genen clinic. S-S-Secret."

"Are Haluk being processed in there?"

"No . . . yes! Ahhh! No! . . . Yes!" The drug was working, but a person with exceptionally strong willpower would be able to resist it. I hoped that Darrel wasn't one of those.

"Who's in charge of the facility?"

He *really* didn't want to answer that one. His eyes darted wildly, a grating moan welled up from his throat, and he thrashed and strained against the plastic cuffs that imprisoned his wrists and ankles. Ildiko held him down. I repeated the question twice before he replied.

"Deputy Security Chief Erik Skogstad . . . in charge. Duty Officer . . . Jim Matsukawa."

Skogstad was the Gala agent who'd been unable to supervise my assassination due to the press of other urgent business. Garth Wing Lee had told me that Skogstad was responsible for Ollie Schneider.

"Is Skogstad inside the facility?" Was there a chance we might nab a primo Gala spook as well as a Rampart turncoat?

"Yes . . . aaah! No! No! He's . . . offworld."

So much for catching two fish in one net. "Where is he? On what planet?"

Once again Ridenour balked, but finally: "Artiuk . . . meeting with the Servant of Servants of Luk."

That was a shocker. The SSL was the paramount leader of the Haluk race. "What's this meeting about?"

"Rumor . . . Big Seven Concern executives came out from Earth."

In anticipation of Rampart's capitulation to Galapharma?

"What are the Concern execs talking to the Servant about, Darrel?"

This time his denial was agonized. "Don't know! Don't know! It hurts . . . Make it stop!" He screamed and fell back, mumbling.

I said, "Rats."

"Perhaps he's hypersensitive to the drug," Ildiko said. "Ease up, Helly. I'll give him a calmative."

She fetched another doser and did the injection. In a few minutes Ridenour relaxed. He asked for water and she put a canteen to his lips. When he seemed to have recovered, I continued the questioning.

"How many humans in your security force?"

"T-Twelve."

"How many Haluk guards?"

"Thirty-two."

"Do only the human guards carry blasters?"

He gave a barely perceptible nod. On Cravat it had been the same. The alien security forces were armed only with stunguns. "How about noncombatant personnel inside the facility? What do they do?"

Two humans were genetic engineers. There were also three human hopper pilots. Twenty Haluk cooks, bottlewashers, and all-around domestics took care of the scut work.

"Very good, Darrel. Now I'm going to show you a picture." I held up Schneider's mug shot. "Look at this carefully. Have you ever seen this man?"

He squinted at the e-book screen. "Looks like . . . that human motherfucker, John Green."

"Is Green inside your facility?" I held my breath in suppressed excitement. "Does he work there?"

"Stays in the administration block . . . plays computer games. Reads. Drinks. Doesn't work."

I tried to get more information about "John Green," but Darrel seemed genuinely not to know.

"How about these men?" I showed Ridenour the other four Rampart ExSec traitors.

He burst into hysterical laughter. "*They're* working! Oh, yes! They're really working."

"What are you talking about? What do they do?"

"In the dystasis tanks . . . sharing their DNA." He was cackling like a madman, eyes squeezed tightly shut. "DNA!" he howled. "Sharing their DNA!"

"Sweet Jesus," Ildiko whispered.

I said to her, "I figured Ollie might have kept back incriminating data that made Galapharma handle him with care. I guess his buddies weren't included in the deal."

Her face was full of horror. "Can we get the poor bastards out of there?"

"Our job is to get *Schneider* out," I said, "and don't forget our people waiting back at the privateer crash site. Maybe we can convince Zone Patrol to raid the place later. There'll be other humans imprisoned there besides Ollie's quintet. The genengineers use them for tissue-culture donors."

I resumed my interrogation of Darrel Ridenour. His hysterical laughter had ceased. The new medication rendered him apathetic and almost docile. He readily revealed the internal layout of the facility, the nature and position of its defenses, and the deployment of human and Haluk forces inside. The three antiaircraft blaster turrets on the roof were operated from a fire control center in the administration module. There were two other ESC-10XA hoppers in the underground hangar. One was inoperative, undergoing routine engine maintenance.

I was drafting a map of the target's interior and discussing assault tactics with Ildy when the cockpit com unit sounded off.

"Hopfrog Two, base. You copy? Frog Two, give a status report. Come back, Frog Two."

Ridenour began to shriek at the top of his lungs. I told Ildy to gag him and went to the command seat.

The base operator said, "Come back, Frog Two. What the hell you guys doing out there? Roasting friggin' marshmallows?"

I did a rat-a-tat on the com pad at the same time that I mouthed broken gibberish.

"Say again, Two? You're breaking up."

I repeated the maneuver.

"Frog Two, go to backup com system. Primary has a glitch. I say, go to backup com, Two. Do you copy?"

One more time on the garble.

A different voice, full of no-nonsense authority, rang from the speaker. "Hopfrog Two, return to base immediately! Duty Officer Matsukawa here. Return to base. Do you copy, Hopfrog Two?"

I did a very brief garble response, shut off the communicator, and sat there thinking. Ildiko was wrapping the five prisoners in a big cargo net and hooking the squirming bundle to the deck tie-downs.

I said, "You ever played gunny on one of these aircraft, babe?"

"On a better one. ESC-15XB. Had twin cannons and a TND torpedo launcher besides the Kagi blue-rays. Pretty much the same targeting setup as the 10XA, though. You got a plan?"

I told her what it was. "What do you think? Tell me straight. You're the assault expert."

"Depends on whether you've evaluated the target correctly, Helly. And whether Darrel told us the truth about its defenses. Given a thumbs-up on both points, I'd say go for it. We've still got the advantage of surprise. But once we start pounding, there's no way we can prevent them sending a subspace call for help—short of taking out the facility's central module and maybe losing your prize, Schneider, in the rubble. If there's a hostile cruiser within striking range, we could end up screwed even if the ground action succeeds."

"I'll check that with Joe right now. You take the right-hand seat. Light the engines and do a run-up on the weaponry. Back in a short."

I clapped on my helmet, hurried outside, and called *Chispa Dos* on the lasercom, praying that the big rock pinnacle wasn't blocking my hat-beam to the orbiting starship.

To my relief, Joe responded.

"I need you to get on the high-resolution scanner," I said, "and do a full-sky search for starships incoming this solar system—especially anything that smells like a Haluk or Galapharma express cruiser."

"I'm ahead of you, Helly. Been combing the ether since we parked. This Bodascon prototype of yours has a really righteous ship-sniffer. Wait one. Gotta resort the swarm—whoa! That's new."

"What?"

"A possible bandit just coming into range at sixty lights, bopping right along at sixty-three ross. What do you know: fuel signature indicates a Haluk vessel."

"Goddammit to fuckin' hell!" I wondered if Eric Skogstad was returning early with a fresh load of Haluk genen subjects.

"She's ex Artiuk. That's their principal Spur colony. Jeez! I never knew the Haluk flew anything that hot."

It was no surprise to me. I'd barely escaped being creamed

by a similarly speedy Haluk starship on the way to Cravat. I suspected that the colossal flagship of the Servant of Servants, which had nearly been the death of me at Helly's Comet, was even faster. "You confirm a Dagasatt system vector for the bandit?"

"That's an affirm."

"Okay, listen up, Joe. You'll have to go out and kill it. We've got no choice. O'Toole's dead, but Ildy and I have grabbed an armed Vorlon hopper on the QT and we're ready to attack. The opposition is bound to put out a subspace squawk when we initiate. If that Haluk boat catches the call, it'll come charging in, loaded for bear. It might even notify the local yokels and we'll have Squeaker gunships up the wazoo."

"You have any idea of the Haluk's shipscan range?"

"Less than yours. Maybe thirty, forty lights."

"If you can delay your assault for about half an hour, I'll be able to nab the bandit with his pants down."

"We'll do our best to oblige. Happy trails, pardner. I'm gone."

I hurried back inside the aircraft, slapped the hatch closure control, and popped off my helmet. "There's a fast Haluk starship coming," I told Ildiko. "Joe will play exterminator. Let's try to stall the attack for at least half an hour so he can—"

"Helly," she said calmly, "a second hostile hopper just came up on the lift out there. Sit down and fly this crate. It's party time."

Chapter 10

We stayed put while a black Vorlon aircraft identical to ours lofted off the pad and approached at a low altitude. It called itself Hopfrog One and tried continuously to make contact with us.

"Uh . . . Hopfrog Two? Is your position hazardous? Is it safe for us to land? Come back to One, Frog Two."

Circling slowly above our position, observers inside the other ship rubbernecked the smokes and us, assessing the situation. The crew of Hopfrog One knew that our engines were powered up. I'd engaged the wave-bender shield, so they couldn't tell how many live people were inside our aircraft. They *could* see footprints and body dragmarks in the sand around us. I hoped they wouldn't interpret the spoor correctly.

"Frog Two, do you have casualties? Can you exit the aircraft and signal manually? Frog Two, if you copy, exit your aircraft."

Ildy and I waited.

"Hopfrog Two, Frog One is surveilling the terrain and then coming in for a touch."

The aircraft's circular flight path widened, taking it behind Corkscrew Pinnacle and momentarily beyond the sight line of the Haluk facility. That was what Ildiko had been waiting for.

She had disabled the Harvey's electronic targeter to avoid alerting her prey. Using the backup optical reticle to track it like a duck in flight, she blew Hopfrog One out of the sky with our HA-5 actinic cannon, vaporizing the top of the rock formation along with it.

We bounced in the shock wave. The columns of oily smoke flattened and coalesced and swirled around the surface of the ground like a mass of tangled inky fabric. A split second later I had us airborne, heading straight for the target, flying through smoke at an altitude of less than two meters.

Abandoning the controls of the too-powerful Harvey cannon, Ildy used the twin BRB-200 blue-beamers to behead the facility's tower. The larger antennas controlling the PHBA sensors and the GBD generator went tumbling down. The dissimulator umbrella winked out. As the upper parts of the surrounding formations lost their fuzziness, drifting smoke began to obscure the ground around the facility itself.

Someone inside pulled his shit together and the small Kagi guns in the defensive ring began peppering us with blue blazes. Our ship's armor held firm against the relatively weak antipersonnel lasers.

A console alarm light began flashing. The ship's computer said: *Alert. Alert. TG-383 target acquisition field seeking this aircraft.*

"The roof turrets!" I yelled.

Three fat white beams sizzled through the smoke above our hopper.

"Easy does it," Ildy murmured. "Their guns can't depress far enough to acquire us." She drilled the east- and west-wing emplacements without significant harm to the building beneath, just as we'd planned. The third turret continued to fire. "Go around so I can take it out."

I sent our Vorlon on a screaming turn barely above the surface of the lake so she could get a clear shot at the north wing. Gouts of futile Kagi photons bathed us like the dew covers Dixie. The blaster in the undamaged turret continued to discharge, exploding great chunks out of the red mountain behind us until Ildy's precision bursts with the BRB-200s melted its firing mechanism.

Rockfalls thundered down from the battered Jukebox formation and splashed into the lake. By now the entire basin was hazy with smoke from the petroleum fires. I had no doubt that observers inside the facility could still see us.

I zoomed straight up to an altitude of fifty meters. Ildy ticked off the small Kagis in the inner perimeter defense one by one, as though playing a video game.

"Atta gal!" I exulted.

She grinned. "Want a job done, hire a pro."

We were hovering directly above the central module of the target. There was no visible activity down below. None of the avalanche material from the butte had reached the facility walls.

It seemed likely that we'd effectively disarmed them. The weaponry left inside had to be light stuff. In a facility like this, the windows were almost certainly bulletproof, impossible to shoot through with portable weaponry—from either side. I didn't think the opposition would be stupid enough to open a window and shoot a homing missile or a magnum HE grenade at us, but I was taking no chances.

I activated the com unit's low-band emergency channel. They'd receive that even with the tower antennas dead.

"Hello, the base! Stand down! Stand down! Do not fire through the windows. If you fire through the windows we'll destroy you with our cannon. You copy that?"

No reply.

"Base, we want to talk to D.O. Jim Matsukawa. Come back, Jim."

Silence.

"Whack the rest of Corkscrew Pinnacle," I told Ildy. "Get their attention."

She took the HA-5 and blasted the broken red-rock column to plasma. A single huge mushroom of scarlet-painted black smoke belched skyward from the abruptly enlarged petro pit at the formation's base, sucking the ground-hugging haze along with it.

"Yeow!" said Ildy.

I called, "Hello, down there! Anybody copy in the base? You in there, Jim? I sure hope you weren't aboard Hopfrog One, ol' buddy. It's gone to the last roundup—along with a bunch of blaster turrets and perimeter guns and that up-standing piece of local real estate just south of your place."

"A duty officer would stay at his post," Ildiko whispered. "He's there."

I knew that. "Jimbo? Naughty, naughty! I know what you're doing, my man. You're sending a subspace shout to that Haluk starship vectoring in from Artiuk. But he'll never get here in time to save your ass. Neither will any of your Squeaky pals. You'll have to negotiate with us if you want you and your people to survive this little faceoff. How about it?"

Nada from the facility. He was a stubborn one.

"You're disappointing me, Jim. Do I have to destroy one of the wings of your installation and kill a bunch of innocent Haluk floaters? I don't want to hit you again. Not unless I have to. Talk to me. Save lives. You listening? I'm going to count to three, then take out your north wing. One——"

"Matsukawa here," said that voice full of no-nonsense authority. "Who are you?"

"Call me Geronimo. You guys have something that belongs to me. Hand it over and I'll go away without any more hostile action."

There was a long pause. Then: "What do you want, Geronimo?"

"It's more of a *who* than a *what*. You have a man in your facility by the name of John Green——"

He broke in furiously. "So that's it! You fucking idiots, you'll never get away——"

"Shut up Jim. I mean it."

He did, while I cheered inwardly. The Galapharma officer obviously believed that Ollie Schneider's confederates had come to rescue him. Far be it from me to correct the misperception.

I said, "The continuing good health of my dear old friend is what will keep you and yours alive, Jim. If he's damaged or he dies, we wipe out the entire installation and call it the John Green Memorial Slag Heap. Do you copy?"

"Yes," said Matsukawa. He was calm again.

"Okay. I'll give you five minutes to suit John up and send him out the front door."

"We'll need more than five minutes, Geronimo. Your friend is still in the sack. He likes to sleep in after a night of overindulgence. Give us twenty minutes, minimum."

"He's stalling," Ildiko murmured.

"Maybe," I whispered back, "but I don't know what we can do about it—short of blowing a hole in the wall and marching inside to collect our prize package in person."

I opened the com again. "Okay, Jim. You've got *fifteen* minutes—not twenty—before we open fire. Clock starts running on my mark. I expect to see John Green come out that south door alone, unmasked and unhooded so we can confirm his identity. Give him a com handset so we can talk to him and make certain you haven't harmed him in any way. Copy that?"

"Affirmative."

"Mark," I said quietly. "Countdown is running."

"Matsukawa out."

"Well, hell!" Ildy said. "That was almost too easy—if Schneider's as important as you say he is."

"He's important enough to write Galapharma's obituary, alive or dead. Which poses a pesky dilemma for our Jim. He'll be consulting with his boss, Skogstad, and I'm betting Skogstad will bump the buck to a higher level still. Maybe even Alistair Drummond himself."

"Oh, man."

"They'll weigh the alternatives, and most of them suck. If they surrender the prize, we win. If they refuse to do it, we still win after we destroy the installation and Schneider, and the big insurance policy comes due. Their best bet is to do neither of the above. I think they'll hand over the prize, then immediately try to take him back. Let's be prepared."

Once again we waited. Billowing smoke spread in a high layer that hid Dagasatt's sun, but things were relatively clear where we were, hanging in midair fifty meters above the target. I'd moved Hopfrog Two southward just a tad so we had a good view of the all-important door.

Ildiko and I put on most of the combat gear we'd discarded

earlier, excluding the backpacks but including the sidearms. The hopper's ground scanner was set to alert us if anything larger than an ant moved in the vicinity of the building below.

She sat quietly, humming an unfamiliar melody and wiping out the inside of her helmet with decrud solution, while I went aft to check on the prisoners.

They were still secure in their cargo-net wrapping, bunched up in a parody of a love pile. Four of them glared ferociously at me and gave loud grunts through their gags, but Darrel Ridenour appeared to be unconscious. I hoped the penverol hadn't shtonkered his brain permanently. There were questions he still hadn't answered to my satisfaction.

And something else . . .

"I think we'll have to take Darrel along with us when we go," I remarked to Ildy. "Maybe these other jokers, too. We need to do a proper interrogation."

"Ridenour's talk about the Big Seven meeting on the Haluk planet got you curious?"

"Damn straight. It's funny, a low-ranker like Darrel knowing a sensitive piece of intelligence like that."

She shrugged. "Rumors fly in isolated little installations like this one. It's hard to keep anything secret. Same thing happens at remote Zone Patrol outposts."

"Something else is bothering me. A weird thing that Darrel said." I shook my head, looking down at his unmoving body. "Damned if I can remember what it was."

"It's been a rough day, man. Too much distracting stuff going on."

"Yeah, right. Death and destruction can really screw up your concentration."

"It'll come to you later," she reassured me, "when you're just about to fall asleep. Always works for me that way."

"Sleep! If we get out of here alive, I'm going to stay in bed for a week."

"Copy that," said Ildiko wistfully.

I returned to the command seat, checked my own helmet—a little ripe inside, but what the hell—and tried to do a mental replay of the Q&A session I'd had with Darrel.

What was it that had struck me? Not a piece of information: an unexpected turn of phrase. Something that slipped past while I was pumped up at the news about Schneider, when Darrel confirmed my hope that the archturncoat was actually there inside the facility, using the alias of—

It hit me. And the bottom dropped out of my stomach.

Darrel had looked at Ollie's picture and said, "Looks like that human motherfucker, John Green."

Human . . .

I whispered, "Shit!"

Ildiko was frowning. "Helly, what is it?"

Maybe it had been just a slip of the tongue, understandable given Ridenour's drug-induced state of agitation. And maybe not.

"A passing nasty thought. It'll have to keep. I want to brief you on what comes next in Operation Q. This race of ours is coming down to the wire, babe, and there's no time for side issues."

Precisely on the fifteen-minute mark the door of the facility opened It was actually a small airlock. A man of imposing physique stood on the threshold, clad in an enviro jumpsuit with the hood off. Behind him was not only darkness, but also a scannerproof force-field that probably screened a heavily armed SWAT team.

The man in the doorway lifted a com unit and spoke. "Geronimo? John Green here."

Oliver Schneider and I had met only once face-to-face, at a wild and memorable Rampart board meeting on Seriphos, where my father announced that he was cutting ExSec out of the loop and placing "Helmut Icicle" and his squad of irregulars in charge of Eve's kidnapping investigation. At the time, Schneider didn't recognize me as the banished black-sheep member of the Frost family.

I figured he'd done his homework by now and might remember my voice. It has a sort of cowboy *je ne sais quoi*. And after fifteen long minutes, maybe Jim Matsukawa had managed to scrounge up a voice-print machine and hook it to the com unit, in hopes of identifying Geronimo himself. Neither of these contingencies fit my present plans.

So Ildy was going to do the negotiating from here on in. I'd prompted her on what to say. Both of us were wearing our helmets, unrecognizable through the aircraft's windshield.

She spoke to the com through her annunciator. "Good day, Citizen Green. I'm Geronimo's deputy, Zsa Zsa. Are you in good health?"

"I suppose so," came the grudging retort.

Through the ship's ground scanner I studied the face of the man in the doorway. He was about fifty years old. His bull-dog jaw and somber dark stare confirmed that he was my quarry, the former Rampart Vice President for Confidential Services and Galapharma mole, Oliver Schneider. He'd gained weight during his confinement on Dagasatt, and also acquired a set of deplorable bags under his eyes and scarlike stress furrows beside his wide mouth. He hadn't bothered with shave-gel for the last couple of days, either. His hair, which I remembered as a spruce crew cut, was overgrown and unkempt.

Disengaging Hopfrog Two's autopilot, I slowly brought the aircraft down. I'd taken control of our weapons system.

"We're friends, John Green," Ildiko announced, "sent by certain of your former colleagues to take you out of here—"

"So you say!" he snapped. "How do I know you aren't a gang of outlaws ready to sell me to Simon Frost like a side of fuckin' beef?"

"How do *you* know," she replied sweetly, "that you won't end up like the four ExSec officers who fled with you—a human vegetable adrift in a dystasis tank while the Haluk siphon off your DNA?"

His mouth dropped open in shock. "How do you know about that?"

"I know a good deal, John Green. For example: five weeks from now, the Rampart Board of Directors will vote on the Galapharma acquisition bid for the last time. It's a virtual certainty that they'll capitulate to Alistair Drummond. Then your usefulness will be at an end. Why should Drummond keep you alive when your evidence against his Concern has become a dead issue?"

"He—He has to. If you know so much, you know *that*."

"I'm sure Drummond made many promises. To you and to the four officers who accompanied you to Dagasatt. But he broke his promises to your associates, didn't he? Why should he treat you any differently?"

Schneider was silent.

I'd brought the Vorlon down to hover a couple of meters above the ground, no more than a long stone's throw from the open door of the facility. The entry was bathed in the faint purplish glow of our targeting field. So was Oliver Schneider.

Matsukawa and his goons were probably sweeping us with six different kinds of spy-beams through the facility windows, and the SWAT team lurking behind Ollie had us cold in their sights. But our ship's own wave-bender would stymie most of the scans, and our hull armor would stop most types of portable weaponry.

I figured that all we really had to fear now was a missile or a grenade attack through that open airlock door. I was gambling that they wouldn't want to endanger the prize by shooting over or around him. The doorway was too small.

Of course, if Ollie stepped aside . . .

Ildy was saying, "We know you must have an insurance policy forcing Galapharma to keep you alive. But think about this: when Rampart Starcorp no longer exists as a legal entity, the damage you inflicted upon it as a secret agent of Galapharma will no longer be legally actionable. Drummond will have nothing to fear from you anymore. The CHW Judiciary can't prosecute a crime against an extinct corporation."

True. But if I'd guessed right, Ollie had also engineered the death of Rampart's Chief Research Officer, Yaoshuang Qiu, and maybe other people as well. There was no statute of limitations on murder.

I didn't want Schneider to think about that. Besides, time was a-wasting. Qastt gunships sent by corrupted local officials might already be on the way from Taqtaq or one of the other refinery cities.

Pulling out my e-book, I wrote, *Show him the stick!* and held it in front of Ildy. She picked up the hint instantly.

"Citizen Green, think carefully. Are you willing to trust your life to a megalomaniac like Alistair Drummond, a proven liar? He's negotiated a secret trade deal with a race of aliens who have always hated and feared humanity. He did this without a thought to the dangerous political ramifications. He was thinking only about profits for Galapharma and setting himself up as the most powerful man in the Hundred Concerns—the most powerful man in the galaxy! He *used* you, John Green, just as he used millions of other people. Now you're worse than expendable: you're a threat."

Oliver Schneider's form had stiffened as she talked. "You've come directly from Rampart, haven't you! You're not outlaws. No outlaw would know what you know."

I wrote another note to Ildy: *Now show him the carrot.*

"If you come with us willingly," she said, "Rampart will petition CHW to grant you full immunity in exchange for freely reiterating your psychotronic testimony against Alistair Drummond and Galapharma in open court. This will strengthen Rampart's case."

"I know." He was still vacillating.

I wrote: *Treason.*

She said, "John Green, try to understand what this conspiracy involves. Galapharma hasn't just plotted to destroy a small rival—it's committed treason. The Haluk intend to wage war against the Commonwealth. Alistair Drummond and his Concern allies are too power-hungry and blinded by greed to see it. They are aiders and abettors of a hostile alien race. Their shortsightedness is criminal. We need your help to thwart this monstrous conspiracy. How can you refuse?"

"I—"

"There's no more time for discussion. Come out of the doorway, John. Walk a straight line toward our ship. No tricks. The people hiding behind you don't dare harm you . . . not while they think they still have a chance to recapture you later. But they won't do that. We'll protect you with all of Rampart's resources. Come out to our ship now."

"I'm coming," said Oliver Schneider.

He took about ten steps toward us, and then everything went to hell.

Understandably, Ildiko and I were both riveted by the approach of the man we'd risked our lives to find. We were alert for enemy fire that might emanate from the airlock or the windows, but we'd forgotten about the lift on the hopper pad a hundred meters or so to our left.

As the defenders had no doubt intended.

Later, I deduced that during the critical fifteen minutes we'd waited for Ollie, the people inside the facility had disconnected the caution lights and other alarms surrounding the circular opening. They'd also hauled the *third* Vorlon ESC-10XA, the one grounded for engine overhaul—but still armed and deadly—onto the elevator platform. The lift lid was now able to whisk back without warning and allow Hopfrog Three to rise and fire on us.

They didn't want to harm Schneider with cannon backflare, so they hit us right in the powerplant with their twin BRB-200 lasers.

The jewel-fuel explosion almost deafened me. I had no chance to use our own ship's weapons. The Vorlon, which weighed about thirty tons when deprived of antigrav lift, dropped two meters onto the stony ground. The right landing gear buckled in the impact and the ship tilted sideways, belly toward the adversary, who continued to fire. Ildiko and I tumbled against the starboard cockpit bulkhead. Our LGF-18 grenade launchers, which we'd propped against the instrument console, clanged on top of us.

Flickering azure beams punched holes in the hull. Electronic systems exploded and spat sparks. The ship interior was full of smoke, and something hissed ominously back in the stern compartment. Ghastly muffled sounds came from the netted prisoners. Hopfrog Two creaked and lurched as the lasers continued to stab at it.

"Out! Out!" I screamed into my helmet, scrambling over the instrumentation, grabbing hold of the manual hatch release underfoot and hauling at it with all my strength. The damaged thing slid reluctantly on its bent tracks, then jammed before it was halfway open.

Ildiko wormed her way through, hauling the launchers with her. I was a lot bigger and I nearly didn't make it. Stuck feet first in the narrow slot, kicking like a fool, I finally had the wit to smack the quick-release buckle on my equipment belt and drop down and out without my sidearms. Blue rays from the big Kagis were zapping holes in the ceramalloy doorframe a hand's breadth from my helmet visor.

As I crashed to the dirt like a sack of bricks, a thunderous detonation shook the ground. A magnum HE grenade round had hit something important over on the hopper pad.

In my helmet phones a satisfied female voice said, "*Viszontlátásra,* assholes."

Suddenly, silence. No more beams, no more booms.

I lay there under the wreck for a few seconds, stunned by the fall, and heard a lesser explosion followed by a muffled *phut phut phut phut.* Standard HE grenade, plus sleepy-gas rounds going off inside a confined space.

"Yes!" said Ildiko. "And that's all, *kisbaba.*"

With shaking hands I retrieved my belt with its Ivanov and Kagi pistols, which still dangled from the partially open hatch overhead, picked up my LGF-18, and crawled out from under the Vorlon. It was perforated like an ebony Swiss cheese with laser hits and smoldering vigorously at the stern.

Ildiko sat on the ground, cradling her grenade launcher in her lap while she reloaded it. "You okay, Chief Inspector, sir?"

"Alive, Lieutenant, ma'am . . . and kicking myself for getting caught like a fat rat in a drainpipe. Congratulations one more time."

Hopfrog Three was now nothing but burning junk scattered around the canted lift platform. Wisps of smoke and pearly pink gas curled from the open doorway to the Haluk facility. I magnified the view and saw a jumble of torn bodies inside the airlock. The inner door had been blown apart.

A dozen meters in front of the facility, lying prostrate with both arms flung out, was Oliver Schneider. He wasn't moving.

"Fired over his head after the hopper blast knocked him down," Ildiko said. "Sorry, Helly. I had no choice."

"I agree. You want to check on our prisoners? I'll take a look at John Green."

I drew my Ivanov and trudged out to him. The sleepy-gas wafting out the facility door hadn't reached him yet and he was conscious, staring at the smoky sky and smiling, as if at some private amusement. He lay flat on his back. The excess flesh had stretched away from his face and throat, giving him the unexpectedly youthful look you often see on embalmed bodies.

Schneider wasn't dead, but there were wounds. Shrapnel bits from the ship Ildy destroyed had struck him along his right side. He had a head injury that bled copiously and his light enviro jumpsuit leaked scarlet in four or five places.

His lips moved. I knelt beside him. The wind was blowing the gas eastward, away from us. I tongued my helmet's annunciator. "Hey, Ollie, old hoss-thief. How ya doing?"

"Asahel Frost?" He began to laugh, and the faint sound was a broken crackle like trodden autumn leaves. "I wondered if it might be you pulling this loony stunt. Troublemaker from the git-go . . ."

"That's me," I admitted.

"They . . . wanted me to step aside fast once I was out the door, get out of range so a squad hiding behind me could hit your ship. Said I would, then didn't." More laughter. "Really pissed 'em off."

"We figured it was something like that."

"Didn't know Jim Matsukawa was planning to hoist the grounded Vorlon. He's a sharp bastard."

"Sorry you got caught."

"That's the way it goes sometimes."

"I don't think your wounds are too serious. We'll have you patched up pretty soon."

He made a faint sound of assent that turned into a groan and a muttered obscenity.

"Ollie, listen. I've got to ask you about your insurance policy against Galapharma. Will it remain in force if we take you off Dagasatt? We don't want your evidence released prematurely if it can be avoided."

"I'll have to make a subspace call to Earth no later than five days from now. Otherwise . . . fireworks start."

"We'll be evacuating you right away. Zone Patrol and Rampart ExSec will come in and mop up the operation a little later."

"One other thing, Frost . . ."

"Yeah?"

"Go inside. Check out the three genetic engineering labs, then do what's right. My four men . . . you know how this fuckin' allomorph eradication process works?"

"Yes."

"My boys . . . the bastards are using them for tissue-culture donors. They're in dystasis, but once they're freed and put through psychoprobing by CHW, they'll go to Coventry Blue for sure. And you know what happens to corporate enforcers inside the walls."

I did. Cruel and unusual punishment didn't begin to describe their fate. "Maybe we can work out the same deal for them that I offered you, if they agree to testify against Galapharma."

He shook his head. "No good. Commonwealth Judiciary will never let all of us walk. Harry Piretti iced Qiu, the CRO. The others took down Clive Leighton and his girlfriend, disposed of Volta, Bransky, and Matsudo, smeared the Starcorp from one end of the Spur to the other." He managed a faint laugh, full of wry satisfaction. "We damn near handed Rampart to Alistair Drummond on a plate before you came along."

"So, bad luck for your sidekicks," I said coldly, getting to my feet. "Good fuckin' luck for you."

If I had anything to say about it—and, unfortunately, I didn't—both Ollie and his gang would end up with the book thrown at them, incarcerated in the Blue Disenfranchised Persons Reserve for the rest of their miserable lives. I felt no sympathy at all for the wounded man lying on the ground and even less for his murderous floater pals.

He knew it, and yet he was actually pleading with me. "You'll get everything you need for your case against Gala from me, Frost. Please! . . . Do my boys, save 'em from Blue, and I promise I'll cooperate fully with the psychoprobers. They'll get more out of me, quicker. You know how it works."

"I'll do whatever I can to get immunity or reduced sentences for all of you. But it isn't my decision."

"Goddamn Throwaway cop . . . might have known . . ."

Ollie's voice faded. His face had gone translucent and his eyes drifted shut. Bits of smut from the burning Vorlon that Ildy and I had hijacked fell on his pale skin like black snow. The blood flow from his head wound had diminished to a trickle.

Hauling out my poncho, I began to ease him into it. He groaned once, thrashed about weakly, and then became a dead weight in my arms. Accoutred as I was in helmet and combat gloves, I couldn't tell whether he was alive or not.

Ildiko came dashing up. "All our prisoners in the wreck are dead. There's a chance the ammo stores in the stern might blow up any minute. Is the prize package still with us?"

"A good question. Help me get him to a safer spot, upwind of the gas and out of range if the wreck blows. Let's try the hopper pad. The lift lid's bent up. Maybe we can take cover behind it."

It was a little under a hundred meters away. We hoisted Schneider together and ran for it. No sooner had we dragged him behind the canted elevator deck than our aircraft exploded, sending a wave of dust, smoke, and diluted sleepy-gas rolling over us.

I lay over Schneider, protecting him with my soft-armored body from the few bits of debris that rained down. I'd lowered the poncho hood over his face, but he spasmed beneath me as AG97 entered his lungs and then fell back limply.

"Shit," I muttered.

Ildy pushed me aside and carefully lifted one of Ollie's eyelids. The eye was rolled back. As we watched, it returned slowly to its normal position, the pupil shrunk to a pinpoint.

"He's alive," she said. "AG97 is supposed to have minimal side effects on a healthy subject. How bad were his wounds?"

"Maybe not too serious. Hard to say." I was struggling to my feet, resettling my equipment. There was no time to discuss the patient. "You put up a tylar tent here and do what you can for him. I've got to get inside that facility and call for the cavalry . . . if there is any cavalry."

"Do you have a fallback option, Helly?"

I surveyed the terrain for a minute. Conical Butte, with its apron of talus, was due west of our position. To the southwest were the original Three Smokes, and behind them, about four zigzaggy kilometers away, the pointed volcanic crags that concealed our tuqo. The intervening plain was rocky gravel with a few boulders. At full magnification my visor showed no patches of cinders or smoky ground.

"If the balloon goes up," I said, "make for the tuqo. Return to the privateer at top speed and tell Mimo to blast off."

"Understood."

"And watch out for survivors coming up the elevator shaft. The gas you pumped in the front door might not have penetrated this far."

I shouldered my grenade launcher and headed for the entrance to the facility. The hideously mangled dead inside the airlock were a Haluk SWAT team armed with heavy blasters and smart-missile launchers. Alarm bells that were already ringing insidiously in my mind cranked up a notch. Darrel had lied to me. The Galapharma agents at the secret Cravat facility hadn't trusted the xeno guard force with lethal weaponry. So what was happening here on Dagasatt?

The inner airlock door had been completely destroyed by Ildy's grenade but the semicircular lobby area beyond seemed relatively undamaged. Signs on four wide-open corridors indicated the way to CENTRAL, GE1, GE2, and GE3.

Red emergency indicators on the walls were flashing, and a computer voice yammered: *Alert. Alert. AG90-type gas attack. Antidote is not in defensive arsenal. Alert. Alert . . .*

Well, that was a break. I hoped the place didn't have autosealing doors. Ildiko had pumped in four sleepy-gas rounds, enough to fill the whole building if nothing blocked it. A few molecules of AG97 sufficed to stun a rhino, and the gas swiftly penetrated all but the most advanced filters. I figured that the opposition should be down, unless the building had compartmentalized ventilation systems, or the occupants had managed to put on Air-Paks or oxygen.

I hustled along the corridor leading into Central, and was suddenly aware that the nagging voice of the computer warning had finally shut off. I'd hung the LGF-18 on my back and drawn my Ivanov pistol. Everytime I passed a closed door, I flung it open in search of conscious combatants. I found none, but there were fallen Haluk everywhere.

I wondered how many of the aliens were illicit sharers in the human genetic heritage, freed from the allomorphism that had limited their racial progress. Even more, I worried about the humans inside this establishment, and whether Oliver Schneider knew or even suspected what they might be.

Most of the Haluk I encountered were in the gracile, fully active state: slender, wasp-waisted beings with slate-blue skin, dressed in natty uniforms, fatigue coveralls, lab smocks, or the kind of casual alien clothing I had seen in the underground establishment of Cravat. The two sexes were only slightly different in appearance. Their skulls were finely shaped and had manes of platinum hair, variously styled. Gracile Haluk eyes were disproportionately large, brilliant blue, almond-shaped, and quite beautiful. By way of contrast, their arms, cheeks, foreheads, and long necks had prominent ridges and carunculated areas that seemed hideous by human standards.

A few of the unconscious aliens were obviously genetically unaltered, since they had entered the transitional or lepidodermoid phase of their allomorphic cycle. The Haluk had evolved on an ancestral world with a very eccentric orbit that carried it dangerously near the sun for half of each four-hundred-day year. The race adapted, regularly changing its body form in response to the increased heat, dryness, and solar radiation flux of the deadly summer.

As gracile Haluk turned into lepidoderms, intelligence

declined and bodily functions slowly began to shut down. Lepidos were asexual, thick-limbed, barrel-bodied creatures able to perform only simple tasks. Greatly enlarged heads, scaled to insulate the sensitive brain, grew massive brow ridges to guard eyes that were now shielded by dark protective pigments. Noses and mouths shrank. As the cycle progressed toward the Great Change, the lepido body acquired more and more scales, at first dark blue, then changing to dull gold. Movement became ponderous and finally ceased. The ultimate testudinal phase was an immobile golden chrysalid in which the Haluk slept—estivated—for about 140 days. Then the cocoon opened and a fully functional gracile emerged, memories and intelligence intact . . . but *way* behind the times.

Even though the Haluk had long since abandoned their appalling home world and settled on more hospitable planets, the annual cycle persisted. It was no longer synchronous, however. Individuals now cycled at different times from their peers, but allomorphism was still vexatiously inconvenient.

Especially for a race that yearned to conquer the universe.

I found Jim Matsukawa alone in the communication room, slumped before a subspace com unit with its viewscreen gone to auto standby. He was a sturdy, well-muscled specimen wearing a red-and-black Galapharma uniform, and although he seemed totally incapacitated, I clamped plastic manacles around his wrists and ankles before tipping him off the chair onto the floor.

Even before I located him, I'd decided that Jim was going to accompany us offworld. As a material witness and potential informant, he was far superior to poor dead Darrel Ridenour and his companions. Matsukawa's testimony was going to corroborate that of Oliver Schneider, justifying a full-scale investigation of this genen site by Zone Patrol and Rampart Security.

Jim's DNA might yield even more interesting evidence.

If the Haluk had actually demicloned the likes of Ride-

nour, a mere Gala ExSec Agent 4th Grade, it seemed possible
that they might also have replicated other humans assigned to
the genen facility staff. In an isolated place like this, a Haluk
demiclone-in-training could easily study the background and
mannerisms of his unsuspecting donor before taking his
place—and eventually moving on to a more strategic venue.

Duty Officer Jim Matsukawa was a prime doppelgänger
candidate. An even more likely—and potentially valuable—
one was Erik Skogstad, who had supervised the entire operation on behalf of Galapharma. In time, a Haluk mole such as
Fake Erik might be able to penetrate the inner circles of
Galapharma security—unless he happened to be driving that
Haluk starship Joe Betancourt was stalking, in which case his
fake-human DNA would soon mingle anonymously with the
interstellar dust floating between Dagasatt and Artiuk.

Taking a seat before the SS com unit, I asked it to tell me
what stations Jim Matsukawa had called within the past hour.
The list was a short one.

1. [Encrypted designation], starship on interstellar course
   within Perseus Spur
2. [Encrypted designation], planet Artiuk
3. [Encrypted designation], Toronto, planet Earth
4. [Different encrypted designation], Toronto, planet Earth

I figured that the first call had gone to Skogstad, or whoever was piloting the approaching starship. The second alerted
Haluk authorities, or Galapharma agents, on Artiuk to the attack on the facility. The third might have gone to Galapharma's home offices on Earth, notifying them of the attempt to
grab Schneider. The recipient of the fourth message was a
puzzler. It seemed unlikely that Matsukawa would call another Galapharma number in Toronto if he had already reported the emergency to Concern HQ. But who else would
rate a priority communiqué?

It didn't look as though Matsukawa had summoned any
local Qastt gunships himself—at least not through the SS

com—but there was always a possibility that others had done it for him.

I sent out a call to Joe Betancourt aboard *Chispa Dos*. Over an hour had gone by since I'd told him to pursue and destroy the Haluk speedster.

He responded at once and told me he'd carried out my orders.

"It was really strange," Joe said, after I'd offered felicitations on his success and his survival. "I hid in a little dust-nebula and did a fairly typical hostile intercept of the Haluk. The ship refused to surrender, even when I demonstrated my superiority, so we engaged and I finished him off rather quickly. You'll never guess what was trash-talking at me from inside that zippy xeno crate."

"A human," I said.

"You got it! But it gets weirder. The pilot recognized *Chispa*, even though I had the transponder-ID blanked out. Flat out accused me of stealing his Y700 prototype! The man was seriously apeshit—madder about his ripped-off ship than about the fact that he was outgunned and outmaneuvered and about to go plasmatic."

"Your opponent was very likely a major Galapharma operative named Erik Skogstad. Mimo sort of inherited his blitzboat as spoils of battle. I'll tell you the story later . . . So, did you get dinged at all in the dogfight?"

"Not a scratch. My three Qastt passengers didn't even realize that anything hairy was going on until it was all over. How're you and Ildy?"

"Both okay. We hit the facility successfully and that's where I'm calling from. Operation Q is just about a wrap. We captured the big prize. Unfortunately, Schneider was wounded by friendly fire during the penetration. I hope we can save him."

A shocked pause. "Well, that's a shit shortcake."

"The four lesser prizes are probably also still alive, but in no condition to be evacuated. I've taken the duty officer prisoner, and he'll be going out with us as a corroborating witness to what was happening in this damned place."

"What *was*?"

"There's no time to talk about it now. The important thing is for us to get out of here, fast. I don't know whether these clowns called for Qastt reinforcements. If they did, Ildy and I will deal with the situation as best we can. But we won't be able to last long."

"Helly, you've got to get away from the facility. Take cover in the rocks, or something."

"Affirmative. That's what I intend to do. How soon can you get back to Dagasatt?"

"Twenty-three minutes suit you?"

"Beautiful! You make good on that, I'll adopt you into the Frost family. Megabucks, colorful kinfolks, horseback rides, sunset barbecues, and all the Galapharma shit you can shovel."

Joe Betancourt howled. "I'll take a pass on everything but the money. I'm gonna need lots to get my charter business going."

"You'll get a bonus, along with everybody else. Now listen: there are other people you have to contact. First, get ahold of Mimo. Tell him to wait until you arrive to give protective cover from orbit. Then he can fly out on an oh-nine-oh course, hugging the bitumen, skip over the volcanoes, and exit the atmosphere over the Empty Sea. Escort the privateer to some hiding place in the system's Kuiper Cloud, then come back for us. Mimo can fly *Chispa*'s gig down for the pickup while you hold off any Qastt that interfere. If our luck holds, there won't be any Qastt—but watch for other Haluk cruisers coming ex Artiuk. I think this facility may have been very important to them."

"I copy all that. Any other orders?"

"Contact Matt Gregoire on Seriphos. Ask her to send any armed Rampart ExSec or Fleet Security starships in the region to Dagasatt to reinforce you. There ought to be a fleet cutter on Cravat, if nothing else. And have her alert Cravat's hospital to expect us with Ollie Schneider—whenever."

"Copy that."

"She'll also have to notify Zone Patrol that we have firm

evidence of human prisoners being held on Dagasatt, and set up a joint Rampart-ZP assault on this place. But not until we're all safely out of here. Tell Matt I'll contact her when we're en route to Cravat."

"Anything else?"

"Just hurry it up, Joe. I'm really sick to death of this fuckin' planet."

Shutting off the SS com, I drew my Kagi pistol and blasted critical modules of the instrument to melted glop. Then I went off hurriedly in search of GE1, the east-wing genetic engineering lab.

The central module had a confusing radial layout, and I was grateful for Darrel Ridenour's floor plan. I loped down now-silent corridors, only occasionally finding a fallen Haluk, and came at last to a heavy door, wide-open. Three unconscious technicians dressed in white coveralls lay crumpled just outside, and it was obvious they had been about to lock the lab and flee when the gas reached them. Two of the techs were Haluk and one was a middle-aged human woman. She wore a translator pendant and still held a key-card in her hand.

I stepped over the sleepers into a dimly lit scene of bizarre familiarity. The laboratory was crowded with row upon row of upright, transparent technocoffins of the type used in the most elaborate forms of dynamic-stasis gene therapy. Bodies submerged in thick bubbly liquid floated inside the containers, suspended on intricate frames and connected to arcane gadgetry. The dystasis tanks seemed identical to those I'd seen in the Haluk facility on Cravat.

Embedded in the gleaming black glass floor was a network of neon-red filaments that connected with the tank bottoms and illuminated the bodies from below, leaving them otherwise in womblike twilight. At the far end of the wing stood a collection of oddball machinery that also looked familiar. Multicolored spheres with pulsating inner lights, linked by more of the glowing red tubing, were mounted on a black glass platform next to banks of exotic monitoring equipment.

To my layman's eye the assemblage looked more like a light sculpture than scientific apparatus.

I started down the nearest aisle, examining the comatose floaters more closely. On Cravat the tanks had held what seemed to be hundreds of gracile Haluk—with the single conspicuous exception of my sister!—dressed in long silvery shifts that left only their feet, arms, and heads exposed. At first I believed the xenos were being treated with human DNA, vectored by the wide-spectrum transferase in PD32:C2, so that their allomorphic cycle would be eradicated.

Later I found out from Eve what was really going on in the Cravat facility. The sickening discovery had confirmed my fears that the Haluk had hostile intentions toward the human race.

And damned if it didn't look like the same sort of thing was happening here on Dagasatt!

With an increasing sense of dread, I examined the silver-gowned beings in the tanks and discovered they were paired. Every other subject appeared to be a gracile Haluk, and alternating with them were humans. Or almost humans. But the allomorph eradication process used a different, simpler technique for transferring DNA.

Direct interconnection of genetic donor and recipient was necessary only for the *demiclone* procedure, which took much longer and was more complex.

This is the way it worked:

First, capture your human. Then place him or her into dystasis. Using PD32:C2 as a vector, insert selected nonallomorphic Haluk DNA into the human subject, in order to preclude rejection syndrome in the alien recipient during the demiclone procedure. About twelve weeks later your demiclone template is ready. As a reversible side effect, the human donor has acquired the superficial appearance of a gracile Haluk—as had happened to Eve, albeit incompletely.

Next, take one nonallomorphic Haluk and place him or her into a tank adjacent to the donor. Transfer an enormous amount of DNA from the modified human to the Haluk recipient, again using the PD32:C2 genen vector. In another twelve weeks or so the Haluk will have become a human-appearing replica of the donor, physically differentiated only by a small redundant gene sequence in the nucleus of each fake-human body cell: a marker programmed into the demicloning process by Emily Konigsberg of Galapharma, unbeknownst to the Haluk.

The big Concern, being justifiably suspicious of the demiclone scheme but forced to accede to it, had made damn sure it could identify the fakes. It had also extracted firm promises from the alien leaders that only a few demiclones would be made, and installed its own security personnel at all of the Haluk genen facilities to ensure that the promises were kept.

Maybe they had been, in some places. But not on Cravat.

And not here on Dagasatt, either.

I knew it was impossible for me and my tiny force to rescue any of the halukoid human donors. Disconnecting a dystasis subject was a delicate medical procedure that took time and special expertise, and we had neither. Later on, if Matt Gregoire managed to convince Zone Patrol to raid Dagasatt for cause, or if Rampart ExSec was granted permission to do so by CHW, the floating prisoners might be freed and restored to their original human form.

Or maybe not, if the Haluk got there first and carried the luckless donors off to another genen facility elsewhere.

As for the demiclones, those rapers of human identity . . .

When Ollie Schneider had said, "Do 'em," he was begging me to give his four friends a merciful death. I didn't have the right to do that. But at that moment I believed I did have the right to do something else, in retaliation for what had been done to the original Darrel Ridenour, to the other innocent human DNA-donors in this damned place, and to my sister Eve, who'd almost joined them.

So I drew my Kagi pistol and went up and down the rows of tanks, first in the GE1 laboratory wing and then in the two others. If the floater looked Haluk, I let it be; but if it seemed human, or almost human, I shot it in the head.

When I was finished I took an antigrav tote that I'd found in one of the storerooms and went back to retrieve Jim Matsukawa—whoever and whatever he was.

We reached the entrance of the facility just as the Qastt gunships began their bombardment.

The first strike was a small one, in some far-distant wing. I had just reached the outer lobby with my prisoner when the building shook. My helmet sensors barely picked up the ensuing sound—but an instant later the facility's computer warning system began telling me what I already knew.

Air attack alert. Air attack alert. GE2 integrity has been compromised by blaster fire.

GE2 was the west wing, the one I had visited last of all before retrieving Jim Matsukawa. More hits made the floor tremble. Since there was no longer any need for communication secrecy, I called Ildiko on the regular helmet intercom.

"Ildy, what's happening? Is it the Qastt?"

"Affirm," came her level reply. "Three small gunships armed with medium-power blasters. Looks to me like they're trying to destroy the facility. Not a whole lot of firepower going, though, and the building is apparently well-armored. The prize and I are okay. What's your status?"

"In the lobby with one prisoner. Any chance you can take the ships with grenades?"

"Not a prayer. They're keeping their distance, hovering just below the smoke deck, altitude niner-three-three." A larger tremor shook the place and the computer announcement abruptly choked off in mid-cry. "Uh-oh! Looks like the west wing roof just breached, Helly. They're pounding the rubble."

Doing 'em . . .

I hopped over the bodies in the airlock and took a peek outside. The air was swirling with smoke and dust. Green photon blasts meteored down at a near-vertical angle, pulverizing the ruins. It was definitely a demolition derby. The Haluk had sent their allies to wipe out evidence of demicloning on Dagasatt. Even though the Squeaker cannons appeared to be only a third as powerful as the Harveys on the Vorlon hoppers, given enough time, they'd do the job.

I said to Ildy, "Have you tried to contact *Chispa*?"

"Affirm, every five minutes until the Qastt showed up. No reply. All this crap floating in the air is weakening the lasercom HUV beam and Joe might not be able to read me. Or perhaps he's still escorting the privateer and out of range."

"Can you take shelter down inside the elevator shaft?"

"Negative. There's a lot of unstable-looking wreckage blocking the way. I didn't want to risk checking it out alone and leave Schneider unprotected. Maybe the two of us can figure something when you get over here. I've got a rappelling cable."

"Right. I'll be making my break in a minute or two."

The Qastt had left off firing on GE2, which was now completely flattened, and began to pound the facility's north wing. My visor had adjusted automatically to compensate for the murky air and I could see the hopper pad clearly. Would the gunners notice me making a break for it, towing my prisoner behind? They'd certainly have IR scanners, but the glow from nearby semimolten debris would tend to futz the blips made by me and Jim Matsukawa. I fervently wished I still had the camouflaging filo poncho I'd wrapped around Ollie Schneider.

The antigrav tote with Matsukawa strapped to it floated over the airlock casualties with ease. Then I took off, and it was a matter of broken-field running through smoke and gouts of green flame while Ildy cheered me on.

I nearly made it home safe. But less than a dozen meters from the pad I tripped over a jagged piece of hopper wreckage, slashing my right shin savagely and taking a header. I was unable to get up again and filled the helmet intercom with agonized curses.

"Hang on. I'm coming," Ildy said.

And she did—just as one of the Qastt gunships tardily noticed ground activity and took a shot at us with some sort of small actinic weapon. A white blast hit the ground three meters to my left. Another zorched the sand just behind Ildy. The

Squeak could certainly see us with the ship's infrared scanner, but he seemed to be using an optical sight, not an auto-targeter, and the range was extreme.

Ildy arrived and hauled me into a sitting position. Another shot, another miss. "Take *him*, dammit!" I indicated Matsukawa. "Never mind me."

She said, "Oh, shut the fuck up."

A moment later she'd rolled me onto the hovering tote. Draped sideways over Jim's body, hands and feet dragging on the ground, I made the rest of the trip dodging ingloriously through fireworks. The Qastt gunner got off one last wild shot before we reached the shelter of the makeshift bunker and dropped off his scanner. The demolition of Hopfrog Three had cracked the elevator piston near its base, tipping the circular platform sideways as well as angling it skyward almost thirty degrees. The elevator deck was about twenty-five meters in diameter, shielding us fairly well from the bombardment of the facility.

"Thanks one more time, *yet!*" I gasped.

Ildy said, "Brace yourself, cowboy. Time to dismount."

She lowered the tote and carefully rolled me off. The pain in my shin was excruciating and the leg of my armored jumpsuit was sodden with blood. Hauling myself into a sitting position, I fumbled for the first-aid supplies in my belt pouch. Ildy used a special blade to cut open the pants leg and inspected the wound. Oliver Schneider's half-visible filo-shrouded form lay close by, along with her grenade launcher. I'd lost mine somewhere along the way.

After a momentary respite, the Qastt gunship was once again firing on us. But it hadn't changed its position and the actinic bursts were still being fired perpendicularly, sending melted blobs of ceramalloy arcing in all directions off the battered elevator platform. Realizing the futility of his attack, the lone gunman broke off. Meanwhile, photon cannons hammered the devastated facility's east wing. The Squeaks would smash Central next. Then they'd move off for a clear shot under our umbrella with their mean greens, and we'd be toast.

Ildy announced, "You're slashed wide-open and this shin-bone's either busted or cracked right through. At least the broken ends are together and the leg's straight. Hand me some dressings and wide tape."

"Never mind that. You still got your filo poncho?"

She was taken aback. "Of course . . . You think we'd do better making a run for it, rather than trying to get down the shaft?"

"You'll do the running, hauling the prisoners. I'm going nowhere. Get Schneider loaded onto the tote on top of my guy. Cut up my poncho, wrap 'em as well as you can, and make tracks for the tuqo."

"But—"

"That's an order, Lieutenant!"

"The tote will carry three people," she protested.

"One poncho can't possibly conceal us all!" I bawled furiously. "Now move your goddamn ass! The Squeaks will turn their big guns on this platform as soon as they finish trashing the building."

Insubordinate mutterings, which I ignored. She began bundling up Schneider and Matsukawa head to feet, with the healthier duty officer relegated to mattress status. I concentrated on bandaging my shin wound, for all the good it was going to do me, gave myself several doses of antibiotic and painkiller, and splinted my entire leg with the useless grenade launcher.

"Give me a hand," I asked Ildy when I'd finished. "I'm gonna try hobbling off into the sunset at an angle from you guys. To hell with sitting here waiting for it."

She complied. "I'll give another shout to *Chispa* on the lasercom when I'm in the clear. And I want to say it's been a real honor to serve with you . . . even if you are a cowboy asshole."

"Feeling's mutual, bull-dagger babe. Now move out!"

She took up the tote handle and turned to go, just as a blast of coherent emerald light struck the platform. The canted structure gave a hideous squall and slowly began to topple.

I hardly knew what hit me. Then I realized it was Ildiko,

virtually invisible in her poncho, whisking around and delivering a vicious double stiff-arm to my middle back. I keeled over on top of the shimmering, packaged prisoners. Bits of junk rained down as two more cannon shots hit the platform with thunderclap detonations. It went *skreeeaawrooom!*

We moved. I clung to Ollie Schneider's hooded head, past caring whether the bastard's neck got broken in the process. Lying on my stomach, my vision impeded by the helmet, I wasn't expecting the final stunning crash of collapsed ceramalloy, punctuated by a cannonade of green flame.

The concussion knocked Ildiko off her feet. At least, I saw her boots go flying. The tote had enough residual momentum to bang into her before stopping in midair, causing me to release my grip on Ollie and flop onto the hard hopper pad. The crumpling platform had missed us by less than three meters, and we were enveloped in smoke and dust.

I heard Ildy's voice murmuring something in rapid Hungarian that sounded like a prayer. My own final words were going to be more profane. Flat on my back, I looked at the sky through the power visor and cussed out the three klutzy looking little alien gunships, still hanging high above us like a trio of malformed vultures. What were they waiting for? One more blast would finish us.

Instead there were three bright flashes, one after the other. Three monstrous explosions reached us an instant later. The Qastt were gone, obliterated.

"Look!" Ildy said in an awed voice. She was on her knees with her hood pushed back. "Here comes the gig."

But she was wrong about the identity of our rescuer. Descending serenely through murky chaos came the elegant, dangerous shape of *Chispa Dos* herself.

Chapter 11

"Cut it a little fine, didn't you?" I groused to Mimo.

He helped me up the ramp into the starship. My leg was numb and well-braced and I could stump along on it fairly well. I felt weird and woozy. Ildy had already gone aboard under her own steam after Ivor Jenkins took charge of the two prisoners.

Mimo said, "Sorry we took so long. It was necessary for us to dispose of a rather large Haluk cruiser before arranging your deliverance. I handled the guns myself. It was a nasty surprise. The bandit appeared unexpectedly as we were escorting Ba-Karkar's privateer through the outer reaches of the Dagasatt solar system."

"Is the little pipsqueak okay?" I asked anxiously.

"Don't worry. He's fine. We sent all of the pirates and the captured Qastt search-and-rescue team to Cravat in the privateer. They were shepherded by a Rampart Fleet Security cutter that arrived too late to join in the fight against the Haluk."

The hatch rolled shut behind us and I felt the vibration of liftoff underfoot.

"Mimo, wait! We should search the rubble of the facility. Some important evidence might still be intact."

"No, *amigo*, we can't stay. A foolhardy Qastt corvette also challenged us as we approached the planet. Fortunately, it recognized that *Chispa* was too formidable an opponent and backed off—but not before warning us that more armed Haluk starships are on the way here from Artiuk and Oruka-

240

vuk. Their mission is to ensure that all putrid untranslatable human invaders are expelled from Dagasatt."

Mimo urged me aft, toward the ship's well-equipped sick bay. I caught a glimpse of the sky outside the ports, which darkened almost instantly. Joe Betancourt had *Chispa* outward bound at illegal exit velocity, no doubt shattering the tranquillity of the Great Bitumen Desert with a horrific sonic boom. In an instant the ports shone with a weirdly rippling curtain of dazzling red and green. I cringed. Joe had accelerated to maximum sublight drive while we were still in the upper atmosphere and set off an ionic conflagration.

Dagasatt was going to pay a price for having harbored a clandestine demiclone facility: our electromagnetic pulse had just fried most of the high-tech circuitry on the planet. I wondered if the Qastt would send the Haluk a bill.

Mimo continued. "There's nothing more we can do here. *Chispa* will be on Cravat in less than an hour. Zone Patrol will deal with the hostile Haluk starships if they dare to follow us, but I think there's small danger of that."

Dagasatt's sun was shrinking to a golden spark. I staggered, momentarily blinded as we made the ultraluminal crossover. When my vision cleared, Dagasatt was lost among the stretched stars.

I said, "Nothing more to do."

My eyes unaccountably filled with burning tears. When I lifted a hand to wipe them away I encountered the hard, slick visor of my combat helmet. A growling sob came from my throat and echoed in my headphones. I drew away from Mimo's supporting arm and stood in the middle of the corridor, swaying. With a violent motion I pulled the helmet off and let it fall to the deck with a muted clang.

An overwhelming surge of irrational anger suddenly engulfed me and I wallowed in it, uttering incoherent obscenities at the same time that I realized I must be spacing out from battle fatigue, delayed shock, and the slew of drugs I'd taken.

"Helly, it's all right! Operation Q is over. A success. It's time to move on." Mimo tried to put his guiding arm around me again, but I stumbled away. He took something from his pocket and spoke into it.

"Damn straight Operation Q is over." My voice was even but too loud. "A great success—if you don't count Zorik O'Toole, who got burned alive, and the two hundred anonymous human demiclone donors who were blown to bits, to say nothing of a crowd of opposition noncombatants that I killed in cold blood, right or wrong. But why worry about them? Hell—we got Ollie Schneider, we got a second witness who might be even more valuable, and we got away! Success! I should be *ready* to move on."

"Helly—"

"But moving on means I have to start fighting all over again. In the Orion Arm, on the planet Earth, in Simon's turf. And I'm so goddamned tired, Mimo."

The old man's grip barely kept me from falling. "Of course you're tired, and suffering from post-traumatic stress as well. You must rest and heal before thinking about what to do next. Meanwhile, trust your friends to carry on your fight."

"Friends . . . ?"

"I'll take him," Ivor Jenkins said. I felt myself lifted in herculean arms, an oddly familiar thing, and carried away.

So tired, Pop.

Time for bed, little buckaroo.

"Leave everything to us," the fading voice said. "Matt Gregoire is waiting on Cravat with portable psychotronic equipment. She was so confident you'd succeed on Dagasatt that she left Seriphos a day after we did, so no time would be wasted."

"Confident?" I forced my leaden eyelids open again. "But I thought she'd washed her hands of me and Operation Q."

Ivor said, "Matt's coming to Earth with us, Helly. She's a witness for the prosecution, too."

"Well, what d'you know . . ."

No more jabberin' now, boy. Good night.

Good night, Pop.

My eyes closed and I slept.

*   *   *

Calm. Competence. Courage.

The message had been all the more terrifying for its banality—an ordinary vidphone call to his Rampart Tower office in Toronto, fielded by his secretary and duly transmitted to his desk: The concierge of the Arizona Biltmore informs Citizen Frost that "the meeting" will take place at 1630 hours, local time, in the Lobby Lounge of the resort.

Only one person would dare to summon him in such a cavalier fashion. So off he goes again in supine response to his master's command—only this time traveling in the opposite direction—at a loss to know why Alistair Drummond requires another vis-à-vis meeting immediately. And in Phoenix, Arizona, of all places.

Surely he can't have found out about the presentation of Rampart's venture credit prospectus . . .

No. Not even Galapharma's spy network extends into the executive offices of Macrodur Concern, the computer software colossus, and most powerful of the Big Seven. The audacious scheme hatched by Eve is still confidential and will remain so. Unless, against all odds, it succeeds—perhaps because Macrodur's chairman, that zany, self-righteous prick, equates a Rampart bailout with flipping Gala the finger.

If only there had been some way to subvert Eve's plan! He'd done his utmost to shoot it down before it ever reached the prospectus stage, but to no avail. In the end she and Simon backed him into a corner, ordering him to make the presentation this afternoon along with them and Gunter Eckert, or give a damned good reason for refusing.

He did as he was told.

Calmly. Competently. Courageously.

The mantra loops in his brain as he leaves the taxi and enters the magnificent lobby of the historic resort, which reflects the architectural influence of Frank Lloyd Wright. The Arizona Biltmore is sparsely inhabited now in the height of the desert summer. Squaw Peak is framed in one of the outlooks. Late afternoon sunshine, partially muted by the climate-moderating Phoenix Conurbation force-field, illuminates stained-glass skylights, pilasters of fanciful wrought iron, and the famous patterned concrete blocks that form the walls. Southwestern pottery and arrangements of tropical flowers are everywhere.

He crosses to the lounge, where a few drinkers in expensive casual attire sip colorful potations and converse in low, well-bred tones.

He has arrived precisely on time and is gratified to discover that Alistair Drummond is not yet here. He sits down at a small table as far away from the other people as possible, beckons the waiter, and orders a Long Island iced tea. It quenches his thirst nicely and he impulsively signals for another, feeling his tension easing. And no wonder, since the innocuous-tasting tall drink contains full shots of vodka, rum, gin, and tequila.

Just as the refill arrives, the Galapharma CEO strides into the lounge and plumps down at the table without a word of greeting.

"May I bring you something, also, sir?" the server inquires.

"Whatever my friend is having," says Alistair Drummond. He is wearing a white Izod tennis shirt and shorts with a cotton sweater knotted loosely around his neck. The leonine hair is disarranged, the hard, handsome face is flushed and gleaming, and he exudes a powerful odor of sweat, apparently not giving a damn whether his companion might be offended.

"Katje Vanderpost," Drummond says in a mild, baleful voice. "Have you brought her around to our way of thinking, lad?"

"I've done some forceful persuading," he temporizes, "painting you as a remorseless hard-charger who'll have his way by fair means or foul. On the surface, she seems as stubborn as ever. But she's got to be a very frightened and demoralized old woman by now, ready to accede to my demands."

Drummond's voice is almost inaudible. "You're lying. You've been afraid to tackle Katje, hoping she'd die before the next board meeting and solve your problem for you. I warned you about lying to me . . ."

"Your spies have it wrong this time, Alistair." He forces a

smile, plucks the straw from his second cocktail, discards it, and swallows a long, fortifying belt. "Why, I called her just the day before yesterday to offer my condolences on Asa's death. She was in a pitiful state, barely coherent—"

"Asahel Frost is alive. I wouldn't be surprised if his mother knows it."

Stunned to the depths of his being, he can say nothing.

"Furthermore, he mounted a massive attack on the secret facility in the Perseus Spur where Oliver Schneider was confined. This happened less than ten hours ago. Schneider was either killed or taken into custody by the attackers. If he's dead, we have approximately one week before damning evidence against Galapharma is made public by his solicitors, according to a prearranged scheme. If Schneider's alive, I think we may assume that Asahel Frost will bring him to Earth in the fastest starship at his disposal—one stolen from Galapharma. Even with refueling stops, the ship will arrive in eight days. They'll need another day or two to prepare the formal depositions for the civil suit and present them to the Commerce Secretariat and the Commonwealth Judiciary Tribunal. But after that . . ."

"Oh, Jesus," he whispers.

Alistair Drummond leans across the table, so close that every pore and drop of perspiration on his face is visible. "Our previous timetable is nullified. Both of us will have to act immediately if we're to salvage the situation. You will arrange for an emergency meeting of the Rampart Board of Directors within one week."

"But that will require Simon's approval, unless—"

"Do it!" Drummond says. "Before the week is up, you will coerce Katje Vanderpost into giving you her voting proxy. Or else bring her *will* to the board meeting, along with the proxies of those charity groups who inherit her quarterstake. Get on with it, you gutless sack of pigshit! You've vacillated long enough."

He sits frozen. It's come, the eventuality he has feared ever since the earlier meeting with Drummond. Katje will never hand over her proxy to him. He knows this, and he has already laid the groundwork for the alternative course of action. She is well-guarded, but the action will succeed because of its utter simplicity. There is not the remotest chance that he will be implicated.

It will be a merciful release for the sick old woman. A good thing, in so many ways.

"Her will," the Galapharma CEO repeats with implacable gentleness. "Ready for expedited probate. The Rampart board must vote to accept my tender before Schneider's evidence is officially submitted to ICS and the prosecutors or I'll be destroyed. And you'll go to Coventry Blue."

His reply is spoken judiciously, without emotion. "There's no reason for either of us to be concerned. I've made very careful arrangements. All I have to do is give the word . . . It'll be done."

The trusted housekeeper and confidant of the old lady has a ne'er-do-well grandson, a young unmarried priest in Albuquerque with divergent sexual appetites. To save him from exposure and disgrace, the housekeeper has agreed to substitute a particular tea bag—when given the order—for the innocuous chamomile infusion Katje always uses as a sleep aid. The simpleminded housekeeper believes that the bogus beverage will merely make stubborn Katje "more amenable" to certain crucial matters of business.

Tonight, he will give the order. Katje will take her final cup of chamomile.

He and Alistair Drummond sit together in silence until the server arrives with Drummond's drink. The Galapharma CEO accepts with gracious thanks and takes a long pull.

"That's delicious," he tells the waiter. "What d'you call it?"

"Long Island iced tea, sir. But there's no tea in it at all."

"No tea? Amazing! You could have fooled me."

"The flavor's deceptive. So's the alcoholic content."

Drummond laughs. "Deceptive, eh? Then I'll have to watch my step, won't I?" He nods at the man across the table. "So will my friend. His glass is nearly empty. Please bring him another."

"Whatever you say, sir," says the server.

"Damn right," murmurs Alistair Drummond.

Cravat is a medium-sized, borderline S-2 world. Humans can survive there without full life support, providing that they endure nineteen inoculations, aren't persnickety about being munched upon by small carnivorous life-forms, and are agile enough to avoid the large ones. Smart visitors wear Class Two envirogear while strolling, and carry high-powered weapons.

Cravat is Rampart's most remote colony, and it harbors no Indigenous Sapients. Poisonously lush vegetation clothes most of its small continents, which yield enough valuable minerals and biological agents to make the place economically attractive to entrepreneurs. The planet is also the sole source of the obscure genen vector PD32:C2, a broad-spectrum transferase agent that finds a modest market among human terraformers. In recent years increasing quantities of PD32:C2 have been purchased from Rampart by Galapharma AC, mystifying the Rampart sales force.

The only permanent settlement on Cravat, forthrightly called Dome, is tucked under a full DF-1500 hemispherical force-field like a model village protected by a bell jar. Rampart personnel stationed there do not consider it a hardship posting. The Starcorp, following my late Uncle Ethan's dictum—"The lousier the workplace, the spiffier the employee accommodations and perks"—has made Dome a beautiful and lavishly appointed oasis in the midst of what its human denizens fondly call the Green Hell.

I can testify to its diabolical charms through personal experience.

Cravat's hospital is small but well-equipped. Its medics took about an hour to heal my broken leg with bonebrace, leaving it as good as new structurally and assuring me that the pain would go away in a couple of weeks. My mental discombobulations received pharmaceutical therapy, since I needed to remain *compos mentis* for a few hours more. I was warned to take it easy now, and catch up on my considerable sleep debt during the voyage to Earth unless I wanted to risk going bonkers.

While I was being pasted back together, Matt Gregoire supervised the care of the two star witnesses. Jim Matsukawa had a smashed nose and other minor contusions suffered as a result of being bottom layer in the antigrav tote sandwich during the final exciting minutes on Dagasatt. He was otherwise unhurt. Oliver Schneider's injuries required more extensive treatment, but he was going to be reasonably fit in short order. Matt placed the prisoners under heavy guard, then went to the Fleet Security office to file some slightly fictitious reports to Zone Patrol concerning recent activities on and around Dagasatt.

Ildiko, Ivor, Joe, and the gaggle of Qastt who had been escorted to Cravat ahead of us, not being in need of hospitalization, retired to Dome's luxurious spa to refresh themselves. (I was informed that the Squeakers demanded, and got, bubble baths.) By the time I joined them in the spa's restaurant, everyone was groomed, garbed, and gobbling quantities of expensive food and drink—the Qastt at one table and the humans at another—all hardship and danger apparently forgotten.

During a lull in the carousing, I dealt each of my three human companions a niobium EFT card primed with the agreed-upon stipend, plus a sizable bonus.

Joe Betancourt cleared his throat, looking slightly abashed. "What will happen to O'Toole's share? Since he had no family, maybe you might consider—"

Before Joe could continue, Ildy broke in. "I'd like to suggest that his pay be donated to the Zone Patrol Benevolent Association in Zorik's name. It's a charity for the survivors of personnel killed on duty."

"Great idea," I said. "I'll see to it myself." Then I asked if anyone was interested in signing on for a second tour in Cap'n Helly's Irregulars, accompanying me and Mimo and Matt and the prisoners to Earth in *Chispa Dos*.

"You know you can count me in," said Ildy.

"I'd go just for the fun of it!" Ivor declared blithely.

"It might not be so amusing if the Haluk try to ambush us," I said. "And by now, Galapharma must know that the Dagasatt raiders—namely us—have their stolen Y700. They'll be watching for its signature. Our trip might be rocky, even if we're riding the fastest boat in the galaxy. Or we might have a pleasure cruise. It's a toss-up."

Joe said, "I'd like to reenlist, Helly, but . . . what kind of fee are we talking about?"

"The same as Dagasatt. For everyone."

"That's very generous. I'm on."

I rose from the table. "You guys finish your meal. I have some business to take care of. Remember, we meet in the Port Traffic Manager's office in two hours. You want to buy any more new clothes or other stuff for the trip, better get a move on."

The nine Qastt, who were all wearing translators, had been seated at a table in the quietest corner. In lieu of Squeak food, they were supping on the least putrid human groceries available: dandelion salad with Angostura bitters, grilled black pudding, squid fritters, kim chee, Icelandic hrökkbraud and Marmite, Bananas Foster, and a big pitcher of scorpion cocktails made with Demerara rum.

I told the aliens they could remain in the spa for three more days at Rampart expense and run a tab up to five grand apiece at the Cravat Mall. This news provoked whispers of wild enthusiasm among all but one of the little people.

"Where my bribe?" Ba-Karkar demanded baldly.

I produced a card and handed it over. "Here you go, skipper. I'll trust you to give a suitable share to Tisqatt and Tu-Prak. And I strongly suggest that you go into another line of work."

"I think about it," he muttered.

Ogu neatly nipped the money card out of her husband's hand and tucked it into her draperies. "He think about it with *significant* intensity!" Tisqatt and Tu-Prak choked back giggles.

The five abducted Qastt agents of mercy received a generous compensation for their unjust incarceration, together with paid passage on the privateer to Ba-Karkar's home planet, where they would be able to catch a transport back to Dagasatt. I advised them to exaggerate the horrors of their ordeal and say nothing about the under-the-table payoff. They agreed that the idea made significant sense, then toasted my good health with scorpions, human-style, and shook hands with themselves in the traditional Qastt fashion of indicating goodwill to all.

Leaving the restaurant, I went to the spa's atrium in search of peace and quiet. I found an open area where the Cravat sun shone through the protective force-field onto planters brimming with petunias, roses, and geraniums, potted palm trees, a pretty little fountain, and a small manicured expanse of terrestrial grass with padded shiatsu lounges parked on it. Sinking gratefully into one and turning on the massage, I took out my phone and called Mimo. He had decided to pass up the spa to take care of the servicing and supplying of *Chispa Dos* for the first leg of the long Orion run.

"Everything's going fine," he told me. "The starport maintenance crew are just putting the finishing touches on our new brig. It's comfortable and secure. All the special supplies have arrived and are being stowed. The servicing should be finished soon. I'm checking out the weaponry systems personally."

I said, "Don't forget our little ceremony at the office of the Port Traffic Manager, Terence Hoy. You have two hours."

He chuckled. "I wouldn't miss it for the world. Are you feeling better?"

"All mended and ready to boogie," I prevaricated. Actually, I felt like the Black Death revisited. "I'm going to take a nap now so I'll be fresh for the festivities. Catch you later, *mi capitán*."

I settled back, thinking idly of my first trip to Cravat, when the Port Traffic Manager had been a man named Robert Bascombe. Poor Bob had died accidentally after I coerced him into helping me investigate Eve's kidnapping. Now, lying there in the sunshine, staring at the swaying palm fronds above my head, I suddenly remembered something Bob had said. A small slip of the tongue, perhaps quite meaningless. But it was worth checking out.

I got Terence Hoy on the phone. "Asahel Frost here. Just a brief question about your late predecessor, Robert Bascombe. He had a wife named Delphine. Does she still live in Dome?"

"Why, yes. Del LaMotte. She's an analytical chemist at our Flutterbug One facility."

I asked for, and got, her phone code. When I reached LaMotte at work and identified myself, her voice grew instantly cooler. I apologized for her loss and then asked my question.

She said, "I don't really remember, Citizen Frost. Bob was always inviting people from Central for the big game hunting, but none of the VIPs stayed with us in our home."

"I understand. But perhaps your husband mentioned a visit by either man to you in passing. They would have wanted their presence on Cravat kept very confidential. Please think carefully. This is no idle query, Citizen LaMotte. It might even be crucial to Rampart's survival."

There was a silence. Then she said, "Only one of them ever came here that I know of. It happened about seven months before your sister's disappearance. I found out only by accident when I overheard Bob speaking on the SS com. He became very upset with me. I was told to forget all about the matter, and I tried my best to do so."

"Who was the confidential visitor?"

She told me.

I thanked her, turned off the phone, and lay there thinking. Was it a damning clue or just a useless bit of trivia? He might have come to Cravat for any number of reasons—not necessarily to meet Elgar/McGrath and inspect the secret Haluk facility.

Not necessarily to plot my death and Eve's destruction.

The atrium smelled of new-mown grass and roses. A soft artificial breeze was blowing. The fountain splashed, palms rattled, and recorded birdsong trilled gently. In spite of the thoughts tumbling about in my fatigued brain, I felt my eyes closing.

I slept—and dreamed of *him*, worse luck.

After a delay that seems interminable, the call to Earth goes through and a man with a long freckled face and auburn hair appears on the com display.

"Who the devil are you," he barks, "and how did you get this number?"

"Your Artiuk associate gave it to me and told me to report. Are you Tyler Baldwin, Galapharma's head of security?"

"Ah . . . Yes, of course. I'm Baldwin. Sorry to be so abrupt. We're in the midst of a major shitstorm here. Is Oliver Schneider still alive?"

"Yes. But no thanks to your stupid Squeaker allies. Their gunships almost nailed him during the big blowup on Dag. He was badly injured."

"It was a mistake. The Qastt were ordered only to destroy the facility, not fire on persons outside. I presume Schneider will recover?"

"He's in the Cravat hospital. They say he'll be okay. Speaking of mistakes, what the *fuck* was that big Haluk cruiser doing, lying in wait among the Dag asteroids? It nearly creamed us!"

"A failure of communication," Baldwin says dismissively. "These things happen. When will Asahel Frost leave Cravat?"

"Soon. Maybe three or four hours. He had to be patched up, along with Schneider and the Galapharma officer who was taken prisoner."

Consternation floods Tyler Baldwin's face. "What officer?"

"Oh. I forgot to mention that Frost brought out the D.O. at the Haluk facility. A man named Jim Matsukawa."

"Matsukawa! What does Frost plan to do with him?"

"Take him to Earth along with Schneider. As a material witness to the illegal activity on Dagasatt, I suppose. They'll both be interrogated psychotronically. Matilde Gregoire showed up on Cravat with portable probe machines. She's making the trip, too."

"You *must* find a way to prevent Matsukawa's interrogation—but without harming him. This is absolutely imperative."

"Are you out of your tiny mind? How am I supposed to do that? There's no way I can get at the psychotronic equipment to sabotage it. Frost and Gregoire have locked it in the wardroom where they plan to do the probing."

"You'll have to think of something," the Galapharma security chief says with harsh urgency. "We can't allow Matsukawa to be questioned."

"But what difference does it make? You'll get both prisoners back when I—"

"This is an order!"

"What about Ollie Schneider? Do I have to muzzle him, too?"

"It's not necessary. But Matsukawa must not be probed!"

"Well . . . I suppose I could try to take him out with food poisoning. You can pick up a lethal bug culture on Cravat just by wiping a Kleenex on the starport tarmac. If I can smuggle it through the decon gate—"

"I don't want the man dead, you bloody fool! Only unable to respond to the psychotronic machines. He must not be harmed in any way!"

"This wasn't part of our original deal."

"If you fail, not only is the deal null and void, but so are you."

"*That's* a terrific incentive."

"Don't take that tone with me. You made the choice to betray your comrades. And don't think you can skip out with what we've already paid you. We'll track your ass to Andromeda and points west." Abruptly, Baldwin's voice moderates, becomes persuasive. "I know it'll be a tough job. They'll guard the prisoners like the Crown Jewels. But find a way and Galapharma will triple the sum originally agreed upon."

"Triple! . . . Wait a minute. I just remembered something. A trick human pirates sometimes used to botch up our interrogations. It could work. Matsukawa will be puking like a pig and feel pretty bad, but he'll survive."

"Explain."

The bizarre expedient is described. "Trust me. It'll work. But you listen to me, Baldwin: I want the extra pay right now, while I'm on the com and able to verify. This is non-negotiable. And the same precautions apply as in your man's original arrangement with me."

"Agreed."

"You'd better tell me how you want to arrange the handover of the prisoners."

"That hasn't yet been decided. We'll be tracking you closely on your way to Earth. Perhaps you might seize control of the ship at one of the more remote fueling stops."

"Just like that!"

"When you've done the job, a broadband summons will bring us to you in short order."

"What's wrong with you setting up an ambush? Gala-pharma running short of heavy cruisers?"

"The Y700 could easily outmaneuver them . . . if it were flown by a competent pilot. And we can't risk the lives of the prisoners in a firefight. Find another way. Earn your excessively generous pay."

"All right. But Gala better be playing straight with me. I'm warning you, Baldwin. I know how to take care of myself."

"Take good care of Jim Matsukawa, my friend, and you'll find out just how generous Galapharma can be."

I slept among the roses and palm trees for fifty whole minutes before my phone buzzed.

"Yes."

"It's Matt. I have Karl Nazarian on the subspace com. I think you should talk to him."

The anxious sound of her voice was like an ice cube down my collar. I sat bolt upright.

"Is it bad news?" I demanded.

"*Plomazo* was attacked about half an hour ago. Karl and the others are all right. They're heading for Torngat Starport for minor repairs."

"Shit! . . . Torngat's about five thousand lights from here, isn't it?"

"Five thousand four hundred twenty-two," she said.

"Where are you?"

"The Port Authority building, on the Ring Promenade right next to the starport terminal."

"I'm on my way."

The spa's concierge knew all about me and my VIP associates. When I asked her for speedy transport, she volunteered to take me herself. But Cravat Dome was so small that the only personal ground vehicles were modified go-carts with a top speed of 15 kph. We rolled sedately to the opposite side of town while I ground my teeth in frustration. The Ring Promenade was a cantilevered floating mezzanine thirty meters above ground level that harbored small shops and office strips, interspersed with living greenery that cascaded over the parapet edge like the Hanging Gardens of Babylon. Matt was waiting for me at the Port Authority entrance as we rolled up the ramp. I thanked the concierge and hopped out.

"This way." She hurried off with me struggling to keep up with her. My freshly repaired leg ached like a sonuvabitch.

The last time I'd seen Matt Gregoire had been a fleeting, unfocused glimpse in Cravat's hospital, just before the medics hauled me away for repairs. She'd been euphoric then, sharing the Dagasatt triumph. Now the onyx-black eyes were somber and her cinnamon skin seemed pale. We didn't speak again until we reached the communication rooms.

She eyeballed the scanner on a locked room labeled DEDICATED COM—RESTRICTED ACCESS. The door rolled open to admit us. Inside was a bank of open-beam subspace transceivers connecting Cravat to Rampart Central on Seriphos, Fleet Security HQ on Tyrins, the Starcorp offices in Toronto, and each of the four Zone Patrol posts serving the Perseus Spur. No employees were on duty. They'd probably been cleared out on orders from Madame Vice President.

Matt sat at the com unit hooked to Seriphos, which was relaying the signal from Karl. I pulled up a chair as Nazarian's weathered face came onto the display.

He said, "Helly. Congrats on the Dagasatt caper. Matt told me about it. I'm sorry to rain on your parade."

"What happened?"

"The time-frame is important. Today at 0720 Zebra *Plomazo* was attacked by three light-cruiser-class starships." He gave the ship's coordinates at the time of engagement. "The aggressor vessels were of human manufacture, highly modified DAS-4 types a couple of rungs below our Y660 in assault capability. They made no attempt to communicate, just popped out of a dust cloud and started zapping. I, um, blew the crap out of them, but it was a close call. There were no aggressor survivors."

"Matt said you sustained damage."

"A minor hull breach. Hector says we're in no immediate danger. We're limping to Torngat, twenty lights distant, for a fix."

"That's not a Sheltok world, is it?" The big energy Concern owned most of the major starship fueling and maintenance stations in the Orion Arm. Since Sheltok was an ally of Galapharma, I wasn't anxious to do business with it. I'd already instructed Mimo to plot *Chispa*'s course using freesoil pit stops, even though the routing was less direct and a lot more expensive than following conventional shipping lanes.

"Torngat belongs to Macrodur. It's a winter resort world serving Sector Six. I think we'll be reasonably secure there . . . for a little while."

I caught his drift. "Right. We'll have to pick you guys up. We can be on Torngat in a little over three days. Our Y700 is big enough to carry everybody."

The old security man pulled a wry face. "Depends on who you include in the 'everybody' bag! Matt told me about your Operation Q crew. I think it's possible that one of them tipped off Galapharma to *Plomazo*'s course. And pretty damn recently at that, or we'd have been hit earlier along the route. There aren't that many private Y660s riding the void. It would have been easy to track us if the bad guys had a sizable observer net—like Gala—and knew what to look for."

"Christ! You could be right. But . . . I don't see how it could have happened. You surely can't suspect Mimo or Ivor of selling us out. And the new crew members signed on after you guys left. Maybe your bandits were real bandits after all."

"*Plomazo*'s too fast and well-armed to attract conventional pirates, even in triplicate. And there was no summons from the hostiles demanding surrender. They came at us with lethal intent."

Matt said, "The leak couldn't possibly have come from my Rampart Central office or the Seriphos starport crew. I made certain that the only people who knew that *Plomazo* carried Garth Wing Lee were personnel who had been vetted in duress for loyalty."

"I'll vouch for Lotte, Hector, and Cassius with my life," Karl stated. "My people are loyal."

"That leaves me and my folks, doesn't it?" I said dispiritedly.

"Seems so," said Karl. "Unless we had stone bad luck on one of our earlier fueling stops, and some informant told Gala security that *Plomazo* was passing through. We altered her ID, not that it helps much with such a distinctive boat. Drummond's spooks know Mimo's your good buddy. They might have put out an early APB on a Y660 starship, thinking you might be aboard, along with Lee."

"It could have happened that way," Matt said.

"I'm supposed to be dead," I reminded them.

"You've been resurrected before," Matt observed. "But I'm more inclined to believe the stool pigeon scenario. A fairly recent tipoff."

I shook my head. "It doesn't seem possible, after all my crew and I went through together."

"But you can't discount the possibility," Matt said. "Who else besides Mimo knew you were shipping Lee to Earth?"

I tried to remember. "Meem and I discussed the matter casually on the flight to Nogawa. We were wondering what Lotte Dietrich was going to find in the data-dump she'd taken from Garth Lee's ship—"

"She found a lot," Karl broke in. "But it'll keep. Go on, Helly."

"Um. We were in the dining saloon, drinking coffee after a

meal. Ivor was clearing the table. The new crew members had already finished eating and were gone."

"So Ivor could have overheard you," Matt said.

I blew up. "It's ridiculous to think he'd betray us!"

"Calm down," Karl said from the SS com. "The boy might not have realized that the information was sensitive. He could have passed it along innocently to one of the others."

"I'll check with him." Matt pulled out her pocket phone, tapped up a code and spoke. "This is Matt Gregoire. Where are you? . . . Good. Do you recall any conversations with Helly or Mimo during Operation Q where *Plomazo*'s mission to Earth was mentioned? In connection with Karl transporting a man named Garth Wing Lee? . . . Did you ever discuss the matter with members of the new crew? This is really important, Ivor . . . Okay. Thanks."

She cut off and said to me, "He remembers the messroom discussion. He swears he never passed on the information to anyone."

"I believe him," I said. "The leak—if there was one—must have come through me, but I'm damned if I can think how. Rats! I feel like a total schlump."

"The attack on *Plomazo* could have been a fluke. A piece of incredibly bad luck, just as Karl said."

"We'll go ahead on that assumption. For now, at any rate."

"You're the boss." Matt turned back to the SS com and spoke briskly to Karl. "Keep a close guard on Lee. There's an especially important question we failed to ask him during his psychoprobe session back on Seriphos. Helly and I will get back to you in a day or two, after we sort things out."

He nodded and ended the transmission.

"Important question?" I inquired dopily.

"Whether Lee himself is a Haluk demiclone."

"Oh, right. My brain has turned to cowflop."

She nodded in humiliating agreement. "The most obvious suspects are Ildiko Szabo and Joe Betancourt, but I'm at a loss to know how either of them could be long-term Gala agents. I picked them out of a hat when you asked me to find recruits for the operation. If either one defected to Gala, it must have been a spur of the moment decision, done for money."

"What are we going to do, Matt?" In the state I was in, I hardly had a clue.

"There's always psychoprobing."

"Aw, geez. Scramble my friends' brains on a fishing expedition? I can't do it, babe."

"Then we simply leave the two of them behind."

"Ildy saved my goddamn life on Dagasatt. She wants to see her folks back on Earth and I promised to bring her along. And Joe took out the Haluk ship that could have sunk our whole operation. He really needs money to start his charter operation, and we need another pilot to spell Mimo and me on the trip."

She thought about it. "If we secure the ship's SS com from everyone except you and me and Mimo, lock up the portable weapons, and do a buddy system arrangement with the crew to forestall crude forms of sabotage, we might be okay. If there is a Gala agent on board, he or she will have to be circumspect to avoid giving the show away—to say nothing of self-endangerment. Our traitor wants to live to spend the loot."

"Let's be up-front with everyone about the possibility of a spy being among us. If nothing else, it'll put the fink on notice." I looked at my wrist chronograph. "It's time for our little melodrama with Terence Hoy. And then we're out of here."

Ollie and Jim, looking crestfallen and accompanied by Fleet Security guards, were waiting in the anteroom when we all trooped past them into Hoy's office. The Port Traffic Manager, who was the de facto governor of Cravat, seemed nearly as uncomfortable as the prisoners. Matt had already warned him what was going to happen, explaining that it was a legal necessity so Rampart could plausibly deny having invaded Dagasatt.

It was plain to see that Terence Hoy fervently wished that the legal necessity was happening on someone else's planet.

Matt instructed the guards to wait outside for a while with the prisoners, then closed the door and checked to make sure that the props were there: a tall folding floorscreen, a vocal distortion device, and a bulky armored combat glove. She herself had brought along a zipped carrier bag that clinked.

Mimo, Ivor, Ildiko, and Joe stood behind the desk with Terence, witnesses to the upcoming proceedings. Matt stood in front. I hid behind the screen, which was set up at the left, arranged so the person in back of it couldn't be caught on the room's holovid recorder or seen by others in the room. I selected an artificial voice from the device menu, put the glove on, and said, "Testing, one-two!"

I sounded like Donald Duck, but nobody laughed.

"Very well," Matt said. "Terence, please activate the recorder."

He touched a pad on the desk console and we were rolling.

Matt faced the holocam, identified herself, announced the time, date, and place, and named those present. The last individual mentioned was one Geronimo, disenfranchised person and bounty hunter.

I stuck my gloved hand out from behind the screen and waggled my fingers in greeting.

"Mr. Geronimo," Matt said, "your desire to remain anonymous is understood and respected. Why have you met with us today?"

"I'm here," said the duck, "to formally offer to Rampart Starcorp the persons of two suspected felons—Oliver Schneider and James Matsukawa—apprehended by me pursuant to CHW Criminal Statute 22, Clause 743A."

"What is your fee?" Matt asked.

"One dollar and other good and valuable considerations."

I stuck out my gloved hand, and she put the coin into it. Then she opened the outer door and summoned Ollie and Jim and their guards.

"Are these men the ones you apprehended?"

"They are," I quacked from my hiding place. Schneider did a double take. Matsukawa stayed deadpan.

"Thank you for services rendered, Mr. Geronimo. I accept

delivery of Schneider and Matsukawa in the name of Rampart Starcorp. Guards, you may take the detainees back outside and wait with them there. And you, Mr. Geronimo, may also withdraw."

She told Terence to shut off the holocam. When its red eye winked off and the door closed, I came out from behind the screen, ditched the glove and the voice disguiser, and stood meekly before the Vice President for Confidential Services. The camera was reactivated.

"Are you the man sometimes known as Helmut Icicle," Matt asked me formally, "who knowingly misused a Rampart Red Card on the planet Nogawa-Krupp after your employment had been terminated by Rampart Interstellar Corporation?"

I admitted it. She ordered me to surrender the card and levied a fine of one dollar. I returned her lucky buck and she pronounced my trespass forgiven. Then she gave me a new Red Card made out to Asahel Frost and announced that I was herewith rehired as Vice President for Special Projects, enfranchised and fully empowered to exercise all duties and offices of the alpha-level corporate position, including that of *praefectus conlegius* of the Commonwealth Judiciary.

She then remanded to the custody of Asahel Frost the persons of Oliver Schneider and James Matsukawa, detainees suspected of committing multiple crimes against Rampart Interstellar Corporation and the Commonwealth of Human Worlds. I accepted responsibility for them, declaring that I would, as empowered by law, interrogate them *sub duritia* en route to Earth, and turn over psychotronic evidence deposed by them to prosecutors of the Commonwealth Judiciary Tribunal upon my arrival in Toronto. (I'd also transmit the depositions via SS com to Eve as soon as they were complete; but their final validation would be delayed until Matt and I were able to affirm them in person.)

Matt thanked Terence Hoy and the other witnesses and declared the proceedings at an end. The camera was shut off. She made three copies of the holovid, gave one dime to Terence, one to me, and kept the third herself.

Then she lifted the carrier bag onto the desk, unzipped it, and pulled out two bottles of Veuve Cliquot NV and a package of disposable glasses. Corks popped and we drank to Rampart's success and the confusion of her enemies. Mimo Bermudez offered expensive Cohiba Robusto cigars in plastic cylinders to those assembled. Mellowed by the champagne, Terence Hoy took two of the Cuban stogies, Ildiko Szabo took one, Joe Betancourt took three, and the rest of us passed.

The necessary business being concluded, we said goodbye to the friendly folks of Cravat, collected the prisoners, climbed into *Chispa*, and set off for Earth at top ross pseudovelocity.

Chapter 12

I'd promised the doctor to rest in bed for at least two days before attempting any strenuous activity; psychoprobing prisoners fit the "strenuous" category in spades. But before I embarked for dreamland I contacted Eve on the subspace communicator to give her the news.

To my surprise, I tracked her down in the Toronto offices of Rampart, working very late in the CEO suite. She was dressed in a summer outfit of silver and carnelian voile that included a smart suit, dress gloves, and an astounding cartwheel hat featuring a heap of silk daisies and an opaque veil that completely hid her features.

My greeting consisted of, "Good God! You look like the Merry Widow."

She laughed, removed the headgear and gloves, and tossed them onto the communication console. "I put them back on again when your call came through. I wanted you to enjoy the full effect of the ensemble. Conceals the mutation rather nicely, doesn't it? I was quite a sensation at Chanterelles when I dined with Gunter this evening . . . and even more of a smash at our meeting with the Macrodur Chairman and Chief Financial Officer this afternoon."

"Macrodur! What the devil were you doing there?"

"I'll explain it all after you've told me your news. Incidentally, I'm very happy to see you alive, Asa. I hope you'll let me inform the rest of the family about your survival. Poor Simon was crushed."

"That'll be the day . . . Ah, rats. You might as well tell the old buzzard that the prodigal son has risen from the dead.

Better keep Dan and Beth in the dark for the time being. They're too tight with Zed, and I don't want him to know I'm on the prowl. Not just yet." I paused for dramatic effect. "Of course, Ollie Schneider's capture should remain top secret until we land in Toronto."

"You nabbed him!" she exulted. "I knew you would."

"Another overconfident female. The fact is, I nearly made a mess of it. But we won out, thanks to a gang of good people. Matt Gregoire and I will interrogate Schneider en route to Earth and transmit his deposition to you as soon as we can. He's agreed to testify freely in exchange for immunity. I'm beginning to think we should file the civil suit without delay. As soon as Ollie's deposition is validated."

"We'll have to examine Schneider's raw evidence and get an opinion from Dan and the legal department, but I'm inclined to agree with you."

"Have you talked to Ef Sontag yet about the Haluk threat?"

She hesitated a moment before replying. "Just a preliminary conversation to alert him that we might submit something interesting. I—I thought we agreed that I'd wait for Karl to arrive with Garth Wing Lee before meeting Sontag."

"Karl's going to be a little late." I told her about the attack on *Plomazo* and my decision to pick up the crew and Lee, balancing the bad news with the prospect that both Lee and Jim Matsukawa might turn out to be Haluk disguised as humans.

"That would be marvelous luck if it's true," she said, sighing, "because we're out of luck with the Fake Emily demiclone. Her brother authorized a disinterment and I sent some of my trusted people to Yorkshire for the body, but the coffin was empty. I presume Gala's agents got there first."

"Rats. What about the Haluk corpse at Tokyo U?"

"We managed to get that—along with a new copy of Professor Shibuya's research data confirming the presence of human DNA and eradication of the allomorphic trait. Your friend Beatrice Mangan is keeping the remains in a private mortuary in Fenelon Falls north of Toronto until we're ready to turn all of our Haluk threat evidence over to the Commonwealth Assembly. Xenoaffairs already has a copy of

Shibuya's report on the body, but it's classified Cosmic and I didn't want to risk having some suborned SXA bureaucrat make it 'unavailable.' "

"It's just what the bastards would do . . . Now tell me what kind of rumpus you've been raising on the Rampart front, Madame CEO. Were you elected by acclamation?"

"Of course! Cousin Zed almost suffered cardiac arrest when Simon renewed my nomination, but it did pass unanimously and was affirmed by stakeholder vote. After I told the board about my new venture credit scheme, Aunt Emma made an amazing little speech, saying how pleased Uncle Ethan would have been at my election."

"Zed must have enjoyed that."

"He sat there with absolutely no expression on his face, while his mother burbled on about how wonderful it was that *I* was willing to fight for her late husband's dream against all odds, while some others, unnamed, were willing to let it die. The rest of the board members were rather nonplussed. So was I, frankly! It was a Mouse That Roared situation. I almost felt sorry for Zed. Emma has always been so meek and willing to follow his lead."

"It sounds like Katje's got at Emma and brainwashed her. Revolt of the Little Old Ladies!"

"Emma may not stay brainwashed," Eve said. "She leans with the wind, and Zed's flying hurricane flags."

"Was Katje at the meeting?"

"No. Simon had her proxy. Do you think Mom used the same arguments on Aunt Emma that Pop used on her?"

I laughed. "Why not? Converts are always the most fanatical missionaries. But never mind that. Tell me about your venture scheme."

She explained it briefly, then told me how the prospectus had been submitted to Macrodur's financial arm, with the Concern's Chairman in attendance. I gave a low whistle of amazement. "Stanislawski met with you himself? That's wild! Did the Archnerd laugh in your faces and send you packing?"

"Certainly not. I told you I'd been doing my homework.

Adam Stanislawski has a long-standing personal animus toward Alistair Drummond. Mind you, there's small chance of the credit coming through unless Rampart is seen to be pulling its socks up."

"Well, it would help if you guys discovered another rozkoz."

I meant that as a joke, referring to the confection more delicious than chocolate that had founded the fortunes of Rampart Starcorp fifty years ago.

But she said, "We've done that already, Asa. Only we failed to realize its true potential. I've done a lot of thinking since the last time we spoke, even revised some of my financial strategy as a result." She paused and seemed to take a deep breath. "The commodity that's going to make Rampart a valued corporate collaborator of Macrodur is called PD32:C2."

My poor old brain was so full of horseshit and gun smoke that it took a moment for the full import of her words to hit me. Then I almost screamed into the communicator.

"*What?* Evie, have you lost it? Or am I speaking to your friggin' demiclone?"

"Calm down! Consider the prospect rationally. Is it really so unthinkable? I'm talking about allomorph eradication only, of course, after CHW makes a new treaty with the Haluk. One having stringent safeguards to ensure that the vector is used for nothing else—especially not demicloning. Rampart would then sell the vector to the aliens directly, at moderately fair prices."

"I can't believe you're saying this!"

But she continued serenely on. "We're assuming Galapharma is clobbered by our civil suit and forced into receivership first. That goes without saying. ICS might even obtain testimony against Gala from the other conspirator Concerns, in exchange for slapping them on the wrist rather than indicting them along with Gala."

"Legitimizing the Haluk trade conspiracy retroactively!"

"It's been done before, Asa. With the Joru, Kallenyi, and Y'tata."

My retort was bitter. "And just like before we'll have funny business going on under the table—embargoed commodities peddled to the aliens on the sly! I know the way it works, Evie. Trying to stop it was my job at ICS Enforcement. Whenever we'd plug one leak in the dike, another would spring up. Except the Joru and Kallenyi and Y'tata don't want to take over the goddamn galaxy . . ."

"I discussed the idea with Gunter at dinner this evening. He thinks a new Haluk treaty might fly. He also understands the realpolitik of the situation: throughout human history, implacable enemies have been transformed into friendly trading partners—given the proper incentive. Dan's wife Norma will be discreetly sounding out some of her Commonwealth Assembly colleagues, and Gunter is feeling the pulse of his contacts in ICS."

"What about Macrodur?"

"Stanislawski and his top execs know about the Haluk–PD32:C2 connection already, and about the existing illegal trading situation between the aliens and Galapharma. We—we had to put a guarded mention of it into the prospectus to show a major profit potential."

I let out a groan of despair. "Oh, Evie."

"The data were submitted under the strictest confidentiality, and we didn't name Gala's fellow Big Seven conspirators to Macrodur. That would have been strategically counterproductive."

An awful certainty had invaded me as she spoke. "And is it *also* strategically counterproductive to submit our evidence of a Haluk expansionist threat to Efrem Sontag right now?"

She did not answer for a moment. "I admit I'm tempted to reconsider our timing of the revelation. You can understand why."

"Well, of course! We wouldn't want to show what scheming fuckers the Haluk really are if the Assembly is debating a new trade treaty with them—and Rampart is using them as a bargaining chip in its pitch to Macrodur. Heaven forbid that we paint the aliens as ravening bogeymen rather than potential customers!"

"You're oversimplifying matters, Asa."

"Yeah. That's me, all right. I'm just an ex-cop and a dive-charter skipper, not a hotshot corporate schemer or a politician. But I've got a nose for bad guys, and all my instincts tell me the Haluk are seriously bad."

"If Rampart is ruined, we won't be in a position to do *anything* about the Haluk. Timing, Asa! It's all about timing, don't you see? And preserving our options."

"That's what Simon said just before I quit Rampart. Now you're trying to convince me that he was right all along. Simon and his fucking Big Picture—"

"We won't bury the Haluk evidence. We'll simply hold it in abeyance."

"I can't accept that."

She drew herself up. "You'll have to. I'm the CEO of Rampart Starcorp as well as a woman who's been personally victimized by the Haluk. And it's my decision that we'll wait on the Sontag presentation until Macrodur gives us a yes or no. Will you continue to stand by me, Asa? Or walk away, as you did with Simon?"

"Evie—"

"Are you with me?"

"Yes," I said.

The half-alien face was less easy to read than one fully human, but her relief was palpable. "Thank you. I give you my solemn word that I will not allow the Haluk threat to be concealed or minimized. The moment Rampart is safe, I'll go to Sontag."

"I believe you."

A ferocious glint came into her eyes. "You know, if our prospectus is accepted by Macrodur, I think there's an excellent chance ICS will approve Concern status for Rampart immediately. Whereupon this comedy will be over—and Alistair Drummond can shit bricks and die!"

"Unless he takes over Rampart before your grand happy ending comes to pass," I cautioned, "in which case the Haluk will continue to lead Galapharma and its confederates around by the nose, as I suspect they've been doing from the start of the conspiracy."

"Drummond's not going to win, dammit!"

"Evie, he's already holding a hand with four aces while you and I are still trying to fill our shaky royal flush. And don't forget there could be a homegrown joker in the pack."

Her indomitable demeanor wilted, just a little. "The possible traitor inside our family . . ."

"My first priority in the interrogations," I assured her, "will be to ask Ollie Schneider if such a person exists. But he might not know the answer. You've got to take the strongest precautions—keep alert for bushwhack tactics from Drummond *or* his inside man. I'm serious about this! The family's in mortal danger. Drummond won't hesitate to use violence to get his way, especially if he gets wind of your Macrodur prospectus. He won't just surrender if he sees his scheme starting to fall apart."

Any more than a rabid skunk will.

"Believe me, Asa. I do appreciate the danger. I'm doing everything in my power to keep all of us secure. We have bodyguards and armored hoppers, and Mom is—Oh, God, I nearly forgot! She wants to speak to you urgently. Ever since I told her to ignore reports of your death, she's begged me to contact you. I didn't dare tell her what shenanigans you were up to."

I caught my breath. "She's not—"

"Her health seems no better, no worse, than before. But I think you should call her at once."

"All right. What the hell time is it in Arizona?"

"Nearly midnight. But Mom sleeps very lightly these days. She'd want you to call now."

"All right. I'll do it as soon as we're finished."

The alien face smiled at me. "Thank you for everything, Asa."

"You haven't done so badly yourself, Evie. I'll get back to you."

"Goodbye."

When the screen went to standby, I made the call to Katje's penthouse apartment in Phoenix. There was a wait before it was put through.

I got up and stalked around *Chispa*'s wardroom, which I'd appropriated as my office and improvised interrogation chamber. The last of the Perseus suns zipped past the viewport like spooked fireflies. We were entering Black Gap, the nearly starless region that separated the Spur from the Orion Arm of the galaxy.

I decided that I was thirsty after the confrontation with Eve. Booze was a no-no given the chemicals pumped into me, so I ordered a big orange juice from the food unit and sat drinking and brooding with the lights turned low.

Over the past six months, my mother had procrastinated endlessly when I urged her to put her quarterstake shares into a trust, not understanding—or refusing to acknowledge—that continuing to vote them herself placed her life in jeopardy. Katje's position, which she'd patiently reiterated to me—and which I had to admit made sense—was that only she could ensure that the Reversionist "charities" she championed would receive the shares' income. In any other arrangement, most especially a trust administered by her children and their legal advisors, there was a potential for declaring her mentally incompetent and cutting off funding to the unpopular political orgnizations, which advocated Insap rights and limiting the power of the Hundred Concerns.

I wondered whether my older brother Dan or younger sister Beth had been putting pressure on Katje since the last board meeting. Or had Cousin Zed resumed his insidious meddling, urging her to make the Reversionists an outright gift of the shares immediately, knowing the money-hungry groups would side with him in voting for the Galapharma takeover?

In my present state of decrepitude, I really didn't want to think about all that convoluted financial stuff. But I dearly loved my mother, so I was ready to give her whatever advice I could.

Her face appeared on the screen at last, devastated by age and illness but as invincible as ever. Her hair was white, tightly curled to minimize its sparseness. The Delft-blue eyes were still bright, but deeply sunken in shadowed sockets. She disapproved of all forms of geriatric genetic engineering on principle, especially those that allowed the rejuvenated elderly to cling to power at the expense of the younger generation. Katje Vanderpost sat in an easychair in the library of her penthouse, wearing a dusty-rose peignoir trimmed with lace of the same color. She looked as though she weighed less than forty-five kilos.

"Asa! Darling, it's so good to see you. Eve refused to tell me where you were. It was someplace dangerous, wasn't it?"

"Of course not," I lied. "How are you, Mom?"

She gave a light laugh. "You know how the doctors are. Always wanting me to submit to some damnfool treatment. 'To keep me going,' they say! But they never say *where*, do they? I'm seventy-eight and my useful work is long since done. Well . . . most of it." Her smile was almost cunning. "Will you be home soon?"

"I'm on my way. I'll see you in just a little over a week."

"That's wonderful. Wonderful." Her head sank and the smile slowly dissolved to pensiveness. "I must ask you an important question."

Here it comes, I thought. "Certainly."

"Are you still a Throwaway?"

"Why, no." What's *this*? "Just today I was officially rehired by Rampart. I'm a Vice President again. A citizen in good standing."

"Oh, good. Gerry Gonzalez wasn't sure it would be legal if you were disenfranchised." She turned away for a moment, then held up an e-notebook and tapped a pad. "There! It's done."

Gonzalez was a fire-breathing young Phoenix attorney, head of LISA, the most vocal of the Reversionist lobby groups. He was also Katje's private solicitor, in spite of the best efforts of Simon, Dan, and Bethany to dislodge him.

"Mom, what are you up to now?"

"Well, I know you were concerned about—about my personal safety, if I retained my quarterstake vote on the Rampart board."

"And about Dan and Beth, too. Surely you haven't forgotten that threatening note Simon received after Eve's kidnapping."

"But the children are very well-guarded. And so am I, of course. I never leave the apartment anymore except for an occasional visit to the Sky Ranch."

"Even so—"

"Asa, dear, the point is moot! No one can pressure me now. I've taken steps, after *very* careful consideration. You know, I thought I'd found the right solution when I decided to vote in favor of the merger at the next-to-the-last board meeting. But your father was very persuasive. He made me realize that I didn't have the right to unilaterally dismantle the Starcorp that Dirk helped to found. On the other hand, I'm determined that my charities not be deprived of the funding they need so desperately."

"So what will you do? Turn your shares over to them now? Or make Gonzalez sole trustee?"

"Oh, no. It would be too much of a temptation, you see. In a Galapharma merger, my quarterstake would increase tremendously in value. I want the charities to prosper, but not at the expense of my brother's dream. No—I've decided to do something completely different. Gerry was dubious when I first told him about it, but he came around in the end. The charities will continue to receive their just due, Rampart will have its chance to survive, and Daniel and Bethany and I will be safe from Galapharma's threats." The blue eyes twinkled as she held up the computer notebook again. "Guess what I've done?"

I scowled. "Mom, no more games."

One shoulder rose in a minute gesture of resignation. I was no fun at all. Then she said it.

"I've just made a deed of gift to you, Asa. My entire quarterstake, free of encumbrance. I know I can trust you to deal justly with the Reversionists. You made your feelings clear about the matter years ago. And I'm also confident that you'll do everything in your power to help Eve save Rampart."

"My God! Mom—you can't do this!"

"Yes, I can," she said, in a voice as bright and hard as the big diamond on her left ring finger. "And I have. The deed was executed and witnessed days ago. All I had to do was finalize it. My will has already been modified to reflect the change. Put a data-dime into your communicator, Asa, so I can send you the transcript."

"Give your shares to Eve," I pleaded. "Or to Dan and Beth. I don't want this."

I've run from it all my life . . .

"Eve, Dan, and Beth will inherit your father's stake and divide it equally, twelve and one-half percent for each of them. But none of them would carry out my wishes in regard to the charities. They simply don't believe that galactic Big Business is an abomination, as you and I do."

"But— "

"Do as I say, dear. The dime."

I took a microdisk from the little dispenser on the console and slipped it into the slot. A red telltale flashed on. Then it turned green. I felt a sick lump in my gut. This wasn't happening.

Katje leaned forward and kissed the com display. Kissed the image of my face. "I must go now, dear. I'm very tired and I suspect you are, too. We'll have a long talk when you get here. Please don't let anyone know about this until we've spoken. Especially not your father. I want to be there when you tell Simon yourself."

I had to smile. "Oh, Katje. You're a wicked old woman."

"Sleep tight, Asa." Her head tilted and a bemused expression came over her. "I don't usually rest too well myself. But I think I will, tonight."

The communicator went to blue.

I stumbled off to my cabin, took the medication prescribed by the Cravat doctor, and hibernated for fifty-one hours.

When I woke up, I went to the wardroom, unlocked it, removed the dime from the SS com, plugged it into my own notebook and called up the data.

It hadn't been a dream. I still owned one-quarter of Rampart Starcorp.

* * *

I had just finished eating an enormous breakfast after my long sleep, and was back in the wardroom preparing the equipment for the first stage of Ollie Schneider's interrogation, when the door chime sounded.

I unlocked the door. Mimo stood there. His Don Quixote face was somber. "May I come in? There's something I must tell you."

We sat down at the conference table. Whatever he had to say, it was bad. I braced myself.

"Helly, your sister Eve contacted us two days ago with some very sad news. About your mother."

An invisible monster took hold of my heart and squeezed. "Oh, no. Katje's dead, isn't she!"

"Yes. I'm very sorry, *mi hijo*. Eve called a few hours after you had retired. She told me not to waken you when I explained that you were under medication and desperately in need of rest. You'll want to call her for the particulars. Eve did tell me that your mother's death was peaceful, in her sleep."

Numbly, I thanked him.

"Matt wonders if you would prefer to postpone the questioning of Schneider."

"No. Give me an hour. Then ask her to join me. We'll carry on as planned."

He nodded and left the room.

I didn't weep; my tears tended to flow at odd, idiosyncratic times and not according to default emotional programming. I'd mourn Katje Vanderpost in my own way, when the time seemed right.

Operating on mental autopilot, with the reality of the situation accepted and yet held firmly at arm's length, I opened the locked SS communicator and placed a call to Eve, only to discover that for some reason she was not available. I couldn't bear the thought of speaking to Dan or Beth. My brother was an icy, methodical type who hadn't hesitated to call Katje a silly fool for resisting the trust arrangement. My younger sister, just the opposite in temperament, was very likely crushed by sorrow. That left only one other person for me to talk to . . .

It was barely morning in the high country of Arizona's Tonto Forest. He would rise early, as was his usual habit when in residence at the Sky Ranch, breakfasting before dawn so he could take a good long horseback ride before the intense summer heat cooked the resin out of the ponderosa pine needles and drove the birds and animals of the plateau into hiding.

The ranch manager said he would transfer my SS call to a vidphone out in the barn, where my father was saddling his horse himself. When I asked if the InSec bodyguards were with Simon, the manager told me that the boss adamantly refused to have company on the dawn ride, insisting on being alone so he could "think." The security people were ordered to follow at a distance as best they could, some mounted and the others riding in a Land Rover.

Simon picked up and gave me a curt greeting. "Hello, Asa. I was wondering when you'd get around to calling. Where the hell are you?"

He was wearing a sweat-stained Resistol straw hat with a silver band and a light cotton shirt. The relayed image was none too clear, but I could discern that his crumpled, unshaven face bore the unmistakable patina of a monumental bender. Simon also had his own way of grieving.

"I'm on my way home," I said. "We're about six days out after refueling at Tillinghast Starbase. I just now heard about Katje."

"Yeah." His gaze intensified as he came closer to the wall-mounted video pickup. "Just *what* did you hear?"

"Only that she'd died in her sleep. Eve left a message with Mimo a couple of days ago. I've been totally zoned out. Recovering from the Oliver Schneider retrieval."

"Uh—Eve told me about that. Good work. I never expected—I mean, when you went back to Kedge-Lockaby I thought . . ."

I knew what he'd thought. But my flaws weren't at issue. "Katje. Was it her heart?"

"No." He lifted his head, and I realized that his green eyes were inflamed more with fury than with sorrow. "It was murder."

"Jesus Christ! How?"

"A cup of tea poisoned with sephrosamine, an exotic compound that leaves no trace in the body. But our Internal Security people found the goddamn used tea bag right there in Katje's kitchen."

"Do they have a suspect?"

"Yes and no. That old housekeeper of hers, Concha Cisneros, left a note before taking a swan dive off the penthouse balcony. Said 'the man' told her the tea would be harmless, that she'd never meant to hurt Katje, that poor Freddy wasn't to blame."

"Freddy? Who the fuck is Freddy?"

"InSec pieced it together. Seems the housekeeper has a grandson, a priest, who was a bit of a chickenhawk. Got therapy, then fell off the wagon. Whoever 'the man' is, he threatened to blow the whistle on pedophilic Father Freddy unless Concha served the tea."

"Alistair Drummond! That filthy bastard has to be responsible. He wanted Mom's quarterstake to go to the Reversionists."

Simon's red-rimmed optics stared at me without blinking. "And now it has. But there's nothing to implicate the Insaplovers or Galapharma in Katje's killing. Nothing at all."

"Probably not." I took a ragged breath. "But it won't save Drummond's slimy hide. I'll skin him alive for this."

Simon uttered an ungodly chuckle. "We'll see which of us gets to him first with the Buck knife."

"Have—have you thought about funeral arrangements yet?"

He shook his head with a sheepish air. "Tell the truth, I don't know what she would have wanted. Dan's going to Phoenix later this morning. He'll see that lawyer of Katje's about her will—what's his name? Geraldo Gonzalez. If she didn't specify, we'll do a cremation and scatter her ashes on the Sky Ranch. If you like, we can hold off the services until you get here."

"No," I decided. "It's not necessary. You just go ahead."

I knew what kind of memorial my mother really would have wanted, and it had nothing to do with preachers and flowers and bone dust blowing in the mountain wind. She wanted justice for the human-exploited indigenous peoples of the galaxy, an impossible dream.

Or was it?

My own youthful ideals in that direction, long since submerged in disillusion and misfortune, gave a wan flicker. Chief Divisional Inspector A. E. Frost had seen his noble ambitions ruthlessly crushed, and Helmut Icicle was too mired in self-pity to care about abused aliens. But Asahel Frost, quarterstakeholder in an *Amalgamated Concern*, just might be able to make a difference . . .

The feeble spark flared mischievously, just for an instant, then subsided back into dormancy. Speculation along those lines was not only premature, it was damn near laughable.

Shows what I knew.

"About Katje's will," Simon was saying. "This Gonzalez fella is a notorious Reversion Party activist. She probably made him trustee for all the groups inheriting her shares. According to Starcorp bylaws, the quarterstake trustee gets an automatic seat on the board and can demand an immediate meeting. Dan and Zed are champin' at the bit, all eager for it, damn their eyes. They just want the hassle over and done with."

"Simon, that's not—"

But he barged ahead with his scenario of corporate doom.

"Gonzalez'll call for a vote on the merger and say 'Aye.' Thora Scranton will join him, voting the Small Stakeholders' twenty-five percent. If Emma Bradbury votes along with them—which I think is most likely—Gala flat-out rakes in the pot. If Emma defies Zed and throws her twelve-point-five in with me, we end up with a fifty-fifty *stalemate* and I have to poll the other board members. You know what that'll mean! Votes against Galapharma: Emma, Gunter, and Eve. Votes in favor: Zed, Dunne, Rivello, Scranton, Beth, Dan, and Gonzalez. Six-four Galapharma—and *adios, muchachos*."

He finally ran out of steam, giving me the chance to say, "Wrong!"

"That's the way it'll be," he said gruffly.

"No it won't, Pop." And I told him why, watching the blotchy color drain from his ravaged face and his mouth fall open in shock and disbelief.

"An unencumbered gift? To *you*? My sweet Lord! How—how *could* she?"

Poor old Simon Frost didn't know whether to shit or go blind. His chagrin was almost laughable. Rescued by the scapegrace son and bent cop!

Twice over, actually.

He finally mumbled, inanely, "Don't tell me you're gonna hand over the stake earnings to that gang of xeno-hugging kooks! If you reinvested it in Rampart—"

"The financial aspect is none of your damn business," I snapped. "The only thing that concerns you is my vote. Me plus you plus Emma equals a winning combo. Even if Emma backs out, you and I still have the 62.5 to flatten the opposition."

"Yes." I could barely hear his voice, and he'd lowered his head so that his face was deeply shadowed by the brim of his beat-up hat. Then he looked full at me, the impact of my words finally coming home to him. "Yes, by God! *Yes!*"

"There's only one way Drummond can salvage the situation now," I warned. "By eliminating you."

"Let the cocksuckin' pencil-dick sidewinder try!" Raging green eyes that were identical to my own blazed like those of a catamount caught by a jacklight.

"He will, Simon. Count on it. Unless you want to change your own will. Pass your entire stake on to Eve, rather than dividing it among her and Dan and Beth."

"Wouldn't be fair," he growled. "Especially now that you got yours."

Oh, boy. "Well, at least start thinking more seriously about your own safety. Lay off the solitary morning rides—for the next six days, anyhow, until I get to Earth and we torpedo the takeover. Eve and I have decided Rampart should file the civil suit immediately, as soon as Schneider's evidence is validated. I want you there in Toronto when we march into the Judiciary Tribunal."

"Dammit-all, Asa, I don't need the likes of you giving me orders!"

"You listen to me and listen good, you old fool! I just about died on Dagasatt collecting Ollie Schneider for you. And I sure as hell didn't risk my neck and get a bunch of other people killed just so a mule-headed old fart could screw things up through his own idiot carelessness. You want to see Alistair Drummond get what's coming to him, you better do what I fuckin' well tell you to do!"

"Huh." A grin broke over his face like sunrise over the Sierra Ancha. "Really think you're hot shit, don't you."

"Lukewarm, anyhow." I cut off the subspace communicator.

Matt and I interrogated Oliver Schneider for only three hours in the initial session, working him so gently that his vital signs almost never registered above the normal range.

The first important question I asked produced a disappointing result. Schneider could not say with certainty whether a member of the Frost family, or one of the Rampart Board of Directors, was secretly in league with Galapharma.

If such a person did exist, Schneider was inclined to put Zared Frost at the top of the list of suspects. Cousin Zed had hired Schneider and encouraged his sweeping reorganization of the Security Department inherited from Karl Nazarian. Zed made no bones about his admiration of Ollie's abilities. He'd rubber-stamped dubious changes in security protocols that gave InSec wider access to sensitive financial and legal material that would ordinarily have been outside the purlieu of that department, changes that had eased theft of data by Schneider's moles and pinpointed field operations vulnerable to sabotage. Zed had also defended the security chief's innocence right up until the moment Ollie and his buddies had flown the coop.

But did Schneider have any positive evidence linking Zed to Galapharma? Not really. My cousin's actions could be ascribed just as easily to naiveté and misplaced trust as to malice.

The next question I asked Oliver Schneider was, "Are you a Haluk demiclone?"

He burst out laughing. He said, "Abso-fucking-lutely *no*!"

The machines indicated he told the truth.

With that out of the way, we simply told him to relate his involvement with Galapharma from the beginning, in as much detail as he could remember. He complied with hardly any prompting from us.

Schneider had been tentatively approached by Quillan McGrath, alias Bronson Elgar, in 2228, around about the same time that I was being set up to take a fall in the ICS. He was able to tell me positively that my frame-up was personally engineered by Tyler Baldwin, Alistair Drummond's head of security, in order to get me out of the picture before the active takeover attempt began. They feared, quite rightly, that I might use my high position in the Enforcement Division of the Interstellar Commerce Secretariat to sniff out a conspiracy aimed at the family Starcorp. Drummond had ordered me killed outright; it was Baldwin who convinced the Gala CEO that my spectacular disgrace would better serve the cause by doing a mindfuck on my father and softening him up for the multipronged takeover assault.

Shortly after I was convicted, Oliver Schneider was hooked and reeled in by Baldwin, agreeing to become a key player in the conspiracy to devalue Rampart. Among other things, he arranged for the murder of Yaoshuang Qiu, a key executive, hatched sabotage schemes, fomented Insap insurrections on Rampart worlds, and engineered the pernicious manipulation of data. Ollie's compensation for the chicanery was a substantial wad of Galapharma stock, plus a humongous amount of cash deposited to a secret account on Saraia-Beta, the notorious freesoil haven for dirty money.

Being nobody's fool, Schneider took out his insurance policy as soon as he entered Gala's covert employ. He prepared two duplicate packets of incriminating materials, including holovids of McGrath and Baldwin made secretly during the recruiting sessions, sealed them, and deposited them with a venerable Toronto law firm of irreproachable character. One of the firm's senior partners, Jaswinder Singh, had gone to McGill University with Schneider and they had shared many an undergraduate romp. Details of these long-ago escapades, narrated by Ollie at unfailing intervals of four weeks while his friend checked his voice with a stress-indicator, formed the simple "code" ensuring that one sealed packet remained in the law firm's vault, and the other in a safe deposit box in Singh's bank. According to Schneider's instructions, if he failed to call Singh and relate a genuine anecdote—or if his voice pattern indicated that the communication was made under duress—the packets were to be hand-delivered to ICS Enforcement and the Chief Prosecutor of the Commonwealth Judiciary. The same procedure was to be followed in the event of Schneider's death, from any cause. Naturally, Singh, the guarantor of the insurance policy, received a handsome emolument.

The next insurance call to him was due in three days. I decided to let Ollie make it in advance. It would be disastrous to *my* corporate strategy to have Schneider's incriminating balloon go up ahead of schedule, and I was already feeling leery about what we might encounter when we approached Torngat.

Further gleanings from Schneider's excellent memory:

After my sister Eve was rescued from her kidnappers, Karl Nazarian's sleuthing fingered Ollie and four of his close associates in Rampart Security as traitors. They fled Seriphos and requested asylum from the Galapharma resident agent on the Haluk planet Artiuk. By that time Elgar/McGrath was deceased, thanks to me, and his position assumed by Erik Skogstad.

Skogstad psychoprobed the fugitive Ollie with exceptional rigor—"Reamed me out like a Halloween pumpkin!"—and learned about the insurance policy. Unfortunately for Galapharma, the Toronto law firm's vault proved to be impregnable—as did the safe deposit box—and Jaswinder

Singh was too politically connected to be coerced and too straitlaced to be bribed.

So Schneider was permitted to live, at least until the contents of his dangerous packets became irrelevant and immaterial to any civil action against Galapharma Amalgamated Concern by Rampart.

Connected to our psychotronic machines, Oliver Schneider readily agreed to hand over the packets of evidence to us, provided that Rampart's CEO reiterated my promise of immunity in the presence of his solicitor friend.

I told him that Eve would be delighted to do so. It was arranged that Ollie would call Jaswinder Singh on the SS com immediately, and make an appointment to meet him at his office upon our arrival in Toronto. Singh, the evidence packets, and Ollie would then proceed with me and my party to Rampart Tower. Shortly after that, Eve, Simon, Dan, and I would draw a legal line in the sand, and invite Alistair Drummond and Galapharma to a shootout at the Rampart corral.

When Matt and I concluded the first interrogation session—and the subspace call to Singh was accomplished—we escorted the prisoner back to the brig. He was suffering only a minimal amount of reactionary discomfort. We planned to limit Schneider's questioning to three easy hours in the morning and three in the afternoon. With six days remaining of the trip to Earth, we figured we had ample time to drain his brain of anything relevant.

When we weren't working on Ollie, we'd grill Jim Matsukawa with considerably less tenderness.

Matt and I had lunch, then returned to the wardroom where we transmitted the results of Ollie's first session to Eve. Then we prepared a list of topics for Gala's Dagasatt duty officer. Among the most crucial:

1. Are the Haluk planning to wage war on the human race?
2. Why are the Haluk producing humanoid demiclones?
3. What does Galapharma know about demiclone production?

4. Where are the other demiclone facilities located?
5. Are you a Haluk demiclone?
6. Who else among the high-ranking Galapharma agents and executive personnel are Haluk demiclones?
7. How many humanoid demiclones exist and where are they?
8. Do the Haluk possess starships capable of a pseudo-velocity in excess of seventy ross? How many? What armament do they carry?
9. What was happening on the Haluk planet Artiuk a few days ago, when the Servant of Servants of Luk met with representatives of Galapharma's trading associates?
10. Who was the fourth person Jim called in Toronto, when the Dagasatt facility was attacked by me?

When we had the answers, we were going to forward them to Eve immediately. Even though she intended to delay her show-and-tell with Efrem Sontag, I wanted Jim's data safe in her files. With a possible traitor aboard the starship, plus God-knew-what waiting for us at Torngat, there was a real risk that we might not make it to Earth.

Unlike the evidence from Schneider, which pertained to a civil suit and had to be personally validated by the interrogators—Matt and me—in order to be legally admissible, information about an alien plot against humanity was "intelligence." Once Sontag had it in hand, it would be evaluated with the utmost diligence even if all of us aboard *Chispa* died, and Alistair Drummond destroyed Rampart.

At least I hoped that's what would happen . . .

When we were ready to begin on Matsukawa, Matt called Ivor on her intercom and asked that he and Mimo bring the prisoner forward. After a few minutes' delay, Ivor replied.

"I'm sorry, Matt, but Jim appears to be ill."

She and I exchanged glances. I asked, "How so?"

In his meticulous, pedantic fashion Ivor told us. "His hands are cold and clammy, his forehead is covered with cold perspiration, and he complains of nausea, weakness, and excessive production of saliva."

"Bring him here anyhow," I ordered. Then I told Matt, "Go get one of those diagnosticon gadgets from sick bay. We'll find out if Jimbo is faking."

"Maybe he's terrified," Matt suggested, heading for the door.

"If that's all it is, we're okay. But if the guy's caught a genuine bug, we'll have to put off the interrogation. Even human sickees give anomalous responses to the machines."

She nodded and went out, leaving me to consider some other technical aspects of the torturer's art.

If Matsukawa really was an alien, it could pose problems in psychotronic interrogation. Darrel Ridenour, the presumed demiclone guard, had reacted atypically when I questioned him with the drug penverol, falling into what seemed to be a coma. Penverol was supposed to be less damaging to the mind than probing, but perhaps the Haluk were abnormally sensitive to any sort of psychoactive messing about. Their mutated genes might be largely human, but that didn't mean their mentalities were. In a mature individual, personality traits and general mental function are only minimally controlled by DNA—as any parent of identical twins, or cloner of racehorses, can attest—which is why the demiclone masquerade was feasible.

I wondered if it might be more prudent to postpone Matsukawa's questioning until we reached professional facilities on Earth. On the other hand—

A chime from the wardroom door.

I opened it and Ivor and Mimo came in, supporting the Galapharma duty officer between them. Matsukawa shuffled along listlessly, seeming uninterested in his surroundings. He did not look frightened. His face was a livid greenish-gray and his black hair and T-shirt were soaked with sweat. Ivor and I sat him down in the barber chair and removed the hand and leg restraints he'd worn. I held off strapping him to the chair and attaching the various sensors.

"Feeling under the weather, Jim?" I inquired in a friendly fashion.

"Yes. Maybe I picked up something on Cravat."

"Not very likely, what with all the precautions they have in place. You want to tell me what seems to be wrong? When did you first feel sick?"

By way of response he gave a throttled gulp, bent forward and vomited between his spread legs.

I muttered, "Shit," and summoned a cleanerbot with my wrist intercom.

Ivor, our ad hoc medic, held Jim's head while he retched and yielded up what was left of his breakfast. In anticipation of the grilling, we hadn't allowed him any lunch. His digestive juices smelled human.

After a while the heaves turned dry. I got him a glass of water from the wardroom dispenser and he sipped it weakly before slumping back in the chair. If he was malingering, he was a thespian genius.

Matt came back into the wardroom, carrying a small instrument and looking grim. "The diagnosticon's broken, Helly. Take a look."

I checked the thing. It wouldn't even power up. "Maybe somebody did a number on it, maybe not."

"I can try to fix it," Mimo offered. "Joe is also handy at repairs."

Ivor said, "Sick bay has a Doc-in-the-Box computer that controls the treatment couch. If we feed his symptoms into it—"

"Aagh!" Matsukawa was suddenly writhing in Ivor's grasp. "Toilet— quick—for chrissake!"

Ivor said, "Whoa! Hang in there, man!"

He scooped the officer up in his mighty arms like a baby and dashed down the corridor toward the nearest john, narrowly avoiding a collision with a small janitorial machine that came trundling along to deal with the mess.

Mimo said, "What shall I do? Clean the chair?" The bot had started mopping the floor.

"I'll take care of that. You help Ivor get Jim into sick bay. Both of you stay with the prisoner at all times until he's back under restraint." Mimo went away and I said to Matt, "I'll search Jim's cell in the brig and you go replay the surveillance holovid and see what he's been doing over the past twelve hours or so. This sudden illness is mighty damned convenient."

We separated, securing the wardroom after us. I went aft to the new lockup facility that had been fitted during our brief stay on Cravat. It was very simple. A block of four small cabins had been segregated from the other passenger accommodations by means of two gates across the main corridor. Any crew member could unfasten the gates. Each cell was a little over three meters square and could be unlocked only by a live iris-scan of Matt, Mimo, or me. All the cell furnishings had been removed except for a bolted-down cot, chair, and table. An entertainment unit was mounted on each cell wall. There were no cabinets or other places where items might be concealed. The prisoners' clothing and effects were stacked on a shelf under the table. An adjoining doorless bathroom held a toilet, an open shower, and a washbasin with a shelf for personal care items. A barred observation window had been cut into the outer cell door. The interior was under constant surveillance from a fish-eye camera and a respiration-rate detector inset in the ceiling opposite the bathroom.

Since we had only two prisoners, the extra cabins had their sliding doors left wide open. The third cell was set up as a sort of lounge for the convenience of crew members pulling guard duty. The fourth served as a temporary holding area while the occupied cells were cleaned or inspected. When Garth Wing Lee joined us at Torngat, we'd just toss him into the empty pen.

I checked out Jim Matsukawa's cell meticulously and found no contraband whatsoever. His e-books were undamaged and so was the game control unit, so he hadn't poisoned himself by eating toxic bits of electronic circuitry. The toiletry containers he'd been furnished with were still nearly full. He hadn't consumed quantities of shave-gel, skin cleanser, shampoo, mouthwash, or pit sauce. I made a mental note to replace the items, just in case the Fungus Among Us had concealed poison in any of them.

As a precaution, Matt had set up the "day shift" guard duty roster to include two people. Joe and Ildiko were never paired. Only Matt, Mimo, and I would pull solitary watches, during the prisoners' sack time. We could sleep while the respiration-rate sensor monitored the inmates, set to wake us if somebody began breathing atypically—or not at all. It wasn't a perfect security setup, but it was the best we could manage under the circumstances.

Matt came along with a holoviewer just as I was winding up my search. I said, "Find anything? I'm coming up with a big fat zero."

"The surveillance record shows nothing unusual on a quickie preliminary scan," she said. "Matsukawa seems to have had trouble with his bowels this morning. It was probably the beginning phase of his illness. During the twelve-hour period he ingested the meals given him, water from his own sink . . . and occasional plastic cups of coffee or pop pushed through the cell bars by people on guard duty."

"What?"

"Guards and the two prisoners, all drinking from the same coffee pot. And the soft drink thermoses were sealed before the contents were poured into cups. I suppose the crew thought there was no harm in sharing."

"Rats! Who passed drinks to Jim?"

"Wait one sec while I check again." She looked into the viewer eyepiece and played with fast-forward and reverse for a few minutes. "Mmm. Everyone seems to have done it except me and thee. Even Mimo." She shook her head as she turned off the viewer. "They were all briefed on the possible presence of a Galapharma ringer among us and the need for extreme caution."

I gave an exasperated sigh. "What's done is done, but it better not happen again. Chew 'em out later. Let's get on to sick bay now and see what the Doc-in-the-Box has to say."

Ivor and Mimo had placed Matsukawa on the treatment couch. He was lying with his eyes shut, breathing regularly. His skin had returned to a near-healthy sallow hue.

"He said he felt much better," Ivor said, "then dropped off to sleep."

I studied the vital-signs monitor above the couch. His body temp was nearly normal and his heartbeat just a tad fast. I didn't know how to interpret the blood pressure and other data, so I entered all the symptoms Ivor had described earlier, plus vomiting and diarrhea, and ordered the computer to provide a diagnosis.

The machine said, *Blood sample, please.*

"Anybody know how to do that?" I inquired.

Mimo shrugged. Ivor consulted an e-book of medical procedures he was evidently familiar with, gently lifted Matsukawa's hand out of a little trough at the edge of the gadget-laden couch, and frowned.

"There should be a sampling unit plugged in here. A device about the size of a deck of cards. But it's gone."

"Beautiful," I grumbled. "Don't bother searching. I have a feeling it's ascended to the great recyling bin in the sky."

"Can't you simply prick his finger?" Mimo wanted to know.

"Our sick bay has no equipment to analyze blood that's outside a patient's body," Ivor said.

I addressed the computer. "No blood sample available. Deliver the diagnosis."

Probability two percent that the patient suffers from a psychosomatic disorder. Probability eleven percent that the patient suffers from a disability induced by a deleterious microorganism. Probability fifty-nine percent that the patient suffers from poisoning. A list of 726 possible toxic compounds and bioagents that may be implicated appears on the display.

Everyone except snoozing Matsukawa let out groans of frustration.

"Treatment?" I asked.

No specific treatment can be recommended aside from bed rest and ample intake of fluids. The patient's condition at this time is not serious.

"Just bad enough to preclude interrogation," Matt said to me in a low voice. "Somebody slipped him a mickey. Or he took it himself."

Mimo said, "We'll have to monitor his food and drink from now on."

I nodded. "Well, if he's not seriously ill there's no reason why he can't go back to his cell. Matt, let's you and me collect Ollie Schneider and bring him to the wardroom. We'll have another go at him and save old Jimbo for tomorrow, when he feels better."

But early next afternoon, just before we were about to attempt interrogation again, Matsukawa's symptoms returned with a vengeance. He collapsed moaning onto his cell floor, dripping with sweat. Then he went into convulsions.

Joe and Matt, pulling guard duty at the time, rushed him to sick bay. Ivor and I came running. The patient had a feeble pulse, his breathing was fitful, and his pupils had shrunk to pinpoints. We plugged him into the Doc-in-the-Box and waited for its verdict with dismal foreboding.

The medical computer ordered us to give Jim several medications. Then it said: *You are advised to transport the patient to the nearest hospital without delay. His condition is critical.*

Chapter 13

It is Alistair Drummond's perverse idea to go horseback riding while he receives the latest progress report, undeterred by the fact that it is August in Arizona, and on most days the air temperature in the unsheltered regions around the Phoenix Conurbation approaches 40 degrees Celsius. However, the Galapharma CEO has taken it into his head to view the Sky Ranch from afar and refuses to be dissuaded. Besides, he says, it should be much cooler in the high country.

So he is forced to make the arrangements, utilizing a guide service having longtime ties to Rampart, with personnel who are experienced and discreet. The booking is done anonymously; the service knows only that he is a Rampart executive of high status with an eccentric guest to amuse.

Copper Mountain, 2,071 meters elevation and some eleven kilometers south of the spread, provides the only vantage point unlikely to be under close surveillance by ranch security forces. The ride is a popular one for tourists in spring and fall—although not in the furnace heat of high summer. Numbers of people are intrigued by the famous Frost domain, which combines the elements of a working modern cattle operation with those of a deliberately archaic family retreat. Traveling the slightly hazardous Copper Mountain Trail on horseback not only provides the curious with a long-range view of the Sky Ranch, but also affords an outing in a beautiful high-desert landscape and the opportunity to poke around a romantic old abandoned gold mine.

Is this oddly chosen day-trip just another control ploy on Drummond's part? He is certain that the Gala CEO doesn't give a damn about southwestern scenery, and wonders apprehensively whether information about the prospectus offer to Macrodur might have reached Drummond in spite of the heroic efforts at secrecy organized by Eve and the others.

God help me if Alistair knows about *that*, he thinks. The news I'll have to give him about Katje's quarterstake is devastating enough. Why, the crazy bastard might just kill me on the spot!

There are dark rumors of such things having happened many years ago, when Drummond was a young site manager working on Galapharma worlds far from Commonwealth oversight. Still, the Chairman and CEO of an Amalgamated Concern would hardly resort to personal violence nowadays, would he? Most especially not on a difficult mountain trail, with a local guide as a witness.

No, he thinks. My neck is safe. For now, at any rate. So whoopee-ti-yi-oh! I'm off to play cowboy with one of the most dangerous men in the galaxy . . .

Alistair Drummond has said he will provide his own transport to the rendezvous. He rents a Toyota four-wheeler for himself at Scottsdale Municipal Airport—he is too well known at Sky Harbor—using a blind-draft Rampart EFT card, and drives 120 twisty kilometers to the trailhead. It is in the middle of nowhere, on a dirt track east of the quaintly named hamlet of Punkin Center. Understandably, he has never taken this particular ride, but the country surrounding the Sky Ranch is familiar enough and he arrives without incident at 0835 hours.

At the trailhead, an arid flat surrounded by forested mountains of moderate height, he finds an empty Mercedes sport utility vehicle—an obvious rental—parked beside a big lemon-yellow Dodge Ram pickup with a matching horse trailer. A sign on the trailer says AMPERSAND GUEST RANCH—PAYSON, AZ. Three horses, saddled and ready, are hitched to the pickup's bumper. Two men sit inside the truck.

The morning weather is mercifully overcast and cool. He gets out of his four-wheeler and settles a broad-brimmed straw hat onto his head. He wears a featherweight Allison jacket with environmental controls, faded old Levi's jeans, and scuffed low-heel boots.

The pickup truck doors open. A pleasant-faced young cowboy, lean as a desert grasshopper, emerges and gives a cordial wave to the new arrival before coming over to greet him. Alistair Drummond also climbs out. He remains near the horses, sipping from a plastic coffee cup.

"Mornin' Citizen Jones," says the young man. "I'm Randy Herrero, your guide." His eyes flicker approvingly over the client's garb. "Guess you've ridden before."

"A little. You can call me Scotty. I hope you haven't had to wait long."

"No problem. Me 'n Citizen Smith have been going over the route. It's pretty steep in places, but we've got good strong mounts. I reckon we should reach a suitable lookout point in two, three hours. You do your sightseeing, we have lunch, then ride back by the long and scenic route if you like. I don't think we'll have to worry much about heat today."

The two men walk back to the truck and the horses. Randy Herrero does a final check of the cinches and the gear. Alistair Drummond gives a curt nod of greeting to "Scotty Jones" but says nothing. His glacial eyes are hidden behind wire-rimmed sun goggles.

In honor of the occasion, he has outfitted himself with brand-new Western wear: black jeans, a black shirt with white piping, a white neckerchief, and a black straw hat. With his tawny hair, chiseled features, and regal bearing, he resembles a parody of an ancient Western movie hero. Drummond has made the common tenderfoot mistake of buying premium-priced high-heeled boots with very pointed toes, virtually impossible to walk in with any comfort until they are well broken in.

Good!

Each saddle has a global navigator, a phone, a powerpoint to plug in envirogear and other effete accessories, two enormous canteens, and a cantle-pack for emergency equipment, food, and personal items. The guide also carries a cased blaster carbine and wears an Ivanov stunner of unusual design on a traditional gunfighter's belt. He has informed the clients that the pistol will coldcock any sort of hostile critter from a blacktail rattler to a cougar and leave them none the worse for wear.

"You need me to give you a hand, Scotty?" Randy asks diffidently, when it's time to mount.

But he adjusts his own stirrups and lofts himself into the saddle. His hammerhead pinto, who is named Paco, stands solid as a rock.

"Guess not," Randy Herrero laughs.

Drummond says coldy, "I'd like some assistance, if you please. I'm more used to English-style tack. Please hold the horse's head."

"Sure thing, Al." The guide helps the second dude get settled on a big blue roan gelding.

"No whip?" Drummond says with a frown.

"Western horses don't take kindly to 'em," Herrero says. "Use the ends of the reins if you really feel you have to. But Bluebell, there, is a sweetie. You talk to him right, he'll do whatever you want." He mounts his own palomino. "I know you two gents want to have some private conversation, so I'll forgo the usual tourist spiel and give you plenty of room. Just don't fall too far behind me, and keep a sharp eye out for rattlesnakes. We got a plague of them sumbitches in these mountains and they do spook the horses. Ready? Let's ride!"

The clients stay well behind Herrero as the party crosses the flat, following his lead through catclaw, ocotillo, and dusty sagebrush. The path is neither clear nor well-beaten, and only an occasional hoofprint or heap of desiccated horse manure indicates that it has been used recently. Copper Mountain, a broad and hulking mass with formidable cliffs, rises ahead of them.

The flat ends in a tumble of rocks, and a more obvious trail becomes visible. Wide enough for two to ride abreast, it climbs steeply up a slope dotted with scraggly junipers, paloverdes, and a few stately century plants with six-meter stalks crowned by candelabras of yellow flowers. The sky is beginning to clear and a faint breeze blows. It is very quiet

except for the clip-clopping of the horses, the clatter of dis-
lodged stones, and creaking leather.

They ride without speaking for nearly an hour.

Finally, Alistair Drummond says in a low tone, "I swept the
saddles for bugs. They're clean."

He controls his irritation. "I told you this guide outfit was
completely reliable."

"Is Simon still determined to file the civil suit immediately?"

"There was nothing any of us could do to prevent it. It'll go
to the prosecutors as soon as Asa and Matt Gregoire validate
Schneider's deposition. But it's not the disaster it may seem
on the surface. Surely you realize that."

Drummond nods. "If the takeover succeeds." He rides on
without speaking for a few minutes. Then: "I saw Katje Vanderpost's obituary. My congratulations. Was her death ascribed to natural causes?"

A pang of red anger and guilt seizes him. But he thrusts it
aside, as he has frequently since that night, because it would
be fatal to acknowledge the full import of what he has done.

"Yes. My InSec people tidied the scene. The poison that
was used leaves no residue in the body. The—the person who
administered it threw herself off the penthouse balcony when
she realized what she'd done. I'd told her the poison was a
harmless coercive drug."

"Convenient. Who did the job for you?"

"She was a longtime housekeeper of Katje's. A simpleminded dupe. Her death was so clearly suicide that we didn't
even have to interfere with the Phoenix Police investigation.
The coroner's verdict cited despondency at the demise of her
beloved employer."

"And Katje's will is being expedited in probate, with the
share-voting rights affirmed?"

"Yes . . ."

"Excellent. When will the board meeting be held?"

"It hasn't been scheduled yet, Alistair." He steels himself.
"Katje didn't bequeath her quarterstake to the Reversionist
charities after all. She changed her will the very night before
she died. No one knew what she was planning except her at-

torney, an insolent young prick who's always resisted the—
um—lures and blandishments of the rest of the family."

"Who got the stake?" Drummond demands in a harsh
whisper. "*Who*, damn you? Don't tell me she bequeathed it to
Eve!"

"It's worse," he admits. "Katje executed a deed of gift,
without any legal encumbrances. She gave her entire quarterstake to Asa. And she did it while she was alive, so we can't
even contest the will."

The CEO of Galapharma stiffens violently in his saddle,
almost as though he has been electroshocked. The roan
gelding shies at the unexpected spasm of the rider, and
Drummond brings it back under control with swift ruthless-
ness. For several minutes he only stares blindly ahead of him.
Then he hauls back with a savage yank on the reins, and
Bluebell squeals, turns, and comes to a dead halt, facing the
other rider.

Drummond says, "I think our relationship must be terminated. As of now."

"If you wish." He manages to keep his own voice equable,
and good old Paco stays calm. "However, I believe I can still
contain the situation. Shall I tell you how?"

Ahead on the trail Randy Herrero calls out, "Everything
okay back there, gents?"

"Just fine! We'll be right along," he replies.

"Your plan had better be a good one," Drummond hisses.
"If my people have to intervene to ensure that the merger succeeds, the fallout will be disastrous for your family—and for
you. I must have Rampart. I *will* have it! You know very well
that the survival of Galapharma depends upon it."

"Yes. I know."

"Tell me what you intend to do." Drummond thumps the
ribs of the gelding, which gives a long-suffering sigh. The
two riders move forward again, side by side.

"I'll kill Asa myself, just before the board meeting. He'll
be on his guard against attacks from your agents once he arrives on Earth, but he has no reason to suspect that I'm . . . a
Gala partisan." He adds pointedly: "What I have in mind can

only be brought off by a member of the Frost family. Someone Asa trusts."

"Hmm," says Drummond. You can almost see the clockwork wheels revolving inside his head as he assesses the prospect of eliminating the middleman.

Let's stamp out *that* notion right away!

"And I'll need your wholehearted cooperation from now on, Alistair—not threats and insults—if I'm to bring it off successfully." He smiles thinly. "As a matter of fact, I'll need a bit more than that. I want a signed letter of intent from you, declaring that I'll be named Chief Operating Officer of the Rampart Division of Galapharma AC, to serve in that position for a period of no less than ten years, at an annual stipend equal to your own. I also require a thirty percent stake in the division—not twenty-five, as we discussed earlier—in recognition of my valued assistance as your personal agent during the Rampart acquisition."

Silence. Then, very quietly, Drummond says, "I see."

"I'm happy that you do. I've sensed our relationship deteriorating for some time now, even though I've done my utmost for you. I'll certainly continue to do everything in my power to assist you, if you'll just cut me some slack. I've thrown my lot in with Galapharma and I can't turn back."

"Especially not after Katje," says the Gala CEO. But his truculence seems to have melted away abruptly. He reaches out to pat the shoulder of the man riding beside him. "Lad, if you want the letter of intent, you shall have it. Holographic, if it'll help prove the wholeheartedness of my . . . cooperation."

"That would be eminently satisfactory."

Drummond's laugh is almost roguish. "I'll scribble it up at lunchtime. How's that? No hard feelings, eh? Damn it all, I apologize for bullying you, for my filthy mannerisms. Blame the stresses of my position. And the undeniable truth that I'm an arrogant bloody bastard!"

"You're a brilliant businessman with a transgalactic vision, Alistair."

And probably half mad with vainglorious ambition . . .

But he doesn't dare dwell on that thought. Calmness, competence, and courage have sustained him through another mortal crisis. He's delivered bad news to the beast yet again and survived. Even more, Drummond has finally agreed to sign the letter of intent that he tapdanced away from back at the beginning of their clandestine association.

Alistair still can't pull off the takeover without him, much as he'd like to!

"Is it all right then?" Drummond demands with arch chumminess.

"Of course. You want to know why Asa's death will immediately assure that the board votes for the acquisition?"

"Lad, I'm all ears."

The explanation is ludicrously simple. When he finishes, they ride on silently for a long time, single file now because of the narrowness of the precipitous mountain trail. The scenery is awesome—soaring pine trees, subtly colored outcroppings of ancient Precambrian rock, the occasional glimpse in the west of the Tonto Basin falling away over a thousand meters, green-black waves of forested hills and buttes rolling eastward. The abandoned gold mine, a sinister opening braced with rotting timbers, surrounded by rusting machinery and collapsed shacks, is passed by when the two dudes indicate they have no interest in stopping.

Copper Mountain has no distinct summit; the laboring horses halt at last on a north-facing shelf of bare rock girt with scrubby trees. Randy Herrero dismounts and comes to hold the heads of Paco and Bluebell so his clients can safely slip from their saddles.

"Here y'go, Scotty, Al. This is the place! You can see damn near the entire Sky Ranch from here, right down on that plateau. Big house right by the creek, not seven kilometers away. Ranch buildings, corral, hopper pad, and control tower to the east, other buildings scattered from hell to breakfast. There's an old mule trail leading up from the ranch to the gold mine. The mountain's not so steep on the north slope. Of course, no outsiders are allowed to use the trail nowadays. You brought power oculars?"

"I did," says the dude known as Al Smith. He produces

them from his jacket and does a slow panoramic sweep. "Very impressive. I'm surprised the Frost family doesn't use a ground-based dissimulator to forestall spying. Or even a Class Three defensive shield."

Randy laughs dismissively. "Why fuzzy up their own billion-dollar view? They own seven sections of land north of here, and it's fenced with high-tech alarms and overhead scans. No hoppers are going to drop in unexpected-like, either—not with the airspace monitored by hidden blaster emplacements. The buildings are out of range of any portable arms, so the Frosts don't give a damn about tourists horse-back riding or hiking around the perimeter. But if you came up any of the surrounding mountains in a vehicle, Rampart ExSec would be all over you like flies on shit."

"Seven sections of land?" The archaic measuring term is a puzzlement to Citizen Smith.

"A section was a square mile in the old system," says the man called Scotty Jones with calm certainty. "Quite impregnable."

"Imagine that," murmurs Smith. He resumes his observations through the powerscope. "Just imagine that!"

The Doc-in-the-Box prescribed oxygen for the patient, to-gether with a medication to relieve the convulsions. It urged us to transfer Jim Matsukawa to the nearest hospital.

"We're only two hours out of Torngat," Joe Betancourt said. "I read up on the place during my last trick at the helm. The winter resort has a big medical facility. They must get a lot of broken bones, to say nothing of hypothermia and *après-ski* hangovers."

I said, "Matt and Ivor, you stay with the patient. I'm go-ing to call ahead and see what kind of arrangements we can make. Joe, go drive the boat. Send Mimo to me in the wardroom."

Back in my lair, I opened the SS com and made contact with Torngat Starport, declaring a medical emergency. The tower transferred me to an ER doctor at the local hospital and I transmitted data from our sick-bay computer to her.

"The symptoms are most consistent with some sort of poisoning," she decided, after studying the information. "Was there any complaint of burning or numbness in the mouth and throat? Or abdominal pain?"

"Absolutely not. Neither yesterday nor today."

"Restlessness or thrashing about? Tremors? Headache?"

"Negative."

"Hmm. And you departed from the planet Cravat?"

"Correct."

She diddled with her own computer and her eyebrows rose. "Goodness! What an appalling little world . . . However, the patient's symptoms don't correlate with any native toxic materials or bioagents. A pity you couldn't obtain a blood sample. Well, all I can say is, get him to us immediately."

"Doctor, the man's a high-risk prisoner. It's imperative that we transport him to Earth without delay." I showed her my Rampart Red Card. "I'm empowered by my Starcorp to offer whatever compensation you deem necessary if you'll send medical personnel to treat the patient aboard our starship."

She scowled. "I doubt it could be arranged."

"*Whatever* compensation is required. To the hospital, officially, and privately to the staff members who agree to treat the patient."

"Stand by," she said.

Mimo came into the wardroom, one of his precious stogies clamped in his teeth. "So it's happened again."

"Yes. He seemed well on the way to recovery, then—pow! It's got to be poison."

"But where would he have got it from?" Mimo said. "He could hardly have been carrying it around with him on Dagasatt, and he had no opportunity to obtain it on Cravat. He was constantly under guard."

"It had to've been given to him here on the ship by our mystery fink. But I'll be damned if I know where he or she could have found the stuff. No chemical we have on board fits the medic computer's list of possible poisons, and you can't purchase controlled substances over the counter in a tightly wrapped settlement like Cravat. The odds are astronomical against there being a Gala agent hanging around Cravat

Dome, equipped with a handy-dandy murder kit for the turn-coat to pick and choose from."

Mimo puffed fragrant smoke. "It's possible—but not plausible—that a disloyal crew member had poison in their possession from the very beginning of the operation, before we left Rampart Central on Seriphos. But this would make sense only if Oliver Schneider were the intended poisoning target. No one knew you would take Jim Matsukawa prisoner."

"Right! Why poison Matsukawa to prevent his interrogation, and not Ollie? Both men are potentially dangerous witnesses against Galapharma."

"But only Matsukawa is a possible demiclone," Mimo said.

I chewed that one over and got nowhere. "Ildy, Joe, and Ivor were unaware of the precise goal of Operation Q when they first came aboard *Chispa* on Seriphos. Even on Nogawa-Krupp they didn't know we were after Oliver Schneider, or that we suspected him of being a Gala agent. Our target individual was merely described as a felonious Rampart employee. The only crew member other than myself who knew that Schneider was the prize was you."

Mimo rolled his eyes.

"God knows, I don't doubt your loyalty!" I hastened to add. "It has to be one of the others—or no one. Maybe the goddamn Haluk demiclones have hollow teeth full of assorted pharmaceuticals. Maybe Matsukawa's just highly allergic to Ivor's cooking!"

"Citizen Frost?" The doctor was back on the com display. "If your corporation is prepared to pay through the nose, we can place a fully equipped medical gig, plus personnel, at your disposal. The gig is a rather sizable mobile hospital." She gave me its specs.

"No problem!" I exclaimed. "Our starship's a big one. There's plenty of room for it in our auxiliary transport bay. If necessary, we'll leave our own gig behind on Torngat."

"Very well. We'll be ready to lift when you arrive in parking orbit." She told me what the outrageous cost was going to be. I promised to arrange a prompt transfer of funds from Earth and thanked her profusely. We said goodbye.

I turned to Mimo. "I was going to ask you to ready our orbiter to shuttle the patient if my little proposal was nixed. Now all you have to do is figure out if we can shoehorn the ambulance into *Chispa*'s belly."

"And of course there's Karl to pick up. Do you wish me to collect him and the others from Torngat?"

I thought for a moment. "Let me give him a shout. It'd be best if they could hitch a ride on the medical gig. Check out available space in the transport bay as quickly as you can . . . And I don't want Joe at the helm when we make our approach to the planet. Just keep him with you on the flight deck when you take command."

He nodded and left me alone.

I called Eve and arranged for the medical payoff, catching her in her Toronto apartment.

She made the monetary transfer immediately, then said, "I've just had a bright idea: as soon as the Torngat medical team is aboard, I want you to have them do a DNA workup of both Matsukawa and Garth Lee. Transmit the data to me at once. Beatrice Mangan can analyze it. If they are modified Haluk, we'll know the genetic tag Emily Konigsberg incorporated into the demiclone procedure. If need be, we'll be able to test other suspicious individuals."

"Of course! I should have thought of that myself."

"You realize that the interrogation data from those two will be inadmissible as evidence until it's officially vetted by Xenoaffairs analysts. Until then, it's just intelligence. Furthermore, without a humanoid Haluk, dead or alive, the only substantive proof we have of an alien demiclone threat is my own little blue body—circumstantial evidence that could be interpreted variously—and your unsupported statement about nefarious activity on Dagasatt."

"I know, Evie."

"Take very good care of yourself, little brother. And of your prisoners." She signed off.

I promptly put in a call to Karl Nazarian, on Torngat.

The starbase's general astrogation office patched me through to the hotel where he and the three members of his crew and Garth Lee were staying. I greeted him and inquired how things were going.

"We're holed up in the smallest, most bare-bones establishment I could find," he told me. "A transient spacers' joint just outside the starport where I can keep our prisoner secure and the crew out of mischief."

The thought of finicky Lotte Dietrich, the dour old manhunter Cassius Potter, and laid-back Hector Motlaletsie carousing among the frozen fleshpots of Torngat made me smile. "Of course. Gotta protect your Over-the-Hill Gang from the temptations of snow bunnies and ski bums. How's Garth Lee?"

"Glum and glummer. We're keeping a suicide watch on him."

"Good thinking." I told him about the Fake Emily debacle back on Earth, and about our speculations, and hopes, that Lee and Matsukawa might also be demiclones. "I'll probe your boy Lee as soon as we get him aboard. We've had to postpone the interrogation of Matsukawa due to a suspiciously convenient illness. Maybe poison."

"Ah."

"He's in pretty dire shape and our diagnostic equipment failed to spot what was wrong. The gear could have been sabotaged. I think you might be right about us having a fink aboard."

"What are you going to do about it?"

"What I hoped to avoid. When you and your people are here to reinforce us, I'll probe Joe Betancourt and Ildiko Szabo. It's got to be one of them. Or nobody."

"You coming down to fetch us, or you want me to take care of transport?"

"I've arranged for a medical gig to rendezvous with us in Torngat orbit a little under two hours from now. Matsukawa needs professional care."

"So you're transferring him landside for treatment?"

"No way. We'll be carrying the local sawbones crew and

their space-going hospital along with us to Earth. I'm going to make certain that all of us arrive in good shape."

"Wowie!" He hoisted his bushy brows in appreciation of the costly operation. "So you want me and my group to come aboard with the medics?"

"That's an affirm. You can get details from Torngat Tower on the gig's takeoff. Go over there right away. We don't want to waste a minute getting our show back on the road. Crazy things are happening on the Rampart scene."

"The repairs to *Plomazo* will be complete in a week," Karl said. "Shall I arrange to have her ferried to Earth?"

"Hold off. We'll see what Mimo thinks."

"All right. By the way, I've used our down-time here on Torngat to make a rough précis of relevant data abstracted by Lotte from Garth Lee's ship computer. You won't have to wade through the raw dump like poor Evie did—not that she has any reason to complain. The material we sent her is prima facie evidence of Galapharma's conspiracy to engage in illicit trade with the Haluk. Nothing about demiclones in the dump, though. And nothing to help Rampart's civil case."

"Don't be too sure of that. My brother Daniel and his overpaid flock of legal eagles might just find a way to tweak that data to Rampart's advantage. Dan's a helluva lawyer. A regular Wile E. Coyote. Matter of fact, Eve used to call him that when we were kids to tease him."

Karl looked puzzled, then nodded in sudden comprehension. "Wile E. Coyote! Classic movie cartoon character. Wasn't he always being outwitted by some speedy desert bird?"

"The Roadrunner. There really is such a thing. They're fairly common in Arizona. I haven't thought about them in years." Or about the way Wily Dan Frost earned his nickname.

Karl Nazarian said, "Helly, I'd better get this outfit of mine over to the starbase. See you soon."

When he was gone, I sat staring at the dead SS display, carried away—as seemed to happen too often lately—to the wild western lands where my Frost ancestors carved out the first Sky Ranch in the late 1800s.

Where my mother and father had honeymooned. Where I'd been accidentally born, a bit prematurely, attended not by the high-priced Toronto obstetrician as my parents had planned, but by the ranch's horse wrangler, who knew all about birthing baby animals. Where Dan and Eve and Beth and I spent marvelous early childhood holidays, pretending we were regular kids, not wealthy and overprivileged Frost offspring who'd someday inherit an interstellar corporation.

I thought about how we camped and played cowboy with Pop, learned about minerals and wild animals and Native American history from Mom. I thought about canyons and rimrock and arid high-plateau forest beneath a blazing sun, tiny elf-owls peeking from holes dug out of tall saguaro cactuses, and roadrunners dashing along primitive dirt trails ahead of a lumbering four-wheeler.

I thought about Mom and Dad together, before the estrangement and divorce that had turned them into Katje and Simon; and all of us kids, laughing and scrapping and liking each other. I thought about the way my family had been.

The way it could never be again, especially if what I suspected was true.

Matt Gregoire finally came to tell me that we'd reached the Torngat solar system and were ready to go subluminal.

"How's Matsukawa?" I asked her.

"Slightly worse."

"Who's guarding Ollie Schneider?"

She gave me a look. "At the moment, no one. He's still sleeping off the morning interrogation session. I've looked in on him once or twice and hooked the breath monitor alarm to my wrist unit. You told Mimo to keep Joe on the bridge. I thought it would be prudent if Ildiko stayed with me and Ivor."

"You're right, of course." I shook my head. "Let me grab a cup of coffee before we go aft."

After I'd helped myself at the wardroom dispenser, we

went together to sick bay. The crossover flash gave us a split second of disorientation and momentarily whited-out the view through the corridor port. Then the stretched stars of hyperspace turned back into steady colored lights on black velvet. In a few minutes we'd be in a parking orbit half a million kilometers above Torngat. The place was supposed to be a winter wonderland. Macrodur Concern, notorious for working its employees like serfs, also provided them with the most opulent vacation spots in the galaxy. The tactic was supposed to be very successful in promoting company loyalty . . .

Ivor was bending anxiously over the patient when Matt and I got to sick bay. An appalling stench filled the room.

"Jim suffered another convulsion and a violent bout of diarrhea," Ivor said. "He's unconscious. I administered medication as the computer ordered. Just a few minutes ago the Doc-in-the-Box advised that his respiration is faltering. As you can see, he's receiving oxygen, but the computer advises that he may need to be put on a ventilator. This is a highly technical procedure and I'm not sure that I—"

"No," I said. "We'll hold off until a real doctor gets here with the proper equipment to diagnose Jim. It won't be long."

"How about taking him to the transport bay?" Ildiko suggested. "Let the medics treat him right there, as soon as they dock. We have an antigrav gurney."

"All right, that's a go," I decided. "Matt, get on your intercom and tell Mimo to notify the medical crew about the respiration problem."

"Let me clean the poor man up before we try to move him," Ivor said, pulling on protective gloves. "Ildy, get a fresh gown from the locker for him and fix up the gurney. Helly, pull that wastebasket closer."

The treatment couch allowed sluicing of the patient in situ. Ivor performed the task very efficiently, cutting off Jim's clothes and washing his soiled nether regions with a hose that sprayed warm water and disinfectant. The nearly liquid excrement swirled away as Ivor carefully turned the sick man's inert body.

"Wait!" I shouted abruptly. "What the hell's *that*?"

One of them got away down the drain, but Ivor's gloved hand, moving fast as lightning, snared the second. As we all came close, oblivious of the lingering stink, Ivor carefully washed the object.

Ildiko provided a kidney dish to receive it. "It must have been in his rectum," she said. "Eeyuk!"

"And not just one," I noted. "Two of them."

Instructing Ivor to finish the wash job and place the patient on the gurney, I carried the kidney dish and its unusual contents to a table with a strong light. Ildiko furnished me with a face shield, gloves, forceps, and a pointed probe. Gingerly, I began to pull the thing apart.

Matt, who had gone into the hall to take care of the message to Mimo, reentered the room to see what the fuss was about. "We're in orbit. The gig is on its way . . . Helly? What in the world have you got there?"

"It looks like leaves!" Ildiko said. "Is it some alien organism?"

The swollen, distorted roll was slightly over thirteen centimeters long. Slowly I took it apart, pulled off a piece, and held it against the light. It was part of a leaf, all right.

"An alien from Havana," I said.

Jim Matsukawa had prudently removed the bands before inserting two of them into his body, but I knew without a doubt that the object in the kidney dish was the sodden remains of one of Mimo's premium-quality Cohiba Robusto cigars.

"Matsukawa is suffering from nicotine poisoning," I said, pulling off my gloves with a triumphant snap. "Administered nonorally. I should have remembered. It's one of those legendary prisoner dodges. A single cigarette makes you conveniently sick as a dog so you get a nice vacation in the hospital, and the evidence gets flushed."

"That would have been what happened yesterday," Ivor said. "When I helped him to the toilet."

"He used only one cigar then," I remarked thoughtfully. "He must have kept the unused ones in their plastic tubes, stashed up his exhaust pipe. The question is, why did he use two cigars today?"

"To be sicker," Matt stated. "Hoping we'd evacuate him to Torngat, where his confederate might help him escape."

Ivor said, "But Mimo keeps his cigars in a locked humidor."

"Don't look at me," Ildiko said. "You know I smoked mine after dinner on our first night out of Cravat."

Matt's face stiffened with sudden realization. "Joe Betancourt took three cigars in Terence Hoy's office. I don't remember him smoking any of them."

"He could have slipped them to Jim in one of the coffee mugs," Ildy said. "Robustos are fairly short—when they're dry."

Ivor's huge, gentle face was twisted with dismay. "Joe is the secret traitor? But that's not possible!"

"Yes, it is," I said grimly. "And he's on the bridge with Mimo." I lifted my wrist intercom, then cursed my stupidity. "No. We can't warn Meem that way. Joe would hear it. We'll have to get some Ivanovs from the arms locker and take him by surprise."

All of the portable weaponry had been secured for the duration of the voyage. Only Matt, Mimo, or I had access to the arsenal.

I said, "Ivor, take Matsukawa to the transport bay anteroom. You two gals come with me."

We dashed off down the long corridor, through the galley and the dining saloon, past the locked wardroom and the open crew lounge, where large ports on the starboard side showed Torngat, half lit, a lovely world with ice-dotted indigo seas and sparkling polar continents.

A heavy door opened into the boarding vestibule, the midships excursion bay, and a cluster of equipment storage compartments. The arms locker was located in the forward section, not far from the short companionway leading to the flight bridge.

Suddenly I froze in my tracks, and Matt and Ildiko crashed into me.

The door to the bridge, about eight meters away, was sliding open. Joe Betancourt stood there, holding Mimo in a hammerlock. His right hand pressed a Henckels 14cm chef's boning knife into the soft area just above the old man's Adam's apple.

I thought: A friggin' *kitchen* knife? Sweet Sue!

But the low-tech weapon, honed sharp as a razor, was doing its job. Blood streamed down Mimo's neck and soaked the front of his white cashmere turtleneck. His dark eyes were wide and glazed and his mouth taut against the pain.

"Hold it!" Joe shouted. "All of you stop right there or I'll kill him now!"

"Okay, Joe. Whatever you say." I held up both hands in surrender but continued oozing slowly forward. The arms locker was less than three meters away, on my right.

"Stand still! I mean it. I'll slit the old fucker's gizzard!"

Blood was flowing freely from the wound in my friend's throat, but there was none of the deadly spurting that would have signified a cut artery. His eyes lost their fixed stare and focused on me. Very slowly, one of them closed.

Yes!

A hoarse groan from Mimo. "I'm sorry, Helly. He took me by surprise at the instant of hyperspace crossover. *Ay, dios mio—que pendejada!*" He began to quiver and slump, as though he were fainting.

Joe gave the old man's locked arm a vicious wrench. "Stand up, you bastard! Keep walking! And shut your mouth. One more word and you're dead."

Mimo obeyed, and winked at me again. He certainly wasn't as badly injured as he seemed to be.

I was still moving. "Take it easy, Joe. Don't hurt him any more. We'll do whatever you want—"

I feigned tripping over my own feet, falling headlong to the deck and twisting to the right. Mimo's knees gave way and he and his captor lurched precariously. Joe was a powerful little guy, but the veteran smuggler was a full head taller, gangly as a stork and an awkward burden when he was a dead weight.

Joe screamed, "Goddamn you!" and pulled Mimo back-ward, cussing a blue streak. As I'd hoped, he thought I was trying to get close enough to jump him. But my actual goal was the arms locker. There was no time to open it and grab a gun. All I could do was prevent Betancourt from obtaining a more efficient weapon, praying he wouldn't make good on his threat to slaughter his sagging captive. I rolled, bounced to my feet, and ended up with my face plastered against the iridocontrolled lock, a mechanism that only Mimo, Matt, or I could open . . . or close.

Eyeballing the lock, I said, "Emergency code alpha-three-one-one."

The thing chimed loudly five times. I sprang away, waiting for Joe's next move.

"Cocksucking sonuvabitch!" he roared. "What've you done? *What?*"

I hoped he'd drop Mimo and come at me with the knife. If he had, I'd have booted his teensy testicles up between his ears and cracked his wrist like a celery stalk. But he caught himself in time, still spewing obscenities, and maintained a firm grip on his hostage's locked arm, which he'd pulled so high that I feared it might be dislocated.

Mimo was on his knees, head down, moaning loudly. Joe had shifted the thin, sharply pointed knife from his throat to the base of his skull.

A shuddering inhalation, then Joe spoke almost in a whisper, squelching his fury with a heroic self-control I had to admire.

"If I stab Mimo in this spot, he's gone. With a slashed throat, he might have a chance if you overpower me—but not with a cut brainstem. Understand? *Understand?*"

"Yes." I straightened and slowly placed my hands on top of my head.

"What did you do to the arms cabinet?" he asked me. "An emergency lock-down?"

I nodded. "Twenty-four hours. No override."

"You're lying! I'll kill Mimo right now. I mean it!"

"I'm telling the truth," I said. "And if you kill him you'll lose the only edge you have. So quit with the bullshit and ease up before he has a heart attack."

Joe Betancourt glared at me, breathing roughly. Then he relaxed the pressure on Mimo's hammerlocked arm. The old man gave a sob of relief and looked at me with a crooked smile. "I tried, *amigo*."

"Shut up," Joe said. "On your feet, gramps!"

Mimo complied, wincing. The knife was still pointed at the nape of his neck.

"You two!" Joe jerked his head at Matt and Ildiko, who had remained unmoving at the far end of the compartment. "Into the excursion bay. Now!"

I went rigid. Properly sequenced, the chamber opened onto airless space. "You sawed-off asswipe! If you intend to——"

Joe's voice was almost weary. "I don't kill people without a reason, Frost, believe it or not. I just want to get 'em out of the way." To the women: "Move it, bitches!"

They sidled into the bay, their faces expressionless.

I said, "What about me?"

"I need you. Close 'em up."

There was nothing I could do but obey. He had me disable the safety control that would have let the women free themselves.

"Okay," he said. "Now back to the equipment maintenance compartment. Make it quick."

Above one of the workbenches was a supply cabinet, and residing therein was my nemesis of old—duct tape. This roll was in a dispenser with a clipper, very handy. Joe ordered me to rig my ankles with improvised shackles, leaving a twisted length of tape about forty centimeters long as a connecting hobble. My wrists were next. I bound them loosely but effectively in a web of sticky stuff until Joe was satisfied. I wasn't helpless, but I sure was mightily discommoded.

"Carry the tape with you," Joe commanded. Then we headed aft.

"Satisfy my curiosity," I said as I ambled along. "Were you a Galapharma plant from the beginning, or did they recruit you somewhere along the way?"

"The latter." He'd regained his composure. "When you sent me to destroy the Haluk starship approaching Dagasatt, I screwed up. Misjudged my ULD micromaneuvering capability during the initial hostile intercept. The Haluk ship was a real schusser, damn near as good as mine. I did him some damage, but then he got a fix on me and I knew I was dead meat. But instead of wiping me out, the bandit wanted to make a deal. Talk about a shocker! He was a human, just like I told you. And he recognized *Chispa* as his own stolen starship. I guess that's why he got the drop on me. He knew the crate's capabilities better than I did."

"Did the pilot of the Haluk ship identify himself?"

"It was Erik Skogstad, like you thought, a guy with a big blond mustache. He offered me a heap of Galapharma boodle— twenty times what you were paying me—if I'd help get Ollie Schneider away from you. Alive. He had to be alive. Old Erik was really worried that you'd kill Schneider rather than give him up. After I accepted the deal, Skogstad made the transfer of funds to my account right then and there. Hey! I was in no position to refuse, was I?"

"Mercy, no!" I said disgustedly. "And did you set up Karl Nazarian for the chop, too?"

"Skogstad wanted to know what happened to Garth Lee, the guy who'd been driving his ship when you swiped it. On the way to Nogawa-Krupp, I eavesdropped on you and Mimo when you were talking about that in the messroom. You hadn't been completely up-front about the mission during the briefing earlier on, and I wanted to know what we were up against. I had a right, dammit!"

"So you told Skogstad what you knew about Lee?"

"Yep. That he was being taken to Earth by a guy named Karl Nazarian, in a Bodascon Y660 that belonged to Bermudez, and that Nazarian probably left Seriphos the same time we did."

Galapharma, using its multitudinous contacts in the Orion Arm, had tracked Karl's ship down and tried to destroy it. Their failure had led to an even more fortuitous chain of circumstances.

I said, "So you made your deal and returned to Dagasatt. And Skogstad limped back to his Haluk base."

"I guess so. He said there were no other high-end Haluk fighters close enough to call in. He seemed certain you'd grab Ollie Schneider, send out a shout for Zone Patrol and the Rampart cavalry, and head for Cravat with the prisoner. When we got to Cravat, I was supposed to contact Tyler Baldwin, Gala's security chief in Toronto, via SS com. Tell him the situation and get further orders." He paused and his tone darkened. "I think Skogstad might have tried to double cross me. A big Haluk cruiser attacked *Chispa* in the Dagasatt system before we could pick up you and Ildy. Mimo took over the guns and clobbered it, but I got to thinking."

"About time! You're an idiot if you trust Galapharma."

"I've been paid in advance," he assured me cockily. "And just in case Gala has a second double cross in mind, I have a little surprise planned when it comes time to hand over the prisoners."

"Does it have anything to do with cigars?" I inquired.

He gave an unsteady laugh. "So you know about the Cohibas! Rotten way to treat a good smoke, hey? But the gimmick worked just fine and dandy. Funny thing, though. Baldwin really came down hard on me about wanting Matsukawa kept alive but not interrogated. I practically offered to snuff Jimbo for him, but he wouldn't have it. He didn't seem to care whether or not you grilled Ollie."

Something didn't quite compute in the proctological scenario, but I couldn't figure out what it was. I would have tried to get more details about Matsukawa's importance to Galapharma, but at that point we reached sick bay and found it empty. Joe knew we'd planned to take Matsukawa to the transport anteroom, so we continued on in that direction. Mimo was quiet, walking steadily enough even though he left a bloody trail. Joe had made a few shallow cuts at the back of his neck to keep his attention.

I wondered morosely whether Galapharma fighting ships were already sharing our orbit, hiding behind dissimulator fields until it was time to close in. They'd nab a real prize package, thanks to treacherous Joe Betancourt. Not only Ollie, Jim, and Garth Lee—but also the Great White Hope of Rampart Starcorp: me. Without even knowing it, little Joe was about to write the finish to our corporate comedy. When the Gala goons killed me offhandedly, Rampart would go belly-up.

Because I had no will.

The last one I'd made, leaving everything to my former wife, Joanna DeVet, was automatically invalidated when I first lost my citizenship. According to CHW law, with me newly enfranchised and enriched, if I should die intestate, my quarterstake would be divided equally among my closest surviving relatives—Simon, Dan, Eve, and Bethany. Only Eve would vote with Simon against the merger. The others—including, I was sure, my vacillating Aunt Emma—would vote in favor, producing the fifty-fifty stalemate that would give Drummond his victory.

You say it's my own fault? That I was a sentimental moron to take Joe and Ildy along on the voyage when I suspected one of them might betray us?

Well, you'd be absolutely correct. But I couldn't have done anything else.

Chapter 14

Ivor Jenkins was shocked at the sight of us—me enmeshed in sticky silvery strips, poor bloodied Mimo, and gore-smeared, manic Joe Betancourt, who sang out with false cheeriness:

"Step away from the patient, big fella! I've got a knife ready to puncture Mimo's lizard-brain if you make one false move."

"He's right, Ivor," I warned. "Do as he says."

"Back against the bulkhead and put your wrists together," Joe commanded. "That's good. Helly, you strap him up."

The young giant stood in appalled silence while I fumbled with the duct-tape dispenser. It didn't matter that the strips weren't applied especially tight. Joe made me wind at least ten meters of the super-tough tape around Ivor's hands. When I finished, he looked like his paws were embedded in a silver basketball.

After Ivor sat down, I taped his mouth and lashed his ankles closely together, leaving him immobilized.

"Excellent," said Joe. He cast his eyes around the transport bay anteroom. The entire right side comprised a docking control console with communicators and monitoring equipment. To the left was a rack holding three space excursion suits and some other technical gear. The room had a big observation window, and beside it was the hatch giving access to the airlock and the passenger lift to the transport bay.

Chispa's orbiter gig, golden in color to match its elegant mothership, was parked well out of the way of the huge exterior iris gate so that the ambulance craft would have plenty of room to dock. A few maintenance bots stood at the ready to secure the visitor, and the bay was brightly floodlit with xenon lamps.

"Now power up this com unit," Joe told me, "and let's see if the quacks are coming down the pike on schedule."

The console had a movable swivel chair. I said, "For God's sake, let Mimo sit down. He's wrecked."

"Okay. You stand aside."

When I did so, Joe dragged the old man up off his knees and allowed him to collapse into the seat. Mimo's eyes were crusty black slits. His head with its crown of frowsy hair periodically lolled onto his breast, and both skinny arms hung impotently at his sides. His skin was the color of wood ashes. Crimson streaks defiled his sweater and pants.

Keeping the knife in place, Joe rolled Mimo to a position as far away from me and Ivor as he could manage. "You know better than to say anything smart," he told me. "Get the medical gig on the viewer, but keep our video pickup turned off. Hail them and explain that we've had a com malfunction, but everything else is peachy-keen. Except the patient, of course."

The tape manacles didn't really hamper my use of the equipment. An impressive red-and-white gig emblazoned with the legend TORNGAT EMERGENCY SPACE-MEDICAL RESPONSE appeared on the scan monitor. It was nearly on top of us.

The ship-to-ship interior display showed a distinguished-looking man with a silver Afro and one of the meanest purple snarls I've ever seen. He was wearing a coverall that looked more military than medical and a nameplate I couldn't quite make out.

"It's about time you came back to us, *Chispa Dos*!" he said furiously. "We've been trying to raise you for fifteen minutes. What's wrong with your video feed?"

"A small malfunction. I apologize. I'm Asahel Frost, Vice President of Rampart Starcorp. Who are you, sir?"

"Dr. Ben Harrison Crystal, medical team commander. What's the status of your patient?"

"He's still in critical condition. We've positively determined that he's suffering from nicotine poisoning." I described the mode of administration, and the doctor rolled his eyes heavenward. "We've brought the patient to the transport bay so you can take him into your vessel for treatment just as soon as you dock."

"Satisfactory. We're matching orbits. Open up."

I clumsily hit the proper control pads. Flashing lights and alarm Klaxons activated in the transport bay. Air vented, the exterior sounds cut off abruptly, and the great gate into space opened like a monster's mouth, revealing the orbiter hanging expectantly in a star-spangled night.

It wafted inside, gave a little skip when it hit our graviton field, and landed right on the bull's-eye. The bots converged to clamp it down and zap it with decon radiation, the gate closed, and I hit the control calling for rapid recompression. Alarm lights flashed again. After a moment we could hear the *ooh-gahs* and the hissing roar of air filling the bay.

Dr. Crystal was still on the monitor. His aspect was one of stony anger, and a few beads of perspiration dotted his caramel forehead. Maybe he'd been dragooned into accepting the unorthodox assignment and was piqued at missing time on the ski slopes.

I checked the safety displays. The bay environment was atmospheric and temperate. I said, "Would you prefer to supervise the transfer of the patient from our control room, Doctor?"

He looked questioningly at someone beyond scan range. Then: "No. Bring him down to us."

"May I ask whether you have the Karl Nazarian party aboard?"

"No, you may not ask," said Ben Harrison Crystal. Then he cut me off.

"Well, you have yourself a nice day!" I muttered, and turned to Betancourt for further orders.

Joe said, "Open the broadband hail frequency."

"So you can call in Galapharma?"

"I'll let you do the honors, shitheel. They've gotta be around here somewhere. Give 'em a shout."

I spoke to the communicator. "Starship *Chispa Dos* is calling any Galapharma AC vessel in the Torngat solar system. Come back, Galapharma."

The ship-to-ship monitor went to white in an audio-only reply. They were playing the same game we'd played with the medical gig.

"Galapharma responding. Go to Secure Channel 6892Z."

I did the switch, and the Invisible Man said, "Stand by for instructions."

"*Chispa* acknowledges."

A long silence ensued.

"Yo, Gala?" I caroled. "You want to tell us what to do next?"

After an interval the Invisible Man came back. "Uh—load the patient James Matsukawa onto the medical gig and wait for instructions. Be aware that your vessel is under our guns."

"We will comply." I silenced the transmitter and said to Betancourt, "Looks like you might have a bunch of confused clowns out there."

"Or they're planning to get cute," he growled. "But I'm ahead of 'em! You're going to haul Jim down into the transport bay. I'm staying right here." He grinned at me. "My ace in the hole is Schneider, in case you haven't already guessed. Gala can snatch Jim and that guy Garth Lee off the medical gig any time they feel like it. But they don't get their hands on Ollie until the loose ends are tidied up and I'm able to zorch on out of here with my skin in one piece."

He pushed Mimo's chair closer to the bay airlock hatch, which was now wide-open. The boning knife glittered in the old man's hair and a fresh welling of blood oozed from the rear of his turtleneck. His head was nearly in his lap, and I decided he must have lost consciousness.

I took hold of the rear tiller of the antigrav gurney and pushed it through to the open platform elevator that would carry us down into the bay. Matsukawa was neatly covered with blankets. His nostrils were stoppered with little tubes feeding him oxygen, and a tiny vital-signs monitor was stuck to his forehead. I could see his chest rising and falling. His face looked peaceful. Maybe expelling the cigars had saved his life.

Who are you, Jimbo? I wondered. Why does Galapharma want to keep you quiet? The Dagasatt facility's no secret anymore, and Gala certainly has no idea you're a demiclone—if you are one. So why didn't Ty Baldwin just tell Joe to kill you if your silence is so important?

I hit the elevator descent pad and started down. Joe Betancourt remained standing in the airlock doorway behind Mimo's chair, watching me.

Below, the medical gig was still buttoned up tight. Vague shapes were visible on its bridge. I made the short trip across the deck and halted with my burden half a dozen meters from the main egress hatch of the ambulance.

For a long moment nothing happened. Then the hatch cracked and lowered on its pistons. Dr. Ben Harrison Crystal came down the ramp, accompanied by two technicians carrying complicated-looking medical equipment.

Following after them were four soldiers in full fighting armor and helmets. They held Claus-Gewitter photon beamers, the marksman's weapon of choice for precision zapping.

The tallest of the troopers asked me, "Are you Betancourt?"

"No. I'm Asahel Frost. Betancourt's standing up there in the airlock door, behind the guy in the swivel chair."

Cheeow!

What in hell?

I instinctively dived to the deck as the trooper fired right over my head. Lying there in shock, I waited for a second laser beam to fry me dead.

"Get up, Frost."

The big shooter stood there impassively, his weapon at port. The other soldiers were hanging back as the doctor and his associates bent over Matsukawa and performed some kind of medical procedure, ignoring the fireworks. I got onto my knees, then shambled upright and risked a quick peek at the anteroom doorway above. Mimo was still there, sitting up. There was no sign of Joe Betancourt.

So much for the turncoat pilot's insurance! I wondered if Ollie Schneider's policy would still work when the Gala troops got their hands on him.

"Frost!" the shooter said to me. "Is that orbiter gig of yours over there locked?"

"It's wide-open. We don't have thieves aboard—only Galapharma scumbags."

"Is your gig fueled and ready?"

"Yes." I figured he'd disable it before leaving so we couldn't use it to escape. When the ambulance was clear of *Chispa*, the shooter's buddies in the Gala fighting ships would energetically disassemble us with their cannons. Karl Nazarian and his crew were probably already dead.

I decided to try a last bluff. "You listen to me! My other friends up in the control anteroom will kill Oliver Schneider unless you back off. That happens, you'll be in the soup, buster."

The big guy laughed.

"This is no joke! Haven't you been told that Schneider has hidden evidence that could ruin Galapharma? He dies, the incriminating poop gets released. You better check with your high command."

He lifted his helmet visor, revealing a beefy face adorned with pale eyebrows, a white-blond walrus mustache, and a sardonic smile. "That's not necessary. You can keep Citizen Schneider—with the compliments of Tyler Baldwin. The game plan has changed."

"Erik Skogstad, I presume. How'd you get here so fast? Steal yourself a new Y700?"

The smile faded. "This time, you get a pass. But God help the lot of you if Baldwin's brother dies from that shit you gave him."

"Brother?" I repeated stupidly.

But the puzzle pieces were about to fall into place.

He turned away and shouted an order in an alien language,

one I'd last heard spoken in a secret laboratory below the noxious jungles of Cravat. Belatedly, I noticed that the three other troopers were wearing armor that was conspicuously wasp-waisted. They escorted the medical party and the patient into the gig.

Skogstad prodded my chest with his blaster. "Go back to the control room now, Asahel Frost. When we have both gigs secured for liftoff, open the bay gate. Don't attempt to interfere with us."

He strode off in the direction of *Chispa*'s orbiter, and I went galumphing to the elevator, my head awhirl with wild speculation. At the top I found an empty swivel chair and the body of Joe Betancourt. He had a great big smoldering third nostril right above the other two.

Mimo was bending over Ivor, sawing away feebly with the Henckels boning knife at the ball of tape imprisoning the giant's hands. "Something very peculiar is going on," he observed in a quavering voice.

"Damn right," I agreed. "But I think I'm starting to get a handle on it. Give me that knife and sit down before you fall down."

He subsided onto the deck, leaning against the excursion suit rack. "*Que gacho*—I'm getting too old for this sort of thing."

I ripped the tape from Ivor's mouth, finished cutting his hands loose, and freed my own. I gave Ivor the knife, telling him to cut the tape from his own ankles and then from mine.

Outside in the bay, both gigs had their navigation lights shining, ready to go. Sealing our airlock hatches—Joe's body and the chair were still inside—I slapped the emergency depressurization switch. The transport bay filled with fog for a split second and then held only clear vacuum.

Ivor was working on my fetters, but I was too busy to notice. The iris gate opened and both of the orbiters zipped away into space. I acquired them on the exterior scanner . . .

And saw on the viewer what I'd halfway expected to see.

A titanic starship was waiting out there, its eleven-kilometer length blotting out the stars behind it. It looked like a warty acorn with a fancy dagger poked through it. The acorn was surmounted by a glowing blue dome, and the hilt of the dagger was studded with gemlike azure ports.

Mimo was studying the viewer with awe. *"Vaya por dios— ese es el Meromero de los Haluk!"*

He was right. It was the same immense alien vessel that had come to the Kedge-Lockaby system to rescue Bronson Elgar and maroon me on Helly's Comet, the flagship of the Haluk top dog, the Servant of the Servants of Luk.

The big ship's transport bay opened and both gigs disappeared inside.

"Will they destroy us now?" Ivor asked quietly.

"I'm not sure," I replied. "As Mimo said, something peculiar is going on."

"Where are Matt and Ildy?" Mimo asked me.

"Safe enough. Joe made me lock them in the midships excursion bay but he didn't evacuate the air."

"But all this makes no sense," the old smuggler grumbled.

"I misjudged the situation," I said, "and so did Joe Betancourt. It wasn't Galapharma who turned Joe and came chasing after us. It was the Haluk. I suspect that the aliens set up Karl's ambush as well, maybe using Gala fighting ships."

"Oh, my goodness," said Ivor. "Haluk demiclones in the Galapharma forces?"

"You got it, kid. Joe told me he was recruited by a Gala agent named Erik Skogstad. Erik drove the Haluk ship I sent Joe to destroy—only Erik *won* that dogfight, and gave Joe the choice of betraying us or dying. Guess who was in charge of the bandit boarding party just now, and gave Little Joe his final kiss-off."

"Erik Skogstad?" Ivor hazarded.

"Go to the head of the class," I said. "He probably came in on the Haluk flagship and intercepted the medical gig. When I talked to him, he implied that his specific mission was to rescue Jim Matsukawa—Ty Baldwin's brother."

"But I've seen images of this Baldwin in certain databases pertinent to my former profession," Mimo protested. "He is surely a Caucasoid, while Matsukawa seemed to be wholly of Oriental ancestry. Unless the brothers were adopted, or were—" He pulled up short in sudden comprehension, spitting a Mexican expletive.

"Brothers under the skin," I said. "Or rather, under the human DNA."

And now I knew the fourth person Matsukawa had called from Dagasatt during my assault.

"Both of them Haluk!" said Mimo wildly. "Skogstad, perhaps Garth Lee and Bronson Elgar as well! *Dios*—are any of Gala's Perseus Spur personnel still human?"

I said, "What I'd like to know is, how many ringers besides Tyler Baldwin have infiltrated critical Big Seven Concern positions within the Orion Arm?"

Ivor said, "Do you suppose Alistair Drummond has knowingly cooperated in the demiclone substitution scheme?"

"Hardly. The asshole had no idea what kind of can of worms he was opening when he began his illegal trading with the Haluk. They're *smart*, dammit! They pulled the wool over Gala's eyes—not only with the demiclone thing, but also with the larger trading conspiracy. Gala and its Big Seven allies sold small numbers of advanced starships and other high technology to the Haluk at inflated prices. The Haluk took the stuff and studied it. Then they built more, only they improved on the originals."

"As the ancient Japanese did," Ivor remarked sagely, "when they first encountered Western technology after centuries of isolation."

"How else could that monster flagship out there have kept pace with us on our trip from the Perseus Spur?" I asked rhetorically. "Do you two remember the sophisticated Haluk gunship that attacked us when we were on the way to Cravat? It was head and shoulders above the usual heaps used by their pirates. They've kept their snazzy new starships under wraps. They probably don't have very many of them yet, just as they don't have many demiclones. The Haluk are biding their time, just as I was afraid they—"

"Look!" Ivor cried in disbelief. "Our orbiter is returning."

"Holy *frijole*," I murmured.

We waited. I tried to hail the approaching gig but no one responded. Eventually the little spacecraft reentered our open iris gate and docked.

"Well," I said with a grimace, "let's see if they sent us a lovely present or an antimatter bomb."

I secured the gate and repressurized the bay. When the warning lights and Klaxons shut down, the gig's hatch opened. Karl Nazarian emerged, followed by Lotte Dietrich, Hector Motlaletsie, and Cassius Potter. Presumably, the Haluk had kept back their beamish boy, Garth Lee.

"They've let Karl and his people go!" Ivor exclaimed. "But why?"

I recalled what Skogstad had told me. "Maybe because the game plan has changed."

Then I thought about the unthinkable notion that my sister Eve had so glibly proposed as part of the venture-credit prospectus to Macrodur: Rampart already owned another rozkoz, a commodity with the potential for generating unlimited profits for the Starcorp and its trading partners. All we needed was a new treaty with the Haluk, so they would become a legitimate market for the genetic engineering vector PD32·C2.

"It's just possible," I said to my friends, "that the Haluk know something that we don't. Something that's caused a one-eighty switch in their strategy."

The newcomers had ascended the elevator. Karl Nazarian was pounding on the airlock door, so flushed with excitement I was afraid he'd have a stroke. I hurried to let him and the others in.

"Helly, I'm flabbergasted!" Karl roared. "Do you have any idea what the flaming hell is going on? The medical gig was intercepted by this unbelievably huge Haluk starship—"

"There were *humans* aboard her!" Hector Motlaletsie spluttered. "Collaborators! They took us prisoner."

"I know," I said. "Are any of you hurt?"

"No," Lotte Dietrich said coolly. "The bastards took my e-books, but I had backup data-dimes stashed in my bottle of whiffenpoppers."

Ivor giggled.

Cassius Potter caught sight of bloodied Mimo. "Nothing wrong with us. But it sure looks like somebody messed up Bermudez. Shouldn't we be giving him first aid? And who the hell is that dead man in the airlock?"

All four of them began nattering at the top of their lungs, while Mimo and I tried to explain. We were all a little crazy at that point.

In the midst of the hullabaloo, Ivor pointed at the external viewer and said in a loud voice, "The Haluk starship is breaking orbit."

Silence.

"Well," said Cassius, with sour satisfaction, "if they intend to blast us to bits, I reckon they'll do it now."

Lotte crossed herself.

The monster vessel came about with surprising agility. We watched its SLD power units brighten, sixteen of them paired along the "blade" of the daggerlike structure, and then it soared away. An instant later the dazzling flash of hyperspatial crossover marked the Haluk ship's transition to ultraluminal drive. It was irrevocably gone.

"How strange," Ivor marveled. "Not that I'm complaining . . ."

"Folks," I addressed the gathering, "I think we'd better be on our way, too."

Anticlimactically, we scattered. I sent Karl and Hector to check on Ollie Schneider. Lotte and Ivor took Mimo to the sick bay. Cassius Potter and I went forward to rescue Matt and Ildy. In less than thirty minutes we had resumed our voyage to Earth.

When we were safely away from the Torngat system, I reported the abduction of the medical team "by Haluk pirates" to Macrodur security and to Sector Zone Patrol. Both were disinclined to believe my story until I submitted our edited audiovisual record of the immense flagship engulfing the two gigs, after which there was a furious exchange of subspace messages.

A certain Commander Newton at patrol HQ demanded

that we return to Torngat at once for psychotronic examination. I said, regretfully, that that would not be convenient—citing obscure statutes relating to the rights of sovereign corporations operating in deep space—but promised to transmit formal depositions concerning the incident from all witnesses aboard *Chispa* just as soon as we could get ourselves organized.

The cops threatened to come after us. (As a mere Starcorp, Rampart had less political clout than Macrodur Concern, which was screaming bloody murder.) I suggested that patrol efforts might be better directed toward analyzing the fuel signature of the Haluk pirate vessel and tracking it down before it escaped the sector. I also pointed out to Commander Newton that our Y700 was faster—and better armed—than any patrol cruiser. We had done our civic duty by reporting the abduction, transmitting a holo of the perp flagrante delicto, and affirming that we'd submit statements. Now we were determined to go on about our legitimate corporate business without interference.

Newton bitched, blustered, and bluffed. I stood firm while dazzling him with fusillades of legal precedents and other official red tape. (Not for nothing had I earned the degree of *Juris Doctor* from Harvard Law School back in the days when Simon assumed I'd become a Rampart exec. My years in the ICS had also taught me a thing or two about bureaucratic arm-twisting.)

Zone Patrol finally backed off, just as I knew it would. In the Commonwealth of Human Worlds, sadly enough, civil authorities almost always deferred to Big Business.

The following days were a time of regrouping, of cleaning up loose ends, and of busy intercommunication between *Chispa* and Earth.

In a brief, informal ceremony, we consigned Joe Betancourt's body to the ship's matter converter, then voided his elements into hyperspace. I couldn't remember which of the Circles of Hell Dante set aside for his ancient group of traitors, but the uncanny emptiness between the spatial dimensions seemed a likely enough resting place for our modern-day Judas.

Matt and I concluded the interrogation of Oliver Schneider two days later and transmitted the data to Eve. She assured us that Rampart lawyers were putting the final touches to the civil suit against Galapharma. There was much moaning and gnashing of teeth on the part of Zed, Dan, and the other Gala partisans on the Board of Directors who counseled delay, but Simon would brook no ass-dragging. It was his contention that filing the suit against Gala immediately would enhance Rampart's image as a dynamic outfit in the eyes of Macrodur's Chairman, Adam Stanislawski. It didn't hurt that old Adam also hated Alistair Drummond's *cojones*.

Prompted by intimations of mortality, I made a new will, bequeathing my quarterstake and the rest of my worldly goods to Simon, instructing him to have Dan register it through Rampart's legal department so it would be a matter of public record. I figured—naively, as it turned out—that if the bad guys knew that Simon would own a clear majority of the shares upon my death, I myself and the other members of my family would be safe from intimidation or physical threat.

Matt took formal depositions from all of us concerning our encounter with the Haluk flagship, then sent a transcript to Commander Newton at Zone Patrol. We couldn't conceal Joe Betancourt's role in the incident, nor that of Jim Matsukawa; but we did our best to keep their motivation murky. I stated truthfully that it was Betancourt who told me to send a broadband summons to Galapharma. The subsequent appearance of the alien ship was a shocking surprise to me. (Semi-truthful, but close enough.) My verbal description of the boarding encounter was brief and chock full of holes. Fortunately, neither Mimo nor Ivor had been in a position to contradict it.

In a sidebar statement, not under oath, I regretted that I'd failed to activate surveillance cameras in the transport bay while the pirates were aboard *Chispa*. In mitigation, I reminded Zone Patrol that I'd been under considerable stress at the time.

Karl and his people said nothing in their depositions about the presence of Garth Lee aboard the Torngat gig. None of the recorded material revealed it, either. My crew loyally declared that they "could not speculate" upon why the Haluk had kidnapped Jim Matsukawa and the medics.

Commander Newton told me that our depositions left a lot to be desired. I thanked him for his opinion and referred any subsequent official queries to the Rampart legal department.

It was a foregone conclusion that Macrodur would submit a formal complaint against the Haluk to Xenoaffairs. There was nothing we could do about that. It seemed likely, however, that SXA would bury the beef, as they had the Tokyo Haluk research, for unfathomable reasons of policy. Even if the secretariat did decide to take action, nothing was likely to happen for weeks—or even months.

I sent Eve a copy of the Zone Patrol transcript, along with an uncensored postscript filling in the blanks. The evidence, I told her rather snidely, could join the growing collection in her secret Haluk files, until she decided to reveal it.

Neither my sister nor I had the faintest notion how to turn the Tyler Baldwin blockbuster to Rampart's advantage. The demiclone Gala security chief was no doubt following an agenda of his own. Only time would tell whether it favored Galapharma and the ambitions of Alistair Drummond, or whether some convoluted sea-change had occurred among the aliens.

The rest of our voyage to Earth was relatively uneventful.

Mimo Bermudez healed rapidly and consumed the remainder of his Cohiba Robustos without sharing, citing therapeutic priorities. He used his convalescence to practice on the guitar and become better acquainted with his magnificent new starship. Meanwhile, he ordered *Plomazo* to be ferried back to Kedge-Lockaby after repairs were completed.

Karl Nazarian, Cassius Potter, and Hector Motlaletsie took over piloting duties, giving the rest of us welcome leisure. They seemed relieved that they would not be asked to undertake any serious clandestine operations while on Earth, and delighted to learn they would receive a generous combat allowance in addition to their other pay.

Matt Gregoire communicated with her office on Seriphos, smoothed out the final rough areas of the Dagasatt flap—at least so far as Zone Patrol was concerned—and dealt with other professional matters that had come up during her absence. Kindly and firmly, she refused to sleep with me. Not even a charity fuck. I told her I understood, then went and thought about how I might bury Alistair Drummond before he buried me. It was better than a cold shower.

Lotte Dietrich commandeered the galley and ousted Ivor Jenkins from his post as *chef de cuisine*. Waist-broadening schnitzel, sauerbraten, strudel, torten, pies, cookies, and other "comfort food" invaded our formerly health-conscious menu, to the delighted horror of one and all. As Karl said, we all needed a little Christmas out of season. Or Hanukkah or Kwanzaa, as the case may be.

No longer plagued by the Inquisition, Ollie Schneider studied e-books of notable vacation worlds, trying to decide where he'd live after he was set free—if he *was* set free—in the plea bargain arrangement. He proved to be a formidable poker player. Even Mimo got skinned.

All of the crew members speculated volubly about what they would do when we reached our journey's end and they were finally at leisure. Matt, Ivor, and Lotte had never visited Earth. The rest, terrestrial natives, had been away long enough to have developed raging cases of homesickness. There were good-humored arguments about the most scenic places to visit, the best museums, theaters, and other cultural attractions, the finest restaurants, the greatest shopping. The only thing everyone seemed to agree on was that Earth's capital, Toronto, would provide a highly satisfactory introduction to all manner of earthly delights—provided that Ollie Schneider didn't win all of their money before they got there.

The only person aboard *Chispa* not looking forward to arrival on Earth was me. Coping with the homicidal strategems of Alistair Drummond would be tough enough; keeping Simon from self-destructing might be even more of a challenge. But perhaps the worst dilemma I faced was how to deal with the family fink.

I'd pretty well nailed down his identity by now, but I didn't dare expose him until the time was ripe—if it ever was. The Frost family's reputation was at stake, and Rampart's integrity as well. The most satisfactory resolution would have been to tell him that I knew, quietly obtain his resignation from the Starcorp, and then let him stew forever in his own vile juice.

Before Katje's murder, that might have been a genuine option. It wasn't now. He'd have to pay a higher price for his unspeakable crime, but I was damned if I could decide what the price should be—or whether I had the right to exact it.

When we were only a day out from Earth, a welcome communiqué from Commander Newton at Zone Patrol informed me that Dr. Ben Harrison Crystal and his Torngat Emergency Space-Medical Response team had been released unharmed on the freesoil planet Linsang. And wonder of wonders, the medics confirmed what we had already told the patrol—that they had been abducted by a hitherto unknown coalition of lawless humans and Haluk, who plied interstellar space in a starship of astonishing proportions.

Newton refused my request for transcripts of the abductees' statements, although he did grudgingly provide me with brief verbal summaries when I reminded him of Rampart's legal rights as co-victim in the crime.

To my relief, Dr. Crystal's team apparently said nothing at all about Garth Lee's presence aboard their gig. Maybe they'd never noticed him among Karl's gang of hitchhikers on the way up from Torngat. Later on Lee might have made himself scarce. Neither did the medics report my conversation with Erik Skogstad, although they did comment on Joe Betancourt's abrupt termination. Maybe they'd been too preoccupied with the patient to eavesdrop.

Jim Matsukawa, man of mystery, recovered fully from self-induced nicotine poisoning. His return to health had been the signal for the medical team's release. The junior

medics speculated that Matsukawa must be a valued hench-
man of the pirates, who somehow engineered his rescue from
captivity on *Chispa* by means of the cigar subterfuge. Dr.
Crystal diagnosed Matsukawa as a cretinoid coprocephalic—
helpfully translating the medical terminology into its Standard English equivalent of "stupid shithead"—who was lucky
to be alive.

Before letting the gig go, the raiders removed all of its
high-tech healing equipment, expressing breezy apologies.
The Response Team and their denuded craft were currently
on their way back home, hitchhiking on a Macrodur transport
diverted from the Redmond-Alpha run.

Patrol Commander Newton told me that the authorities on
Torngat were greatly relieved at the happy outcome to the abduction. (Pirates will be pirates, and these had proved more
gentlemanly than most.) On the other hand, Rampart might
expect to receive a bill for additional charges from Torngat
Emergency Space-Medical Response to refit the stripped gig.

Newton wanted to know why we'd had Matsukawa in our
brig. I told the truth: he was a material witness in an upcoming civil case, legitimately in our custody. ZP could
check with the Port Manager of Cravat for verification, if
necessary.

Newton said he would. And he'd be reporting the entire
fishy incident to the Secretariat for Xenoaffairs.

I said I really didn't give a damn.

Eight standard days and fourteen hours after leaving
the Perseus Spur, *Chispa Dos* entered the Terrestrial Solar
System.

I insisted on taking the helm when we touched down on
Earth at the enormous Oshawa Platform Starport in Lake Ontario, fifty kilometers east of the Capital Conurbation. It was
a perfect day in August, puffy white clouds in the sky, the
cobalt-blue lake sparkling with sunlight. Over on the shore,
the gorgeous skyway-connected towers of Toronto shone beneath the faint shimmer of the force umbrella like colored
spears entwined with gleaming ribbons.

Earth. I decided I was glad to be back after all.

Mimo was in the right-hand seat on the flight bridge. I settled *Chispa* into the docking cradle and shut down the SLD engines. Our internal graviton field cut off. We sat quietly, waiting to be towed away to the underwater hangar facility.

"Earth gravity," I said. "Never thought I'd feel it again. Not nearly as strong as Dagasatt's. I'm almost ten kilos lighter. My sorry old muscles should have more oomph in them, too."

Mimo laughed. "That's the conventional wisdom. However, your activities in the next few days will likely be more cerebral than physical, *amigo*."

I stretched, flexed my pecs, made a fist of my right hand and slapped it solidly into my left palm. "That's right. Cerebral. A little necessary business to take care of in the capital, then maybe something completely different down in Arizona at the Rampart Board Meeting."

"Would you like me to accompany you?"

"Thanks, Mimo, but no. What happens next is between me and my family. A few days, and it'll all be resolved. You enjoy the capital for a while. I'll give you a call when the dust has settled and you can come down to the Sky Ranch. We'll relax together. I'll show you my old boyhood haunts."

"Certainly. That will be very pleasant."

"Don't worry. I've got my battle tactics all worked out. The good guys will triumph and the bastards will never know what hit 'em."

"I have every confidence in you, *mi hijo*."

We grinned at each other, neither believing a word the other was saying.

Chapter 15

"Asahel Frost has made a will!" Alistair Drummond thunders. "My legal people just found it in the public record and called it to my attention. Why didn't you inform me?"

He decides to tell a prudent lie. "Because I didn't know about it myself until this morning."

"So much for your bloody brilliant plan! . . . And if that weren't bad enough, my investigators in Toronto have managed to ferret out another Rampart bombshell. I wonder if you can guess what it is."

Drummond's face on the vidphone screen is a mask of ferocity, deeply tanned from his Arizona sojourn except for the area that was shielded by sunglasses. The ice-colored eyes set in startling ovals of pale flesh are no longer unreadable; they have the glaring wide pupils of a goaded predator poised to strike.

"The venture credit prospectus!" the Galapharma CEO says. "Did ye think I wouldn't find out about it, ye treacherous buggerin' lump of shite?" A torrent of curses, some of them impenetrably Scottish, pours from the phone.

But he remains withdrawn and silent, oddly immune to the beast's raging, mulling alternatives now that Asa's death can no longer ensure passage of the takeover vote. There must be another way to exert the necessary leverage. There must be.

Drummond leans closer to the telephone's video pickup. His hair is disheveled. He wears the black cowboy shirt with its top pearl snaps open. A vein in his neck is throbbing. After his lapse into Caledonian, he has reverted to the purest Home Counties diction, full of withering contempt. "The prospectus. My agents inform me that Adam Stanislawski is about to accept. Do you know what that means? Of course you do! You helped draft the prospectus. You stood by as it was submitted, knowing it could mean the ruin of all my plans—of Galapharma itself. And so you're *dead*, you conniving scrote! . . . No, that's too easy! Why should I have you killed when your own family will see that you're sent to Coventry Blue?"

Then he has it. Thanks to Drummond's ranting.

His voice is a whipcrack. "Alistair, shut up."

The enormity of his insubordination actually silences the beast.

"You won't lose Rampart. I've thought of another way. And Macro's venture credit infusion will only increase the value of your new acquisition. Stanislawski won't withdraw out of spite after a Galapharma merger. He's a practical old Polack—and a political whiz. If he's decided to enter a venture scheme based on PD32:C2's prospects, he must have already sent up a few trial balloons in the Assembly concerning a new treaty with the Haluk. And liked what he heard. Alistair, we can still win this thing. I can do it for you."

The Galapharma CEO has listened impatiently. Madness flickers in the black wells of his eyes, striving to take control; but in the end the rational portion of his mind supervenes. He blinks and pulls back from the phone lens. Stalling a little further, he screws a fresh giggle-stick into his jade cigarette holder, lights it, and takes a deep drag. Behind him is the understated elegance of his villa at the Arizona Biltmore.

"Very well." As though he doesn't really care. "Tell me your new idea, lad."

"Simon has scheduled the board meeting for this afternoon, at the Sky Ranch. I'll get his proxy before then. And Asa's, too." He explains how.

Drummond is openly skeptical. "You haven't got it in you!"

"Try me."

"Hmph. All right. But if I decide that you've failed—or you attempt to pull some scam—I'll institute my own fallback action. It *won't* fail."

"I'll call you when I have the proxies in hand. Would you like to attend the board meeting and make your ultimate pitch in person?"

Caught by surprise, Drummond bursts into uproarious laughter. "Oh, yes! I accept your kind invitation." He is still laughing as the phone display goes dark.

There was really only one costume appropriate for both Toronto and Arizona on that memorable day. So I was wearing my good old poplin briar pants, the Navajo-motif Pendleton shirt—getting a little frayed around the collar by now—and my beat-up Gokey snakeboots. I'd worn the duds a lot during my six-month stint as a Rampart VP, prowling Spur worlds in search of baddies. They were my armor against creeping corporate respectability.

The day was a touch too warm for the waxed-cotton hunting coat, so to complete my outfit I borrowed one of Mimo's belts that had a massive silver buckle, along with a bolo necktie with a cabochon Mexican fire-opal on the slide. I carried a briefcase in which I'd stowed a notebook, a hard copy of Ollie Schneider's deposition, and a Kagi pistol in an innocuous-looking closed holster.

When Matt Gregoire showed up in *Chispa*'s boarding vestibule with Ollie Schneider in tow, she studied my ensemble with a knowing little smirk. "Killer threads! Seems to me I've seen them before."

"When first we met," I concurred airily. "When you and Ollie and the Rampart Board of Directors first clapped eyes on the dreaded Helmut Icicle back on Seriphos—and froze your livers."

We cackled in unison. Schneider stood there looking dejected—as well he might. After we finished with him, he was going to lodge in the CCID Detention Facility in Elora until the resolution of Rampart's civil case against Galapharma. It was a glamour slammer where the inmates were pampered, but it wasn't freedom.

Matt looked marvelous in corporate mufti, an oyster silk pantsuit and a matching silk boatneck tee that set off her cinnamon skin to perfection. Her only jewelery was a pair of small Tyrinian gemshell ear-studs. She wore a stun-glove on her right hand, and her other wrist was linked to Ollie's by an unobtrusive security cable.

The ship's computer said: *Ground transport has arrived.*

The three of us went into the excursion bay and cycled the lock. Outside on the deck of the submarine hangar was a gleaming black robolimo. The front door opened and out stepped my cousin Zared Frost. He smiled at us without offering to shake hands, which was understandable under the circumstances.

"We drew straws to decide who'd do escort duty. I won. Welcome to Earth."

The President and Chief Operating Officer of Rampart Starcorp was a moderately tall man in his mid-forties. His carefully styled hair was glossy chestnut. An aquiline nose, high cheekbones, and a thin, decisive mouth made him the most good-looking member of the Frost clan. He was also one of the smartest. Only a limiting innate conservatism and a deficiency of that elusive entrepreneurial quality called "drive" had kept him from being designated crown prince of the family empire.

His own father, my late Uncle Ethan, had sadly kissed Zed off as having "not a lick of fire in his belly." Ethan's will had divided his quarterstake between his wife, Emma Bradbury, and Simon to ensure that Zed would not gain control of the Starcorp. But my cousin had never given up his ambitions.

Now he swept open the door to the rear limo compartment and ushered Matt and Schneider inside. "I'm sure you two won't mind if I have a few private words with my cousin Asa on the way into town."

Matt said, "I understand."

Ollie gave a bored shrug.

When Zed and I were seated side by side in front, I said, "We'll have to make a short detour before going to Rampart Tower. To pick up Schneider's lawyer. He's in the Simcoe Block."

Zed gave the destination to the car and we sped up and

away to the Oshawa Collector. Moments later we were thirty meters high in the limpid summer air, westbound on the upper level of Queen Elizabeth Way, heading for the corporate spires of downtown Toronto.

"I'll make this short and sweet, Asa," my cousin said. "What will it take for you to vote your quarterstake in favor of the Gala merger?"

I pretended to consider. "How about your head on a platter with an apple in your mouth?"

Zed turned and seized the strings of my bolo tie in both hands, hauling me toward him. "I'm serious, damn you!"

Matt Gregoire was rapping anxiously on the closed glass partition separating us. I appreciated her concern, but I wasn't worried.

Reaching around and entwining the fingers of my left hand in Zed's designer coiffure, I hoisted him ceilingward out of the leather bucket seat beside me. He shrieked—more from shock than from real pain. Hair is a merciful handle. Try yanking a large wad of your own some time.

"In less than five seconds," I told him, "your nose will be smashed against the navigation console of the car. Or you can let go of my tie and we'll take it from the top."

He turned me loose. I reciprocated. He flopped back into his seat, making soft gasping sounds.

"Violence is not your *métier*, Zed," I remarked. "You're an amateur and I used to be a pro. Also, my muscles have pumped up a bit from living strenuously on high-grav planets, whereas you have mainly exercised your charisma."

"Fuck you."

"Why should I vote for the Galapharma takeover?" I asked him.

"It'd be best for all of us." He turned away to stare out the windshield, smoothing his mussed hair continuously with a trembling hand. "You know what happens to people who get in Alistair Drummond's way."

"Some of them get marooned on comets," I said lightly. "Some get semimorphed into Haluk. And some are given poison and die in their sleep."

"Don't you think I know that?" he cried hotly. "His gorillas have threatened me, too—and Jenny and the children! Even my mother! After Emma made her foolish little speech praising Eve at the last board meeting, I was told to modify her thinking—or expect to receive my inheritance from her before the next vote on the merger is taken. Drummond is insane, Asa! What kind of a man would order the deaths of two harmless old women?"

"A desperate one."

"Then let him have what he wants! We can't fight him. What difference does it make if Rampart becomes a division of Galapharma? For God's sake—we'll profit hugely from the deal, all of us!"

I said, "You don't understand the Big Picture."

"And *you* don't really give a damn about the Starcorp!" he bellowed. "Or Simon, or any of the rest of us except your precious big sister. I've worked my ass off for Rampart for twenty-three years! *You* thumbed your nose at it and went off to play cops and robbers until you fell on your face. Then you have the monumental brass to come waltzing back out of nowhere, pulling a snow-job on Simon, telling the rest of us you know what's best—"

"Saving Eve, rousting Gala spies and saboteurs from Rampart's woodwork, corraling the one material witness who can nail Drummond's hide to the barn door." I chuckled without humor. "Some brass. You could use a little yourself, Zed—stuck up your spine."

"You—you—you *cowboy*!"

I guess it was the worst epithet in his vocabulary. I had the feeling he would have laid hands on me again, if he'd dared. His eyes were darting wildly. One hand clenched into a fist and the fingers of the other scratched reflexively at the fabric of his pants leg. Cousin Zed was a man approaching the end of his rope.

I didn't say anything. After a while the anger and tension leaked out of him like grain from a punctured feed bag. He slumped in the leather seat and I saw tears trickling from his eyes.

"Asa," he finally said in a hoarse voice. "I'm scared out of my fuckin' mind. So are Dan and Beth. They've told me so. Drummond's brutes must have threatened Simon and Eve, too. Please! Be reasonable. You can solve everything—"

"I'm doing my best to do that," I said. "In my own way."

"You'll be the death of us all." He said it almost matter-of-factly. "Unless I can convince you to vote in favor of the merger."

"You can't."

He eyed me askance, his face full of desperation. "You wouldn't even have to go to the board meeting and face down Eve and your father. If you gave me your proxy I could—"

"Zed. No."

He gave a great sigh. "Then it's on your head. Whatever happens."

"If it makes you feel any better to believe that, be my guest. But there's a quote by a Brit named Edmund Burke that I used to have mounted on my office wall at ICS. Joanna embroidered it for me—can you believe it? It said: 'All that is required for evil to triumph is for good men to do nothing.' I got to feeling pretty pessimistic about that philosophy after I got Thrown Away. Now I'm maybe ready to give it another shot."

"You're a self-righteous bastard." His voice was faint, resigned. "You don't care who gets hurt."

I nodded. "Simon would probably agree with you."

"Go to hell," he said dully. "Go to hell."

After a while the limo's computer said: *Now arriving at Simcoe Block. Please indicate the office you intend to visit so that the proper skyway may be selected. Default is the underground parking lot.*

I said, "Law offices of Falwyn, Singh, and Bloomberg."

We zoomed up the spiral skyway with inertialess ease and exited at Level 62. A uniformed flunky came to greet us.

"I'll wait with the car," Zared Frost said in a dead voice.

So Matt and Ollie and I left him.

Our business didn't take long. Jaswinder Singh, a bearded man wearing a butterscotch-colored suit and a matching

turban, had a mournful expression and dark liquid eyes
that took in my casual garb with cosmopolitan insouciance.
After the introductions, he embraced his old college chum—
hampered only slightly by Schneider's being shackled to
Matt—and commiserated briefly.

One of the incriminating sealed packets sat on Singh's
desk. (Ollie had told him to destroy the other one.) The
lawyer had Schneider open the container and verify its contents. Then Singh said to me, "As I understand it, you now
wish me to accompany you to Rampart Tower, where the
formal offer of immunity will be vouchsafed by Rampart's
CEO."

"That's correct," I said.

"Very well. I'm ready to proceed." He rummaged beneath
his desk and produced a case to carry the packet in.

"There's one other small thing you might do, if you're
willing," I said diffidently. "It would save us considerable
time and enhance our goodwill toward the prisoner. Rampart
would expect to be billed for your services, of course."

"What's that?"

I opened my own briefcase and took out the notebook
primed with the dime of Schneider's deposition. I handed the
hard copy transcript to Singh for his examination, explaining
what it was and how it still required interrogator-validation
by an independent officer of the court before becoming admissible evidence.

"Matt Gregoire and I are the interrogators of record and
both of us hold *praefectus* status," I concluded, powering up
the notebook. "I'd like you to do the validation. I know my request is somewhat unorthodox, but I have good reasons for
not using a Rampart legal officer in the procedure. You may
duplicate and retain the data for your records if your firm
intends to act on Schneider's behalf during the upcoming
proceedings."

Singh frowned at the scene on the notebook's flatscreen as
the preliminary statements played and the recorded questioning began. He flipped briefly through the bound sheets of

the hard copy, then tapped the notebook's Pause pad and spoke to Schneider.

"Ollie, do you want me to validate this deposition? It would be better if I examined it closely first—"

"Nah. Do it, Windy. I really want Rampart's goodwill enhanced. And if you'll represent me, I guarantee I can pay my bills . . . if you don't object to sheltered funds."

Some subdued laughter. I tried without success to imagine this dignified, middle-aged Sikh lawyer as a hell-raising undergraduate named Windy.

Jaswinder Singh lifted his hands in a gesture of agreement and called in an assistant with the proper data-amending equipment. Ten minutes later it was done. Schneider's validated deposition was transmitted safely to Rampart's legal department computers and incorporated into the body of the civil suit, just as Eve and I had arranged it during my flight to Earth.

And there wasn't a thing the family fink could do about it.

Rampart Tower in Toronto pales in comparison to the grandiose structure on the planet Seriphos that serves as the working corporate headquarters. The tower is a nice enough building, a hundred stories high, with three skyways providing direct access from the high-road network in addition to a hopper pad and the usual basement connection to Underground Toronto. But in those days, Rampart itself only occupied the top fifteen floors in the tower; the offices below were leased out. It was a fairly typical setup for a Starcorp of moderate size that had great expectations.

Our small group was subdued as we disembarked at the uppermost exit of Rampart Tower's skyway. Simon's assistant, Guido Cabrini, met us in the glass-enclosed porte-cochere, accompanied by two uniformed InSec guards.

"These gentlemen will relieve you of your prisoner," he said to Matt. And to Singh: "You and your client will be taken to one of our lounges until your presence is required. There will be something to eat."

Cousin Zed had slipped away almost as soon as the limo

stopped moving. Matt and I followed Cabrini's suggestion that we freshen up in the opulent executive washrooms before going into the meeting. When I returned to the foyer, Matt was already there, admiring the spectacular view while Cabrini pointed out landmarks.

"—and just to the south of us, at the edge of the Inner Harbor, is Galapharma Tower. Four hundred stories high. The Concern's offices fill every square meter of space."

Matt's lips were twitching suspiciously. "What a striking architectural style the Gala building has. So . . . erect!"

Guido Cabrini grinned. "It does have a rather emphatic masculine aspect, doesn't it? Capital wags have many colorful names for it. The Galapharma headquarters in Glasgow is three times larger, but not nearly so evocatively designed . . . Would you please come with me to the conference room? The attendees are just finishing a buffet lunch."

We followed him down a sunny corridor decorated with potted plants and generic artwork. Since this uppermost floor was dedicated to the most rarefied commercial machinations, it gave the appearance of being nearly deserted. The occasional ranking minion wafted by, doing a double take at my nonconformist appearance.

The conference room was a huge circular chamber enclosed in floor-to-ceiling window. The 360-degree view of the Capital Conurbation and the glorious blue lake was breathtaking. In its center was a fanciful stone construction that would have served as a multiple fireplace in winter; in August it was an artificial waterfall adorned with native and exotic flowering plants. Around the room's perimeter were furniture groupings—couches, low tables, and serving credenzas, as well as com units, computers, and other equipment, well-camouflaged so as not to disfigure the ambience of managerial elegance. A much larger circular table with more than a dozen chairs and individual recessed data terminals stood on the room's north side—perhaps coincidentally out of eyeshot of Galapharma Tower.

When Matt and I were led in and announced by Guido Cabrini, there were three distinct groups of people waiting, conversing in subdued voices and munching from plates of tidbits. The Rampart contingent included Simon, Eve—in another Merry Widow disguise, veil and all—Dan, Zed, and old Gunter Eckert, Rampart's Chief Financial Officer.

Not quite mingling with them were the governmental representatives—three people from the Interstellar Commerce Secretariat and four from the Office of the Chief Prosecutor of the Commonwealth Judicial Tribunal. I recognized only two of them: Undersecretary Vernon Kildare of ICS, one of the few among my former superiors in the Enforcement Division who had not believed me guilty of the trumped-up charges; and Special Prosecutor Hildegarde Lambert, indefatigable nemesis of corporate villains, known in the halls of justice as Broom-Hilda in celebration of her sweeping Wiccan style.

Matt and I acquired cups of coffee and plates of fancy edibles. Cabrini went around reciting the names and titles of the bureaucrats for our benefit and we nodded and smiled a lot. Then the executive assistant withdrew from the room and Simon took charge.

My father had eschewed his customary ranchman's outfit for an archaic linen ice-cream suit complete with a vest, a black string tie, and a striped shirt with French cuffs. He looked almost like Mark Twain without a mustache. His green eyes were aglitter and he broadcast vibes of barely repressed glee.

"Ladies and gentlemen, let's all sit down any whichaway at the big round table. Bring your vittles and drinks along. We all know why we're here, so let's cut to the chase and do what's necessary. Hilda—maybe you'll sit beside me. Asa—you, too, on the other side."

Well, well. I gave Matt an ironic look and went to do my parent's bidding. Eve waggled fingers in greeting and Gunter smiled. My brother Dan, looking strained and even more colorless than usual, gave me a curt nod. Zed seemed to be in a state of shock, staring blindly out the windows, refusing to meet anyone's eye or respond to attempts at conversation.

Many of the government lawyers stared at me with frank

curiosity. Cosmopolitan Toronto did not harbor too many birds of my exotic species. I presumed everyone present knew of my checkered background.

Hildegarde Lambert said, "You've been a long time rehabilitating, Asa, but I'm happy to see you back. Especially under such novel circumstances."

I said, "Thank you, ma'am" in my best bashful cowpoke style.

Undersecretary Kildare murmured, "Is this blockbuster your doing?"

"I didn't start the fight, Vern. But I may help to finish it."

Simon scowled me into silence. He didn't bother to rise, but plunged right into his presentation.

"The terminals in front of each one of you will furnish a running summary of my introduction. You may also consult them ad lib for background, specifics of evidence, or whatever other sort of data strikes your fancy." He swept the gathering with a slit-eyed look of raw triumph. I noticed that he'd dropped his folksy western drawl and reverted to Standard English. "Everybody ready? This meeting is to announce that Rampart Interstellar Corporation is filing suit against Galapharma Amalgamated Concern. It's our contention that Galapharma conspired to damage and devalue Rampart for the purpose of forcing its stakeholders to accept an unsolicited and hostile acquisition bid. Among other torts, we allege industrial espionage, sabotage of equipment, theft and subsequent malicious use of data, extortion, subornation of Rampart employees, and incitement of Rampart-World Indigenous Sapients to riot with the express purpose of causing injury to Starcorp installations. You can read all the subsidiary stuff later. In our suit, pursuant to Statute 129 of the Interstellar Commerce Code, we are demanding as redress the maximum damages set by law—that is, all assets tangible and intangible of Galapharma Amalgamated Concern, as shall be ascertained by a Receiver appointed by the Commonwealth Judiciary Tribunal."

A pause. A deep breath. The blazing Frost grin, accompanied by a heartfelt "Whew!" Then he leaned his elbows on the table and folded his hands under his chin. "That's the bare bones of it. The boring legalities are in the computer. What I'm going to do now is tell you the meat of the story."

His tale of corporate iniquity took less than half an hour and held them spellbound every minute. He was funny, profane, and full of fiery indignation, a hard-charging small-time operator on the verge of crossing over into the Big Time being cut off at the knees by an unscrupulous and soulless business rival.

He touched only briefly on important criminal aspects of the conspiracy—my frameup and the attempts on my life, the murder of Yaoshuang Qiu and the others, Eve's kidnapping, Gala's treaty violations—saying that he'd leave those matters in the able hands of the Judiciary.

Now and then he'd ask a question of me or Matt Gregoire or Eve, to which we gave brief answers. He told his audience about Gala's prime motivation for the scheme—its desire to control the Perseus Spur and open up a vast new market for human products among the Haluk. He and Eve explained the use of PD32:C2 in eradicating Haluk allomorphism.

Nothing was said about the demiclone scheme, nor was there any suggestion that the Haluk might pose a threat to the human hegemony in the Milky Way.

Simon gave a highly edited account of the retrieval of Oliver Schneider by "motivated bounty hunters," provoking cynical chuckles and at least one catcall of "Atta boy, Asa!" from an anonymous suit.

Then my father wound up his presentation. "The crucial deposition of Schneider, together with certain other important evidentiary material supplied by him, forms the core of our suit against Galapharma. My son Asahel and his associates, together with Rampart Vice President Matilde Gregoire, risked their lives to bring this material witness to Earth. He's here today, along with his attorney, to petition for immunity in exchange for his testimony. Rampart is willing to grant his request, since he has fully cooperated with his interrogators, and Special Prosecutor Hildegarde Lambert has also graciously concurred."

The door opened and Ollie came in, unshackled, flanked by Jaswinder Singh and trailed by the two security guards. There was a small commotion, during which holocams and other recording equipment were set up by the junior suits, following Dan's instructions. As Rampart's Chief Legal Officer, my older brother supervised the small ceremony that followed, in which Eve and Broom-Hilda declared that Ollie would get off scot-free if he repeated his testimony freely in open court, skewering Gala sixty ways from Sunday.

And that was that. It was 1400 hours. The lawyers from the Prosecutor's Office took away their data to prepare the indictment. The ICS officials withdrew to weigh the criminal aspects of the case; later they would make recommendations to the Tribunal. In the Commonwealth of Human Worlds, civil law violations applicable to corporations took precedence over mere criminal proceedings.

Oliver Schneider and Jaswinder Singh returned to the executive lounge to await the arrival of CCID marshals, who would take the precious prisoner off to a country-club pokey, guarding him en route like a ton of transactinide treasure.

When all of the non-Rampart people were gone, Simon stamped the floor with his boot, punched the air with his fist, and hollered, "Yee-*haw*!"

Gunter, Eve, Matt, and I roared with relieved laughter.

"We're gonna eat 'em up!" Simon exulted. "Peel that slimeball Drummond like a catfish and fry him up for supper! Asa—did Zed tell you about Macrodur?"

I shot a glance at my cousin, who was standing somberly with both hands thrust into his pants pockets, his face blank as a hardboiled egg. "No, he didn't."

"They've accepted our prospectus," my brother Dan said in a completely neutral tone. "Eve had your friend Beatrice Mangan provide Macrodur with a copy of the Tokyo research confirming eradication of the allomorphic trait in the body through substitution of human DNA. It was enough to convince Adam Stanislawski."

"Ain't that a sockdolager?" yipped Simon.

I turned to my sister. "Congratulations, Evie." I lifted the veil of her cartwheel hat and kissed her blue alien cheek.

"We still have to vote down the takeover and send Drummond packing," she said. "The other members of the board are waiting at the Sky Ranch."

"We'll do it, and then we'll have the biggest party on God's green earth!" Simon declared. He seized Matt Gregoire by her upper arms and whirled her around. In their white suits they made an oddly consonant pair. "How's about it, gal? You're coming down to Arizona with us—right? And where's the rest of Asa's gang? Karl and the Mexican smuggler and the rest of 'em?"

"Settling in at the King Edward Hotel." Matt extricated herself gently. "And so will I—at least for the next few days." She smiled at me, then continued more gravely. "There'll be plenty of time for partying after the Rampart board takes care of necessary business. And after the Frost family unwinds. Perhaps Citizen Cabrini can call me a taxi."

Dan said, "Certainly. I'll speak to him." He used his pocket phone. "It'll be at the porte-cochere in a few minutes."

Matt squeezed my hand. "I hope you'll throw a barbecue when I visit the ranch. I've always been curious about them. And I'd like to see cactuses and tumbling tumbleweeds."

"Cactus, yes. Tumbleweeds are pests that were eradicated from the ranch before I was born. But maybe we can find some on the Navajo Reservation. They have neat rock formations up there, too."

"I'll look forward to it." She went out.

I turned to the others. "I presume we have an armed hopper to take us to the ranch. It'd be a sorry thing if we were ambushed by Drummond's hoodlums this late in the game."

"It's waiting on the roof pad," Dan said.

"There are a few things I must pick up in my office before we leave," Eve said, dashing for the door. "I won't be five minutes."

When she had gone, Cousin Zed ambled off toward the conference room john. "I'm going to take a leak."

Gunter Eckert hesitated a moment, then smiled sheepishly. "Oh, hell. Guess I'll follow Zed's example. That was a pretty exciting meeting."

Simon said, "I'm gonna have me a shot of rye to celebrate." He opened the nearest liquor cabinet. "How about you boys?"

Dan hesitated, looking around the suddenly emptied room. Then he smiled and reached inside his jacket. "Nothing for me, thanks . . . and nothing for you two, either."

He pulled out an Ivanov stun-pistol and aimed it at my face.

Simon dropped the rye decanter. It smashed, and the smell of fine Canadian whiskey stung our nostrils. "Holy fucking shit! Dan, have you lost your *mind*?"

"Not him," I said. "Not Daniel Scott Frost, Esquire. His mind's tracking on ultraluminal drive."

"To the pad elevator!" he commanded. "Fast—before the others get back."

"What is this?" Simon whispered in disbelief.

"He's a Galapharma stooge," I said. "Probably from the beginning."

"You knew?" Dan seemed genuinely surprised. "How?"

"Your little visit to Cravat was the only thing that gave you away. When I first arrived there, hunting for Eve, Bob Bascombe the Port Traffic Manager momentarily mistook me for you. Called me by your name and said, 'Welcome back.' Later, I checked with his widow and she told me you'd made a hush-hush visit and gone off by yourself—supposedly on a hunting trip. Your Cravat excursion wasn't in any of Rampart's executive flight logs, hence it wasn't just an innocent jaunt. You went to check out the Haluk installation, right?"

"Of course," he said coolly.

"Was it your idea to demiclone Eve?"

"The clone would have been my puppet if she became CEO. I knew Simon and the board would never consider *me* for the top slot. Not good, gray Dan—even though I was the best possible choice."

"Haw!" Simon barked in derision. "In your dreams! Even Zed's got more moxie than you, Danny-boy!"

My brother smiled. "My dream is about to come true—thanks to Alistair Drummond. He's agreed to put me in charge of the Rampart Division of Galapharma."

Simon said, "Sweet suffering Christ! Then he's a bigger wackadoo than I thought."

"That's enough!" Dan said viciously. "Get into the elevator, you old fool—or I'll give you a three-dart shot right now."

A lethal stun-chemical dose for humans.

"Come on, Pop," I said.

Simon was still spluttering. I took his arm and led him across the big room. Dan followed, not too closely, keeping the pistol close to his own body. Smart. He opened the elevator doors, herded us inside the spacious car, took a position in the right front corner and touched the control panel. We ascended.

"I didn't think you'd make your move until we got to the ranch," I remarked. "Figured there'd be too many witnesses here. Stupid me. Wile E. Coyote wins a round."

The doors opened into a bubble-shelter on the very summit of Rampart Tower. A ten-seater Garrison-Laguna hoppercraft, armored and discreetly armed, waited on the pad outside: secure transport for nervous upper management.

"You drive, Roadrunner." Dan slipped right into our childhood nicknames without missing a beat. "Pop sits beside you and I'm behind, ready to give him a triple if you screw up."

"Gotcha," I said. We boarded the luxurious machine. I said, "Where to? Gala-schlonga Tower over yonder? Or do you plan to kick us out of the aircraft over Lake Ontario?"

"Nothing so crude. Your deaths wouldn't bring about the appropriate outcome. My intention is to keep you alive in a safe place until Gala and Rampart are well and truly married and the civil litigation has been quashed. Your conditions of confinement will be either comfortable or odious. The choice is yours. If you give me your proxies so that I can vote your stakes at the board meeting—"

"Stick your head up your ass," Simon told his oldest son, "and eat a turd sandwich."

Dan was undismayed. "You may change your mind when I show you the alternative." To me: "Get us out of here now. Request a low-altitude nonexpress vector to Mississauga."

I complied. We lifted off the pad and soared into the northwest at a sedate velocity under the guidance of Toronto Air Traffic Control.

"Where are we going?" I asked. "Some hideaway up in the North Woods?"

"Not nearly so far," Dan said. "Tell the navigator to take us to the Blue Disenfranchised Persons Reserve."

Chapter 16

We landed in a gated hopper park and made our way on foot through a narrow, filthy lane to the turpitudinous enterprises lining Peel Road. On that bright summer afternoon the sidewalks of the Blue Strip were nearly deserted, as Dan had doubtless anticipated. Most of the few cars cruising the streets had registration tags from distant places: tourists from the boondocks window-shopping the X-rated attractions.

"Why the hell have you brought us to this friggin' sinbin?" Simon demanded wrathfully.

"For some attitude adjustment," Dan said. "Then I'm going to ask you again for your proxies."

"Ask till you turn blue, you two-faced snake in the grass! You underhanded young weasel! Shoot me dead in the goddamn street. Go ahead! Kill me like you killed your poor mother, you cunt-lappin' polecat. See what it gets you."

"Keep walking," my brother said.

Simon and I proceeded together, attracting no attention in spite of his tirade. Dan followed a good two meters behind with the Ivanov tucked in the pocket of his charcoal silk sport jacket. He had warned us that the weapon was still set to the three-dart lethal mode. Disposal of our bodies would pose no problem in Coventry.

At the end of the block was a large building with a facade that gleamed as fluidly black as the tar pits of the Dagasatt Bitumen Desert. Its sign said SILVER SCYBALUM. A few well-dressed idlers stood on the sidewalk in front of the establishment, staring into the front window and laughing.

"This is the place," Dan said. "Before we go in, I'd like to call your attention to the exhibit in the display window."

"Alien critter," my father growled, not bothering to hide his disgust. "Criminal exploitation, I'd call it."

Dan said, "You're wrong, Pop . . . Asa, tell him what that thing is. Or was."

"It's not a genuine alien, Simon. It's a human genen transform. A prison inmate who's been morphed with dystasis therapy. God only knows why the poor devil ended up like this. Perhaps he got on the wrong side of a convict kingpin and this was his punishment. This dive features performances by counterfeit aliens. You can probably purchase their sexual services as well."

Simon's eyes were goggling. "But—how can the authorities allow—"

"The prisoners inside Coventry Blue are lifer Throwaways," I explained. "Every one has been convicted of some major corporate felony. They have no rights. And this particular DPR has been under the control of the inmates for over thirty years, with the tacit permission of the authorities."

"That's disgusting!"

Dan laughed. "Nonsense. It makes for a more effective deterrent. And a source of innocent merriment for the capital citizenry. Anything goes inside Coventry Blue! Whatever depraved amusement your imagination can conceive is available, at a price. You'd be shocked to know how many corporate and government notables are regular visitors."

Two gigantic doormen, dressed as antique comic-book astronauts, flung wide the double doors when Dan spoke to them in a low voice. We were obviously expected. The three of us entered a lobby tricked out like a set from a 1930s movie serial. A bevy of muscular transvestites in provocative "sci-fi" costumes converged on us. Their melon-sized breasts were bare, with nipples saucily painted to match their different colored outfits. They wore bejeweled open helmets crowned with droll little faux antennas.

"Welcome! *Bienvenida! Konichi wa! Allo!*"

Simon muttered, "Great blazing balls o' fire."

"We are your hostesses—the Bitch Gals from Outer Space! The Silver Scybalum will be your passport to erotic delights beyond human comprehension! The fee is only two kay. For each of you, of course."

Dan stopped them in their mincing tracks. "Can it, girls. We have an appointment with King Farley. My name is Daniel Frost."

"Wait just a nanosec," said the tallest bitch, a vision in pansy-purple with a baritone voice. She went behind a counter and used a phone. The other hostesses pouted at us.

"Go right in," the baritone said. "Follow the arrows. The king will come to meet you."

An unobtrusive door slid open briefly to admit us, then closed with a solid *clunk*, secured by an old-fashioned solenoid lock. Dan herded us down a ramp to a wide, curved corridor that seemed to encircle some central architectural feature. It was dimly lit and dirty. The inner wall was full of closed doors with numbers on them, and murky secondary hallways. Green arrows blinked on the outer wall, showing us which way to go. This area of the funhouse had none of the trashy splendor of the foyer upstairs. Its ramshackle plastic and wooden structural members, wiring, and plumbing were largely exposed. I had the impression that we were behind the scenes of a firetrap theater.

The tumid rhythms of Ravel's "Bolero" came faintly through flimsy walls of particle board. I heard a distant spatter of applause.

Then the creature appeared, slithering—there's no other way to describe his means of locomotion—out of one of the dark side passages like some mythological caricature. Simon and I stopped in our tracks, gaping.

He was only about 130 centimeters tall, with the dried-apple face of a little old man—nose and chin almost touching, squinty black eyes buried in puddles of wrinkles, a mouth full of tiny, artificial-looking teeth. His body, in contrast, was elaborately muscled. He might have been an over-inflated action-figure doll wearing the wrong head. He was dressed in a skintight garment and crested hood of some remarkable reflective material that gave him the appearance of having been dipped in iridescent molten metal. The suit featured an undulating whiplike tail and a glistening ithyphallic codpiece with obscene motility. At least I hoped the damned thing was fake . . .

The creature said, "I am King Farley. I own the Silver Scybalum." He oozed closer to Simon and me, eyeing us with horrid appraisal. My father shrank back in loathing. "Are these the two subjects?"

I tensed instinctively, ready to jump the little abomination and use him as a hostage. King Farley pointed an index finger at me and a blue spark did a Tinkerbell hop from its electrode tip to my breastbone.

An invisible branding iron seemed to sear my flesh. I let out a scream, staggered, and would have fallen if Simon hadn't caught me in his wiry arms. He uttered a volley of profanity and asked if I was badly hurt.

I told him I was okay and regained my balance within a few moments. The tiny bastard in the silver lizard suit was a walking taser. It was the same electroshock technology Captain Ziggy Cybulka had used to knock me ass over teakettle back at Mimo's place.

Dan was saying, "This is the pair I spoke to you about, King. Before we conclude our negotiations for their—um—sojourn, I wonder if you might show them some of the transform possibilities?"

"Why, sure!" shrilled the manikin. "Today's pretty slow. Most of the pets are just hanging out in the bullpen. Just take a peek through here." He threw open a ramshackle pair of shutters that covered a grubby window on the inner wall. "Every single one an authentic reproduction! Every single one available . . ."

Dan motioned with the Ivanov. "Look carefully. Imagine the possibilities! Then decide whether you want to give me your voting proxies or not."

We looked.

Hieronymus Bosch would have loved it.

During my tour of field duty in the ICS, I'd seen a considerable number of grotesque xeno life-forms. Simon, a veteran galactic traveler, had also encountered his fair share. But King Farley's crowded "bullpen" was a revelation to both of us, simultaneously fascinating, stomach-turning, and pathetic. The dismal holding area imprisoned at least fifty beings—all different, most having not the slightest resemblance to anything human—resting apathetically or moving about in frenetic agitation.

"Takes only about three months in dystasis to do the makeover job," Farley said chattily. "I got talented staff."

As my father and I watched, a hatch slid open at one side of the pen and a hulking Bitch Gal armed with a high-tech cattleprod moved into the nightmarish throng. She beckoned to one of the creatures, a thing with long silken hair and garishly colored ischial callosities that resembled a cross between a dwarf mastodon and a mandrill baboon. It meekly followed the hostess out to whatever duties awaited it.

King Farley closed the shutters. "That's enough, I think." He folded his shimmering pneumatic arms and said, "Well?"

Simon was aghast, his gaze darting from his impassive older son to the smirking pimp. "Dan, you can't be serious—"

My brother reached into his inside jacket pocket and brought out an electronic document slate with an iris-reader. "Here's the proxy form. Both of you imprint it. Then you can spend the next two years wearing your own bodies, living in one of the king's town houses."

"Not a top squat," Farley remarked with a shrug, "but comfortable enough. Decent food, warm in winter. Better than most of our Coventry Blue inmates enjoy. Otherwise, into the tank—presto, change-o! Makes no nevermind to me. I get paid the same, either option."

Silently, I held out my hand. Dan gave me the slate and I lifted it to my eye. My brother smiled broadly and handed the document to Simon.

The old man was staring at Dan in sad astonishment. "For *Rampart*? You want to be boss-man that badly? Everything you've done . . . your mother's death, what you were ready to do to Eve . . . and now this. Just so you could run Rampart! Daniel, I just don't understand."

"You never did," my good, gray brother said, thrusting out the proxy slate. He wasn't smiling anymore.

Simon eyeballed it.

Suddenly, two of the muscular transvestites from the lobby were standing in the corridor. One wore a bubblegum-pink costume and the other was clad in turquoise satin. Both of them held prods.

"Our business is concluded, Citizen Frost," the kingpin convict said to Dan. "I'll expect the agreed-upon emolument at your earliest convenience. You can go out the way you came in. Chantal and Pepper will escort the other two gents to their accommodation in Dannemora House."

King Farley slithered away with amazing rapidity, waving his tail, and Dan turned to go.

"It's not over," I told my brother.

"Alistair Drummond will be at the board meeting in Arizona to present his latest tender in person." He glanced at his watch. "Just a little over two hours from now. I'll give your regrets to him and the others. They'll understand why you didn't care to be present. Goodbye, Asa, Simon. We'll talk again in a couple of years and discuss your future."

Then he was gone.

My father and I exchanged glances. His rangy trail-boss features had gone flaccid. He looked dazed and old.

"I'm Pepper!" chirped the pink Bitch Gal. She topped my height by nine or ten centimeters.

"I'm Chantal!" said the turquoise slut. She was a bit shorter, but still had maybe fifteen kilos on me. "Let's move right along to your new home, dahlings."

"You guys take bribes?" I asked hopefully.

They burst into merry chortles. "Isn't it *precious*!" said Pepper. Then she zapped me in the groin with the cattleprod.

I collapsed on the filthy floor, moaning.

"Now, now," Pepper crooned. "That was only the minimum setting, sweetie. Hardly enough to toast your tiny chestnuts. Upsy daisy!"

I rolled over, fumbled onto my hands and knees, head down, still making doleful sounds. Pink Pepper was telling nothing but the truth; the shocker had delivered small voltage, and it had missed my family jewels and hit my inner thigh—a distinct owie, but hardly enough to disable a fit male human.

"Up up up!" urged Pepper cheerily.

"Oh, Jesus," I wailed. "Gimme a minute. Oh, God, that hurts."

"Poor baby." Chantal laughed. "You should wear them ring-tucked, as we do, and they wouldn't be so vulnerable."

Shaking my addled head, I caught a glimpse of the turquoise bitch standing next to Simon, baton hanging carelessly at her side.

I got up, Mr. Wobbly, face all squinched with pain. Pepper had her stick raised, buzzing gently, ready to deal me another zotz if I misbehaved. Praying the thing had a deadman switch that would deactivate it when dropped, I stepped close, used both my forearms to clobber her weapon arm, and got a two-handed grip on her wrist. Then I pivoted sharply, bringing her arm over my shoulder and shattering her elbow. The prod fell out of her hand. I kicked the back of her knee and Pepper went down howling. Then I stomped the bridge of her nose with the heel of my heavy snakeboot.

No more noise. Maybe no more Pepper, if I'd managed to drive her broken nasal bone into her brain.

Snapping out of a state of momentary bamboozlement, Chantal came at me like a fury, swinging her hissing baton like an electrified baseball bat. One touch and I was fried. I dodged and flung myself at her, encircling her upraised arm and neck while locking my hands and squeezing with all my strength. Her silly helmet went flying. She fell over backward with me on top of her, forcing the pinioned arm and head forward.

A noise like a wet stick cracking.

Chantal went limp.

"Holy fuck," whispered Simon.

"Yeah." I climbed to my feet and went about retrieving the

cattleprods. "That one's neck is broken. You want to check out the other?"

Simon complied. "I don't think she—he—whatever—is breathing."

"We're outta here, Pop." I gave him one of the weapons. "Move! And for God's sake, watch where you wave that prod."

Bless King Farley's villainous heart, he'd forgotten to turn off the green directional arrows. We found the ramp without getting lost, dashed up it—

—and came smack against the locked lobby door.

I rapped on it with my weapon: *shave-and-a-haircut*.

"Who's there?" a voice fluted.

"It's Pepper and Chantal, dahlings!" I called in falsetto. "And you'll never guess what kind of goodies we've got!"

Buzz. The old-time lock let go and the door opened. A Bitch Gal in golden lamé managed one terrified squeak before I jolted her full-power between her hormonally enhanced boobs. The tall dollie in purple tried to flee into the street, but I grabbed her by her gem-studded belt and delivered an electrical goose.

"Okay," I said to Simon. "I'm going to yank open these front doors. You burn the left-hand doorman and I'll do the other one."

His green eyes were glittering with vitality again. "Got it. But dammit-all, Asa, how're we gonna get shut of this fuckin' calaboose? They got walls with razor wire, Kagi guns—"

"And tourists. Just do as I do. On three. One . . . two . . ."

We burst through the doors, delivered the volts, and watched the spacesuited gorillas topple like a pair of silver-clad refrigerators. The thrillseekers gathered at the display window watched with their jaws hanging open. A couple of cars slowed and the occupants lowered their windows to see what was happening.

I waved my baton in salute. "Just part of the show, folks. There's always loads of *fun*! At the Silver Scyba-*lum*!"

I grabbed Simon's arm and dragged him toward a smelly

gangway that led around to the back of the building. "Now run like your pants are afire."

We took off at a gallop. The area behind the Blue Strip was a far cry from the tarted-up main thoroughfare. Aside from the parking lots and guarded lots for visiting hoppers, the buildings were shabby and bleak, dormitories or structures originally dedicated to various inmate services in the failed experiment of a "village" governed by the prisoners themselves. Of course there wasn't a guard to be seen. They almost never left the area around the main gate unless a visitor called for help on a pocket phone. Sometimes not even then . . .

Nobody followed us—but that didn't mean we were home free. I had no doubt that King Farley and his freakish court had already discovered our escape, but they had to find a way of nabbing us without frightening the paying customers. I figured we had a few more minutes before the balloon went up.

The first hopper lot we passed was nearly empty, except for a raggedy attendant snoozing on a stool outside a shack. The few aircraft sitting in it had their security fields turned on. The second lot, where Dan had landed the Garrison-Laguna, looked more promising. The G-L and my wayward sibling were gone, but another pair of visitors were entering the gate on the way back to their transport. The man and woman were middle-aged, wearing identical Hawaiian shirts and woven palm-leaf hats with feather bands. They had loaded carrier bags bearing the logo NANKI-POO'S TOY SHOPPE.

"Yo!" I called out in a friendly fashion. "Hey, there, folks. Hold it just a minute, please. Did you enjoy your visit to Coventry Blue?"

Expressions of guilty apprehension. Nobody ever wants to answer a customer survey. They scuttled toward a sleek Mitsubishi-Kondo that sat isolated in a far corner of the lot.

The attendant, half zonked on some intoxicant, regarded us without interest.

I said to Simon, "Let's cut out those two dogies and grab their ride. Cattleprods on medium zap."

"Christ!" He was staring over my shoulder, appalled. "What the bloody blue blazes is *that*?"

I turned to look. On the Strip about two blocks away was a tall building crowned by a revolving neon sign: CASINO ROYALE—LOWEST ODDS ON EARTH. Skidding around it onto the back street came a scarlet motorcycle with a cowl shielding the rider. Flickering strobe lights of red, white, and blue decorated the thing from stem to stern.

I heard high-pitched hornet screams. A brace of small missiles smacked into the fuselage of one of the parked, field-screened hoppers and set off its intruder alarms and more bright flashing lights.

The loopy attendant grinned. "Far out!"

"Allenby magnum stun-guns!" I yelled to Simon. "Do the jackrabbit! We can't let those people take off without us."

Stun-fléchettes flew around us as we dodged and side-stepped, doing a zigzag run across the lot. The terrified tourists had dropped their shopping bags and were fleeing toward the Mitsubishi.

I heard the roar of the motorcycle growing in volume and glanced back. The machine must have been traveling at 120 kph over the broken, potholed pavement, bouncing a meter or more into the air whenever it hit a bad patch, each time returning safely to earth with a resounding *wham*. Fortunately for us, the maneuvers of the daredevil driver played hell with his weapons targeting system, and the parked hoppers partially shielded us.

The Hawaiian couple were climbing into their aircraft as I reached them. The missus cried out, "Willis! Hurry! Hurry!"

The hatch was almost shut when I blocked it with my cattleprod and began wrenching it back open. Once again my mighty muscles did their stuff. A string of stun-fléchettes hosed the hopper hull a couple of centimeters above my head but the door was slowly yielding.

"Go away!" the tourist lady wept, kicking at me hysterically with her sneakered foot. "Oh, I knew coming here was a mistake!"

Her husband had the engines turned on. I felt the Mitsubishi lurch as the antigrav engaged. Simon was on top of me as both of us shoved our way inside, pushing the poor woman from her banquette onto the deck.

"Willis! Willis!" she screamed. "Help!"

He looked over his shoulder, his face irresolute. I was afraid he'd abandon the controls and come to his wife's rescue. The door had shut.

"Lift off!" I yelled, "Lift off, for God's sake, or we're all dead!"

The hopper jolted skyward at an oblique angle like a badly aimed bottle rocket, coming to a halt at the 200-meter emergency holding level when Willis's frantic pawing at the controls threw the navigator into Reboot mode. He tumbled out of the pilot seat and came at me with his fists cocked.

"Whoa, there, pardner!" I seized his wrists and held him firmly at bay. "We're not crooks or convicts. We're innocent tourists like yourselves. The bad guys are trying to kill us. They stole our hopper."

Willis was getting a close look at us for the first time—me with my gaudy fire-opal bolo tie, Simon in his once-elegant suit, now much the worse for wear.

"How do we know you're telling the truth?" wailed the lady on the floor.

Simon reached down and tenderly helped her back onto the seat, switching on his charm like a megawatt floodlight. He pulled out a business card and presented it with a flourish. "Ma'am, I do sincerely apologize. And to you, too, sir, for commandeering your aircraft in such a boorish fashion. My name is Simon Frost and I'm the Chairman of the Board of Rampart Starcorp. This other gentleman is my son, Asa. I'll just ask him to unhand you now."

I let the tourist go, giving him my friendliest smile. He was about sixty years old. His features had a slight Polynesian cast, he was in excellent physical shape, and he wore a professional spacer's chronometer on his wrist. His wife passed him Simon's card and he looked at it with suspicion.

"May I ask your name?" my father inquired suavely.

"I'm Willis Kanakoa. This is my wife, Leilani Peterson. What's this all about?"

"You're in North America on vacation?" I asked.

"Yes," said Leilani. "Who was that brute on the motorcycle shooting at us? Are his confederates going to come after us in a hopper?"

"No, no," laughed Simon. "Convicts don't dare try to follow decent folks out of Coventry. Their chip implants would set off alarms. We're all perfectly safe now."

"Hmph," Willis grunted dubiously. "Well, I think you two—"

Simon broke in. "Citizen Kanakoa, would you be interested in making a great deal of money just for taking my son and me someplace we have to go? A brief two-hour flight. You might even like the place well enough to stay and visit."

"Where's that?" Willis asked.

I said, "Arizona. You'll love it there. Much quieter than Toronto."

"Baldwin?" Alistair Drummond barks into the vidphone. "I'm having a serious problem with our agents assigned to this area."

"What's the trouble, sir?" The Galapharma Security Chief is speaking from Concern headquarters in Glasgow.

"Insubordination. Your bloody bastards here in Phoenix won't carry out my orders."

Tyler Baldwin's eyes narrow and his voice changes its timbre, becoming less obsequious. "Sir, I've actually been informed about that matter already. A request of particular delicacy."

"As a matter of fact, it was. I asked for a certain piece of equipment that I need for the Rampart board meeting at the ranch this afternoon. Your people won't give it to me. Flat out refused. They referred me to *you*!"

"Yes. Well, you might want to reconsider—"

"Get on the blower right now and tell your flunkies to obey orders!"

Baldwin says, "I regret to say I can't do that, sir. Not with the situation in such a critical state of flux. What . . . I presume you intend to do with the equipment is simply not expedient. Not in the best interests of the other Concern trading partners in the Haluk consortium."

"Damn you—what d'you think you're playing at?" Drummond roars. "Do as I say or you're finished! Terminated! Do you hear what I'm saying? Not only fired, but—"

The phone screen goes to standby. Tyler Baldwin has ended the transmission.

The other Concern trading partners?

Baffled and furious, Drummond sits frozen before the desk in his villa at the Biltmore. What does Baldwin mean? Has news of the imminent filing of the civil suit by Rampart leaked out? Or have the Big Seven conspirators learned of the Macrodur prospectus? Did that lot of stone-faced fuckers at Bodascon and Sheltok and Carnelian and Homerun think he, Alistair Drummond, was going to concede defeat?

The telephone chimes. If it's Baldwin again, with more insolence—

He stabs at the Open keypad. The face on the screen is that of Daniel Frost. The screen graphics indicate that he is calling from a hoppercraft in flight.

Dan says, "I have the proxies of Simon and Asa."

"Well, I'll be gormed!" murmurs Alistair Drummond.

"When we get to the ranch, I'll feed Eve a line of bullshit to explain the absence of Simon and Asa at the board meeting. She won't be able to do a thing about it. The CEO can't cancel or postpone the vote because I now hold the convening privilege of a majority stake. We're scheduled to meet at 1530 hours local time. I'll pick you up at the hotel half an hour before that and fly you to the ranch myself."

"Most satisfactory," Drummond says.

Damn near astounding!

He touches the End pad, sits back and closes his eyes. When he is once again in control of himself, he mulls over the new development, especially as it applies to his earlier frustrated request.

It occurs to him that someone else in the Galapharma organization, a local Concern executive not under the thumb of Tyler Baldwin, might be persuaded to furnish the piece of equipment he needs—or a reasonable substitute. In spite of the unexpected triumph of Daniel Frost, he still fully intends to carry out his own ultimate solution of the Rampart problem, a solution that particularly includes the egregious Daniel himself.

Smiling, he touches the phone's keypad and calls up a new number.

Simon and I briefly contemplated transferring to a speedier rented aircraft, but I was afraid that King Farley would have notified Dan of our escape by now. Wile E. Coyote wouldn't panic. He'd put out a credit-card-theft alert, ensuring that we'd be nabbed and detained if we tried to obtain any sort of commercial transport. Picking up a Rampart hopper in Toronto might have been a risky move for us, too, if Dan had spun some wild yarn to the corporate flight office.

So we stuck with bemused Willis and Leilani. Like most visitors to Coventry Blue, the Hawaiians had illegally suppressed their hopper registration to preserve their anonymity. There was no way King Farley or his biker buddy could identify our getaway vehicle to Dan, the Gala security forces, or anyone else.

We had effectively vanished.

As we flew southwest at over 1,500 kph, Simon wanted to contact Eve to tell her what had happened. I nixed the notion. It seemed to me there was a very real possibility that Dan had gone back to Rampart Tower after dumping us in Coventry and picked up Eve, Zed, and Gunter for the flight to Arizona. He might have told them that Simon and I had decided to fly down separately, or recited some other cock-and-bull story. If we tried to call Eve on her personal phone while she was aboard the Garrison-Laguna, Dan might somehow be alerted to the situation and panic. At worst, he might harm Eve and the others in some act of desperation. At best, he'd put off the vote.

I didn't want either thing to happen. I was counting on my brother being unwilling to confess the Silver Scybalum fiasco to Alistair Drummond. I wanted the Galapharma CEO to attend the board meeting at the Sky Ranch, to come out of his spider-hole of invulnerability.

His insane chutzpah deserved an appropriate reward. Perhaps I'd be the one to give it to him.

It was 1440 hours when Willis Kanakoa's Mitsubishi arrived at the Turkey Spring Guardhouse at the southeastern corner of the Frost family spread. It wasn't the main entrance to the ranch. That one, providing convenient access to the Phoenix Conurbation, was situated thirty-five crow-flight kilometers away on the western perimeter, near the Jakes Corner crossing on Tonto Creek. The only people who used the eastside gate were ranch employees who lived in Globe or in the remote little town of Pleasant Valley about twenty kilometers to the north.

August is monsoon season in Arizona, and masses of ominous purple thunderheads were building up south of Copper Mountain and Greenback Peak as we went into a holding hover.

Willis said, "Don't think I want to be flying around here when that weather arrives."

"Don't worry. This is where Simon and I get out." I instructed him to hail the guardhouse and ask if he could touch down for a minute or two and check out a possible malfunction in the hopper's throttle. The transponder ID was working again, so the Hawaiian registration of his aircraft was evident: just another tourist, snooping around the Sierra Ancha wilderness and getting into trouble.

Sky Ranch guards have standing orders to be reasonably polite to rubberneckers. They told Willis to come on down and they'd do what they could to help. He landed on the pad beside one of the small Saxon-15 hoppers that ExSec used to patrol the spread. There was also a Rampart Jeep parked there, and a couple of pickup trucks that probably belonged to the guards.

"Time for us to say goodbye, folks," Simon said to the Hawaiians. "Remember what I said: call me day after tomorrow. If Asa and I are still alive then, you're invited to the biggest goddamn barbecue this territory's ever seen. Now get outta here."

My father and I climbed out of the Mitsubishi and it took off at once. The heat was excruciating, even though we were at an altitude of over 1,800 meters, and the air was dead calm. We trudged to the guardhouse, a small building set among tall ponderosa pines. Not far away was the tall locked gate flanked by scanner masts, with a sign posted on it.

> PRIVATE PROPERTY OF RAMPART IC
> ABSOLUTELY NO PUBLIC ACCESS
> DANGER! CUIDADO!
> LETHAL DETERRENTS IN USE

A uniformed man with the holster of his sidearm unfastened was standing at the open guardhouse door regarding us warily.

"That you, Pete Halvorsen?" Simon called out.

"Good God!" the guard exclaimed. A smile broke over his weathered face. He hollered to somebody inside, "Julio, never mind reportin' in. You get on out here! It's the boss, for chrissake!"

Another guard appeared, older than the first. There were jovial curses of surprise. Simon knew both men, but he cut short their chatter after introducing me.

I said, "Julio, did you get around to telling Central Security that you had visitors out here?"

"Nossir," said Julio Perez. "I was just getting on it when Pete said it was the boss."

"Good. We don't want anyone to know we're coming in."

"What's up?" Pete asked.

Simon said, "We got some bad shit comin' down, boys. It's nothing I want to explain to you right now. We need a Jeep ride in to the main house."

"Sure thing," said Pete. "I'll take you. Ol' Julio can keep an eye on things here."

"We'll drive ourselves," I said.

"Suit yourself, son. Key's in the rig. Remote control for the security checkpoints clipped on the sun visor. Reckon you know the drill."

"Do you have a stunner we can take along?" I asked. "And a Claus-Gewitter or some other kind of blaster?"

"Well, shoot!" said Pete. "You planning a home invasion?"

"Got an extra Ivanov," Julio said soberly, "and a Harvey HA-3 if you want some important artillery. I'll get them."

"Perfect." I turned to Pete. "Remember, don't let anyone at the main house or the Central Security station know that Simon and I are coming in the Jeep. You get any inquiries, say that Julio's driving around on road inspection or something."

"I understand." The guard's face was grim. "You can count on us."

Simon clapped him on the shoulder. "Tell you later 'bout the reeraw. With luck, it won't amount to anything."

Julio came out and handed me the guns. "You take care. And keep an eye on Copper Creek when you cross her. Might flood out suddenly. Helluva big storm coming."

"Wouldn't surprise me," Simon said glumly.

The two men went back into their air-conditioned guardhouse. I slipped into the driver's seat of the Jeep and started it up. A moment later the back gate to the Sky Ranch rolled open and we drove inside.

The time was 1505 hours. The board meeting was scheduled to begin in twenty-five minutes, and it would take us at least that long to get to the house via the winding dirt road.

Eight members of the Rampart Board of Directors have gathered in the living room of the ranch house, awaiting the arrival of the ninth and his special guest. An atmosphere of decorum prevails. No one speaks of looming calamity or exhibits unseemly enthusiasm in anticipation of the event they all know will shortly take place. The weather provides a useful topic for small talk.

The living room is a place of mellow oaken beams, polished floor tiles, and informal furniture upholstered in subdued southwestern Indian motifs. An enormous unlit hearth overflows with potted ferns and jars containing sprays of pink, white, and green orchids. Beyond a wall of glass doors, closed against the oppressive heat, a broad terrace overlooks a stupendous vista. The house stands on a rise in the midst of a sparsely wooded plateau and it is almost completely encircled by mountains. The peaks to the south stand in striking contrast to a backdrop of towering cumulonimbus clouds—brilliant white at the tops and nearly black at their bases. Lightning flickers redly in their depths, and from time to time a distant growl of thunder is audible, even inside the heavily insulated house.

In the absence of Simon, Eve Frost has assumed the role of host. She wears a hooded robe of sparkling salmon-colored fabric, and her Halukoid features are frankly revealed. She serves crystal tumblers of sangria to those assembled and is particularly solicitous of her elderly aunt, Emma Bradbury, who seems to be the only one among the directors who does not understand the enormity of what is about to happen.

Zared Frost, President and COO, stands near the patio doors with his close associates, Leonidas Dunne, Chief Technical Officer, and Gianliborio Rivello, Chief Marketing Officer. Zed seems to have regained his executive poise. The three men watch the monsoon begin to engulf the mountain rampart with a gray curtain of falling water. They discuss the prospects of the Arizona Diamondbacks baseball team in the World Series.

Sitting together at a cocktail table made of polished petrified wood are Thora Scranton, a director-at-large who controls the twenty-five percent of Rampart stock owned by the Small Stakeholders, Gunter Eckert, the veteran CFO, and Bethany Frost, the Assistant Chief Financial Officer. Thora is an elegant woman of ample proportions, whose air of maternal calm conceals a ruthlessly pragmatic mind. Beth, a brilliant mathematician, is the designated successor to Gunter. Her election to the board after the death of Yasser Abul Hadi was pressed by Zed, Gianni, Leo, Emma, Dan, and the late Katje Vanderpost over the objections of Simon, who considers his younger daughter still too immature to play a leadership role in the Starcorp. Beth, like her brother Dan, to whom she is devoted, strongly favors the Galapharma merger.

A houseman in a white jacket slips into the room and whispers to Eve. She says to the others, "It seems that Dan has arrived with his guest."

A murmur, almost a sigh, sweeps the room. Then there is silence except for the intensifying drumrolls of thunder. A moment later Daniel Frost enters, his presence almost completely overshadowed by the flamboyant man following on his heels.

Alistair Drummond seems almost to be enveloped in an aura of crackling energy, as though he has managed to siphon ions from the impending storm. His cowboy costume, far from looking inappropriate, gives him the aspect of a Western stalwart of old. Supremely self-confident and smiling, he approaches Eve Frost, takes her dusky blue mutant hand, and inclines his head in a courtly gesture that is just short of mockery.

"Thank you so very much for allowing me to attend your board meeting, Eve! I can't tell you what a great pleasure it is to meet you at last."

She nods, turning away from him almost at once to address the others. "It's time for our meeting to begin. Please gather in the chairs around the fireplace."

Those who are not already seated take their places. Only Eve and Alistair Drummond remain standing. He silently declines to take the chair she has indicated.

"Ladies and gentlemen, this meeting of the Rampart Board of Directors will now come to order. We will dispense with the reading of the minutes by our esteemed Secretary"—an ironic nod to Dan—"and move on immediately to the principal business at hand, our consideration of the acquisition bid by Galapharma Amalgamated Concern."

"I move that the Galapharma tender be accepted," says Daniel Frost.

"I second the motion," says his cousin Zared.

"The motion is now open to discussion." Almost in relief, Eve sits down on a padded stool to the left of the fireplace.

Dan says, "Since this matter has been extensively discussed and voted upon by the board before, I would like to invite my guest, Alistair Drummond, Chairman and CEO of Galapharma Concern, to tell us the advantages that may accrue to Rampart Starcorp, its stakeholders and employees, should this motion be passed today."

Drummond steps forward and begins to speak. His voice is well-modulated and forceful. Its faint Scottish accent, perhaps deliberately intensified for the occasion, lends an exotic charm to even the most banal recitations of statistics. He has brought an electronic display slate with him in a large case, and its muted holograms illustrate and elucidate his remarks.

As he winds down to a conclusion, the onrushing storm reaches the buildings of the Sky Ranch at last. A clap of thunder shakes the main house, provoking startled laughter. Rain descends in a torrential cascade, rattling on the roof and sluicing the terrace windows. Outside, it has become almost as dark as night.

The living room lamps brighten automatically, compensating for the gloom. So do Drummond's splendid holos. Offhandedly, the Galapharma CEO makes mention of the impending participation of Macrodur in the new venture credit program and acknowledges the near certainty that a new treaty with the Haluk will be approved. The data are all smoothly incorporated into his grand new schema. He seems to have thought of everything.

His presentation comes to an end and a few people applaud. Smiling, he deactivates the display and replaces it in its case, which rests on the beautiful table of petrified wood. "Are there any questions from members of the board?"

No one says a word.

Eve rises. "Then I call for a vote by the Rampart stakeholders and their representatives. First: Emma Bradbury, with twelve and a half percent of the corporate stake."

"Aye," Emma says, almost dreamily.

"Next: Thora Scranton, representative of Rampart Small Stakeholders, with twenty-five percent."

"Aye," says Thora.

"Next, Asahel Frost, with twenty-five percent."

Dan holds up the document. "I hold the proxy of Asahel Frost, and vote aye."

"Madame CEO?" says Gunter Eckert. "Point of order."

She nods. Eckert says he wishes to examine the proxy document. Dan hands it over and the old man makes a minute examination, finally shrugging and returning it. "The document appears to be authentic, but I insist that it be verified by an independent technical authority before the results of this vote are inserted into the public database."

"I agree wholeheartedly with Gunter's quite legitimate request," Dan says.

"Very well," says Eve. "The final stakeholder vote is by Simon Frost, with thirty-seven and one-half percent of Rampart stock."

Again Dan lifts the document. "I hold the proxy of Simon Frost and vote aye."

"And I once again stipulate verification." But Gunter's voice is tired and perfunctory now and he is staring into his lap.

"A vote of Rampart stakeholders has been taken," Eve says, "and acceptance of the Galapharma tender is unanimous, subject to the verification of the two proxies. Do I have a motion for adjournment?"

"I so move," says Zared Frost.

"I second," says Gunter. "And God help the lot of us."

At this point the glass terrace doors burst open. A tremendous gust of wind and rain batters the living room, sending lamps, throw pillows, and precious Native American pottery flying, lifting small rugs from the floor, and causing the window drapes to billow and crack like torn sails in a gale.

Emma Bradbury and Bethany Frost shriek and cower in their club chairs. Eve turns a serene face to the invading storm, almost seeming to welcome it. Daniel Frost is a gray statue, clutching the proxy document to his breast like a talisman against disaster. Leonidas Dunne and Gianliborio Rivello leap up, mouthing curses, and dash to secure the flailing French doors before they shatter.

They fall back in confusion as two tall figures, drenched to the skin, step past them into the living room.

I kept on walking, reached Dan's paralyzed form, and ripped the proxy slate out of his nerveless hand. "This document is null and void. It was obtained under duress and is completely worthless." I flung the thing onto the floor tiles and crushed it under my boot.

Behind me Simon bellowed, "Damn right! And this fuckin' farce ends right now."

Alistair Drummond turned without a word and strode toward the door.

Dan shouted, "Wait! You can't leave!" He started after Drummond, taking hold of his shoulder, trying to stop him.

Incredibly, Drummond halted, reached into an inner pocket of his vest, pulled out a small but powerful Lanvin actinic pistol, and shot my older brother in the chest. Then he spun about and ran down the hall toward the front door, leaving chaos behind him.

I headed in the opposite direction, to the French windows that led onto the terrace. "Simon!" I yelled. "You've got my proxy. Take another vote and transmit the results to the public database immediately!"

"Gotcha!" said Pop.

"Eve—you get on the com to Ranch Central Security. Tell them to expect my orders." Then I was outside and moving.

Water impounded by the parapets, falling too heavily to drain away, made a shallow lake of the flagstones. I splashed across it, hopped over the rail, and bounded through ornamental shrubs and smashed flowers.

A monster bolt of lightning illuminated the grounds around the big house. Even then, visibility in the downpour was less than fifty meters. A planting of slender cottonwood trees was bent almost flat by the wind and sturdier pines tossed and moaned.

The Jeep was where Simon and I had left it, pulled up on the formerly pristine irrigated lawn at the end of two horrendous ruts. I spotted a couple of blurred red taillights going down the front drive. It looked like Dan's Range Rover. For an instant I wondered why Drummond hadn't taken the Garrison-Laguna, which was parked on the house landing pad. Then I realized that a hopper would need security clearance to penetrate the Sky Ranch's scanner net. If it tried to break through, the automated Kagi installations would shoot it down.

Diving into the Jeep, I fired it up, hit the Max Traction control, and roared off the lawn in reverse. Clots of turf and muddy water sprayed roof-high. I reached pavement, shifted, and tore off in pursuit of Alistair Drummond.

The Rover's lights, dim red eyes bouncing and jinking, were still in sight. He was heading south to the T-junction where the blacktop ended, about two kilometers from the house. From there, all the ranch roads were unpaved. The west leg of the T, well-graded gravel, led to the main entrance and the Phoenix Freeway. The east leg, rougher and with fewer bridges over the creeks and arroyos, was the utility road Simon and I had come in on.

Drummond turned east.

I got on the com. "Security Central, come back to Helly Frost."

"Yes, *sir*!"

"Get on the global positioner. Nail down Mr. Dan's green Range Rover going along the East Road and feed it to the navigator in"—I checked the ID of Pete's Jeep—"Rampart Patrol Three-two."

"Roger that. Acquiring target. Downloading. You got it, sir."

I switched on the nav display. There we were, two blips half a klick apart. He was pulling away. "Thanks, Central. Can you send aircraft to cover the east gate?"

"That's a negative right now, sir. As soon as this monster storm cell moves through we can go flying. Estimated plus-minus seven minutes. We'll alert the East Gatehouse, but—"

"Do you have any ground units between the house and Copper Mountain Cutoff?"

"Negative. And I gotta tell you that West Fork Copper

Creek is running bank-high. Your bogey won't ford it and neither will you."

"I copy that. Stand by."

It was taking almost all of my attention to keep the Jeep on the road. I was barreling along at nearly 90 kph on a rough, devilishly slick track in a vehicle that was only about a third as massive as the one I was chasing. The Rover stuck to the ground much better than I did. It had a more powerful engine, too. The Jeep windshield was doing its damnedest to stay clear, but the amount of water flowing over it threatened to overwhelm the ionizer.

I slowed down and shifted part of my vision to the navigator. In just a few more minutes Alistair Drummond was going to butt up against that torrential creek, at which point he faced some uncomfortable options. He could turn left and drive cross-country over the plateau until he foundered, or he could turn right onto an exiguous two-rut trail that headed toward the summit of Copper Mountain, eventually dead-ending near the abandoned gold mine. The opposite side of the mountain was much too steep for vehicular travel. Only horses or hikers could make it down that way.

If he was smart, Drummond would pull off somewhere along the track and ambush me. I wondered if he had any other weapons besides the nasty actinic peashooter he'd shot Dan with. Most of the ranch ground vehicles carried a stunner, at the very least, to cope with rampageous wildlife. I had my trusty Harvey, which would bring down a tyrannosaur.

Provided I got it in my sights.

The rain seemed to be abating and we were back in daylight mode. I was coming up on a rise, so I stopped the Jeep. Since I had no oculars, I grabbed the Harvey blaster and went out to do a fast recon through its powerscope. It was suddenly cold outside. The air temp must have dropped nearly twenty degrees. Lightning still flared occasionally, but the principal fireworks had passed to the north.

I stumbled up the road to the top of the ridge, crouched behind some rabbit brush on the verge, and swept the land below with the scope. There was the creek, bordered by bebb willows and alamos and brimming with a brown, foamy torrent. No sign of the Range Rover.

I strained my ears and heard a laboring turbine engine, the sound intermittent among the rumbles and dull thuds of retreating thunder.

I skidded back to the car and consulted the navigator. There he was, the crazy dude bastard, heading up the mountain—and rather briskly at that. I notified Security Central and told them to send armed hoppers to the area but not to land or fire on the bogey until I gave the order.

I got rolling again and turned onto the cutoff road in pursuit of my prey. Then I switched to Channel 16 and called Alistair Drummond.

It took a few minutes for him to notice the little green telltale blinking on the com console, figure out what it meant, and come back to me.

I said, "You know the track you're on ends up near the mountaintop. You're finished, Drummond. You might as well give up."

A laugh, soft and eerie, came out of my speaker. All he said was, "It's your family that's finished, Asahel Frost. And the day will come when I put an end to you as well."

"Drummond? You want to explain that? Drummond?"

There was no reply.

Jesus . . . Of course that's what he'd do!

Still driving, I got back to security and told them to patch me through to the house and my sister Eve. Interminable minutes later I heard her voice say, "Asa? What's happening? Did he get away?"

"Never mind that! Did Drummond leave anything behind? Anything at all?"

"Only the case with his holo display. Why?"

"Get out of the house!" I shouted. "Get everybody out of the house now! The bastard's going to kill you all. There's something in that case!"

Silence.

"Eve! Do you understand?"

"Yes," she said. And was gone.

I prayed, and I drove like a fiend, pushing the Jeep to its limits, cracking the undercarriage against rocks, scraping the sides on hairy switchbacks, winding up to the summit of Copper Mountain while the rain diminished and the beauty of the Sky Ranch spread out around me.

Dan and Eve and Beth and I had played on this mountain when we were young children. We'd been forbidden to enter the derelict gold mine, so of course we did. One time, a black-tail rattler hiding just inside the entrance struck at Beth. I crushed it with a rock. Another time, Dan found a nubbin of quartz with embedded metallic specks that gleamed in the sun. He knew it was real gold. The rest of us sneered, but we thought it was, too. Lucky Dan! He said he'd reopen the mine when he grew up, dig out the gold, and get rich. We all sneered at that as well, while we halfway suspected he might do just that. Wily Dan!

Wile E. Coyote.

Too young yet to know that, in a galactic economy, gold wasn't all that valuable. Even the wily can miscalculate. Sometimes fatally.

The trail was almost too narrow to drive on now, hacked from living rock, incredibly steep and with sheer drops into Copper Creek Canyon far below. It had been built for mule-drawn carts and not modern vehicles, but if the Rover had made it, my Jeep would, too. I kept moving, traveling at less than 7 kph, and finally reached a lookout point close to the summit where most of the Frost spread was visible.

The clouds were beginning to break and a few beams of sunlight appeared. Where were the damned hoppers? Finally I saw them, three specks rising from the big landing field north of the main building—

And an expanding bloom of orange fire.

No.

I screamed, "No!" Did it over and over again.

The fireball turned black and became an umbrella of smoke.

Could they have made it out in time? I reached for the com,

saw the green light blinking, touched the pad to open Channel 16.

"Say goodbye to them, Asahel Frost!"

Something large went hurtling overhead, flying off the sheer-sided switchback just above me. At first I didn't realize that it was the Range Rover. Then the car was clearly visible, turning over and over so very slowly until it struck the rocks two hundred meters below and disappeared in a second fireball, much smaller than the first.

I started driving again, out of it. Uncomprehending.

In my shock and grief I had the ludicrous idea that if I reached the old mine where we'd played as kids everything would be different. A proper happy ending. The sun shone on the wet rocks. A bird was singing. The hoppers were coming and a red telltale blinked on the com unit. I ignored it.

The top. The muddy, rock-strewn level area in front of the broken-down shacks and rusted machinery of mysterious function. The precipice where Alistair Drummond had plunged to his death. I opened the car door and got out, taking the Harvey with me.

At the dropoff I used the gunscope to spy out the wreckage. Smoke coiled up from amid some scrub oaks and stunted ponderosas. Two ExSec hoppers were heading down into the canyon to investigate. Another one circled high above Copper Mountain, checking me out.

My hands were shaking a little so I dropped to one knee to get a steadier view—

Chweek!

The beam from the small actinic pistol missed me by centimeters, fired from the direction of the mine-shaft opening.

Oh, you crafty bastard!

He had ambushed me after all.

I ate mud. Rolled sideways, bruising my body on sharp rocks, found a boulder the size of an office wastebasket, puny shelter for someone my size.

Chweek! Chweek! Chweek! Chweek!

Fountains of goop and puffs of chipped rock. I was almost

out of his range and it was nearly impossible to shoot a gun that tiny with any kind of accuracy. But Alistair Drummond was doing all right, peppering me from the shelter of the mine entrance. He scorched my right thigh. It hurt like hell. Another beam caught me on the shoulder, setting my sodden shirt afire. I slapped the flame out. Then one of his shots sent a chip of rock into my left eye. My vision on that side dissolved in red fog.

Okay. That does it!

Heedless of the deadly white beams, I fired my Harvey into the rock face above the dark opening. Once. Twice. Three times.

Thunder returned, echoing across the crags, making the ground shudder. Tons of ancient rock cascaded down, loosened by my big blaster. Rocks poured into the old mine entrance, collapsed the supporting timbers, refilled the hole, obliterating it.

I stood up, burned and half blinded, a muddy wreck.

But Alistair Drummond was buried. Just like a rabid skunk.

Slowly, I shuffled back to the Jeep. The red light on the com unit was still blinking. Collapsing behind the wheel, I touched the pad.

"Asahel Frost here." My voice was slurred. I'd bruised my lower lip, too.

"Asa—it's Eve! Everyone in the house got out in time, including the staff. And Dan. He's alive. Are you all right?"

"Could be better . . . You get that board vote into the public record?"

"Oh, yes. Rampart's safe. Galapharma can't hurt the Starcorp now. We've won, Asa, whatever the outcome of our civil suit."

"How's Simon?"

"Subdued. Shocked. Rather pissed off because he'll have to postpone the big barbecue. But never mind that! Tell me—what's happened to Alistair Drummond? We had a report from security that his car had gone off the mountain."

A Rampart hoppercraft was hovering immediately overhead. I could hear someone calling out to me on the annunciator.

"Evie, I'll be down there before you know it, and I'll tell you everything. Gotta go now."

"Goodbye, Asa. Love you."

I shut down the com unit. Outside, an amplified voice was saying: "Exit your car! You are surrounded. Exit your car! Surrender and you will not be harmed!"

I said, "Easy for *you* to say."

Then I climbed out with my hands raised over my head and waited.

DEL REY® ONLINE!

The Del Rey Internet Newsletter...

A monthly electronic publication e-mailed to subscribers and posted on the rec.arts.sf.written Usenet newsgroup and on our Del Rey Books Web site (www.randomhouse.com/delrey/). It features hype-free descriptions of books that are new in the stores, a list of our upcoming books, special promotional programs and offers, announcements and news, a signing/reading/convention-attendance calendar for Del Rey authors and editors, "In Depth" essays in which professionals in the field (authors, artists, cover designers, salespeople, etc.) talk about their jobs in science fiction, a question-and-answer section, and more!

Subscribe to the DRIN: send a blank message to
join-drin-dist@list.randomhouse.com

The Del Rey Books Web Site!

We make a lot of information available on our Web site at
www.randomhouse.com/delrey/

- all back issues and the current issue of the Del Rey Internet Newsletter
- sample chapters of almost every new book
- detailed interactive features for some of our books
- special features on various authors and SF/F worlds
- reader reviews of some upcoming books
- news and announcements
- our Works in Progress report, detailing the doings of our most popular authors
- and more!

If You're Not on the Web...

You can subscribe to the DRIN via e-mail (send a blank message to join-drin-dist@list.randomhouse.com) or read it on the rec.arts.sf.written Usenet newsgroup the first few days of every month. We also have editors and other representatives who participate in America Online and CompuServe SF/F forums and rec.arts.sf.written, making contact and sharing information with SF/F readers.

Questions? E-mail us...

at delrey@randomhouse.com (though it sometimes takes us a little while to answer).